a/ca

THE ICE KING

THE ICE KING

MICHAEL SCOT

NEW ENGLISH LIBRARY

Copyright © 1986 by Michael Scott Rohan & Allan Scott

First published in Great Britain in 1986 by
New English Library, Mill Road, Dunton Green, Sevenoaks, Kent.
Editorial office: 47 Bedford Square, London WC1B 3DP.

Typeset by Rowland Phototypesetting Limited
Bury St Edmunds, Suffolk
Printed in Great Britain by
St Edmundsbury Press, Bury St Edmunds, Suffolk

British Library Cataloguing in Publication Data
Scot, Michael
    The ice king
    I. Title
    823'.914[F]   PR6037.C75

    ISBN 0-450-06110-8

CHAPTER ONE

THROUGH THE narrow rock opening the wind came screaming off the sea, flattening the undergrowth and the flames
of the bonfire until it roared in answer. Wood cracked
explosively, lashing showers of sparks into the eddying
air. Against the sudden light the horned head stood out
sharply, tossing this way and that among the little knot of
struggling figures. The circle of watchers bellowed and
jeered as they fought, panting and cursing, to force it
forward. But all the voices, and the terrified bleating of
the beast, were swallowed up in the wind's whine and the
answering rumble of surf far below. The tall tree swayed
and bent back against the sheltering cliff face, its boughs
rattling in a clacking rhythm. The things that hung from
them seemed to be dancing to it.

The sound, or the sudden waft of corruption that went
with it, maddened the struggling ram still further. The
black face ducked down and jerked up violently, twisting
to one side. One horn scored a jagged, welling line across
a bare chest, and flicked red droplets hissing into the fire.
The man fell back with a yelp, and the shrilling beast half
leapt, pawing frantically at the empty air.

Another horned shape swept across the circle of light,
huge and upright, stooping over the beast before it could
break loose. Careless of the flailing horns, an arm snaked
under the neck and around, tightened, and jerked sharply
back, catching the ram's head in the crook of the elbow and
choking it instantly silent. The beast threw all its weight
forward, but the arm was a broad, immovable collar. Two
men pinioned its legs, and the horned figure jerked the quivering creature into the air; instantly it was half conscious.
He took a few clumsy steps forward with his burden, and
the circle round the fire swayed forward with him. The man

1

with the gouged chest sat up, moaning. No one paid him any attention. Another two steps, and the horned figure was at the flat rock under the tree, throwing a fantastic shadow across it. He hefted the huge ram as if to hurl it down, then dumped it more gently onto the rock. It lay twisting feebly.

He gestured, and two figures little shorter than himself strode out of the circle. One held a length of rope and a tall staff, cloth-bound at the top, the other a great logging axe. The horned figure snatched the staff impatiently, twitching the rags off the gleaming blade and into the man's face. He ducked, and looped his rope around the ram's neck, pulling it smoothly together till it vanished into the fleece, then let it hang loosely from his hands. There was a rippling murmur from the watchers. The horned figure struck the rock a ringing blow with his spear-butt, and then again, more lightly, tapping out a softly regular rhythm. He began to chant in time with it, and the watchers echoed him raggedly. The fire flickered and swirled as figures circled it, faster and faster, feet drumming the earth. The chant grew louder, the horned helmet bobbing and swaying till sweat ran from beneath it, gleaming across neck and shoulders. Swaying wisps of smoke whirled out of the fire, rasping at eyes and nostrils. The ram, aroused, began to twist and kick. The horned figure shouted, and the watchers crowded suddenly around the rock. The rope-holder braced a foot against the rock, tensed, and heaved. The loop snapped taut, and the ram's body jerked with the force of it, drawing the neck right out beyond the enveloping wool. The axe swept up into the shivering leaves overhead; the spear whirled in the horned figure's hand till its blade pointed down, and in that instant thrust hard. There was an exultant yell from the watchers as the axehead clipped the leaves apart in its downward plunge – then a leaden, snapping sound, a gritty metallic ring, and the rope-holder fell backwards. The watchers sprang aside from the leaping sprays of red; again the fire hissed and sizzled. The horned man was probing with his spear, as if picking out some delicacy. He jabbed sharply, then raised the spear at arm's length, staring at it almost dreamily as the impaled head rose above his own.

2

He grinned suddenly and whirled it around over the heads of the onlookers, spraying the ones who didn't move fast enough. He swung right round, shouting, and in the same movement swept the speartip high into the tree, slicing off twigs and leaves and fragments of what hung among them. With a meaty thud the head was impaled on a broken branch. He jerked the spear free and bayed out a single word, the others echoing him, a name and a defiance flung in the face of the seawind. Then they cheered as the carcase was gutted over the stone, and two of the men began to skin it roughly; stakes for the spit were already being set up by the fire. But the horned man stood for an instant, gazing up into the tree. Then he turned, and with a wild yell hurled the heavy spear into the air, high over the others' heads, across the bonfire. The flames roared up to meet it, filling the whole glade with light.

Far below, out on the choppy waters of the estuary, the man in the small dory saw the faintest flicker of light high on the cliff face, swelling and fading in a moment. He laughed.

'Some berk out on the paths!' he remarked to the big black German Shepherd beside him. 'Need more'n a torch to be safe up there, an' all. Where some folk'll go for a bit of –' He broke off, swinging the wheel around to send the little boat into the lee of the huge structure that straddled the centre of the channel.

'Talking of torches . . .' He pulled the tazer from his belt and swept it across the dark, choppy water ahead. The truck-tyre fenders lining the jetty gleamed wetly black in the beam, and he twirled the wheel one-handed to bring the little boat smoothly alongside, right under the sign that read:

SAITHEBY SHIP EXCAVATION
by the
FERN FARM PROJECT
NO UNAUTHORISED LANDINGS
ON THIS DAM AT ANY TIME
WARNING: GUARD DOGS PATROL NIGHTLY

3

'Which means you,' he grunted to the dog as he looped the painter round a handy upright. 'So 'op to it.' Even in the shelter of the coffer-dam's high seawall there was plenty of swell to bounce the little craft around, and the dog had a difficult jump. That seemed to disturb it, and it stood whimpering at the edge as if about to leap back again.

' 'Ere, don't you bloody dare!' barked the guard, and hastily swung himself up after it – too hastily, because he missed his footing on the spray-soaked metal ribbing and fell with a crash that rang hollowly through the jetty and wakened odd echoes in the dam. The dog jumped and hunched, snarling. The guard was so startled he forgot to swear.

'What's up wi' you, then, you great soft pillock? Fine bloody guard dog you're turning out to be.' He hauled himself painfully off the soaking walkway. 'C'mere and get a leash on you, then – c'mon.'

He pulled the walkie-talkie from his belt and thumbed it on; the light glowed and static whispered. He clicked it off and replaced it, looking up at the looming bulk of the dam. He sniffed, and checked over the tazer as well – but only the flashlight button. He was careful not to touch the two others, the ones in line with the two stubby barrels under the light. He knew only too well what the barbed dart-tips inside could do. Satisfied, he swung the beam round to the ramp that led up to the dam, unlocked the gate, and urged the dog through. It went willingly enough, trotting at his side as usual, but when they reached the walkway at the top it plunged ahead suddenly, straining at the lead, and stopped short, quivering. The guard felt the lead shake with the tension in the animal's body; he heard it sniff and growl faintly, and bent down to put a hand on its harness. It jumped at the touch.

'Eh, boy, eh,' he whispered. 'What's all this, then? If there's someone there why don't you come right out an' bark like you're bloody trained to? Eh? Shall I let you go find it, eh? Eh?' He flicked open the quick-release catch, but the dog did not spring forward as he expected. It stood, still tense, still sniffing at the turbulent air. Puzzled,

4

the guard swept the high-powered torch beam all across
the top of the dam, and up and down the levels of scaffolding that supported the seawall. Nothing moved except the
dancing shadows, and here and there a tarpaulin flapping
in the wind. The only sound came from the dark pit at his
feet – the soft patter of the sprayer system. He leant over
the single railing and turned the beam downwards; the
fountaining mist of water iridesced like a rainbow before
it drifted down onto the dark, hummocked shape at the
centre.

Quite a bit of it clear now, thought the guard. *Looks
like some bloody great whale, all buried in the mud* – He
winced as the wind turned, and the stench of the exposed
estuary bed – dead seaweed, dead fish and centuries of
sewage from the town that flanked it – struck him in the
face. 'Aw God – smells like it, too. That what's worrying
you, boy? Can't say as I blame you. Come on, let's have
yer leash on again. Too cold to linger. Get our rounds
done – slope off 'ome sharpish. Must be mad, them all,
diggin' away in that shit'eap. Be lucky if they don't catch
something. Serve 'em right, too. Past's dead. Should let
it be – who needs it?' He looked up, as the briefest flicker
of pale light on the cliffs caught his eye, but it was already
gone. He snorted, and looked down into the unbroken
darkness of the pit.

'Thousand years it's been down there. Could've left it
another thousand, for all the difference it makes.'

'. . . and now local news, and a special report from
Saitheby, where the Fern Farm archaeological project has
once again been making headlines. Two years ago they
came up with the only known remains of a pagan Viking
temple. Today they've chalked up another first, in a rather
unusual spot. From the middle of the Saithe Estuary, Tom
Latimer reports . . .'*

A raucous cheer went up from the dig workers gathered
round the TV screen. Latimer acknowledged it with a
wave of his beercan and his best weather-worn grin. He
was glad he'd decided to spend the evening with the

5

diggers, partly because they were the best company he could hope for in a town that rolled up its pavements after six, but mainly because of a very foxy lady called Pru Ravenshead, now sitting just out of grab range and smiling. Latimer liked English girls, especially English girls with a tasty dash of blue blood. A rugged Aussie newshound with tales to tell from all the world's trouble spots was just what she needed – even if said newshound *was* beginning the long slide into middle age. Experience. Girls like Pru valued it.

The setting had him a bit nonplussed, though. The diggers' quarters had all the heady luxury of a north London squat. It had been some Victorian fatcat's house during Saitheby's brief fling as a fashionable resort; in harder times it had been turned into offices for the local council, and about ten years ago it had been gradually abandoned and neglected until even the mice moved out. It had walls, a floor, and most of a roof, but not much else – the diggers slept on the floor, and lived off sticks of furniture the thrift shops had thrown out. Proof that archaeologists were universally nuts – as if he needed any more! Even Pru. She had a home of her own, the bloody great manor her folks had up at Fern Farm. What did she need to come down here for? Not even a TV – he'd had to bring his monitor in from the van. Now, in their so-called common room, he lounged in the doubtful comfort of a clapped-out armchair, dodging the broken spring he'd been warned about, and cursed the mess the local news editor had made of his material. At least they'd left his commentary alone.

'It's more than a thousand years since the Saitheby ship caught fire and sank into the chilly waters of the Saithe Estuary,' said his own voice. The wide-angle shot over the dam had worked well, at least. *'Over the centuries the ship, turned right over on its belly, sank deep into the preserving mud, its back broken, its upper timbers scattered. And there it stayed, until just over a year ago a team of archaeologists from the Fern Farm site tracked it down at last. Massive funding came from the British Museum and from Rayner College, Texas, which is running the project. The team used*

6

it to build this dam, and started to pump out the water that barred the way to an astonishing archaeological first.'

On the screen, figures were moving along the planked walkways in the shadow of the towering seawall, anonymous in their yellow oilskins. A perpetual mist of fine spray drifted across the exposed estuary mud, half concealing the bewildering array of timbers, markers and multicoloured tags that was the Saitheby Viking ship.

'This morning the team began the tricky job of moving the ship, timber by timber, to its new home at the Saitheby Museum . . .'

The camera moved in to frame a long, low mound flanked by a wooden catwalk, glistening with mud in the hazy light. Oilskinned diggers were kneeling along it, chatting to each other and occasionally glancing along at the great slab of a man who stood at the far end. A swift change of shot showed him in close-up, gesticulating furiously at the crane operator up on the dam wall as a web of chains and canvas was lowered into position. Looking up, he shook his hood back to reveal an almost classically handsome young face, given a hint of toughness by a nose that had obviously been broken and reset, and by the concentrated intensity of his expression, lips compressed and blue eyes glittering under heavy eyebrows.

'Let's 'ear it for J.R.!' suggested a raucous Liverpudlian voice from the back of the common room. ' 'Ip, 'ip –' At least three other diggers replied with a resounding Bronx cheer.

'Handling this critical stage of the operation was site supervisor Jay Colby, of Rayner College. The first and most crucial part of the ship to be moved was the main section of its keel – a single oak timber more than thirty feet long, mud-soaked, waterlogged, and ready to crack apart under its own weight at any minute . . .'

The camera pulled back to show the diggers very gingerly easing the heavy keel out of the mud and sliding it onto the cradle, inch by painful inch. Equally slowly the crane cable was taking up the slack, lifting the cradle into shape around the great dark beam, until at last the cable and support chains quivered with the tension and a hair-thin line of daylight suddenly showed under the en-shrouded shape. The diggers hastily slid their fingers into the gap, steadying, supporting, almost caressing the delicate weight. Inches, a foot, knee-high – the diggers were rising to their feet now, with infinite care – waist-high, chest-high . . .

'To begin with, it all went by the book. But then . . .'

The crane was taking the actual weight, but the diggers had to prevent the mass of timber from shifting or twisting. They were having to reach up to it now as it swung over their heads towards the waiting preservation tank. One overreached, slid on the muddy catwalk, and lost his footing; his neighbour spared a hand to try and steady him, and lost his footing, too. They fell heavily, knocking into the next along. She staggered, stayed upright, but lost her grip on the keel. There was a faint moan of stressed timber, and suddenly the massive beam was turning with the torque of the tautened cable, ponderously slewing over and down and beginning, with dreamlike, unstoppable slowness, to slide out of the tilted cradle.

Even on the screen, it made some of the audience gasp. Latimer smirked to himself. There was a sudden rush, a massive figure bowling the panicky diggers aside, darting under the falling end of the beam – Colby, catching it, holding it, bowing down under that immense weight. The camera jerked slightly, then zoomed in on him as his wide shoulders split the heavy oilskins at the seams. His face was purple, rigid with effort as he struggled to hold back the ancient weight of wood. Balanced as he was on the edge of a teetering catwalk, it didn't look possible.

'Like holding up a house!' someone muttered. Colby was visibly shaking with the effort, but the beam slid no further. In the instant before the diggers collected their wits and ran to help him it almost seemed to move back slightly. Then other hands caught it, and Colby's face relaxed. The camera moved back to show him and the other diggers gently manoeuvring the laden cradle down into the tank.

'Ey,' said the Liverpudlian at the back, 'for 'is next trick 'e turns green and busts out of 'is shirt –'

8

'Oh shut up, Neville,' said Pru. 'He may be the Hulk, but he saved the keel, didn't he?'

Again the camera closed in on the central mound. *'But it was two hours after that moment of drama that the archaeologists made their most spectacular discovery so far . . .'*

More outer planking had been stripped from the hull, and its ribs stood bare out of the mud like the carcase of some giant sea-beast. Between them something was just visible above the slimy surface, and diggers were carefully cleaning it with trowels and small water jets.

'A thousand years on, site director Wilf Jackson was about to uncover what had broken the back of the Saitheby ship, the secret that lay hidden under its hull . . .'

The camera moved in to frame a low plank-and-trestle bridge thrown across the open centre of the hull, and the man who knelt there, enthusiastically playing a water jet over the dark object beneath him. As the camera came nearer he shut it off and looked up. He was somewhere in his thirties, smallish, spare, with dark curly hair and a pleasant-looking face. He wore a neat ring of beard round mouth and chin.

'This is really very exciting,' he was saying. *'Superb. I'd even say unique. Look here – it seems to be covered in pitch or something similar, but it's definitely wooden. And ironbound. You may just be able to see these traces of decoration on the banding. And this here may well be a keyhole for the simple locks they used. That's significant. It means they valued the contents very highly.'*

'You're saying it's a treasure chest?' came Latimer's off-camera voice.

'Not quite,' said Jackson, with a demure smile. *'I think that might be going a little too far, just at the moment. But it could be – it certainly could be. It wouldn't be the first time that treasure had been found in a shipwreck, after all!'*

The screen image dissolved to a view of the fully excavated chest, a blackish rectangular shape about four feet by three, and quite deep. The dark metal banding was corroded but clearly visible under the irregular coating of pitch. The view cut to a shot of it being lifted in a cradle

9

and swung high over the edge of the dam into the wide hold of one of the project's two tenders, a converted fishing boat, waiting at the jetty.

'The chest is immensely fragile after its long spell on the seabed, and the mud may well have seeped in – though Dr Jackson thinks the pitch has protected it. Now it's being taken ashore for careful conservation treatment. Over the next few days it'll be opened, and examined minutely. Almost anything could be inside. And I'll be on the spot with regular reports. From the site of the most exciting archaeological find since the **Mary Rose***, this is Tom Latimer, in the Saithe Estuary.'*

Latimer reached out a long arm and clicked off the set. 'Well?' he asked, looking hard at Pru. 'Every shot a ruddy little work of art, right? Really caught that dicey bit with the keel –'

Pru was looking puzzled. 'Yes, it was very good – but you didn't say anything about the other chest, the one underneath –'

'Bit of Press cooperation there. Old Prof Hansen, see, he asked me to say nothing about that till you folks've actually got it out. Bit sharp about it, he was. Seems he only let Jackson take number one out so fast because it was going to crush number two into safety matches. Could damn well stay there tonight and get done properly tomorrow. In the meantime he's got ants in his pants about treasure-hunters.'

'What I don't follow,' said Neville, 'is how you spent the whole day under our flaming feet with that overgrown Box Brownie and only got five minutes of film.'

Latimer chuckled. 'Not even that, squire. That was a three-minute slot they gave me – not bad, by their standards. That's how ENG works – electronic news gathering to you. In the old days they'd've had a whole film crew up here. Now there's just me and the box of tricks. I get tons of stuff and shoot it back to them down a phone line. And they get their mad axemen to work cutting it to fit the slot they want to use it in. Like to see some of the stuff they didn't use?'

There was a general rumble of interest. ' 'Ow about

some shots of Evil K-Neville?' bellowed a burly, curly-haired man with a local accent.

'Ey, thanks, Harry,' chuckled Neville. 'Always fancied 'aving a fan club of me own.'

Latimer turned the monitor back on, changed channel, and switched on the ENG unit attached to it. He clicked a cassette into the combined camera and recorder and set it to rewind. The interviews, that would give them a few laughs. And let Pru see herself on the box – they always liked that. He scrabbled for another beer, listening to the rising wind rattle the tall windows, and grinned over at Pru.

'Pity the poor bugger out on that dam tonight!'

The guard had made himself as comfortable as he could, in a niche under the seawall scaffolding where crates and tarpaulins formed a windbreak. It was still draughty, though, and every gust made the flame of his butane lantern flicker. There was no real lighting on the dam except for the self-powered hazard lights around the walls. He toyed with the idea of bringing one in, but lighting the place deep red or green didn't appeal – it was spooky enough already.

'Probably drive *you* daft, wouldn't it, you great soft gowk?' he remarked to the dog. 'Specially the way you are tonight.' He'd had a fine time settling it down, and even now it was nervy and aggressive. It lay curled up at his feet, but keeping a wary eye on the darkness beyond the lamp's charmed circle, growling softly at every creak, and every large wavelet that slapped against the side of the dam. 'Know what? You're getting on my ruddy nerves, you are.' He listened to the sea rising, and thanked God those nutty professors had had the sense to build a sheltered jetty. The dory would be safe from anything less than a full-dress storm, and there'd been no sign of one on the weather maps. Still . . . He looked at his watch. Midnight plus fifteen; might as well check in. He thumbed the walkie-talkie's call button.

It was a full five minutes before a sleepy voice crackled

out of it, leading off with a tinny yawn. 'Securiguard, Stockton – that you, Lees?'

'No, it's his frigging mutt!'

'Oh aye? That's what you get up to, is it? Ah well, keeps you warm, I suppose. Owt to report? Caught any treasure-hunters yet?'

'On a night like this? You're joking. Hear that wind?'

'Christ, thought that was static. Getting a bit high isn't it? Forecast was light to medium and scattered showers.'

'Yeah, well, you're ten flaming miles inland. Might be medium there, but it's blowing 'ard out here. Not dangerous yet, but –'

'Ay, well, you hang on where you are, even if it does start to blow. You'll be safer on that dam than running for shore in a small boat.'

'Couldn't I just go now?'

'A night they've paid for, a night they get. Treasure-hunters might not worry about the weather, and then where are we? The dig could sue us blind. Check in again about five and we'll see. Dunno what's eating you anyway. Fifteen years I've been running this show and never lost a man yet –'

With a snort of disgust Lees switched him off and put the radio back on the table. He sat for a moment contemplating the lamp and the coffee Thermos, all that stood between him and five o'clock. Then he pulled a slightly soggy copy of the *Daily Mirror* out of his pocket and turned to the racing page, weighting it down with the radio. The boss was right – mad bastards, some of these fishermen, and not too fond of the dam. Mostly because it blocked their easiest channel in, but the ones he'd talked to seemed a bit superstitious about it as well. If they got drunk enough they might just risk coming out and seeing what they could pinch. Or just mess it up – loosen a few bolts, even, and blame the result on the weather. He looked out, and saw the moon shine momentarily through the scudding clouds, silvering the dam wall, leaving the pit a pool of shadow. The dog's eyes were wide and gleaming. It looked chilly, and felt it. He shuddered, huddling closer to the spluttering lamp. Heaven help any-one he got his hands on tonight!

Latimer touched the start control, and chuckled as the first face materialised out of a jumpy blur. Nothing like starting at the top – and the great Viking expert looked pretty much like a Viking himself. The figure that came striding into shot was nearly as tall as Colby, though much less bulky, and the face that filled the close-up had the slightly gaunt look of the well-trained athlete. Latimer remembered him saying that a few seasons' fieldwork kept him as fit as anyone in their forties should be. It was a slightly piratical face, tanned and hard-planed under red-dish hair, tousled and windblown, showing flecks of grey. The bladelike nose and neatly pointed red-grey beard heightened the impression, and only the calm intelligence in the eyes countered it. Or did it?

'*Professor Halfdan Hansen,*' said Latimer's commentary voice, '*head of the Archaeology Department at Rayner College, Texas – and, as one of the world's foremost Viking scholars, director of the whole Fern Farm project. But Professor Hansen –*'

'Hal.'

'*Hal – can you tell us how you go from digging up a temple to digging up a ship?*'

The tall man smiled slightly. '*It's very simple. We just listened to what people were saying. When we found the temple, we realised that people here had been telling folk-tales about it for centuries. But because they were folktales, fairy tales even, no one bothered to take them seriously. A big mistake. So we also listened to the local fishermen – they tell stories about something called "King Henry's Ship" – I don't know which of the Henrys it is supposed to be. They say it sank in the estuary. Once in a while they would find some timber fragments in their nets. We had one of these radio-carbon dated, and suddenly everyone was very excited! Then we began to search. We had much help from scuba clubs along the coast. I thought it worth the effort – this must have been a seagoing community.*'

'Community – you mean the temple?'

'Indeed. What is a god without worshippers, a church without a congregation? All your newspaper cartoonists, they have fun with the temple, but they forget it must have been supported by a local community – farms, maybe a village where Saitheby now stands. And the Vikings who settled here were a seagoing people. There may well be the remains of a boatyard somewhere beneath the seafront at Saitheby, but they will not let me rip it up.'

Latimer still wasn't sure whether or not he had been joking. The regret in his deep voice sounded all too real, and in his sea-green eyes there was a definite gleam. Humour or fanaticism? The Dane was a quiet giant, but a baffling one – to Latimer, anyway. His English was precise, almost formal, those eyes constantly narrowed in the light. The diggers seemed to find him friendly and approachable, yet when Latimer had approached him –

'Just a simple feature, Prof. A personality spot, for *Timescape*, the history show. You know – like they did of you last year –'

'I did not like that much. And for a young man like Mr Colby – it is out of the question, I am afraid.'

'Why?' Colby was a natural – rising young archaeologist who looked more like the college football hero. After that business with the keel –

'I am afraid I cannot tell you why. It would hardly be in his best interests.'

'Oh come on now, Prof. It could *make* him!'

'He is made anyway, once his doctoral thesis is published. I have seen the draft, and I have no doubts. He is brilliant, far more so than I was at that age. In time I hope he will surpass me, so I am not holding him back. I can only repeat, it is out of the question. And I know he will agree.'

Latimer smiled. Outwardly Hansen had kept cool, but after a couple of minutes he had been so het up that his Danish accent had started to come through. There was almost certainly a story there, though maybe not for *Timescape*. Hell! He'd let the tape run on! The recording had cut abruptly from Hansen to another figure, evidently

14

female even with her back to the camera. She was conspicuously not wearing yellow oilskins – instead she had neat blue waterproof overalls and a matching rainhat. Curly black hair spilled out under the brim. She was perched on a pile of boards to one side of the hull, hunched over something that looked like a sketchpad, but was attached by a cable to the case at her side.

'Hi there. You from Rayner? Tom Latimer – **Timescape**.'

'Mmh?' A natural camera face, thought Latimer. Could've been a model with those strong bones, that skin, those great big googly eyes, and oh, that body. If only –

'**Timescape**,' he was repeating. 'TV – archaeology – you know.'

'Oh – uh, yes, hi. Jessica Thorne – Jess – California. I'm with Rayner, yeah. But you don't want me –'

'No?' Latimer grimaced. Could he just quietly turn this off?

'No. See, I'm not an archaeologist. I just run the computers round here.' She waggled the sketchpad. 'Graphics tablet, see? Linked to my little smart terminal here. Have to keep a complete record of the finds, map them out as we uncover them, layer by layer, then just phone the results right on through to the Rayner database. They can make a 3D reconstruct of the whole site, track down scatter patterns, maybe pick out parts we've missed. Fun job, I guess, and it pays my stay over here, 'cause I can do research for my doctoral thesis. In anthropology – folklore. That's my real thing. Hey, d'you always hide behind cameras when you talk to people?'

That got the audience reaction Latimer expected. 'Funny,' said Neville, 'you never struck me as a shrinking violet.' Pru giggled. Latimer winced, and again as his screen voice said, 'Hey, folklore, that's fascinating. What's it about, then, this thesis?'

'Sure you wanna know? **The Cult of the Horned God in Western European Myth and Folktale**. Get that?'

'Er – loud and clear. Hey, you know where I come from, Aussie-land, the abos have some really wild stories –'

'Uhuh, I've heard some. Dreamtime, Wandjina, that kind of thing –'

15

*'Yeah, yeah. Fascinating. Listen, that thesis of yours –
I'd like to hear more. Maybe some time soon we could –'*

Latimer stabbed a long finger hard down on the fast
forward wind button, and the beginnings of the pass he
had made on camera – and the instant put-down – vanished
into a speeded-up gibber and blur. 'Time for another
beer,' he grinned, and headed for the pile on the rickety
table.

He was just opening a can when a voice next to him
said, 'Bust yer balls, did she?' and he almost snapped off
the tag. 'Shouldn't worry about it,' Neville added, also
reaching for a can. He sighed regretfully. 'She does it to
everyone – well, almost everyone.'

'Meaning everyone except you, uh?'

'Me? Perish the thought, wacker. I don't mess with
other fellas' girls – rather roll me own.'

'Go on, mate, laugh it up. You're on next.'

The guard jerked upright in his chair, suddenly awake and
staring wildly round. Everything was dark. The dead lamp
rolled gently on the table, snuffed and toppled by the great
gusts of wind. But something louder than a falling lamp
had snatched him back from the brink of sleep – a rending,
explosive crash from outside. The dog pressed back, snarling, against his legs, tail down and ears flattened, hunched
down ready to spring. Another gust made the tarpaulins
bulge and flap like vast wings, dry and leathery. Shivering
in the sudden waking chill, he had a confused image of
the dam broken and the sea pouring in to reclaim its own,
the ancient hulk, rotten ribs gaping, sailed off down the
tide by a crew in the same condition . . .

Grimly he shut off the gas still hissing from the fallen
lamp, and snatched up the tazer. No more sounds, so the
dam was still holding. The moment he touched the dog's
lead it bounded out of the cubby ahead of him, growling
and casting about in the flurrying wind.

'What is it, boy? Eh? What d'you smell?' He swept the
beam down across the jetty to where his boat bobbed
whitely on the black water. Nothing broken there, anyway.

And it hadn't been in the seawall overhead, or he'd have heard it more clearly; if anything was going, then, it was at the far end. He set off round the creaking walkway at a fast trot, with the dog loping beside him. Another minute and he'd have been out cold, literally caught napping. Anything serious and they'd have had his guts for garters. They might yet.

Panting, he reached the far end of the dam and stood for a moment. Nothing was different, nothing was wrong. The sea boomed just as loudly against the wall down here, the metal and concrete piles rang just as soundly. No more strange noises in the wind, and not the slightest tremor in the guardrail. He risked swinging himself out on it, one-handed above the hungry licking of the water beneath, to shine the tazer along the lengths of the outer walls. Not the slightest flaw visible in the cladding, and no frothing that might indicate an underwater leak. He'd have heard that anyway, chuckling nastily to itself. He swung his leg back over the railing, ignoring the futile plucking of the wind, and sat for a moment, gnawing his lip. Whatever made that crash hadn't been small – it meant damage, maybe serious damage. He stepped across the narrow walkway to the lower inner rail. The pit beneath him was a pool of darkness, so still and deep he almost expected to see his own reflection on its surface, as on water. He hesitated a moment, listening, and when he heard nothing more he thumbed on the beam and reluctantly tilted it down into the pit.

It glanced quickly across the metal walls, the bright plastic tags and white tape of the chessboard squares, the dully gleaming mud beneath. It dazzled over pools of water from the sprinklers, past them onto the great hummock at the heart of the pattern. He gave a gusty sigh of relief as he saw the gaunt, gnawed-looking ribs still upright and intact above the carcase of the hull. But then he saw past them, and relief died. In the mud that filled the belly of the hull a hole gaped like the rotten hollow of a tooth. Wide, deep, irregular, as if something had been torn violently from the mud. Jagged fragments sticking out . . . One wall of the cavity collapsed softly inwards. Only a

17

minute ago, right enough. Furiously he swept the beam round and about the pit, snarling to match the dog. Nobody. A complete cock-up, doubled. The one thing he was here to look after . . .

Suddenly he froze. There had only been his boat at the jetty! They couldn't possibly have got away that quickly, unless that crash had been a biggish hull – a fishing boat, say – bumping the lee wall of the dam . . . No way. He'd seen the news, too. These chests were big, a ton weight, and they hadn't had a crane this time. They were still here somewhere.

He flashed the beam onto the opposite wall, over the main steps up from the pit. Every few minutes the sprinklers washed them clean, but they were muddy now. He swore violently, and was about to run round again when the moon shone clear of the clouds for an instant. In that moment he found himself staring at a figure on the opposite walkway, an unmistakable silhouette against the sudden glitter on the sea. A woman, a tall, slender woman in a stance of rigid surprise . . .

The dog growled once, loud and fierce. She spun sharply on her heel and ducked into the shadow of the seawall. With a half-formed shout the guard sent the beam scything after her – too late. As she vanished into the tangle under the scaffolding the beam barely glanced on her flank, and the guard grunted with surprise. Smooth, dark, and slickly glistening – she had to be wearing a wetsuit. Her head had been clearly outlined, as if by wet hair. He turned and pounded back along the walkways, the dog straining at the leash and yipping with breathless anger. He kept one finger on the quick-release trigger for the leash, and in his other hand the tazer, thumb between torch-beam and firing-button. If whoever that was had really been crazy or determined enough to come swimming through seas like these, he'd better take them very, very seriously.

Latimer sent the tape skating further down the reel, past a hopeless attempt to interview a young digger called Paul, to the point where Neville's face rose like a moon

18

with moustache and horn-rims from behind some hull timbers.

'*Neville Battley, in everyday life a local government officer in Liverpool, is one of the most experienced volunteer diggers. Neville, this is your second season here – what makes you spend your hard-earned holidays this way?'* The on-screen Neville twitched his toothbrush moustache cheerfully. '*Knee-deep in clag, you mean? I dunno, really. The sex, maybe. Or the drugs – plenty of that, there is, drugs. Mostly it's spending the rest of the year polishing up me bum on office chairs.*'

'*But why archaeology? Had you done any before?*'

'*Oh aye. Spent a fortnight once scrapin' out me granddad's aquarium. Never found 'im, though. Got a thing going for me diving suit, mind you – oo, that rubber –*'

The camera was developing a distinct shake, but Neville was interrupted in mid-quiver by a harsh shout from off-screen. '*Battley, you stupid s.o.b.! Shut off that sprayer before you wash out the whole section!*'

Neville snatched up the dribbling sprayer and held it up in a snappy Nazi salute, heel-click and all, thrusting two fingers over his already Hitlerian moustache.

'*Jawohl, mein Führer! Ve hear and obey!*' All the diggers in the audience cheered as the picture cut off hastily. Latimer looked at Pru, who'd been cheering with the rest.

'That was this guy Colby? Not so popular, is he?'

Pru was blushing. 'Well . . .' She seemed to be almost writhing with the effort of saying anything unkind. 'I suppose he's nice enough really. But when we're all pushed together like this things get sort of exaggerated – everyone living on top of each other all the time –' *With you I like that idea!* thought Latimer, '– and he's brilliant, really, but a bit too arrogant about it, I mean he and Wilf – oh dear –'

Jackson's smiling face popped round the door as if she had conjured him up. 'Evening everyone! Pru – oh, hallo Tom. Quite a gathering, eh? Except Jay, of course. He'll come rolling in at three in the morning and fall over everybody.'

'He lives here, then?'

19

Jackson pursed his lips. 'Just about everyone does. It's cheap, you see. We archaeologists don't earn much; not till we reach Hal Hansen's level, with books and broadcasts and guest lectures and so on. So *he* has a room at the Two Ravens –'

Pru laughed. 'Nobody minds that, really. He needs his privacy to work – and he comes down here often enough.'

Jackson smiled again. 'He does come slumming now and again. I was hoping I'd find him here, actually. Any idea, Pru?'

'Well – he did say he was going back to the Ravens to do some work. But I saw Jess get into his car, so he must be giving her a lift home.'

Jackson's smile became very knowing. 'Ah yes. Tom, you've met Ms Thorne? I see you have. She's our other anti-social type. She'd rather go off and live like a hermit on a *particularly* windy clifftop at Fern Farm.'

Latimer blinked. The Fern Farm estate was miles out of town; quite a lift home. Well, well. So the iron lady did have a soft spot, after all? Hansen – old enough to be her father, and she bit your head off for making a simple suggestion. Typical, bloody typical . . .

'Don't listen to him, Tom,' Pru was saying. 'She's very comfortable, really. And it's a beautiful view. We keep an old caravan – or would you call it a trailer, like Jess does? Anyway, we keep it there to rent to tourists sometimes. She took it when she came over for the temple dig, and liked it so much she's taken it again this season. I don't blame her a bit, really.'

'Well, at least no one wakes her up at three o'clock in the morning,' sighed Jackson. 'What's all this gear, Tom? Holiday snaps?'

'Just a few interviews they didn't use tonight. Get to see yourself, then?'

He'd asked the right question: Jackson was positively glowing. 'Yes, actually – in the cafe where I was eating. Made me feel like quite a celebrity. Er – listen, Tom, I hate to bother you, but could you get me a copy of that bit? With the interview. Not for me really; it's more for Pru –'

20

'Sure,' said Latimer. 'No problem, squire.' *You jammy bugger,* he thought. *You and Pru, eh? So that's why she dosses down here.* 'There was one of Pru as well,' he added aloud. 'Haven't seen that yet – we were savin' all the treats for the end.' He grinned at Pru, and saw her blush all the way up to her hairline. *Three cheers for the English rose.* 'Let's have it now, eh?'

There was a rumble of agreement from the diggers. He clicked a second cassette into the machine, and Pru appeared on the deck of the tender boat, kneeling by a pile of plastic-swathed timbers she was labelling.

'For one dig volunteer,' said his voice-over, *'the whole Fern Farm project has a special significance. Prudence Ravenshead. Pru, hallo.'* She dimpled prettily at the camera. *'The whole project's pretty much a family affair, isn't it?'*

She laughed. *'You could say that. It did all start when we were having new power lines put in up to the house, because ours are always going wrong, you know, and blacking the whole place out, and then they found some paving and a buckle, and the local history people and the Museum started a little dig, and called in the British Museum, but they couldn't afford it on their own so they called in the Texans because they've got lots of money and Hal Hansen's an absolute Viking fanatic and . . .'*

'And so you're working under Rayner College supervision now,' he interrupted, to dam the flood. *'Your family have been landowners round here for a long time, haven't they? How long, exactly?'*

'Oh gosh, I don't know really. Almost for ever, we're in the Domesday Book as the local squires, and we've got a coat of arms from somewhere, it's the sign on the Two Ravens you know, but that sounds awfully snobbish, doesn't it? There's really nothing special about us now.'

Latimer froze the frame on Pru's particularly winsome smile, and grinned over at her. 'Wouldn't say that, exactly.' He could never use that clip, of course, but it had been a useful lead in to chatting her up, whether or not it actually made it to the screen – he could just blame that on his editor.

Jackson touched his arm. 'Tom – you're up here for news, aren't you? But had you thought of doing something else – a little feature piece for *Timescape*, maybe?'

Jeez Louise, thought Latimer, *he's not reading my mind, is he?*

Jackson steepled his fingers. 'You see, the archaeology of this area – well, it's my speciality – my doctoral subject. That's why I'm site director here. And I have some fascinating ideas –'

If they're anything like mine you're some kind of perv. 'Okay, we'll have a chat about them some time soon,' was what he actually said. 'Over a pint, maybe.' He looked around. The party atmosphere had definitely died, and the diggers were chatting softly among themselves; even Neville had dampened down. What the hell had done that? Couldn't be Jackson, could it? 'By the way, talking of features, I had an idea of centring one on your Mr Colby, after his showstopper this morning. But Prof Hansen stood on it hard.'

Jackson's smile hardened. 'Yes, well, he would. Colby's his star doctoral student – his protégé, really. But it's no use hiding it from you, Tom, that there was some opposition to his appointment here.'

'Doesn't he know his stuff, then?'

'Oh, he's brilliant,' admitted Jackson, 'but I prefer *my* supervisors to have more practical knowledge. That matter of the keel – it was Colby's insistence on raising it in one piece that led to the accident. The rule in such cases is to section the timber. But Hansen backed him, of course.'

'Why "of course"? What is it with those two?'

Jackson looked around theatrically and lowered his voice. 'Well, strictly off the record, I believe the professor feels rather responsible for him. You see, a couple of years ago when Colby was a senior student at Rayner – and some kind of football star – you've heard of American college fraternities? He was president of one. They often have bizarre initiation rites for freshmen – sometimes they go too far . . . I believe the boy in this case never recovered consciousness.'

Latimer whistled softly.

'Indeed,' said Jackson. 'An unfortunate accident – no question of charges. Even the family money wouldn't have saved him from being expelled, but Hansen stood up for him. Perhaps because he was such a promising student, perhaps . . .' He shrugged. 'You know Hansen is close to Jessica Thorne? Since around that time, I believe. Before that, she and Colby had been friends.'

'Uhuh,' said Latimer. 'Really put my furry little foot in it, didn't I? Thanks for telling me. No wonder Hansen didn't want publicity. Well, he won't get it. No story in that – not for any news outfit I'd want to work for.'

He made sure Pru heard that. She had been hovering around anxiously.

'We're making coffee,' she called over. 'Want some?'

'And something stronger in it?' suggested Jackson.

'Why not?' said Latimer. *Now what's going on here? I wouldn't blab all that to a newshound I hardly knew. Not sure I like this guy – or is he just a bit naive? Well, either way, he's not going to hang onto Ms Pru for long. She's not the dumb blonde she makes herself out. Give her half a chance, and she'll run.*

The guard and the dog came pounding up to the shadowy seawall and plunged, without stopping, into the maze of tarpaulin-draped equipment at its base. He'd flashed the torch-beam over it as he ran, and seen nobody, so they had to be hiding in here somewhere. He flicked the dazzling beam to left and right, but its intensity only seemed to deepen the shadows – shadows that hopped and twitched startlingly with every little tremor of the light. The wire cage that screened off the main generators cast a confusing grid over everything, breaking up the outlines.

Behind the generators – had he heard the faintest rustling? He squinted cautiously through the mesh, and saw nothing. He snorted impatiently, stepped round – and fell back with a yell as something dark whirled up in his face, all but triggering the tazer. But as the gust died the scrap of canvas fell away again, and he leaned back against the cage, trying to slow the heartbeat that thundered in his ears. He hated being spooked. He'd been made to look a complete bloody idiot, and almost wasted a valuable shot. Well, he'd make good use of it now; someone was going to suffer for this.

He suddenly became aware that the dog was whining at his heel, straining the lead again, but in an unexpected direction. It was facing the narrow stairway – little more than a ladder with wider treads – that led up to the two higher floors on the scaffolding. He stared. They must be pretty well spooked themselves to hide up there – now he just had to search each floor in turn, keeping an eye on the ladders. Maybe they were only panicky teenagers – he thought about shouting up to them to stop pissing about and come down –

He looked up sharply. The faint, slow creak had come from above – from the boards of the first floor. He waited a moment in silence, breathing shallowly, and heard it again. It seemed to come from directly over his head: a soft, gradual sound like the measured footfall of someone infinitely patient – and very heavy. They would need to be, to make solid boards creak like that. They seemed to be moving closer to the stairwell . . . For a moment he braced himself, expecting a sudden rush down out of the dark. Then he heard another footfall, and a different, sharper creak, and remembered suddenly that the stairway to the second floor was, naturally enough, right beside the first. And he realised, too, that the top of the wall would make an excellent vantage point for someone to signal any pickup boats he – or she – happened to have waiting around . . .

With a furious hiss the guard triggered the leash release and cracked it, whip-like, off the dog's collar. In the same movement the animal sprang for the stairs with a ravening growl and bounded up them, claws clacking on the rubber-sheathed metal. The guard was right on its heels, torch full on now and searing away the dark. It was a manoeuvre they'd often rehearsed in training. Anyone waiting to attack the guard met the dog, and anyone attacking the dog would find the tazer a shocking experience.

The guard jumped the last few steps, caught a stanchion,

and swung himself up round it, in the same movement sweeping the beam right round the first floor. Only shadows leapt out at him. Then he looked up, shouted, and jabbed his thumb hard on the trigger button. There was a flash, a bang, and the tazer jerked in his hand as the little streak of silver spat down the torch-beam, straight at the leg that was just lifting off the last step up.

But with a spanging smack of metal it struck sparks off the stairs and ricocheted away into the shadows. Snarling, the guard jerked its tail of fine wire free of the little pulley inside the barrel – the dart had discharged its voltage now, and it was useless. Then he was off after the dog, now bounding up the last few steps. Again he leaped, and swung himself up on the supports of a fuel tank, squinting into the wind that was suddenly whipping at his cheeks. The top of the wall formed a high parapet to this floor; it offered little shelter, and not much was kept up here except the gravity-feed tank for the boats and generators. The only place anyone could possibly be hiding was at the far end, behind one or two low stacks of boxes swathed in glossy black plastic. The dog stood facing them, growling faintly, and the guard's face twisted into a lop-sided grin. There couldn't be room for more than two back there, so the one shot he had left would be enough.

He bent down to the dog. 'Well, boy? Going to go flush 'em out for me, are you?' It growled, once, more savagely than he'd ever heard it growl before, but it didn't move. 'Well? What're you waiting for, yer great daft gowk – the tide?' He jerked its collar forward, and finally had to nudge it with his boot. It went then, but not bounding forward as it was trained to; it went low on its belly, ears back, hackles rising, with a continual singsong snarl of menace. A sudden chilly qualm of realisation crept over the guard. The dog wasn't hunting something out – it was stalking it, stalking something it saw as a serious threat . . .

He plunged forward, but in that moment the dog also sprang, onto and over the pile of boxes and back down on whoever was behind them, taking the topmost boxes with it. He winced at the impact. The brute was as strong as most men, and the way it was now, half crazy with fear, it was quite capable of ripping somebody's throat out, and where would they all be then? He *had* to get it off – with the tazer, if need be. But then he saw it thrown back and away, rolling over and over almost to the edge of the inside railing, with nothing but open space beyond it and the pit far beneath. It was stopping, barking, snarling, gathering for another spring at the dark figure rising out of the wreckage. He swung up the tazer. The one that moved first –

The figure's head turned, and he jerked the beam away from the dog. But before it made contact there was a flurry of movement, a black blur rising in the light towards him, and he stabbed the second trigger in the instant before he dived aside. The flash, the bang, and the thump of connection were almost simultaneous, and as he hit the wall and dropped he felt the boards spring and vibrate under the crashing weight that struck them. Dizzy with relief, he hauled himself quickly up against the wall – and then he choked. Against the turbulent sky in front of him, the figure was also standing – the same slender female silhouette he had seen below, the same slim shape that had just been hit by a dart carrying an electrical charge calculated to stun, even hospitalise, the strongest man.

The foul smell of the pit seemed to grow stronger, as if the seawind caught it up like spray. Suddenly he could hardly breathe for it, and shook his head violently, choking on the rankness of the air. In that instant there was a rush of feet and weight slammed into him, forcing him back against the wall, pinning him there. Fingers touched his face almost caressingly, choosing their place. Then they closed – hard.

He screamed through teeth he could not open, shook his head violently and only increased the terrible strain on his neck. The heel of the chill hand was under his chin, forcing it up and back with the slow strength of a hydraulic press. He battered at the arm beyond for a futile instant, and then, in desperation, he grabbed the wrist and heaved. The grip broke, and he kicked upwards, trying to put a knee in his enemy's stomach, bracing himself against the

26

seawall. But again the fingers closed, and his head sang with the pressure. Through distorted eyes he saw the shadowed head stoop over him, and then he felt his spine bend back against the seawall, creaking. Between pain and pressure he could hardly breathe, and the blood roared in his ears. He tried to claw the fingers off his face, but a terrible, numbing tingle was growing in his arms, and he could hardly control them.

Then the clouds broke again, and momentarily the moon came out.

The guard gave a single, tearing, convulsive shriek, and the sheer violence of it jerked one leg free. He wrenched it up, connected, and with the last shreds of his strength he lashed out his foot. The killing grip tore loose, gouging agony over face and throat, and the force of his kick shot him upward and back, out over the parapet of the wall. The glittering water careered crazily under him for an instant, he threshed his arms hopelessly for grip or balance, and then air, sea and sky were whirling around him in an insane kaleidoscope –

The mirror broke with a hammerblow, and shattered him to shards. He sank into chill darkness and pain, fighting to breathe against a new and harsher weight. And after an age, an agony, there was air to gasp, and light. Above him the wall, and for a moment it seemed he would be hurled against it. His fingers scrabbled on rusty metal. Then, from above, came a single shriek of yelping agony and a terrible crash, and his fingers tore loose. The cold current whirled him around and past, outwards, seawards. A spark of orange flared in the blackness, and he clutched at that, too. But it was far away, high on the cold cliffs above him, and like the last ember of his consciousness it flickered, guttered, and went out.

CHAPTER TWO

Wilf Jackson's usual twinkling charm was wholly absent from his face, and his neat beard twitched with indignation. 'Damn it, this is ridiculous! You come bursting in on me at six o'clock in the morning, you drag me off down here saying something terrible's happened to the dig – and now you say you don't even know what it is!'

Detective Chief Inspector Giles Ridley of the Saitheby area CID gave a deep sigh and stared out to sea. The waves were grey, the sky was grey, and the drizzle that passed between them was grey. Autumn was creeping into what was left of his soul, and he himself had been rooted out of bed at five twenty-nine precisely – a ghastly hour anywhere, but here it should be illegal. He forced a note of awful sympathy into his voice. 'Afraid I can't tell you more than I know myself, Mr Jackson. Sergeant Harshaw was on duty when the call came in, and he's out there now. But we'll be there in a minute.'

Thank God, Ridley added to himself, though Jackson only snorted irritably. He should have called the police launch back instead of trusting himself to this fibreglass bathtub the dig people called a dory; its blunt bow plunged and wallowed like a hippopotamus among the white horses skipping along the bay. He felt unwell, unwashed, un-shaven, and horribly awake. His only consolation was that the others didn't look much better, and serve 'em right; this was their stupid business. Jackson, according to the patrol car that fetched him, had been rousted out of bed at the diggers' lodgings – apparently with the Ravenshead girl. Nice kid, terrible taste. He himself had found Hansen in bed at the Two Ravens, though the landlady hadn't been sure he would; the great professor hadn't come back by the time she'd gone to bed. In fact, it appeared the great professor was often out on the tiles till the small hours – nice work if you could get it, this academic lark. Now he loomed in the stern by the wheel pulpit, as grey and grim as the cliffs above, so that it was a surprise when he spoke.

'Some act of vandalism, that was all you said. And our security guard? I do not see his boat –'

'No, sir,' said Ridley absently. The dory, turning to come alongside the jetty, was momentarily broadside on to the swell, rearing and rolling. He swallowed heavily, not sure whether he was glad of his empty stomach or not. 'It's missing. And so is he.'

Ridley flung the painter to the uniformed men waiting on the jetty. They looked almost as pasty as Jackson, and that was something to think about: they were local men who wouldn't be upset by half a mile of choppy sea. And by God, there was Bill Harshaw looking cheesy too!

The burly sergeant stepped forward to help the new arrivals up, and was introduced. 'Morning, Professor, Mr Jackson. You'll know your way fine, of course –'

As they moved ahead Ridley leaned over to Harshaw and said softly, 'Now, Bill, what the hell's going on? You all look like you'd seen a ghost, and . . . What the bejasus is that smell? Something dead round here?'

Hansen, overhearing, smiled faintly. 'I am afraid the smell is perfectly normal, Inspector,' said the tall Dane before the sergeant could answer. 'We have simply gotten used to it. In this profession one may – *Gud i himmel!*' The tall man swayed to an invisible punch, clutching violently at the walkway guardrail. Beside him Jackson looked as if he'd been hit by a bus.

Ridley, coming up the ramp behind, couldn't see what had stopped them dead in their tracks. In the pit below them spread out a scene he had seen many times on the TV news, and it didn't look any different. At first the sheer size of the place baffled him; on TV it had looked impressive but somehow easier to take in at a glance. From here it looked like a two-storey steel-walled courtyard, still half-built in scaffolding. Or some weird sports arena, with banks of lights glaring down through the drizzle and the fine mist from a dozen sprayers onto – what?

He realised why it seemed so chaotic. The high brown-black mound of the ship, which had seemed so impressive on TV, looked absurdly small now, with a shredded rag draped carelessly across it. But there was more to it than that, more and worse. The neat rows of white tapes which had formed a chessboard grid across the pit floor, with the hull at its centre, were gone – tangled, torn up, strewn around like streamers after a party. Over a great swathe of the floor the bright Day-Glo labels, which elsewhere sat neatly attached to things in the ground, were crumpled and trampled into the mud. It was almost as if the ship itself had shrugged off everything the archaeologists had tried to impose on it – as if a door to the past, painstakingly coaxed open, had been brutally slammed shut.

Ridley felt a sudden sharp tremor in the guardrail he was leaning on, and saw Hansen leaning over beside him, gripping the rail with a white-knuckled intensity that was almost frightening; the policeman felt that with a touch more effort the metal would twist like a corkscrew. And his face – for a moment Ridley seemed to be looking at an image in wood, a carved Viking with staring eyes, bared teeth, beard bristling. Embarrassed by the naked emotion, Ridley hastily looked back down at the ship – and wished he hadn't.

He had seen unpleasant things enough in his career, early and late in the day, but never after a rough half mile of sea. His all too empty stomach convulsed painfully, and he turned aside and retched slightly behind his hand. Nobody noticed. The thing he had mistaken for a rag had leaked a slug's trail of dark glistening liquid down the timbers. He moved a few steps along the walkway, and saw, scattered across the other flank of the hull and the mud below, a ragged trail of fragments that looked like scraps from a slaughterhouse – raw dark flesh, gobbets of offal and foul pallid tangles of entrail, white shards of splintered bone. For a moment he found it impossible to see what they had once been part of, let alone believe they had come from a single body. Then he saw an unmistakable patch of tan and brown hide, an entire limb with the knuckle joint showing bare, as though torn out bodily by the roots, and near it the hollow curve of a ribcage, mangled and empty. Then it was possible to see the small triangle of jawbone, lying as if flung far from the trampled pinkish paste that must have been the skull, recognisable only by the single eyeball that had spurted out of it.

'Oh my good God. Bill, that must be –'

'The dog, aye, sir. But Lees 'imself, not a sign.' Ridley raised an eyebrow, and Harshaw shook his head. 'Not 'im, sir. Known 'im for years, and 'e was real soft on animals. But since t'boat's gone –'

'– you reckon chummy took it? And maybe Lees – or . . .' He made a tossing movement towards the water.

Harshaw nodded heavily, and Ridley pursed his lips. The two archaeologists were still staring grey-faced down at the mayhem. Time to seize his advantage and slip in a few questions before they could snap back.

'Anything missing, Mr Jackson – Mr Jackson?' Jackson's neat features were sagging with shock. 'Professor Hansen?'

The craggy face turned towards him. 'I would have to go down there. And I think you will not wish me to, yet.'

Ridley blinked with surprise. The voice was calm, the words spoken with a care that minimised his accent. Cold fish, this one – or cool. 'In a moment, sir. When the photographer's ready Sergeant Harshaw will take you through –' He stopped short. Jackson had sprung to life, leaned forward for a moment and then gone racing around the walkway to the far side. He gave a sudden wild yell and waved.

'God! Hal! *Hal!* They've got the second chest!'

Hansen exhaled sharply, and his head sagged forward. He stared down at the walkway for an instant, but spoke as calmly as before. 'That was only to be expected, I suppose . . .'

Ridley collected his wits. 'Excuse me – the *second* chest?'

Hansen gave an utterly mirthless smile. He strode along after Jackson, and pointed down at the gaping hole between the hull's bare ribs. 'We were hoping to keep that a secret from the public, for the moment.'

'So who *did* know?'

Hansen shrugged. 'All of us on the dig, naturally. And that television fellow Latimer –'

'He was with us down at the house until late last night,' muttered Jackson as he came back.

Ridley coughed diplomatically. Another one who'd been reading detective stories, too ready to start plastering alibis over the landscape. 'We're not chasing anybody, yet. The chest's just one factor. I don't suppose you've considered other motives?'

They both looked nonplussed. *Specialists! Can't imagine anything more important than their load of little Viking knick-knacks!* 'You don't know, for example, just how much local ill-feeling there is about this set-up of yours?'

Hansen mouthed an O of understanding. 'The fishermen, you mean? They do not like the dam obstructing the main navigational channel. Yes, I can understand that. But they can still get by. And it is only for two seasons, it will bring in much tourist income, and we obtained the council's permission . . .'

'Even so. They don't think much of the council either. And there's a trace of something else. You most often hear them bellyaching about wasting time and daft university types, the usual class warfare claptrap, but there's a real resentment underneath. They don't like what you're doing here.'

'Superstition? They are not savages, they are Yorkshire-men with very hard heads –'

'Aye, hard-headed enough – but old-fashioned with it, and bloody-minded. A couple of drinks and that resentment gets blown up out of all proportion – it can turn violent.'

Hansen thought for a moment. 'But surely it would not go this far? This guard of ours, is he not a local man also? Well. And the chest is not merely destroyed, but emptied. You must forgive me for thinking only as an archaeologist, but I remain sure that whoever did it came for what that chest might contain – came, perhaps, a long way. And

32

were such people that the lives of a man and a dog did not mean much to them.'

Ridley twisted his mouth. Normally he'd never bandy theories with anyone but his own people, but this Hansen was definitely in a position to throw some weight around – especially with the Press. Time to touch the forelock. Besides which, his reaction might be interesting. 'Give me *some* credit, Professor. First thing I thought of – except that Scotland Yard keep tabs on the high-grade villains in the antiquities game; any of 'em come within a hundred miles, they'd just love tipping the word to us locals. Up till now, well, no offence, but you've not been churning up the kind of stuff that would interest them. It was only yesterday you found that chest, the news wasn't broadcast till late evening, an hour or two at most before – well, this. We're examining all the possibilities, but I can't imagine a pro coming running that quick – not when the chest hadn't been opened, and he didn't know there was a second one. And if he did, he'd be more likely to have a go wherever you've got chest number one – your lab, of course – than out here. Eh?'

'The waste of it!' exploded Jackson before Hal could answer. 'Criminal waste! What could have been in that chest – the opportunities –'

Hansen smiled sourly. 'I should not be too worried, Wilf. You can still tell *Timescape* all about number one. And say to the newspapers how you are defying the new Tutankhamen's Curse.'

Jackson's face collapsed in a self-righteous glower, suggesting that Hansen's shaft was all too accurate. Ridley looked sourly at the pair of them. *Academic types! Squabbling like a pair of teenyboppers.* There was some excuse for Hansen, though; the man was obviously under terrible strain. A change of subject was indicated. He raised his voice. 'Box Brownie boy ready yet, Bill? Okay, send him through and take the prof in after. You understand, Professor? We want to know what's obviously missing, near as you can tell us. Also anything there that shouldn't be – tools, anything like that you're not one hundred per cent sure about, okay?'

33

Hansen looked glum. 'That will present a problem. We obviously do not know what was in the chest.'

'Mmmh. The first chest? If you had a look in that, could you guess . . .'

Hansen shook his head sharply. 'Not a safe guess! When I travel, I might pack one bag full of clothes, another of books – you follow? In any event, it is not so simple. Whatever is in that first chest will need microscopic examination and testing before we dare move it, let alone remove it – understand, I am not being finicky. Without stringent conservation work it might crumble to nothing – meaningless as evidence for either of us.'

Ridley nodded. 'I understand. And you really can't even hazard –'

'I cannot!' said the tall man firmly. 'Not yet. We may have lost the greatest treasure since Sutton Hoo, or nothing at all.'

And a right little can of worms that opens up, thought Ridley as he watched the photographer go tottering down the steps. Suppose there was something valuable, and one of the diggers – maybe even Hansen or Jackson – just happened to want the money more than the glory? Professional archaeologists couldn't expect to get windfalls under the treasure-trove law on stuff they'd dug up. Or there was nothing, and somebody didn't want to lose face – Hansen? *Doesn't seem like his style. Jackson? Wouldn't have the guts. Bit extreme for either of 'em, this. Maniac's work. Doing that to a poor bloody mutt –*

'The dog!' said Jackson suddenly, as if reading Ridley's mind. 'Last night's guard, it was – forgotten the name – older chap, broken nose . . .'

'Bill Lees, aye. So?'

'Well, I may be wrong, but wasn't there a dust-up over that dog of his? About, oh, six weeks back?'

The professor glared at the supervisor, ran a hand through his thick red hair, and clutched at it for an instant. 'Something we should know about?' inquired Ridley politely.

'If only to dismiss it,' grunted Hansen, no longer cool; Jackson's return shot had hit the nerve. 'A stupid business

– one of my supervisors a few weeks ago, working late on a light summer evening. The dog was not used to seeing him, it growled at him and I believe tried to bite him. He does not like dogs, and I believe they generally return such feelings.'

'Seems so. And?'

'He was nervous, perhaps. He was foolish enough to kick it, and it did bite him, not badly, before Mr Lees could restrain it. There was an argument.'

Ridley and Harshaw exchanged expressionless glances. 'Oh aye? And, who was this dog-lover, just by the by?'

'A young man called Colby – Jay Colby. He is one of my departmental staffers –'

Harshaw's finger twanged the rubber band that secured his notebook. 'Well now, sir. I'll *bet* there was an argument –'

'All right, Bill,' said Ridley quietly. 'Perhaps we'll send Mr Jackson down to look around just now – I'd like a word with you first, Prof. If you don't mind, that is.'

Hansen shrugged with weary fatalism, and Harshaw bustled Jackson away out of earshot. Hansen watched him go, and, surprisingly, smiled. 'Poor Wilf! I hope you do not think we are bickering like that *all* the time. This has come as a blow to him . . .'

'His big chance, you mean? Can't blame a man for being ambitious, Professor . . .'

'Oh no, I agree. And he is a very knowledgeable man, a real expert in his chosen field. But he seems hypnotised by this television nonsense. Myself, I would be glad enough to be rid of it, except that it helps to interest people in the subject.'

Ridley smiled wryly. The abominable snowman was definitely thawing a bit. 'For recruiting, you mean? I wish TV cop shows did. Seems to give them all the damnedest bloody ideas of what we do . . .'

'I can believe that. For recruiting, yes, to raise money for expensive projects like this – and to make John Q. Public see why it is worth delaying that new freeway or office building a few months, so we can save vital knowledge it would obliterate. People must be informed, so that they know why they must care for their past, their inheritance – perhaps not as passionately as a good archaeologist does, but enough.'

'I see,' said Ridley thoughtfully. 'This lad Colby – is he a good archaeologist? Does he care passionately?'

Hansen nodded. 'I had him in mind.'

I'll bet you did. To defend him, though? Or what?

'In fact,' continued Hansen, 'he is probably the best single doctoral student at Rayner's graduate school in all my time there. Since he quit football he has been dedicated to his subject, single-minded –'

'Aye – but he's still got some leisure time, hasn't he? What'd he do with it back home?'

The tall man hesitated. His fingers rasped over his thick beard. 'Sport, I guess, mostly – tennis, swimming. I believe he once took up judo or something of the sort. And he rides motorcycles – he has one here.'

'I know. I've seen it. Must've set him back a bob or two, eh?'

'You mean, was it expensive? Probably. I am no expert.'

'And he could afford something like that? A student?'

'Many times over. His family is wealthy even by local standards – and the locality is Texas. He has a considerable income, and they indulge him. It is a miracle he is not more spoilt.'

'I wonder,' said Ridley thoughtfully. 'Doesn't just zoom around alone, though, does he?'

'Hardly,' said Hansen, and his face took on a strange sour smile. 'A number of girls seem to have found him impressive –'

'I mean with friends – a group – other bike enthusiasts . . .' Hansen hesitated again, and Ridley pounced. 'Come on, Professor – does he hang around with biker types?'

'I believe sometimes,' admitted Hansen, as if a tooth was being extracted.

'Tough types? Hell's Angels?'

'I believe he did at one time – he had rather a disturbed adolescence, and –'

'Aye. Well, he's doing it again.'

Hansen's face clouded over, the heavy brows knitting

36

to form a solid storm-front. 'Here? Just what are you talking about, officer?'

'Chief Inspector,' Ridley reminded him coolly. 'I'd better spell it out. These last few years we've had the usual crew of layabouts on this patch – pretty pathetic bunch, Saitheby lads but no different from any dole-queue dropouts anywhere else. They get pissed, make a lot of noise, chase girls who don't know any better, duff each other over, that sort of thing – trouble enough, but not *real* trouble, if you follow me. At worst, pinch a tourist's handbag or a car to joyride. But this last year they've changed, and it's no improvement. Your Mr Colby starts hanging around with them now and again. Suddenly the petty theft more or less stops, and yet they've more cash than ever to throw around. They're more organised. They go roaring round the roads in convoy showing off and making a bloody nuisance of themselves. Almost no casual violence – but a couple of what looked like pitched battles with toughs from the fishing boats and the farms. One or two of them are turning into really nasty pieces of work – rumours of gangbangs, that sort of thing. And I personally am damn sure they're getting drugs from somewhere. Do I need to make it any clearer?'

Hansen's eyes blazed. 'Yes,' he said with startling ferocity. 'I believe you do. Rumours – implications – do you know, have you any idea how ridiculous it is to imagine Jay Colby doing anything to damage this dig? Anyone who knew him would find the idea absurd! I think you had better be damn sure you have solid proof before you start involving any member of my staff!'

Ridley hated anybody trying to intimidate him, but taller men most of all. 'Proof?' he barked. 'Let me tell you – *yes, Bill, what the hell is it now?*' He yanked the little walkie-talkie from under his coat. 'I see,' he added, less irritably. 'Okay, I'm on my way – no, you stay here and get the gen from Jackson and the Prof. Okay. Ridley out.' He turned to Hansen. 'You heard? They've found Lees, alive – just. Washed up a few miles down the coast, on some rocks. Exposure and a skull fracture, so he's not telling us anything yet; still, I'd better get down there and see. But listen here,

37

Prof – I'm not implying anything, not yet. But ask me where I'd find somebody in this area crazy enough to do . . . that,' he nodded down to the depths, 'it'd be that little bunch. And your Mr Colby's mixed in with them.'

The dusk was drier than the dawn, but darker. It settled clammily over Saitheby, blanketing the cheerful layers of red pantiled roofs; the little town, crouched in its steep-walled rift in the cliffs, seemed to fold in on itself under the shadowy weight. Jess Thorne, waiting down by the harbour for her bus home, felt as if everybody else in town had retreated behind those rows of glowing windows and left her shivering out here. There was plenty of light from the big dockside lamps, brighter and whiter than ordinary streetlights, but there was no warmth in it; it was bleak in the extreme, especially gleaming on the muddy black estuary water, and it made the town beyond seem vastly more remote.

She shrugged; she was going soft, that was what – too dependent on Hal Hansen's car. So he wasn't back from talking to the cops yet, so what? She'd managed well enough on the bus for the first week or two. For the tenth time she looked up the hillside, and felt ridiculously comforted to see the cheerful lights of a bus that might be hers come snaking down through the newer part of the town, momentarily silhouetting the high-roofed Victorian buildings, gleams of gothic fantasy against the sullen cliff face. In the tallest one of all, lights blazed yellow from uncurtained windows, and she grinned. She'd be infinitely more comfortable in her trailer than crammed into Dracula's Castle up there with all the rest. The sheer press of people there made her itchy, the permanent tang of damp, laundry, stale cooking and underwashed bodies hanging in the air. And most of all the lack of privacy – all of them living in each other's pockets. She had to be free to breathe the clean air above the cliffs, without anyone to note her comings and goings. It was worth a little extra trouble, an occasional lonely wait and long walk, to get that. As long as this bus didn't turn off before the bridge . . . It did, and Jess swore. God alone knew when hers'd be along now.

Then a sudden scraping sound made her jump, a dragging rasp that echoed along the empty sidestreet behind her. She looked around sharply and saw movement in the deep dark pools between the streetlights. Something large walked there, quickly but oddly, with a swaying, lurching gait that reminded Jess of a bear. Abruptly, it plunged forward into the light, caught hold of a lamppost and swung around it with a blood-curdling rebel yell.

'Why sure it is Miz Scarlett O'Hara!' drawled a deep voice. 'Evenin', mam, you look like a million dollars. Shall we dance?'

Jess let her shoulders sag with a sigh. 'Jay . . . You crumb, Jay, you really made me jump there, you know that?' She peered more closely at the swinging figure. 'You look like hell . . . Jay, are you drunk again? Have you been fighting?'

'I cannot tell a lie,' he carolled. 'I did it with my little hatchet! Hey, I really showed the scaly bastards, you know, nine of them or maybe ten and they got their fuckin' clocks well and truly *cleaned*, excuse *me*! Goddam fishermen, try an' tell me I can't drink where I want to in this town! C'mon, let's dance, dah-de-dah –'

Jess rubbed a weary hand over her eyes. 'Oh Jay . . .' She heard the wary tenderness of her own tone, and it infuriated her. It was snapping at he needed, not sympathy. 'For the love of God, Jay, you're an educated man – can't you grow up or something? I mean, quit acting like you're Indiana Jones!'

The big man guffawed. 'Pardon me, mam, you seen my bullwhip lyin' around? Man can't be a real ark-ay-ologist withouten a bullwhip'n'a purty gall, can he now? Well, guess I'll have t'settle for the one – c'mere!'

'The Hero is Back!' said Jess sardonically, evading his clumsy lunge. 'A born bullwhipper, that's you. Hands off, Jay, you don't know where I've been.'

'But I know where you're goin'!' he hissed melodramatically. 'Back to that lonely ol' tin trailer up there on the seacliffs. Why d'you like living up there all on your lonesome, Jess? Whaddya do all night long? How come Hal doesn't come sleep there? Or drag you off back to his nice little room at the pub?'

She looked at him levelly. 'Hal doesn't own me, Jay. Any more than you did. The difference is, he isn't fooling himself –'

'You mean he lets you kick his ass around!' growled Colby. His massive hand flickered out and clamped around her forearm. 'But there's more differences than that – aren't there? He's an old man. Jess! You're wastin' your time with him – come back with me! Now, to my room! It's real snug up there, you don't want to hang around freezin' your ass off on a night like this –'

Jess managed to yank her arm free. 'Forget it, Jay! That's all over, remember? Finished – *fini – finito –* washed up! Got that? Times change! Other places to go –'

He grinned like a dog. 'Aw, c'mon, Jess . . . We had good times together, we really went places –'

'Did we, Jay? Did we really? Don't kid yourself. It wasn't that great.'

'Not that great? Ah c'mon now, Jess – Hal ever make it five times in one night?'

Jess pursed her lips tight with annoyance. 'You want to talk performance? Okay, we'll talk performance! Jay, if you'd ever really cared a damn about women you'd have realised they might want something more than a battering ram play and a row of notches on the bedpost –'

'Hell, you never had any complaints at the time! That's just all this feminist batcrap you've been pickin' up, Jess – why'd you ever let that come between us?'

'You know damn well what came between us, Jay. And it's still there.'

He stood very still, hands on hips, head thrown back, staring down his dented nose at her. 'Meanin'?'

She sighed. 'You and your little frat buddies.'

He didn't move. 'That was an accident, and you know it. Still get nightmares about it. Sure do appreciate your flingin' it in my face . . .'

'I wasn't talking about that!' She breathed out raggedly, between clenched teeth. 'Oh Jay . . . You think I couldn't see it? Where you were really at, who with? And I was just an ornament, a status symbol – a full scorecard to prove you're a real man, Mr Colby, and never mind . . . Forget it. But I'm never going back . . .'

He caught her hands, more gently. 'Hey, look, so maybe I did neglect you a bit – so maybe I hadn't quite got my emotions centred up yet, sure, that happens at that age, when you're too young to know what you really want – what you value. So I was a dummy then, I drove you right into Hal – you goin' to torture me for it now? Jess – I need you, Jessie, Jessica. Come back . . .'

His huge hands clasped her shoulders gently, though she tried to wriggle out from under. She glared up at him, but he towered over her as few men could, his gaze sweeping her up and down, stripping her, she realised, in memory. 'You look great, kid,' he said in a husky whisper she remembered well. 'Fit for a king! C'mon, Jess, you still go for me – c'mon, just once – just for tonight even – for ole times' sake – Hal'd never know –' He was pleading like a little boy, unable to believe he'd be denied something.

'With you bragging all around the dig? Forget it, Jay! – Why don't you go sleep it off, huh? – Jay, will you let go of me or . . . Dammit, Jay, I mean it! If Hal –'

He smiled slowly, shaking his head, and drew her closer to him. A glassy intensity was creeping into the pale-blue eyes, although one was blackened and puffy, and his blood-bordered nostrils flared to catch her scent. She could sense him wanting her as he'd used to, coming a triumphant mass of bruises off the football field. Like something he'd earned – battle honours, a cup for the victor, none but the brave deserve the fair. The thought of that made her flesh crawl now.

Jess's crossed hands shot upwards, stiffened into blades, and chopped hard into Colby's biceps. He grunted and let go, and she stumbled back in a defensive crouch – knowing, though, that he would not return the blow. For all he enjoyed a fair roughhouse, he kept a tight rein on his strength these days. Now he was looking at her, eyes brimming with the agonised surprise of a rejected child.

41

But that weapon also had been used on her too often before. 'That's it, Jay! That's enough! Any more and I put another dent in that nose of yours – and start screaming loud enough to bring down every copper in town, you hear? You hear?'

He glared at her with the petulant resentment of drink, and stumbled forward. Jess retreated carefully.

'Jay – I'm warning you . . .' She wasn't scared, not exactly. She could handle Jay, she'd had to before. He was no rapist, but with the drink to help he was quite capable of going too far, persuading himself that it was what she really wanted. The least traumatic thing would be a convenient exit, but there weren't any. She looked around frantically, but there was nobody else in sight and no sign of her bus, even across the harbour. There was an engine sound, though, approaching, a flash of lights from the bridgehead and the sound of a big car rumbling across the old swingbridge. When she saw it was a Range Rover Jess leaped up and waved, snatched up her bag and sprinted towards it as it came purring down the dockside. The passenger door was flung open, and she bounded up into the high passenger seat. Hal Hansen smiled across at her. 'They told me you had gone for your bus. Were you talking to somebody there?'

Jess shook her head. 'Nobody important.'

The Range Rover rumbled off down the empty street.

'But soft,' squawked Neville in a ludicrous falsetto. 'What fairy footsteps steal upon mine ear? Size 12 by the sound of it. If found, return to Thomas Jefferson Colby III, spinster of this parish.'

'Shut *up*, Neville, he'll hear you!' hissed Pru, fighting her giggles and losing. 'You know what he's like when he's had a few, honestly, he's worse than Daddy –'

The common-room door swung open, and Colby filled the gap, gazing disdainfully around at the happy squalor like a Roman patrician entering a slum. A somewhat drunken patrician, because he spoiled the effect with a rasping belch.

'But soft,' Neville trilled again, 'what wind from yonder blighter breaks?'

Pointedly ignoring Neville, the immense young man weaved out across the room, steering a perilous course between the piles of old magazines and paperbacks littering the floor. An abandoned beercan squashed under his foot. He bumped into the bare melamine table, clattering its jetsam of unwashed crockery and coffee-mugs, kicked one of the fifth-hand wooden chairs out of the way, and staggered up against the rows of open cubicles on the far wall, crammed with stale sneakers, laundry clean and unclean, items of cooking gear and other personal relics. Things spilled out as he bounced along the wall. 'Ach, watch it, y'drunken booger!' grumbled a heavyset man from the depths of the less dangerous armchair.

Colby manoeuvred his bulk around to face him, and leered nastily. 'Aw, we're getting kind of fastidious all of a sudden, Hardwicke, aren't we?' he growled. 'Given up sniping at other folks's pheasants? Or looking up little girls' skirts?' Pru clapped a hand to her mouth, but all Harry Hardwicke did was cackle.

'Nay, lad – not yet. So you'll joost 'ave to wait yer turn!' He was the dig's crane operator and driver, seconded on a programme for long-term unemployed. He was also the town character, a short, massive man in his mid-thirties with coarse, gypsyish good looks, now running to a beer gut. His persistent tastes for poaching and teenyboppers had got him into trouble before, but he was no child molester, and most people liked him. He heaved himself up to face Colby, and his chest and arms were almost as formidable as the younger man's. 'Now – you going t'pick those oop like a good lad?'

Colby's reply was cut short by the sharp rapping of a heavy pipe in a metal ashtray. 'That'll do, the pack of ye!' A copy of *The Scotsman*, erected like a wall, crumpled down, and the thin face of Forbes, the senior supervisor, peered over it. 'Ye're no' fit company for civilised men. Away wi' you t'yer bed, Jay – it was where ye were gaun' anyhow, wasn't it?'

Before things could go any further, Pru sprang to scoop

43

up and return the fallen items. Colby's gaze, bleaker than the light of the bare ceiling bulbs, swept across them all for an instant, then he stumbled around and went banging and clattering up the decrepit staircase to the first floor 'bedrooms'. The title was a hollow courtesy for rooms as big, bleak and empty as the rest of the building. There was nothing in them but bare walls and boards where the diggers could stretch out air mattresses and campbeds. The wealthier of them managed a few luxuries – reading lamps and transistor radios. At least they were roomy, a welcome, sometimes necessary escape from the noise and bustle downstairs – and from occasional embarrassing situations.

They heard him go, listened to his boots clatter across the boards above and the rending crash as he slumped down on his big old-fashioned campbed. Pru sighed deeply. 'Ah, don't let Gentleman Jay get to you, pet,' said Harry cheerfully. 'You know 'e always apologises in the morning.'

'Yes, I suppose he will,' said Pru, a little too brightly. 'Still, I think I'd better be going up myself . . .'

'What's the 'urry?' demanded Neville wickedly. 'The Mighty Wilf's not back yet . . .'

'Aye,' grinned Harry. 'T'night is young. Fancy a round o' cards?'

'With you?' she smiled. 'You'd want to make it strip snap, and I don't think we could stand the awful revelations really, could we, Neville? Nighty-night!' She shut the door softly and began the long tramp up to her own room on the top floor. It suddenly seemed longer and more depressing than it ever had. She wished Wilf would come back. He seemed somehow less eager to, these days. And people seemed to be getting at her about him, laughing – the Mighty Wilf – it was so unfair. Nobody got at Jess, and Hal was just about old enough to be her father. Well, nobody would dare get at Jess; it must be nice to be all tough and independent like that. Pru was trying, but it didn't seem to come easily to her. Taking up with Wilf had been part of making it happen; he was dapper, charming, terrific fun in bed, and above all interesting. The places

44

he'd been to, the things he'd seen, the way he had caught her up in his involvement with archaeology . . .

Even if that did make him a bit too ambitious – especially lately . . . Well, you had to be, didn't you? Though Hal Hansen stayed so charming – but then he'd reached the top now, hadn't he, and didn't have to push any more?

Moving down here, that was another part of her ambition, away from her strict and disapproving parents to a place where everyone else was sloppy, scruffy, and easygoing like her. Nowadays she only went home for the occasional bath – there were none here – or when her parents were away, but even then it felt like going back to jail. Whatever the problems, this had to be better, didn't it? If only Wilf would come back . . .

Their room was better than most – Wilf had seen to that – but she could hear the wind rising and whistling around her as she undressed, and she was shivering in draughts, real or imaginary. She slipped hastily under the duvet and tucked it in around her. Was that rumbling sound the wind? She giggled. No; Jay's snoring. She'd have to be careful, when Wilf got back. Everything echoed in this place – everything . . .

A long, slow creak echoed in the stairwell. Then another, and another, a slowly accelerating fusillade of sounds with a descant of giggles and squeaks. The card players all looked up at the ceiling.

'My God,' groaned Forbes. 'They're at it again! Them, and yon wind, and Jay snoring – will we never get ony peace an' quiet in this place?'

'Could be,' said Harry. 'You know ol' Wilfie overloads the power sockets in that room something awful? One more gadget plugged in there and 'appen 'e'll be getting a new kind of bang. Teach 'im to mess around wi' Pru.'

'Aye, and maybe blow 'er backwards out of her knickers,' said Neville, finishing his deal. 'C'mon, lads, where's your cash?'

'In your bluidy pockets, mostly,' said Forbes distastefully. 'Want to sit in on my hand, Paul?'

Paul Harvey looked up from his archaeology textbook and smiled uncertainly. 'Not my game, really. Sorry – *what . . .?*'

All of them jumped. The wind had risen to a tearing, drumming howl that grasped the windows and shook them. There was a long rasping slithering sound, a moment of silence, and then a spectacular popping crash from outside.

'Slates!' said Forbes. 'It's takin' the slates right aff the roof. And will you listen to it creak? This place isna' safe!'

'Ee, sure it's not Hurricane Wilfie at it again?' asked Harry, grateful for the diversion from an unpromising hand.

'That'd put anyone off their stroke!' chuckled Neville.

'Don't know about that,' said Paul. 'It hasn't interrupted Sleeping Beauty, has it?' An exceptionally loud snore vibrated through the ceiling. 'Is he always like – well, the way he was earlier?'

'Ach, no,' said Forbes reassuringly. 'He'll be sorry for that the morn. He can be gey friendly – specially if you've a real interest in the subject. Takes it very seriously – and himself as well, sadly, so he's no' sae ready to take a joke. But he's a damn good supervisor – look at the way he was organisin' everybody to get the excavation back in order today, wi' the cops tramplin' roond in a'body's way. Don't blame him for hittin' the bottle after that.'

'It's what else 'e hits,' muttered Neville. The wind roared and battered the windows, and another slate went crashing down into the street. High overhead the roof creaked and groaned as if a great weight rode down on it. 'Ah, well, on wi' the game . . .'

'Sorry, Nev,' said Harry hastily, forcing an elaborately unconvincing yawn. 'Proper shagged out, I am. Gotta pack it in for tonight . . .'

Hastily he rammed his cards back in the pack, but Neville managed to fish them out and examine them. 'I've got news for you, 'Ardwicke,' he muttered. 'I've sold you. Better pack your bags, they'll be 'ere for you in an hour . . .'

The offender stared at him, deeply shocked. 'Ee, you

46

wouldn't take advantage of an exhausted man, would you?'

Exhausted or not, Harry's senses were those of a poacher. The first faint sound flipped him into instant wakefulness from the depths of a confused but intriguing dream. At first, though, he wasn't quite sure he was awake. Then he realised that the willowy gauze-draped female form bending over him wasn't a stray fantasy. It was Pru, golden in the glow of the streetlights, wearing only a very floppy old T-shirt that was translucent enough to reveal all sorts of interesting things.

'Eeee!' said Harry happily. From that angle it was obvious she wasn't wearing anything else.

'Hssh!' hissed Pru. 'There's something funny downstairs, and Wilf won't do anything, I don't think he believes me but I know there was something, I mean he said it was the wind but you don't imagine a sound like that, not twice I mean –'

'Mmmnhh? 'Ow's that again, flower?'

She seized his shoulder. 'Listen!'

He tried. It wasn't easy. Colby was still snoring like a hog next door, on the far side of the room Neville was muttering in his sleep, and the old house was a chorus of grumbling and groaning in the savage wind. But he gradually filtered these out as he would the thousand sounds of a wood at night, to concentrate on the single sound that mattered, the hesitant movement in the undergrowth, the soft chattering of pheasants dozing on low branches. But what he isolated now was no natural sound, and he couldn't place it. The ticking creak of lifted fence-wire? The squeak of a rusty shotgun hinge? Something metal, moved, strained . . .

'I hear it, pet . . . Somewhere downstairs, eh? Neville! *Neville!* Wake oop, y'dozy booger!'

Neville's moustache twitched violently, he snorted and his eyes flew open. They took in a rear view of Pru in her T-shirt, bending over Harry, and kept on opening. But he heard the sounds when they were pointed out.

'Could be visitors,' whispered Harry. 'Could be them bastards as knocked over t'dam, eh?'

Neville swung out of bed and into his tracksuit trousers in one movement. 'Want a coat, luv?'

Pru, suddenly aware of the exposure, managed to smile, look embarrassed and whisper 'Thanks!' all at once. Harry flashed a look that said *Spoilsport!* only too clearly, and rummaged around for his jeans.

They made an odd procession on the dimly-lit landing, Harry in jeans that barely stayed up over his beer gut and peep-show Y-fronts, Neville in an old tracksuit, and Pru in his crumpled raincoat which came down to her knees, carrying her little handtorch. Neville carried a steel strut from his campbed, and Harry grabbed a pick-handle from one of the tool stacks – better than nothing, but not much. The sounds were hard to locate out on the landing; they seemed to be coming from the rear of the building, which would put them directly under Pru's room. They crept over to the door of the room below hers, and listened. A minute of silence passed. Their breathing and their excited heartbeats sounded so thunderous in the silence they were afraid they might miss something. But after one minute, perhaps two, they heard the same stealthy creak.

'Anyone sleeping in here?' hissed Neville.

'Don't think so.' Harry hefted the pick handle in fingers that were suddenly sweaty, and eased the door gently open.

The orange-lit windows seemed to leap out at him, but the room itself was solid darkness. They heard something stir on the floor, there was a flurry of shapeless shadow-motion and a silhouette whipped upright against the window.

'Who is it? Who's there?'

Neville breathed out sharply. The voice was Paul Harvey's.

'Ssshh, Paul! Sorry,' whispered Pru shakily. 'We heard something –' And just then it came again, louder, long-drawn out, a grinding tortured creak of metal against stone. And everybody looked down at the floor.

'T'ground floor!' whispered Harry. 'There's storerooms

48

or summat down there . . . C'mon!' He noticed Paul come padding out behind them, gestured him back, but gave up as he fell in next to Pru. Well, why not? He'd have done the same himself.

The staircase down was a nightmare, because they didn't want to alert anyone with the torch. Harry, in the lead, had never tried going down it in darkness, and he wasn't enjoying his first attempt. He was used enough to things looking different in the dark, to the tricks moonlight could play with your sense of direction. But here there was only reflected light, broken into scattered shadows by the gnarly carvings on the banisters. And the hallway below was worse, like wading slowly down into an ice-cold inky pool, the tiled floor chilling his feet numb. He couldn't see where the rear storeroom door was, even whether it was open or closed – Christ, they might be in already, standing next to him –

He touched the doorframe and stopped so suddenly that Pru bumped into him, with the faintest of squeaks. The door was closed – maybe even locked? His fingers walked across the peeling paint of the panels, found the cold brass doorknob and rotated it very slowly. The action was heavy, but it turned, and he could feel the door give a little and spring free – unlocked, and what was on the other side? Neville's heavy hand touched his shoulder, and he sensed him slide across to the far side of the door. Pru and the lad would be facing the door, ready with the torch . . . Taking a deep breath, he flung the door back with a ringing crash. The torchlight flickered and spilled out – into a completely empty room.

With a rasp of anger Neville stumped across the cold brick floor and wrestled with the heavy shutters on the window, closed tight and sealed with generations of dusty cobwebs. Harry joined him, and the old hinges whimpered as the panels swung open. Pru's little circle of light fell upon a row of very grimy windowpanes, opaque with dirt and minor cracks – but visibly intact. 'Well, bugger me!' said Neville flatly. Harry looked around. It was a largish room, with bare whitewashed walls; it couldn't have been emptier, and these were the only windows there were.

'It was coming from here, all right!' said Pru tremulously, clutching the coat around her. 'You all heard it – didn't you?' Overhead there was a buzz of confused voices. Harry rubbed the back of his neck, shook out his curls with a sigh; he'd never live this one down. But suddenly Neville leant forward, peering through the end window, and swore. He reached up and clawed at the window catch, then with a heave he sent the whole lower sash leaping upward, and a blast of cold air came spilling in with the grey light of dawn.

'Chr-rr-ist!' breathed Harry, and Paul echoed him.

'Oh my God!' quavered Pru.

The windows were barred. Outside, six rods were set in the masonry, blackened with paint or dirt, each of them a good half inch thick and visibly cemented in. But at the base of the rightmost pair the cement was cracked and splintered, and about halfway up the bars themselves had been bent and twisted apart. Neville leaned out. The bars still stopped his burly shoulders – just.

'See owt?'

'Not a thing. Street's empty. God, what's that?' He pulled himself hurriedly back in, wiping at his bare arm. 'Bloody cold – felt like –'

Droplets spattered the window, and a flurry of flakes rode in on the wind.

'Sleet?' said Pru, unbelieving. 'Already?'

CHAPTER THREE

'WHAT I can't understand,' Paul Harvey protested, 'is what they were after. What'd they want – the furniture?' There was a ripple of derisive laughter from the thirty-odd diggers sitting at, around, or – courting disaster – on the rickety common-room table.

Harry, sprawled in his springshot armchair, smacked his lips and made vague clutching gestures at Pru. 'I reckon it were t'white slavers, after a tasty young body.'

'No chance,' said Neville. 'What would they want with 'er when they can 'ave a ruddy magnificent specimen of man'ood like you?'

'Ee, lad, I never knew you cared. Give us a kiss – or better still, make us a coop o'coffee! All this boogerin' about in the dark, I miss me beauty sleep.'

' 'Ark at the ruddy Yorkshire Marvel,' grunted Neville. 'Anyone'd think you'd scared 'em off single-'anded. What about the lovely Pru, eh? Not to mention yours truly and the audacious Mr Paul – 'e was up just as late as you! You should be makin' us coffee!'

Paul laughed. 'I'll make it – hate to see a grown man cry. Anyway, it'll be a change to have the kitchen free, with all you shower in here.' With only three Calor gas cookers between thirty diggers, it was usually jampacked, but today everyone wanted to hear about the break-in, and air their own pet theories. The commonest, naturally, was that it was somehow linked with the raid at the dam.

'But I can't see how it *can* be!' said Pru. 'I mean, all the finds and that sort of thing are down at the Museum, and we don't exactly leave diamond rings lying about, do we? I mean, gosh, I don't even have a decent pair of earrings down here.'

51

Harry grinned. 'Aye, not since we ripped t'ruddy floor oop looking for t'last pair.'

'No, seriously,' Paul shouted over the sound of a boiling kettle. 'If someone's got it in for the dig, then they'd come here, wouldn't they?'

Neville's grin faded. ' 'Ow d'you mean?'

'Well, the way Colby goes around duffing up fishermen . . .'

'Ay, you've got a point. Might just be 'arbouring 'ard feelings, some of 'em.'

'Can't imagine why – just 'cos they were flattened by a two-hundred-and-fifty-pound Texan thug. Here, coffee's up, come and get it.'

'Oh, super,' said Pru. 'If I don't have some soon I'm going to be asleep all day.'

Harry looked grave. 'Ee, can't 'ave that, petal. Soom dirty booger'd take advantage of you.' He made another grab, and Pru squealed in mock indignation.

'Put me down, Harry, you don't know where I've been. Oh –'

The buzz of conversation faltered and ran down as one by one people registered the blocky outline that had quietly appeared in the doorway.

' 'Lo there, Inspector!' said Harry, unabashed. 'Lookin' for soombody, were yer?'

'Well, not you, my lad – for once.' Ridley hesitated, as if weighing up which approach would be best. He seemed to come to a decision at once, and smiled apologetically. 'Sorry to just breeze on in like this, but your doorbell seems to be an archaeological relic. Anyway, if you've all got a moment – and maybe a spare drop of that coffee –'

'Takin' yer life in yer 'ands, Inspector!' grinned Neville, pushing an overfilled cup across the table. 'We didn't know Mr Paul only made it 'cause he wanted 'is socks washed –'

Paul made a rude gesture at him. Ridley carefully ignored it, slumping down onto a creaky chair with a deep sigh. 'As long as it's hot and wet and preferably strong – God, that's welcome! First thing I've had this morning, and it was another five o'clock start.' He looked around him keenly. 'Which is what brings me here, as it happens.

Any of you hear anything unusual in the street last night?'

Harry and Neville exchanged glances. 'Depends what you mean,' said Harry uneasily. 'Soombody were messin' about wi' our cellar windows, maybe tryin' t'break in –'

'Oh aye? So that's what all the argifying was about? Should've reported it at once. I'd better have a look-see.'

Ridley stared at the mangled bars, poked at an untouched one, and turned to the expectant audience of diggers. 'Well! They're not just for show, those bars – they're solid. Looks as if somebody was using a strainer – what the Fire Brigade use to get kids' heads out of park railings. Garages have 'em, too. But why – well, the police, as they say, are baffled.'

'So're we an' all,' said Harry. 'Nothin' 'ere worth nickin', is there?'

'Not a lot,' said Ridley. 'And it doesn't seem to have much bearing on my main problem.'

'What's that, then?'

'Death, causes unknown, one. An old gippo tramp called Wally Rogan. Found down on the corner there with his head bashed in.'

'Might've been one of our slates,' suggested Forbes, one of the upstairs sleepers. 'I was forever wakin' up and hearin' them go rattlin' down the roof wi' the wind –'

'Yes, we did think of slates,' said Ridley wryly. 'There's enough of them in the road. But none with the traces you'd expect, nor in the wound neither – well, I won't put you off your breakfasts. Maybe he just got blown against something – it was wild enough weather. Mind how you go, if you're out late; it got another fellow, too – young lad, took a tumble down the South Cliff steps and broke his neck. Not much doubt there; patrol'd logged in black ice on the road above, so the steps were probably –'

'Jesus, you're jokin'!' burst in Harry, sounding so alarmed that the diggers stared. 'It's only early bloody autumn –'

'Early, right enough. Makes you think, doesn't it?'

'Oh Lord,' breathed Pru, 'that's perfectly *dreadful*!'

'Kin say that again an' all,' said Harry. 'Think I'm off south for the winter –'

'Sort that out with your probation officer first. Well, I'll send one of my lads up today to take some statements and maybe fingerprint those bars. And when he's done that, why don't you screw those shutters closed? Then if you hear anybody fiddlin' with them –'

'Drop a sewing machine on 'is bonce?' suggested Neville. 'Or let Colby off his chain?'

'I'd rather you just called us,' said Ridley severely. 'Much safer all round. But since you mentioned your pal Colby – I wanted a word with him while I was about it, and he doesn't seem to be here . . .'

'Ey, they really notice things, these cops!' said Harry admiringly. 'No, 'e's buggered off.'

'When? Last night?'

There was a unison groan from the diggers. 'No sich luck,' said Forbes. 'Came in pissed an' spent the night snorin' like a bluidy steam train.'

'So he was definitely here all night?'

'Oh aye,' said Neville. 'Got up about six, shaved 'is tongue and went for a swim – 'is patent hangover cure.'

'A swim? Where?'

'In the sea, of course,' chuckled Paul.

'At this time of year? At dawn? God above, he must be a polar bear . . . Where would he go? Would he still be there?'

'Probably swum right out to the dam by now,' Neville grunted.

'The dam? That's half a mile of open water!'

' 'E's done it once or twice, in good weather –' Ridley's brows rose sharply. 'Now don't get me wrong,' Neville added hastily as Paul and the others glared at him. 'Always in the daytime – nobody'd last at night, it's bloody freezing! Even Colby's not daft enough –'

'So everybody keeps telling me,' grunted Ridley. 'But somebody else might, mightn't they? If they'd seen him do it? Somebody with a wetsuit, maybe . . . Well, you tell Mr Colby I'd be obliged if he'd drop by the station for a little chat as soon as possible – maybe this evening. I'll still be there – I've got to waste this morning helping the lads on crowd control for the Odd Dance. As if we hadn't enough on our plates! Thanks for the coffee – and I'd sooner have your socks, Paul, than Neville's here. Bye!'

'Cheeky sod!' said Neville, watching Ridley stump off down the hill.

'Not a bad bloke for a cop!' said Harry cheerfully. 'Right stiff-necked booger 'e was when 'e came oop first, but 'e's mellowed. Well, c'mon, folks – tender'll be waitin', and we'll 'ave to fight our way through t'tourists if we 'ang around.'

The streets were already filling up with gawkers and dawdlers as the little knot of diggers straggled down towards the quay. By the time they reached the boat the performance was just starting, with the usual quick lecture, squawked through a battery bullhorn, on the Dance's history – how it was the most spectacular of Yorkshire's traditional sword dances, took great skill and timing, and had been revived around the turn of the century but was probably a survival of some ancient sacrificial rite. They watched with varying degrees of boredom as the dancers lined up in their familiar Morris costumes, ribbons and bells shivering in the seabreeze, flexing their thin steel 'swords'. The accordion wheezed, and the dancers hopped and skipped in shifting lines, then suddenly peeled off outwards and went bounding round in a wide ring. Every few steps each dancer turned to face his neighbour, and they clashed their swords in an X shape. Then the tune changed to a faster rhythm, and the circle split as the dancers went springing diagonally across it in pairs, clashing swords as they went. When it reformed the lead dancer was skipping in the centre of the circle; it closed around him, the swords flickered upward and then with a clatter and a shout they closed around his neck. The audience gasped – and then the circle broke, and the lead dancer was holding up the swords, blades interleaved in an intricate star-shaped knot. Applause scared the seagulls off the quay, and the tender's helmsman seized the chance to start up the engine and move away from the jetty. Behind it the dancers were launching into the first interlude in the long Dance performance, a mummers' play.

'Could liven up the end a bit,' suggested Neville, sitting in the stern with the others. 'Sacrifice a tourist or three . . .'

'More'n last year already,' Harry observed. 'Like a flamin' antheap. They call 'em summat like that in Cornwall, don't they – ants?'

'Emmets,' sighed Pru. 'Pretty accurate, isn't it? And you just wait till the temple site's open next year. The town'll be absolutely *stiff* with them.'

'Shift the Dance out to the temple,' suggested Paul. 'Then the tourists won't have to come into the town at all.'

'Not a bad idea, lad,' grinned Harry. 'Let the nobs cope – it's all a bloody middle-class thing anyway!'

'Rubbish,' sniffed Pru. 'Most tourists aren't middle-class – look at this lot, miners half of them with their huge cars. And anyway, it's their money keeping workers here in jobs – all except you, that is –'

'Aye, we all know what the tourists keep Hardwicke in,' leered Neville. 'The little female ones as don't know any better, any'ow . . .'

'Can I 'elp it if I'm irresistible?'

'Ask me again when you are,' said Pru, 'if ever.'

'Can tell they grew up together, can't you?' Neville remarked to Paul.

'What as?' laughed Paul. 'Beauty and the Beast?'

'Oh aye,' said Harry. 'My old grandda' were gardener up at Fern Farm – real old upper-class lackey.'

'He was *sweet*,' said Pru. 'Not like you at all. So we used to play together –'

'Aye,' breathed Harry, with a huge smack of his lips. 'Doctors and Nurses, ah!' Eyes closed in ecstasy, he shot out his feet, slipped and sat down hard in a frozen patch on the cockpit floor.

'It's a judgement,' observed Pru, as he picked himself up, cursing fluently.

'Ice!' he growled. 'Ice in friggin' September –'

56

'What's so terrible about that?' asked Paul. 'You and the cop were getting quite steamed up about it – why?'

'Ah,' said Harry sagely. 'Answer's all around you, ain't it? T'cliffs.' He waved a large paw at them. 'They Vikings were bloody awful town planners – stuck us down in this ditch. Okay if you're goin' by sea, but all t'roads coom in over t'cliffs, like, an' they're steep as 'ell, aren't they? Bloody dangerous even in a heavy rain. Coom winter it only takes a bit of ice an' snow, and you can't get through 'em. Rest o' country's just sweepin' their path, we're bloody near cut off!'

'Yes,' Pru sighed. 'Quite a few towns in the area are the same – Robin Hood's Bay, for example. And if it's freezing at night this early in the year we could be in for a hard winter.' She laughed. 'I don't know what Harry's worried about – he makes a fortune then, they're always getting him in to drive extra relief lorries or snowfans; it's about the only time of year he's always holding down an honest job!'

'Aye,' said Neville. 'That's what's really worrying him. It's a terrible shock to 'is system.'

Harry snorted. 'I just don't like it, way t'weather's going.' He cocked a poacher's eye at the clouds, sniffed around in the clear fresh air. 'And there's more t'coom. Might look fine for t'bloody tourists now, but you mark my words! We'll all be glad enough of our beds t'night.'

A great surge of wind came howling landwards, whipping up the harbour to froth, bending the trees and the TV aerials, sending the tourists' litter on a wild leaping dance through the narrow streets. It washed over the night-locked town like an invisible wave and welled up and over the cliffs on either side. Up by Fern Farm, parting the hedgerow, it caught Jess Thorne's old trailer caravan in strong malicious fingers and heaved it so it rocked like the boats moored far below. The occupants hardly noticed, rocking in a rhythm of their own, crying out as harshly. The woman rode the man, her rigid arms on his chest the pivot for a sharp mechanical thresh and thrust of her

57

haunches, heaved up, struck down with a brutal, aggressive emphasis. His hands, busy between her legs, moved out, slid up along her flanks to her small firm breasts, circling her nipples, then clutched quickly, urgently, back at her haunches, parting them, fingers digging in, adding their convulsive strength to the force of her thrusts. If they felt, then, the bed quiver and surge under them, it only echoed the intensity that linked their bodies, a harsh gust that arched and stiffened them like filled sails. Then it fell, the sails quivered, slackened, sagged. She tumbled down onto his chest and lay gasping.

He stroked her back slowly for a moment, then ran his fingers through her black curls, dimly aware that at some time in the recent active past he had strained his arm, for the moment caring not a bit. He nuzzled at her face, and with a liquid little chuckle she pressed her lips gently against his. Her eyes fluttered open, and he caught a rare unguarded tenderness in her gaze. She reached out, stroked his chest, caught at the silver chain he still wore and toyed gently with the heavy silver pendant she had given him, replica of a Thor's hammer amulet they had found together at Fern Farm. Then another sharp gust drummed on the metal wall, followed by a harsh rattle of raindrops; she looked up, startled, and rolled off him.

'Oh wow,' she sighed, 'I keep thinking that's somebody knocking –' and then abruptly she shut up.

He looked at her keenly. 'Jess, I know normally you prefer to sleep alone – and of course I understand, I too like to be independent – but since the weather is so bad, I could stay just for tonight.' She flashed him half a smile, ducked her head down into the pillow for a moment, didn't answer. 'It is not just on your account. After all, I am not overly anxious to drive back in all that – I'm very comfortable where I am.'

'Mmh. Yeah . . . Oh Hal, I don't know. I keep wanting to say yes, but – I don't know. Maybe I'd get to like that too much – get too used to it – you'd get too used to me – I don't know. Better not.'

Hal shrugged, carefully nonchalant. 'As you wish, *kaereste*. At least my bed in the pub will not blow away. It seemed to me you might need some extra weight to hold this rattletrap down.'

She chuckled. 'Guess what we were doing should've hammered it down nice and firm. I'll be okay, Hal – honest.'

'Of course you will. It is one of the reasons I love you.'

She kissed him again, brushed the hair back off his forehead and smoothed down his beard. 'Mmmh. And I love you too. You're so goddam beautiful and patient and understanding and – and – you fuck like a gentleman!' She gave a deep dirty giggle, then swung over suddenly. 'And wow, you make a mess of me – I'd better straighten up . . .'

Hal watched her disappear into the tiny shower cubicle, smiled a little sadly, and began collecting his scattered clothes. His arm hurt him as he dressed, and he winced. Patient! Understanding! Great, marvellous. It just got to be a strain now and then, that was all.

When they were both dressed, him in his day clothes, Jess in the old trail shirt she slept in, they kissed again. She held him even tighter and longer than usual, as if trying to make something up to him. Or, he wondered, did she really want him to stay? Should he have tried harder? But that might have ruined everything, and he couldn't risk that, not now. They said their goodbyes lightly. As he unlatched the rickety door the wind almost snatched it from his hand. With a last smile to Jess he tumbled out into the rainsoaked grass and slammed it shut behind him. The wind was at his back as he tripped and stumbled through the showery darkness to the road and his car, half lifting him and frogmarching him along as if he was some kind of intruder here, being thrown out. He felt enough like that already. But as he reached the fence he turned and saw a patch of gold in the uniform grey. She was watching at the open upper half of the door, silhouetted against the yellowish battery light. She looked smaller somehow, lost and forlorn – or was that just his wishful thinking? He waved, and saw it returned; she'd blown him a kiss, something he'd always thought rather childish – it made him smile. Give it time – time. But at

59

his age, how much could he waste? The pain in his arm struck as he slipped into gear, and he thought of Helga, and how she was always acquiring odd little aches and pains, as their marriage sailed closer and closer to its inescapable rocks. When the Range Rover's high headlights swept across the flank of the van the door was closed.

The drive back to town was better than he'd feared. The wind seemed worst at the clifftop itself, spending most of its force there. And at least it was blowing inland; it couldn't bowl the van over the cliff – though it was well tethered down, and had a solid fence and hedge behind it too. The rain came and went in brief fusillades, heavy enough to make him drive carefully but no real problem. He had set out well after eleven, and heard the half-hour chime from St Hilda's as he rounded the last corner before the pub. Just as well; it would be another long day –

He stared, and slowed to a crawl. The blue light pulsed around the little square, flashing and flickering from rain-washed windows. The car beneath it was ghostly white in the shadow, and the arm that flagged him down looked disembodied and sinister. As he pulled in behind it the rain came hammering down with redoubled force. The other car's passenger door was flung open, releasing a cold gleam of courtesy light; he pulled up his anorak collar, grabbed his keys, swung out, and ran for it. He piled in in a tangle of arms and legs.

'High bloody time, too!' said Ridley savagely. The car stank of tobacco and every kind of human odour, overlaid with cheap disinfectant. 'I'd've had a patrol out on your tail if I could've spared one. What kind of director d'you call yourself when you can't be found in an emergency?'

'Emergency? What emergency? And surely Wilf Jackson –'

Ridley snorted. 'Mr Jackson's got a cold, it seems. Isn't stirring at this hour for anyone. Says he's just the site director anyway, and the Museum's your baby –'

'Rubbish, I – the Museum? Has something happened there?' He felt his face tighten. 'The lab –'

'Yes,' said Ridley flatly. 'A break-in – a smash-in, more like. Place turned upside down. Like the dam – only worse.' His fingers writhed on the steering wheel. The rain drummed and danced like smoke on the white bonnet.

'Worse? How?'

'The nightwatchman. Like the dog.'

'*Gud i himmel –*' Hal sagged back in his seat, seeing a heap of ruin rise before him, bloody and nightmarish. The smell in the car was choking, sickening him, and he thrust open the door to the cold wind. 'I must go there at once – see what –'

Ridley reached across him and slammed the door shut. 'Not without my say-so,' he said, still tonelessly. 'There's a murder investigation going on – remember?'

Hal caught hard at his temper, and sighed. 'Yes. Yes, God damn it. I liked old Grindrod. But it is everything I have been living for, for years –'

Ridley nodded. 'Yes. I'll take you there in a minute. But you can help with some background first. You've been with Miss Thorne this evening? All evening?'

'I suppose Wilf told you. Yes, since we left the dam – about six, half past.'

Ridley clicked on the courtesy light and began to make notes. 'And have you seen Mr Colby at any point –'

'Inspector –' Hal began angrily, and then stopped. 'No, neither of us. I do not know where he would be. Out with his friends, perhaps –'

'No, he isn't; I've had a word with them. Some bloody friends! If that boy's so bloody brilliant as you all say he is, what's he want to hang around with a crew of no-hopers like that for? You'd have thought an educated type, an archaeologist –'

'I am flattered,' said Hal wryly. 'But I could tell you a thing or two about archaeologists, even famous ones – Schliemann was a real bastard. Belzoni was a faker, an ex-circus strongman and a bit of a thug, Wheeler a woman-iser and poseur, Carter . . . Well, we are not immune to human weaknesses, I have my share, and so has Jay – more than his share, perhaps. But never – *never!* – would he do anything like this! I am no psychologist, but I think he has a deep need to belong – and to dominate what he belongs to, to stand out; that is the sports star –'

'Sounds like a teenager to me – immature.'

'You may be right. He had the kind of hellish childhood only the rich seem to manage. It does him credit that he has come so far now – he has immense drive, almost fanaticism. A legacy of his Bible Belt background, perhaps – we have much trouble with fundamentalists at Rayner. He has escaped that, thankfully, but he still needs to believe in something. And when he does he takes it seriously, and tries to make others do the same. He has always been good at recruiting for our archaeology classes.'

'I'm not impressed,' grunted Ridley. 'He's got a violent streak – he brawls –'

'But never badly. Believe you me, I have seen worse at Oxford rugby club dinners, and they are your future prime ministers, are they not?'

'Not the way I vote. All these things you've been telling me – warp 'em a bit, and know who you end up with? Charlie bloody Manson, that's who! Only with brains and money this time.'

'Bullshit!' said Hal forcefully. 'That trick you could play with the normal faults of anyone! The fact remains that with that fanatical streak he would not – *could* not – do that kind of damage to the dig! He practically worships archaeology! And he simply would not kill anybody –'

'What about the fraternity –'

'*Because* of that! All the more because of that!' Hal's face hardened. 'How did you come to hear of that? Never mind, I can guess. But can you not see what I am getting at? That now, after that traumatic experience, he might still behave irresponsibly, yes. But he would take extra care nobody got hurt –'

'Oh, I can see it all right. I just can't afford to rely on it – wouldn't be doing my job. He's gone too far once – oh, I know it was an accident and everything, but you'd be surprised how often these accidents are really signs of underlying disorders –'

'Such as?'

'Oh, I don't know. Beginnings of a breakdown, maybe?

Been working hard, has he, Colby? Under a lot of emotional stress?'

Hal flushed. 'You seem to have done a thorough job of picking up gossip –'

'My job.'

'Maybe. But that could apply to any of us –'

'D'you know the English saying about no smoke without fire? That fanatical streak you mentioned, isn't that a bit odd to start with? Mightn't it turn back on itself, turn to hatred –'

'Every man a gutter psychologist!' said Hal disgustedly. 'Well, I am not. Anything is possible, madness makes its own rules. But I can tell you, if madness had gone that far we would surely have noticed. *Satans*, we know more of him than you –'

'I wonder. And need it be madness?'

'What do you mean?'

'Ever hear of Angel Dust?'

'The name only, perhaps.'

'Well, I'll tell you. It's some kind of tranquilliser vets use on bulls, elephants, anything large. But it can send people clean bloody wild, raging mad – and aggressive. Like neat Navy rum – Portsmouth lads nicked a sailor on that, normal-sized bloke but he ripped the steel door right off his cell. Made a terrible mess of himself and never felt a thing. Angel Dust's worse.'

'So? How can you connect this awful stuff with Jay?'

'Just that I spent a bit of time on the telex yesterday, via London. Not often I get a chance to do that, not abroad. Know who I got hold of?'

Hal nodded resignedly. 'The Rayner campus police –'

'Right. And the local sheriff's office. And they told me a few things about your Mr Colby that might even surprise you. Did you know he's a known drug user?'

Hal groaned. 'Oh, Ridley, you do not understand, that is just pot, attitudes are different over there! Half the faculty are afloat on the stuff – not me, but then I do not even drink much –'

'We're talking about over here, Prof. The good word is that that gang of his've been getting their paws on drugs,

63

pot, some cocaine, maybe other things. They're enough of a handful without that. And I've every reason to believe Mr Jay bloody Colby's their source –'

A sudden wild screech made Hal jump. Swearing, the inspector reached for the dashboard handset. 'Ridley? Aye – where then? Has it, by God – all right, cover it up, we'll get forensic boys to take a shufti as soon as we can spare them. Ridley out.' He turned to Hal. 'Well! What d'you make of that?'

'Not much. The local accent still defeats me at times.'

'Oh aye, I forget. C'mon, I'd better be getting you on up to the Museum.' He started the car, slipped into gear and did a highly illegal U-turn round the war memorial, tyres splashing and lapping on the wet surface. 'They've found the guard's boat, a mile or two down the coast – at Oddsness. Not washed up, though – beached.'

'Beached?' Hal thought furiously. 'But then – it was used, not just set adrift. They must have planned to use it. That does not sound like somebody on Angel Dust to me – more like treasure-hunters . . .'

'You've got a point there, Prof,' conceded Ridley sourly. 'But then how come they didn't use the boat that landed them? I don't know what the hell to make of it. Oddsness? If you ask me, the whole bloody place should be called Odd . . .'

Hal smiled. 'You find the name funny? You are not a local man, then?'

'Nope, I'm a southerner. Been here eighteen years, but that's nothing, bloody blink of an eye. That's a local type of name then, is it?'

'Oh yes – a very old one, in fact from our special period. It probably means the ness, the peninsula, where Oddi had his farm. Oddi was quite a common Scandinavian name, you see. I believe it still crops up in Yorkshire as a surname –'

'That's right, there's a fella on TV called Oddie. Funny – you read about the temple and the Viking town and that in the paper, but you don't think you're actually living in it . . .'

Hal smiled wryly. 'So much for our publicity! That is

64

just what we have tried to get across to local people – why we mounted the display at the Museum. This was the heart of the Danelaw, the great Viking colony in England – an independent kingdom, even, with its capital at York. But that did not last; the settlers soon blended in with the locals – they were good at that. They took on English laws, left their old gods for Christianity. In the end the English were able to throw out the last Viking king, a man called Erik Bloodaxe. It was one of his local gauleiters who built the temple here. He must have been a real religious fanatic, wanting to draw – or force – people back to worshipping Odin.' Hal looked out at the rain-lashed roads. The car was climbing sharply through the winding streets towards the outskirts of town, moving out among the rows of high Victorian terraces in the lee of the cliffs. 'It was bound to fail, of course. Most Vikings were not religious fanatics; they tended to be tolerant, and Christ was a friendlier sort of god than Old One-Eye. It seems the temple came to a bloody end –'

The car surged round and onto the gravel drive that led up between the Museum's high black gates, glistening with the damp. Ridley looped it around the forecourt towards the end of the east wing, then swerved sharply to avoid the ambulance parked there. He looked at the three policemen and one ambulanceman who were carrying something over to it in a black plastic sheet, something limp, lolling, shapeless. 'Some things do,' he said quietly.

Hal Hansen's door was open before the car stopped, and he set off across the gravel towards the Museum's main door. Ridley called him back. 'You won't need to go in that way,' he said, a little sadly. Hal looked at him, then plunged around the corner of the new extension.

'B-but – but that was armoured glass!' he stammered to Ridley, at his side. 'With an ultra-violet filter – we ordered it specially from Germany –'

'Believe in buying British myself,' said Ridley, contemplating the remains of what had been a wide bronze-tinted picture window. 'That's where they got in – all broken inwards, see? But the Forensic boys say it's pretty strong, that glass. Take more than a sledgehammer?'

'Certainly! A car might break it –'

'Or a motorbike?' Ridley shrugged before Hal could answer. 'Just a suggestion. The grass is pretty churned up, but we've not found any tyre tracks. Well, it's inside you're interested in – hey, careful!'

Hal, stepping through the shattered opening, stumbled and almost fell against the jagged edges. But he caught himself, staring unbelieving around the room. '*Fanden i helved!* They have destroyed the place!'

Just behind the window stood a row of display stands the size of a small room. Now they held shattered ruins of painted wood and imitation thatch. Life-size figurines, human and animal, lay splintered and contorted among the debris, sickeningly suggestive of what else had been done. In all the neat semi-circular glass cases that flanked the walls, not one pane was intact. All the round central cases were broken – some had had the whole top smashed off them. Glittering in the soft overhead lighting, the fragmented glass washed across the floor like a flood of ice. And among it, scattered, spilled and trampled, lay the precious things it had protected.

Hal Hansen shambled forward like a man in a dream, shaking his head as if to deny the ruin he was seeing, another devastation of his life's work. He knelt down to sift through the glass-strewn fragments with careful fingers. 'Can I touch them?'

'Be my guest. We'd never get prints or fibres off that stuff.'

He moved through the room, picking up pieces here and there and placing them reverently back in the cases. But after a minute he stopped, thought, then went back to the stands and began pulling the debris about. Then he stood up and turned to the policeman. 'Ridley – I do not understand . . .'

'What was on those stands, then?'

'Nothing – nothing real, I mean. Just a reconstruction – Viking house interiors, an exhibit about the Fern Farm community. We had almost finished it . . .'

'Valuable? Expensive?'

Hal looked at him emptily. 'Why yes – in terms of time,

66

of hard work by dedicated people, skilled craftsmen. But to a thief, nothing. Absolutely nothing!' He kicked out at the remains with startling savagery. 'Nothing worth stealing! So they smashed it instead –' He stopped abruptly, stared down at the mess, and then around the room. 'They *have* taken things from here! Reconstructed chairs, a table, a loom even, with weaving . . .' He looked around again in utter bewilderment. 'Ridley, I cannot make sense of this. They have chosen pieces from all over the display – chosen, yes; the carved bone comb and its case have both gone, though they were not displayed close together. So these people are not just vandals, drunk –' He paused significantly. 'Or drugged. But they cannot be professional art thieves either.'

'Why? Because they've gone for less valuable things?'

'No! Because they have chosen stupid things – look, they have taken much jewellery, gold things, yes – but only the more or less intact pieces. And here there were fragments of a large gold armring, with a brass replica to show how it actually looked. They have just swept aside the fragments, which you can see are gold, and taken the replica – I do not understand. It is what children might do.'

'And the caretaker? Some kids. You didn't see him.'

'I said I did not understand – I had better look into the lab now. After this it cannot come as a much greater shock.'

But it did, none the less. The first thing he saw was the high window at the far end, shattered like the other. 'Only outwards this time,' said Ridley. 'Must've been in a hurry by then.'

The mess in the room itself was appalling, the neat rows of workbenches shoved harshly aside. One or two were toppled right over, another smashed down the centre as if by a heavy weight, their contents strewn over a thick layer of stinking mud spread out from the far corner. 'The tank!' hissed Hal. '*Satans*, they have tipped over one of the holding tanks – for preserving the ship timbers – no, the one with that *forbandede* chest! *That's* what they were really after! Look –'

'Yes, I see,' said Ridley grimly, looking at the pile of black splintered timbers, some still half held together by a buckled band of metal, one carrying a twisted hasp. 'Just like on the dam.'

'I wish to hell we had never found the goddam things!' snarled Hal. 'Wilf and his treasure chests –' He stood for a moment, staring around him, hands clenching and unclenching. 'Whatever was in the chest has been taken, that is clear –' He stopped, stooped, came up with a blackened twist of metal the length of his hand. 'And it probably *was* something valuable, really valuable – look at this here!'

Ridley poked at it vaguely. 'What is it?'

'A knife-hilt – with what looks like gold wire ornament. I'd know this if it came from the excavation; it must have been in the chest. With who knows what else?' He laid it carefully on the edge of a bench, squelched his way over to the window, leaned on the low sill and took several deep breaths. Outside, under the glare of portable searchlights, the wide lawn was roughly marked out with tape into rectangles. Policemen in rain capes were combing the sodden grass, some on hands and knees, picking up objects and putting them into numbered plastic bags. Hal shook his head. 'It looks like a dig – a ghastly parody.'

'I never would've thought of that,' grunted Ridley. 'But I suppose they do have something in common. Any new ideas?'

'Only one. *I* could cheerfully kill whoever did this.'

The inspector glared. 'I hope you're not serious. I've got enough troubles on my hands.'

'Perhaps I am not. I suppose I should be thankful. Apart from the chests we seem to have lost remarkably little real dig material – more has been spoiled than stolen. Insurance will cover the rest. But – it is like seeing your own home burglarised –'

There was a sudden sharp crackle from Ridley's battered anorak, and he hauled out a small grey walkie-talkie. 'Ridley? Yes, I'm here – Museum, north window – got me? Where're you? And – uh-huh – with you in half-a-mo'!

Out.' He jammed it back in his pocket. 'Bill Harshaw. They've found what might be a trail up the cliff path there, with a few likely-looking odds and sods about. You'd better come confirm the lead –'

With surprising energy Ridley pulled himself up and out through the shattered window. Hal followed, more stiffly, feeling he'd pulled several muscles earlier in the evening. They trotted across the starkly lit patch of lawn, keeping well to one side of the search, and round to a gate in the high hedge beyond; a constable on guard there shone his flashlight at them. Ridley commandeered it; he shone it on the bent gate and shattered lock, and on the metalled path beyond, where perceptible scuffs and smears showed in the glistening mud at the edge. A hail came from above, and they hurried out and up.

'That is certainly one of our exhibit labels!' said Hal, examining the torn strip of art board. 'And this here in the bush is from the spinning and weaving case – wool, authentically dyed. The colour is unmistakable.'

'I'll say,' said Ridley, dubiously examining the garish hank of orange caught in the gorse. 'Any more, Bill?'

'T'lads are following the marks higher up –'

'Hey, Sarge!' came a voice from the darkness. 'Coom on up 'ere a minute –'

The track was getting steeper now, and the ground already dropping away to one side. When they rounded the next corner it was actually a part of the cliff face, falling about twenty feet vertically into an overgrown patch behind some Victorian cottage gardens; the rowan tree rooted there rose level with Hal's feet. The torch beams picked out a patch of violently churned-up mud in the path.

'Bit of a barney, looks like,' said one of the younger CID men.

'A struggle,' translated Ridley for Hal's benefit. 'What's this here? Scuffmarks – hell's teeth . . .' They led to the verge, the narrow strip of grass between path and cliff – and through, in short straight smears, and over.

'Summat's gone over, ey?'

'Or somebody,' growled Ridley, shining his light down

onto dense obscuring undergrowth. 'Can't see a thing. What about a ladder, eh?'

'We called. They're bringing one. And for a car to cover t'other end of t'path.'

'Good. That's at the clifftop?'

'Aye, and it's the only way out – that or falling off. Path's listed dangerous, that's why t'gate were locked. If chummy's still on it somewhere we've got 'im.'

'He won't be,' sighed Ridley. 'He's had time enough to scarper. Anyway, I'm not risking you lads scrambling up a dangerous path in the dark – ah, the ladder.'

Hal helped lower it slowly down into the shrubbery, and jumped when he felt it hit something softer than ground, something that turned over at the impact. Ridley swore, and twisted the ladder to part the bushes. His flashlight beam shone straight down onto an upturned face, eyes closed, ashy white – except for the livid bruise across it.

'*Jay!*' barked Hal.

'Oh, Jesus!' said Ridley, and saw the body stir, the face turning feebly away from the light, an arm coming up to shield the eyes.

Colby was conscious and sitting up by the time the CID men had got down the ladder, and obviously not badly hurt. He insisted on climbing up the ladder himself, reeling and lurching and spreading his massive weight over the gasping men helping him. Hal and the sergeant were barely able to haul him in over the top. 'And now,' said Ridley, when he'd recovered his breath. 'I've called you an ambulance, Mr Colby, but since you insist you're so well, perhaps you wouldn't mind explaining how you came to be down there?'

'Sure,' said Colby hoarsely, massaging his neck and one shoulder. 'I got hit.'

'You got hit. Who by?'

'Dunno. Didn't see – One of those motherfuckin' treasure-hunters, I guess; it was dark, and – say, you guys know what the fuck happened down at the Museum?'

'We were hoping you would tell us, Jay!' said Hal forcefully.

The big man shook his head, winced and clutched his

70

neck, sat for a moment rocking. 'What's to tell?' he said between his teeth. 'I'd been out having a couple with the guys – but after that bawling-out you gave me, Hal, figured I'd better be a good boy tonight, go home, bed early, maybe stop in at the precinct when I passed and see you, Inspector –'

'Which you didn't.'

'Well, sure I didn't, I was down there, wasn't I? I never got back. I'd left the bike 'cause I was drinking, I was walking back, came by the bottom of North Cliff there –'

'When?'

'Maybe about half ten, quarter of eleven, I wasn't looking –'

'All right. Go on.'

'So I heard a real loud crash from up this way, maybe a voice shouting, then the alarms. Well hell – after the other night? I just thought *treasure-grubbing bastards* and came up here at a dead run.'

'Oh aye? Never a thought of phoning us?'

'Well . . . I didn't think there'd be time –'

'And you wanted to get your hands right on them, anyway?' grunted Ridley.

Colby looked sulky. 'Suppose I did? I mean, you tell him, Hal – that stuff's priceless, it's history they're smashing up there. I thought it might be some of those fishermen who've been bellyaching about loss of business – incidentally, that's balls – and I know I can handle them, I could settle them without dragging any fuzz in. So I ran up, I saw two figures come out, cross the lawn –'

'Two? You're sure of that?'

'Two together. Might've been more ahead, maybe.'

'What'd they look like?'

'Who could see? Jesus, I was half a mile away, it was dark, it was raining – they were just . . . figures. Not even clear silhouettes, they were carrying piles of stuff.'

'I see. So you ran after them? You didn't shout or anything?'

'No. I was trying to run quietly, surprise them . . . Don't think they heard till I was almost on them, too.'

'What happened then? What'd you do?'

71

'They were about here – it was real dark, they were still just shapes. But hey – I guess they must've been men, I can say that much –'

'Why men?'

Colby gave a hoarse chuckle. 'You seen many chicks my size? Not even Jess, huh, Hal? One was at least my height. Anyhow, all I remember is running up, then – *boff!* – the ceiling fell in. I guess they hit me. Then threw me over, or I just fell. Stupid.'

'It may have saved your life, Jay,' said Hal severely. 'That was a damn stupid risk you took! You didn't know, but they'd just murdered the nightwatchman.'

'Jesus Christ!' said Colby, tried to sit up too suddenly, and sank back groaning. Ridley shone a torch onto Colby's face, studied the oval bruise that striped across it, smeared with blood from his nostrils and from lesser scratches. He held his broad flipper of a hand over the bruise for an instant; the shape was the same, but nearly twice as wide.

'Ambulance is 'ere,' said a voice in the darkness. 'Is it a stretcher, or can 'e walk down a bit?'

'Help him, lads,' said Ridley. Somebody moaned. 'Shut up. One of you travel with him, get a statement. He's to come help us with our inquiries the moment they let him out of hospital – make sure he gets the message, right?' The three policemen swore and struggled to help the big man onto his feet. Locked together like a group of drunks, they staggered off into the darkness. Ridley tugged at Hal's sleeve. 'Way you were talking there, you sounded as if you believe that story of his, straight off.'

'Why yes,' said Hal drily. 'As it happens, I do. Don't you?'

Ridley made a low frustrated growl. 'I bloody well don't want to – but, yes, I do. Or I'm beginning to – I don't *disbelieve* it, let's say. I can't find any reason to. That bruise was no fake, nor the fall. The bushes're all smashed there, a bit of cliff came with him – lucky he didn't break his neck. And if he hadn't fallen chummy might've broken it for him.'

'Aye,' said Harshaw, puffing his way back up the path.

72

'Somebody bigger than him? Who're we lookin' for now – Boris bloody Karloff?'

'Maybe. Whoever it is, they've obviously got it in for the dig. I'll arrange some extra security, but you'd better tighten up your own arrangements too, Prof.'

'I will, believe me –' Hal shivered. 'Can we talk about that indoors? I'm freezing, and it's raining again –'

'It's not, you know,' said Harshaw, shining his torch beam out into the dark. Small specks glittered and danced. 'It's snowing.'

CHAPTER FOUR

THE WIND whined along the winding streets of the little town and twisted around its rooftops. The houses were huddled stacks of greyness, relieved only by the occasional speck of gold escaping between drawn curtains; sunset had drained the bright colours from their walls and paintwork, the red from their rooftiles. To Jay Colby, looking down the steep coils of Hill Street, it seemed as if time had faded with the daylight, as if Saitheby's past and present hung suspended in a brief moment of shadow. Soon the streetlights would come on and reassert the twentieth century, but for now they were still thinking about it, sullen red smears in the gloom that might have been reflections from cooking fires, a forge, the embers of a ritual balefire on the hills. For now he could see himself stalking down an older street, between rows of wattle and plank walls on stone foundations, tramping down muddy board steps or rough cobbles, a long sword slapping against his thigh, in time with the soft rippling ring of his mail-shirt –

The chill wind sliced painfully across his bruised face. His sinuses ached and began to run, and he hesitated to sniff too hard in case he started his nose bleeding again. He shivered, and pulled up the furlined collar of his expensive bomber jacket. He was feeling light-headed and slightly sick; a full day's grilling by the police had undone any improvement brought about by the night in hospital. Not that they'd worked him over, except verbally; it was their goddam asshole stupidity that had got him so worked up, their mindless moronic obsession with the idea that he – he, of all people – could possibly have been the one who'd –

Anger and humiliation knotted his muscles, and he

74

shuddered again, feeling the aches return in his bruised back and ribs. *Me, of all people! Sweet friggin' Jesus, how many times do I have to tell you I was trying to friggin' catch them! And if I had* – He smiled grimly, despite the bruise, and slipped back into his favourite fantasy. How would *they* have dealt with these wrecking bastards, these vandals, grave-robbers, secret murderers – how would the Norsemen have treated crappy scum like that? If he'd been born one of them – not those farmer types who'd let the old faith slip, but the later ones, the warriors who'd reconquered the place in the days of Erik – then he'd have known what to do. No warrior's death for them – the snake-pits, burning, chaining them to a skerry for the tide to take care of . . . Back came the sickness and the mass of wincing pains, and he snarled. A pair of passing teenyboppers actually *giggled*. His favourite fantasies held little comfort for him tonight.

And he'd have to face the boys like this, with the bruise on his face like the brand of a contemptuous slap. What would they think, that cocky asshole Kingfield, dumbo Ashe? Ten to one they'd know all about the fuzz, too – where would that leave him, in their eyes? Maybe too low, too close to their own level. And that could be dangerous. More than once he'd had to whip them into line, stop them making stupid jokes or coarse corruptions of things he knew were vitally important, sacred. He'd left his mark on one or two – easy, like taming animals. That was all they were; put on a good enough show, play natural leader of the pack, and they'd never question it, just roll over and wave their little legs in the air. But let the act slip, the mask drop, and what then? In nature, the pack could be merciless. And while he could whip any one of them, maybe any two, could he take them all at once? Not the way he felt now. The hospital guys had said nothing was broken, but there were other things breakable besides bones, things as slow and hard to heal. He'd have to stop off at the doss and pick up his bike, whether he felt well enough to ride it or not. Tonight was important – crucial. He'd have to bluff it out, distract them – lay on something special, some entertainment. Toss them a girl, maybe –

but it wasn't so long since the last time, and it could cause more cop trouble if she turned squeamish. Something better . . .

Paul Harvey stared dubiously down at the so-called hamburger in front of him. The plate was oval, the rest of it barely filled by a spoonful of tinned peas and an inadequate scoop of frozen chips. Over these the burger, overflowing its inadequate bun, was leaking greyish grease; more flowed out as he nervously dug in his fork. In the first mouthful greasiness seemed to be the main distinction between burger and bun. No bloody wonder the cafe was empty! Still, it was cheap, warm and bright, an oasis in a gloomy twilit desert; the only decent pubs had all seemed too crowded and too expensive. The cash saved eating here would let him go to the pub with the rest tomorrow evening. But that thought somehow didn't cheer him up; in an odd way he almost felt more comfortable here, on his own, than in among the crowd of diggers. They all seemed to know each other too well, to have things to talk about he couldn't latch on to, private jokes he couldn't understand. He was the latest arrival, probably the last: there was nobody else who'd come this late, and nobody else his own age. Should that matter? He couldn't quite see why. He didn't feel like a child, they didn't seem to be treating him like one – and yet he couldn't fit in on their level. Jess, for example – he really disliked her, she always seemed to be turning her razor-sharp tongue on him and he couldn't keep up with it. There were some unattached girls, as he'd hoped there would be, but all in their twenties; if he made a play for one, even one of the plain ones, she'd be bound to laugh at him, or go all big-sisterly – which would just about be worse. The people he got on best with, oddly enough, seemed to be the older ones – Neville, and Harry, even Hal in his rather distant way. The thought almost choked him on his burger. God, was he looking for father-figures or something? It certainly didn't feel that way. There was Jay, after all – no ancient, and he was easy enough to get on with, whatever some

76

others said. But after hours, of course, he seldom hung around with the diggers. And Pru – she was definitely okay, but she was always letting herself be messed about by that scrote Wilf, God alone knew why. If she ever saw through Jackson, he might just have a chance there . . . If.

The crash of the door, bell tinkling, and a burst of raucous laughter made him jump. He groaned inwardly as he saw two oafish biker types saunter in, swinging crash-helmets, and squeeze in behind the big table opposite. The surly middle-aged woman behind the counter turned even surlier at the sight of them. Before the door had shut itself it was flung back again, and a whole crew of them streamed in, leathers squeaking and boots clomping, carrying a stink of sweat and oil and cheap cigarettes. And last of all, to Paul's surprise, came Jay Colby.

So these were his famous friends! Paul had seen them only once before, anonymous menacing shapes surging along the main street on deafening, smoky bikes. Now, dismounted, he found them a lot less impressive; they were mostly ordinary local yobbos, and substandard ones at that, paler, weaker specimens than their contemporaries from the farms or the fishing boats. Only two came anywhere near Colby's size, a great rawboned thug with a skinhead crop and small lifeless eyes, and a fat ox-like character with a doughy, stupid face fringed with unkempt red hair; the American, undoing his sleek racing-style helmet, literally towered over them all.

Colby was just slumping down in the last chair when he registered Paul, shrinking back into his corner. All he did was wave and smile before shouting to the woman for ten large coffees and every doughnut in the place. Paul smiled and returned the wave, then tried to look genuinely interested in what remained of his hamburger and not to stare at Colby's bruise. Gossip about last night's events had filtered through even to Paul, and he was impressed by the way Jay had gone haring off after those maniacs; imagining himself in that position, he decided he'd have tiptoed away and called the cops. Perfectly sensible, and yet the thought made him uncomfortable, inadequate somehow; he wished he could be brave rather than sensible – or did he?

The bikers were in a rowdy mood, hurling obscure insults at each other, and an uncomfortable feeling began to grow on Paul that some of the row might be aimed at him. He fought down an urge to leave hurriedly, abandoning his dinner; they'd know he was afraid of them then, and he'd learnt how school bullies reacted to that, the hard way. Still – he cast a quick, nervous glance at the door, and caught Colby's eye. The big American mouthed something he couldn't hear, then rounded on his friends and growled 'Shaddap!' They subsided, but Colby still got up, strolled over and perched on his table.

'Hi! What you eatin' there – Jesus, not one of Ma Ashe's burgers, that's playin' with fire!'

'It's okay,' said Paul defensively, forcing himself to swallow a last slimy mouthful. 'Keeps me going –'

'Yeah!' grunted Colby, with a wealth of meaning, 'they tend to. Worse than Mexico, this place – you could catch the Viking Twostep, Erik's Revenge. What on earth makes you eat in a hole like this, anyhow?'

'Oh, couldn't be bothered cooking, got a bit bored with the pub,' Paul mumbled. 'And all the decent cafes crawling with tourists –'

'Yeah, always are on Odd Dance days,' agreed Colby. 'God knows why, it's about as entertaining as senior citizens' disco night.'

'Not real folk-dancing at all, is it?' Paul agreed. 'Ye Olde Tea-Shoppe stuff –'

'Ye Olde Crap!' laughed the American. Then he stopped, looked round at the sullen knot of bikers, and thought for a moment. 'Wasn't always that way, though. Times were it was real, religious, meaningful . . .'

Paul nodded. 'Yes, I read something about that . . .'

'Aw, you mean all the Victorian guys, Cecil Sharp and the rest? Okay, but they were just speculatin' – I *know*.'

'How'd you mean, Jay? You've found out something new? While you were doing your thesis?'

'Thesis? Shit, no – in a thesis you tell them exactly what

they expect to hear! You take my advice, don't try anything too original in yours – wait till you've got it, then they can't touch you.'

'I'll have enough trouble getting my first degree . . .'

'You? Hell, no, forget it, guy like you can walk through that same's me. The secret's being interested – really livin' your subject, see? And you're the type okay. All this, the dig, it isn't just a big giggle or cheap holiday or degree experience or another rung up the ladder or whatever – you *care*. It means something to you, what we're comin' up with – bringing the old world back to life. The whole Norse thing – the dragon ships, the swords, the myths, gods, giants, heroes –'

'Maybe. I did expect more of the dig people to feel that way –'

'They sure as hell should, but they don't. Jeesus, look at Jackson, what's he care? He'd be just as happy diggin' up gold potatoes –'

'But Hal cares, doesn't he?'

Colby's face clouded. 'Once he did, I guess. Now he's so goddam established, he's dried out – knows his stuff okay, but like the pages of a book. Putting flesh back on it, tits, balls, the rest, that'd scare him. There're things I've come up with I'd never want to tell him – but I'd tell you. Such as a real, genuine ritual that's as old as that boat out there –' Colby's voice had dropped to a murmur, and there was a frosty glint in his eyes. 'That might just interest you, right?'

'You mean – something Viking? Christ, Jay, that's impossible –'

'Sshh,' said Colby quietly. 'Hush up, for now. Come meet the boys.'

Paul suddenly liked that idea a lot less, but he'd look a prize idiot if he refused. He got up and followed Colby awkwardly over. Colby waved at him. 'Hey now, you guys – this is Paul here, friend of mine from the dig. Good guy. Paul, that's Billy on the end, Rat, Charlie Boot, the Hog –' The nicknames were pathetic, shadows of toughness that fooled nobody. Paul wondered if he was supposed to shake hands or something, but nobody offered; they waved or grinned idiotically, mumbled 'Hi!' amiably enough. Colby left the ox and the thug till last. 'And on this end here Joe Ashe – yeah, this is his ma's place, why else you think we'd risk it – and Steve Kingfield.' Paul noticed they were the only two he'd given surnames. Ashe grunted something into his ragged beard, Kingfield just looked at him with dead eyes as if he was something the cat dragged in.

'Take a seat, Paul,' said Colby, looking round at the counter; the woman had retired to the kitchen behind and was angrily clattering pots and pans. 'See, what I was telling you – it was through Joe here I found out about it. Just when I came here, last year – I'd gone down to the season's first Odd-Dance performance, wasn't thrilled but Harry'd told me it was a good place to pull tourist chicks. Caught Joe hangin' round my wheels, we got to talking, smoked a little something. I was puttin' down the dance, and he told me he knew the *real* one and the special place for it. Came down in the family, right, Joe?'

Ashe glared suspiciously at Paul and said nothing. Colby leaned across and prodded him hard in his beer belly, and he looked sullenly down at the stained tabletop. 'Aye, well. Me grandpa, soom of 'is mates, they used to go oop there for luck fishin'. Took me once, when I were just a nipper, made me learn t'words 'n' all. Steve's pa were there 'n' all, Hog's uncle, Boots' grandpa – they made us all learn 'n' swear never to tell. But they're all dead now. Us, we did it a couple of times, for fun like, but didn't reckon much on it. Not till Jay coom along.'

'Yeah, he mentioned he an' his friends still had a go sometimes. Didn't think much of it at first, till he told me a few of the details and I could piece together what it genuinely was. Paul, it was real! Guess you can imagine how I felt –'

'Real? How d'you mean, real?'

Colby's eyes blazed under his heavy brows. 'It was the Odin rite! The ancient ritual of worship to the god! The ritual they used at the Fern Farm temple, more'n a thousand years after it was destroyed – real, live and damn near intact! Now d'you understand?'

80

All Paul could do was goggle. 'You mean – people round here still worshipped –'

'Hell, no! *They* didn't know, they'd forgotten. These boys'd never heard of Odin till I told them.' Colby rapped a long finger on the table. 'See, the way I see it is, it must've been some of the local pagans going on worshipping the old gods in secret – probably 'cause they were afraid the harvests and the fish catch would fail, we know that's how the Norsemen saw things. Then later their descendants forgot the actual god behind it all, just kept it up as a fertility ritual – or to spite the Church. Maybe in the Middle Ages or whenever they thought it was witchcraft, devil worship, I don't know. I do know they had a hell of a witch scare in these parts later on.'

Paul shook his head, with an incredulous half laugh. 'But – Christ, Jay, it's just not possible! It couldn't really have gone on that long, could it?'

There was an angry rumble from the bikers. 'Easy, boys,' soothed Colby. 'He's only asking. Sure it could, Paul. You've been reading about the other dances round here – country's lousy with 'em, isn't it? Well, what've they all got in common?'

Paul shrugged. 'Lots of things – steps, patterns, chants – they all use swords –'

'Right!' snapped Colby. 'And they damn near all have kind of a ritual beheading, don't they? Makes it likely they were pagan rites once, too, doesn't it?'

'Well – yes. But there's nothing secret about them, they're out in the open –'

'Sure. Which is why they don't look like much any more. The Christian Church got to them, it sanitised them, castrated them. Ever seen that old Anglo-Saxon cross in the Scotch churchyard? It's been out in the wind an' weather all these centuries, it's almost worn away, you can't read the inscription. But the ones like it that got buried in the ground, they're still pretty clear. That's the way it is with the dance – believe me. Sure, something was bound to leak out from time to time – so you got the witch trials. And I guess somebody in Victorian, Edwardian times blabbed to some collector or other. But either he

81

didn't know very much, or the collector was too goddam ignorant to see what he had, he just forced it into the straitjacket of the local sword-dance style. Saitheby had to have a local dance, it had to be like all the others, right? Very Victorian. But even that version's got a little somethin' extra, hasn't it? Guess that's why it's so popular with the tourists. And meanwhile the real dance just went on.'

'But you say its meaning got forgotten –'

'More like blurred. There's a chant that went with it, sounds just like nonsense rhymes now, but anyone who knew Old Norse could still pick out the words. There're all kinds of things in it, words, acts, that didn't mean a thing to these guys, but they hit me like a ton of bricks. See, all anybody's ever found about the ritual is a few fragments in the sagas, the Eddas, other sources. An' now here was the whole damn thing on a plate – just a bit covered in dirt, like any find. Wipe away the dirt, and – Jeesus, I went wild! I had to see it, take part – and when I did –' He shrugged. 'That was it. I knew. The boys, they'd just done it for fun, 'cause it was somethin' secret. An' the place was good for takin' chicks, right?' The bikers guffawed knowingly.

'Still is,' chortled Charlie Boot.

'So,' said Colby. 'But we don't show them the Dance. I've been studying it ever since – cleaning it up, refining it, taking it back to its original form. It's fascinating.'

'Yes,' breathed Paul, vastly excited. A whole mass of things suddenly made sense, most of all what bound Colby to this weird bunch of yobs. 'It's fantastic – it's like being in on opening Tutankhamen's tomb or something.' Colby nodded, flattered by the comparison. 'Jay – you don't think I could –'

Colby shrugged. 'Think of any other reason I'd've been telling you all this? But listen, you watch out, y'hear? This isn't just me researching my next paper or whatever, something I'd sell TV rights on to Latimer or something. I take this seriously, and so do the boys, now. This isn't dead book archaeology, this is *alive* – right, you guys?' There was a deep, menacing rumble of agreement, a scrape of heavy boots on the floor. Paul swallowed.

'Right,' nodded Colby. His massive hand landed on Paul's shoulder. 'So no rubbernecks, no gawkers, and – no offence – nobody who can't keep his mouth shut. I'm not going to be laughed at by a load of moronic hick tourists. You want to come along, you join in, and once you're in, you stay – okay?'

Paul nodded, threw up his hands, hardly able to talk. 'Sure,' he said breathlessly, accidentally imitating Colby. 'I don't know – this is amazing – you're sure you guys don't mind?'

'Oh naow,' said Kingfield mildly, mocking Paul's accent, 'daon't mind a bit, do we lads, eh? More the bloody merrier.'

Despite himself, Paul bridled. 'If you don't want me along you can fucking well come out and say so –'

Kingfield shrugged. 'All the same to me, sunshine. Jar or two and a Jay special and we'll all be happy as fuckin' Larry, won't we? C'mon, I need a drink.'

Colby grinned at Paul, and began to get up. 'So what else is new, Steve? Hey, time's a'wastin'. Joe, Hog, Charlie, go pick up some stuff at the liquor store, catch us up at the trailhead, okay?'

'On you this time?' grunted Ashe hopefully.

'Whaddya mean, this time? Since when've you had a nickel to your name, lardbutt? The whole evening's on me – isn't it always?' He pulled out a heavy roll of notes, passed out a few and threw one down on the table. He caught up his helmet, and paused to glance out of the grimy window. 'Moon's rising. C'mon.'

An hour later, Paul Harvey was freezing, wet and frightened.

The sky above him trailed a tattered cloak of cloud across the moon. Behind him was a sheer height of windswept basalt cliff, beneath him a thirty-foot drop into surf that growled and leapt like an angry dog. Its foaming crests were steel-tipped by the wavering moonlight, the spray it flung up and around him became a volley of icy arrowheads through his clothes. Underfoot it added to the half-frozen slush on the narrow path. His only consolation was that Colby's gang were shuffling along as nervously as he was – except, that is, for Colby himself.

The big American strode along as casually as he would along a country lane, hardly sparing a glance for the ground he trod, never looking back at his struggling companions. That was what alarmed Paul most of all.

As they left the cafe Colby had genially waved him aboard his own bike, a massive matt-black and silver beast, called something like ElectraGlide, in startling contrast to the battered bikes around it. He had clambered onto the wide pillion, steadying himself awkwardly on Colby's massive shoulders, clutching frantically as the machine bellowed and surged away under him. The wind needled his eyes and sucked the breath out of him, and they were already down across North Bridge and snarling up Hill Street before he realised he was riding dangerously – and illegally – without a helmet. But Colby was just a vast slab of leather-clad back in front of him, tense and quivering with the effort of controlling the bike, and when he tried to shout the wind lashed the words away. He gave up, hung on tighter and ducked his head down for shelter.

He'd expected the ride to last hours, but it was only minutes before the huge bike slowed, swung and bounced violently underneath him. Something scraped at his leg, and in his hunched position he saw shadowy gorse bushes sliding by; they'd left the road, and were travelling slowly enough for him to look up. Without warning Colby swung violently off the saddle, toppling him; Paul landed awkwardly, half-crouching, and saw the American run the bike heavily into a thicket ahead. The other bikers were also covering up their machines in the bushes.

Paul picked himself up shakily and looked around. They were in a small stand of trees, within sight and sound of the main road leading up along the cliffs; this couldn't be the place so convenient to take girls. Then he looked over to the other side, and in the dim moonlight saw the broken-down fencing that cut off the narrow beginnings of a cliff path, the weathered danger notice dangling drunkenly from it. He turned to look for Colby, determined that however far it was home he'd be happy to foot it – stuff the ritual. But Colby was in the middle of a noisy knot of bikers, and before Paul could open his mouth a bottle was thrust into his hand; right now that seemed a very good idea, and he took an experimental swig. It was Scotch, malt Scotch at that. He took another swig, because it was a rare treat and quietened his shakes; *good* malt Scotch. These guys had expensive tastes for bikers – developed at Colby's expense, evidently. He swigged again – and suddenly a hand jogged the bottle, so that a good third of the stuff cascaded down his gullet and he had to swallow or choke. It burned his throat, leaving him gasping and speechless, and before he'd recovered Colby was shouting something, a hand was at his back and he was being propelled forward to the fence, bundled over a gap where someone trod the barbed wire down, and out onto the first uneven steps of the path. And now the whisky was churning his stomach and fogging his mind, and he was inching along a narrow thread of pathway, caught neatly between the gang and Colby – Colby, whose friendly, confiding manner seemed to have slid away like a discarded glove, completely. Colby, whom he'd been relying on among this gang of thugs and yobbos –

He swallowed and inched his way onward, out and around a thin edge of headland, and up towards an out-thrust, isolated portion of cliff that faced northward across the estuary. He looked out to avoid looking down, and was surprised how close the new lights on the dam seemed. He looked a minute longer, and almost bumped into Colby, who'd stopped dead beside some glossy-looking bushes growing in the remains of an old rockfall. The enormous silhouette paused for an instant, then plunged straight at the central bush – and through. Strong hands at Paul's back shot him through next, so hard he stumbled and got scratched. The bushes were thicker and deeper than they looked. Beyond them everything was dark, and he thought of caves; he could hear the sound of water trickling nearby. But he seemed to be sitting in short damp grass, in a wide open space. As his eyes adjusted he could see it in front of him, a bare grassy floor, slightly dished.

Steep rock walls ringed it right the way round, broken only by the cleft. In their shadow lurked dense shrubbery, through which he could hear the bikers crashing and cursing, and a few trees, thin and stunted – except for one majestic shadow that nodded against the open sky, near where the rising moon just topped the wall. Their arrival had been carefully timed.

By the time Paul had collected enough of his wits to stagger up, the bikers were gathering around him again. There was a sudden sharp crackle and a glimmer of light in the tree; somebody was lighting a fire in the centre of the dip. 'J-Jay?' he stammered. 'Th-this is the place, th-then?' The mixture of drink and fright he heard in himself made him cringe.

'Sure is,' said Colby's deep voice from behind him, as warm and friendly as ever. 'And quite a place it is – I'm no geologist, but I guess it was a cave once, till the roof fell in. There's a stream back there, maybe that carved it out – makes it kinda damp, but the fire'll warm us up. And the ceremony. You'll see.' A couple of the bikers guffawed, a harsh mocking sound, and all the reassurance melted away.

Paul rounded on them, still clutching his half-empty bottle by the neck. 'Whas' – what's that supposed to mean?'

'Hey, hey,' said Colby smoothly, 'hang on, Paul, don't go getting all aggressive – you're as bad as these dumbells. Settle on down, y'hear? An' if you're goin' to hit a body with that bottle, at least finish it first. And you guys, can it, y'hear? He's with us, he's goin' through with this same's we all have, and when he does he's one of us, right? Hell, he gave you a chance to object back at the cafe – now you just button your fuckin' lips, y'hear, or I'll do it – if he doesn't beat me to it!' He turned to Paul. 'You heard? There's no ringside seats at this – this is religion, demands respect. You want to see, you've got to be part of it, an initiate – a brother. We are, all of us – we've all faced the same tests you'll have. Nobody'll ask more than that, understand?'

Paul looked up at him for a moment, then nodded

dumbly. It all sounded reasonable enough – and yet there was something new in Colby's voice, under all the reassurances, a soft gloating that was almost worse than the bikers' laughter. But he was here, and backing out might be more dangerous than going ahead – and scared or not, he was still excited by the whole idea. 'As long as that's all,' he said thickly. There was a heavy crackle, and the fire blazed up. Shadows reared up against the rock wall, swollen troll-like silhouettes of the gang. And above them loomed the great tree, a broad ash, its branches swaying and rustling softly – but oddly bowed down, by things that hung from them, like strange fruit –

Paul swallowed hard, trying to choke down the swell of vomit in his gullet. He had seen bare bones before, even human ones in trenches up at Fern Farm; he had helped sort them in finds trays, washed and cleaned them for museum cases. This was only a sheep's skull. But there was still flesh on it, hanging in shreds, putrid and maggot-run. A gust of wind whipped the fire to roaring, spun eddies of smoke into the dancing branches. There were other things hanging there – dark grotesque things. Bones. Birds and animals, half rotted. Animal heads, impaled on branches or lodged in crooks, heads with jaws that sagged or had fallen away completely, shrivelled half-mummified heads, bare bony skulls. The flower of the tree was death, its fruit corruption.

Paul turned away, gagging, and found Colby watching him, arms folded, an unreadable expression on his hard features. 'Just sacrifices,' he said calmly. 'Just like in the Bible. Only the offerings aren't burnt. They hang there for the ravens to take, and the heroes feast on the bodies.'

Paul couldn't say anything; he hardly dared open his mouth in case he was sick. He just shook his head and made as if to turn away. Colby caught his arm in massive fingers, gentle but immovable. 'Now listen here. You're here because you wanted to be. What's so wrong with the sacrifice? It's just a feast, like an ox-roast, a barbecue, only the head's not thrown away, it's offered. Anyhow, there's none of that tonight, no feast. This is special – an

87

initiation. And we're running late.' He turned to the lounging bikers and clapped his hands sharply. 'Shape up, you guys! Hog! Apps! Dig out the gear! Ashe! Charlie! Staves – jump to it! Steve, c'mon, break out the stash! Let's go-go-go!' He grinned down at Paul. 'That's the secret of handling these guys. You've got to organise them – like a team. Keep 'em on the hop – like this . . .' Kingfield was straining to lift the end of a large flat boulder. 'Hey, Steve, ya mother, can't you get anything up today? C'mon, shift ass!' Kingfield snarled and narrowly missed dropping the boulder on his foot. Instantly Colby ducked, seized the sides and in one violent heave ripped the whole stone free of the ground. The biker had to fling himself aside as he toppled it down with a thud. Beneath it was a small chamber lined with flat stones. Out of it Colby scooped two clear plastic boxes with what looked like rolls of tinfoil inside, handed them to Paul and with another heave toppled the stone back into place. Kingfield slouched off towards the fire, grumbling, while Colby chuckled softly and began to prise open a box. 'See what I mean? Show 'em who's boss an' they'll jump through hoops for you. But you've gotta come up with the carrot as well as the stick . . . And here it is.' The first twist of foil was full of what even Paul recognised as joints, fat and neatly rolled. 'C'mon, let's go warm up.'

Paul shook his head dazedly as he was led over to the fire. Back at the cafe he'd thought the ritual explained the link between Colby and the gang. But now, dimly, he could see there was more to it than that, and it made him deeply uneasy. They were sitting in a neat, almost formal, circle around the fire, passing a bottle from hand to hand. Colby thumped himself down at a vacant spot, patted the ground for Paul to join him, and tugged a burning twig out of the fire. He lit one of the joints, took a deep drag, and – as Paul had been afraid he would – passed it to him. Paul had been offered a joint once before, at a school party, refused nervously and been half thankful and half annoyed with himself ever since. He hesitated more than ever now, but Colby frowned at him. 'C'mon, it won't bite. Hell, the whole Rayner team was floatin' on the stuff the year we took the Bowl. Fitter bunch of guys you never saw, some of 'em real bright too.'

Paul shrugged as nonchalantly as he could, and took a deep slow drag, imitating Colby. It was like inhaling a garden bonfire, and he coughed and spluttered. The Hog, next man along, took it from him, inhaled sharply and, to Paul's relief, spluttered nearly as much. Paul didn't notice any difference in himself, but by the time the joint came around again he was feeling less nauseous, less afraid, and didn't cough this time. He grinned at the Hog as he passed it on, and got a grin of sorts in return. Somebody threw more wood on the fire, and the heat became hard to bear in the confined space. The others were stripping off bike jackets and shirts, and Paul did the same. Looking around, he noticed that all of them had a mark roughly painted or tattooed on shoulder or chest – three intertwining triangles. He knew that mark. He had seen it every day, in the Museum, the labs, the ruined walls of the Fern Farm temple itself and the boat-graves around it – a three-sided knot, mazy, intricate, endless.

The half-finished joint reappeared again with what seemed like surprising speed. As he took another long pull he realised that the bikers were standing up, retreating into the shadows. He made to follow them, but Colby's hand pressed him back down. 'Just hang on there, kid. Relax, smoke a little, watch the fire. We're goin' t'set things up.'

Relax? Paul sighed and slumped over on his back. He'd seldom felt more relaxed; he was even getting to like the taste of this stuff. The branches and their burdens danced grotesquely over his head, but now they seemed more funny than horrible. All those nodding heads –

Abruptly somebody was back, helping him up, plucking the stub from his hand and flicking it into the fire. A large hand moved in front of his face, and Colby's voice told him to sniff sharply. He obeyed without thinking, and almost sneezed as his nose suddenly filled with something fine and powdery. But almost at once it faded into a sharp, soothing tingle, and the muzzy world around him seemed to explode into brightness.

89

'What'd I tell you?' said Colby's voice with a very peculiar ringing echo. 'The very best crystal, pure. Dynamite.'

It sounded like the funniest thing Paul had ever heard, and he was on the verge of creasing up with laughter when the row of figures trod into his vision, circling the fire with slow, solemn ungainly steps. In their hands, held upright, were long spearlike staves, which they drummed lightly on the ground in midstride. One by one their voices took up the soft insistent rhythm, soft words half-chanted, half-muttered, in accents so thick he couldn't catch a single syllable. His head was reeling, but he felt a wild urge to join in, to drum and chant, and leap up with their fire-shadows on the rockface above. He tried to jump forward, and found he was held fast. Heavy hands clamped each of his arms, others fell on his shoulders and forced him down to kneel before the circling dancers. 'Hey, stop it, Jay –' he bleated, and then as he struggled feebly he realised it was someone else holding him, weird figures it took him a moment to recognise as Ashe and Kingfield. Like the dancers, they wore strange jumbled costumes – rough cloaks and jerkins of fake fur scraps, ragged leather jackets so covered with heavy studs they looked like armour, denim tops and combat jackets stiff with silver paint, a genuine age-blackened deerskin with antlered head still attached and worn like a helmet, old crash-helmets painted bronze, some with cheekbars and nose-pieces added, others spattered with black-and-red swastikas and SS runes, studded wristlets, crude swords and axes cut out of scrap metal, and here and there the cheap replica Viking jewellery sold in the town's souvenir shops. Ashe wore a crash helmet with a metal face-mask added, Kingfield a Nazi helmet with horns on the sides. Somewhere else, at some other time, Paul might have found it all funny – the gimcrack outfits, the leaden-footed dance. But here, between the dark and the flickering firelight, it took on a sinister rightness and reality of its own. With the artificial clarity of drugs he saw beyond the dancers to their looming, leaping shadows; the costumes were surely to make *them* real,

90

to recreate them as they'd hopped and flickered in this place a thousand years gone by.

Dimly he became aware that his clothes were being pulled off him, that he was being wrapped in a rough, stale-smelling fur. He hung there, past resistance now, swaying to the drum and hiss of the chant. Suddenly there came a shout from the background, and the dancers stopped, swung, froze in strange uneasy poses, staves held out high.

From the wings of shadow an immense figure came striding out to stand between him and the fire. Paul gasped at the sight of him, a massive shape wrapped in a robe or cloak of thick fur over which, like some feral crown, rose a high helm of gleaming, sculpted metal, a writhing, slithering mass of serpent patterns that gripped and clawed and throttled at each other, writhing upwards as if to escape. Out of the helm rose two high, twisted metal tubes in the shape of immense horns, but tipped with gaping dragonhead finials. The dragonhelm bent and tossed like an angry bull, and the dancers cheered raggedly.

The horned figure swung around to face the dancers. He spoke. 'This is the young bear. This is him we offer. Let your eye see him, your choice be on him. Let your spear strike for him, your shield shelter him. Let your gates open for him, your meat fill him, your mead fire him. Let your ravens fly at his shoulder, your wolves feed from his hand – and your steed bear him.'

The hands jerked Paul to his feet and hauled him staggering back, right to the base of the ash tree. His bare heels scraped painfully against a rising edge of rough stone, and he scrabbled to find a footing on it. As he stood there swaying, he heard a sudden rustle in the branches above, looked up, and saw a rope flung over and come twisting down toward him. On the end of it was a noose.

He cried out and tried to struggle, but the dragonhelm was suddenly thrust right into his face. Its front was a mask, and behind it he saw eyes he knew, blue and glinting with chilly amusement. 'Shut it, kid!' hissed a voice. 'Think we'd do this for real? Feel that rope – let him feel it, Charlie! See?'

Paul twisted it confusedly in his fingers. The noose was roughly plaited out of what felt like dry grass. 'Easy with that!' hissed Colby. 'You'll break it! It's about as strong as a daisy chain – this is just a ritual, get it? You've got to go through the ordeal – like Odin in the Edda story – you've read that, remember?'

'Yes,' mumbled Paul, 'he hung on the tree – speared –'

'Okay,' whispered Colby. 'A sacrifice to himself, doubling his power. We're sacrificing you – but not for real. We spear you with the blunt staves, pull you up – then the noose breaks an' you're through. You're our brother. But you mustn't flinch, got that? Got it – no flinching?'

'Sure, Jay,' said Paul giddily. 'Got it . . .'

The helm swept up and away from him, the hands let him go, and he stood there alone on a high flat stone under the tree. One end was stained, by moss or lichen perhaps; he couldn't make out its colour in the firelight. He saw Ashe and Kingfield join the circle, and heard Colby's shout. The dancers echoed it.

One by one they clapped their staves together in an X shape, a sharp fusillade of sound that echoed deafeningly between the walls. As each man clapped his staves he swung to the left, and the circling began again, slower and yet more dizzying. The dancers were moving now like stalking animals, circling each other in pairs, staves held out at arms' length, upright, threatening. It was a weird echo of the Odd Dance as he'd seen it, but infinitely more beautiful, more terrible, fierce and tense. Now the dancers were half man, half animal, growling deep in their throats, their movements more instinct than skill: each in turn became hunter and hunted, staves in play like stabbing spears, a rhythm of alternate life and death. All the weighty clumsiness had somehow drained out of the dancers; they leapt and spun and flickered like creatures without weight or substance – or was that their shadows he was seeing, echoing the ritual, carrying out their own strange dance with fluid intensity, amplifying it to serve their own dark purpose?

The spear-staves rattled and clashed, faster and faster – until one pair of dancers on the far side of the fire fell away, spun, and with a single wild cry came leaping right across it and towards him, the stave-spears stabbing at his throat. He froze – and they clashed, hard, blunt and harmless, against his chest. The dancers reeled aside – and another pair came yelling, leaping. Again the impact, hard enough to shorten his breath, bruise a little, no more. Only his shadow – skinny, attenuated, absurd – was transfixed. Three more pairs came, struck, fell back, and he was proud, he hadn't flinched once. What now? The wisp of noose tautening?

But the dancers were falling back, and again the horned man stood before him. Colby had cast aside his cloak, and now wore only a short kilt of fur. The firelight glinted on his tanned skin, stressed the heavy muscles with shadow. In his left hand he held a thin rod, like a barked willow withy; Paul could see it flexing. In his right hand was a staff like the others – except that metal glinted at its tip. Slowly, steadily, he extended it until the sharp blade touched Paul's chest. The slight touch of chill seemed to clear Paul's mind for a moment; he suddenly thought 'I must look like Saint Sebastian or something . . .' and almost laughed. But the spearpoint kept on coming, slowly, steadily, until there was a sudden sting of pain. Then the point swung away, a faint touch of red at the tip. Paul felt the warm trickle running down his chest, and sagged with relief. But as he looked down he saw the face under the helmet, the cruel lines of the mouth, the half-smile tense, twisted with appetite, and began to glimpse something about Colby he'd been too blind to see before. But then the tall man was gone, charging away around the fire, the dancers leaping and shouting behind him. The seawind gusted in through the crevice, lashed the fire to frenzy. Now the horned man stood, facing him through the flames.

Overhead the leaves began to rustle, to chuckle with the things that hung among them. Two branches scraped slowly against each other, the rasp of staff on staff. The flames leapt up, the shadows went scuttling back as if to shelter behind the horned figure. He swung the spear back above his head, stood poised for an instant – then hurled it forward with all his strength. Paul gasped involuntarily – but the spear never left the throwing hand.

He saw the light glint on it as it fell safely away from him, hypnotic, eye-catching, compelling. The moment of fear was washed away. The blunt wand came lancing forward, launched high in the air, arcing over the flames – the only motion in a world fallen suddenly silent. The flames, a curtain risen in the wind, hung motionless. The horned man did not move. The shadows were still, waiting. Only the staff quivered, spun, as it glided towards him through the dead air.

It spun – and as it touched and entered the flame curtain, it writhed and twisted like a tortured snake. It changed.

The flames glittered on a red-gold tip, on a shaft laced with bronzed serpent patterns, stiff embodiments of tormented energy, heralds of agony.

He opened his mouth for a cry of fear – but there was no sound. His tongue was as slow, as leaden as the world around him. The light of the unmoving flames traced out patterns on the spearblade, rich intricate markings heavy with meaning in his mind. And in answer to the summons he saw there, two new shadows joined the dance.

Forward they plunged from the night beyond, and it was as if it had poured into them, swelled them, made them solid. On either side of the horned man they came, towering higher even than he, long limbs dark-sheened, hands stretched out spider-like in the blazing light. Strands of darkness swept and tossed across their faces, like seaweed over the drowned, lank matted manes overhanging, overshadowing their eyes. Silent their coming, silently they stood . . . and watched . . .

Something touched his chest, a cool, betraying touch like a finger that pressed hard into the skin – a sharp, sharp fingernail that pressed slowly, infinitely slowly down, parted flesh from flesh, probed deeply, irresistibly through fat and muscle, that cut a channel and let in the frozen flame. Chill, searing pain lanced deep into his chest, drew in his breath in a single shrieking gasp, while all the time his mind cried out against it, against the impossibility of it, against the slicing thrust of a stave he had seen was

94

light, blunt, harmless. Then the wind yelled in the tree above him, and lashed the branches upward, and his own unbelieving cry was cut off by a whipping pressure on his throat that swept him up and off the ground with his feet kicking vainly for a foothold. In a wrenching haze of agony he saw the two great shadows advance, and a small figure that shrieked and ran headlong between them, plunging helplessly out into the dark with a falling wail of terror that echoed even through the roaring in his ears. Pain bent him rigid like a bow; the shadows swept down among the dancers, blotting the horned figure from his fading sight. Then explosively, silently, the taut cord of agony snapped, and the world fell inward into darkness.

CHAPTER FIVE

'EARLY THIS morning it was they found him,' said Ridley. His face was as grey as the drizzling sky beyond the window. 'Couple of blokes after shellfish at low tide. Looked like a floater, our Mr Kingfield – as if he'd drowned, I mean. We soon realised he'd come off the cliff, though – roman-candled.'

'I'm sorry?'

'Don't ask. Like parachutists when the chutes don't open. Call it violent compression on impact. He was a long way out from the cliff – as if he'd been pushed. Or thrown. Could have taken a running jump, even. So we searched the clifftop, the paths, and we found this cleft, clearing, I don't know. Hidden by bushes once – all trampled flat now. Christ, what a bloody sight! WPC found it first, tough little biddy, but she was heaving her guts out. Had to haul her off to hospital first – shock.' He shook his head. 'They were all dead in there. Dead or dying.'

'Paul?'

'Him. And the others.'

'What others?'

'Those fucking bikers, who d'you think?' snarled Ridley, then caught sight of Hal's expression, as horrified as his own. 'Sorry. Sorry, Prof. Thought you'd have worked that out. Dear God. Like after a bomb. Just – broken, spilled. Dismembered. Two or three still alive, but no chance, not after the big freeze last night. Two died before we could get 'em out, third one – well, he won't be hanging around long.'

Hal poured out some more coffee. There was no one else in the pub's little dining room, which was just as well. Ridley's eyes were haunted by what he had seen, and Hal was struggling to come to terms with his own responsibilities. He'd seen the boy every day at the dig, talked to him once or twice, but never really noticed him as a person. Yet every single digger was supposed to be in his care, and the volunteers most of all. In his trust – and how had he repaid it? Letting Paul get mixed up with . . .

He started, almost overbalancing the coffee-pot.

'The bikers? You mean those friends of Jay's? So where is he? Is he –' he fumbled for the right word '– is he involved in this as well?'

Ridley looked up. His face was unreadable, but set hard under its fleshiness. 'He wasn't one of the casualties, if that's what you mean. But he was seen with them yesterday evening, and the lad was with him. That bloody great bike of his was parked with the others on the cliff road. He didn't come back to the digs, he's not on the dam, and he's nowhere bloody else we can get our hands on him.'

'*Herre Gud*,' said Hal. It came out as a dry whisper. A wave of guilt washed over him, and another feeling he couldn't quite understand – or wouldn't, because it was too strong and he didn't trust it. He daren't think out the implications, not yet, not without knowing more. 'But – what was done to them? A – a bomb, you said?'

'No I bloody didn't say. Just made me think of Brum – Birmingham. I was in uniform then, helped sweep up. Present from the fucking IRA. Ordinary pub, ordinary people, just drinking, having a good time . . .' He snorted contemptuously. 'This? No comparison. It wasn't ordinary or anything bloody like it. Drugs – evil stuff. God-awful costumes – Nazi rubbish, that kind of thing. The one who's still ticking – thick little lout, Charlie Boot they call him – he may talk, may not. May not live long enough. But no explosions, nothing like that. Just force. Sheer physical force. Somebody did all that with their plain bare hands. Except for the b . . .' He hesitated.

Hal caught his breath. 'Except for the boy? For Paul?'

Ridley's face was bleak. He didn't seem able to go on.

'Listen, Inspector, it is my responsibility to contact the boy's parents, to tell them what has happened. What must I tell them, then? How did he die?'

97

'All *right!* The bastards hanged him – strung him up on a tree full of rotting meat with some kind of leather thong! And he had a bloody great stab wound in his chest – right through him, as though he'd been harpooned! That enough, or d'you want the bloody path. lab to give you chapter and verse?'

'That will do very well,' said Hal tightly, moving to get up. 'We had better go. You will want me to identify him, I suppose . . .'

'Aye, if you've done with your breakfast.'

'You imagine I have any appetite now? Paul dead, Jay missing . . .' And then he stopped and sat down again, hard. 'One moment. Hanged. And then stabbed. What with? *What did they use?*'

Ridley stared at him. 'What the hell has that got to do with anything?'

'Just tell me, please.'

'Don't know. Haven't found it yet. There was a spear of sorts – painted broomstick, throwing knife bolted on the end. Even blood on it –'

'And that was the weapon?'

'No. Couldn't possibly have made that wound. Wrong shape – too small. Just what's eating you, Hansen?'

Hal didn't seem to hear him. 'Stabbed,' he muttered, 'stabbed and hanged. From a tree.'

'An ash tree. So –'

'Yes, it would be an ash.'

'So this means something to you?'

'I – cannot be sure. It may not be important.'

'Christ, you academics drive me up the wall! This isn't a bloody doctoral thesis; there's no time for poncing about and writing fifteen bloody drafts! *I'll* decide what's important, Hansen, and if you've got ideas, any ideas at all, you bloody well spill 'em. I don't give a damn how crazy they are or who they drop in the clag. We do happen to be talking about mass fucking murder!'

'Yes, yes of course. But I find it crazy myself. This hanging from a tree – the spearing, too. It is a rite the Vikings used: a sacrificial rite.'

Ridley's eyes widened. 'Sacrifice? Like at Fern Farm?'

'Exactly like. Mostly animals, but sometimes humans –
slaves or captives, as a rule. All sacrifices to Odin, the
god of battle. They used to call the hanging tree Odin's
horse . . .'

'That so?' Ridley bit his lip. His anger seemed to have
been overtaken by a mood of cold, bitter calm. 'Sounds
like someone's been getting ideas. Look, you'd better
have a shufti at some of the stuff – forensic crew's still
working up on the cliff, but we'll drop by the station on
the way back from the hospital. If you've got time, that
is.'

'For this? Of course. We had better go.'

The mortuary drawer creaked and clanged shut behind
them. Ridley nodded sombrely. 'Thanks, Prof. That's all.
Unless . . .'

'Unless?'

'You've probably seen all you can take, but the other –
casualties – are here as well. Still in those bloody costumes.
You might see something – something important . . .'

'Yes, yes.' The high tiled room was clammily cool, but
Hal could feel sweat prickling his forehead and neck. The
image of the boy's face, relaxed and empty in death,
haunted him. His fault. His responsibility . . .

Ridley gestured to the hovering assistant, a skinny young
man who counted off the tiers of drawers with a wagging
finger before seizing one and hauling it out with a ringing
crash.

'Oh Christ,' said Ridley weakly, 'can't you be a bit more
bloody careful with – that? You can sec the state it's in.'

'Ey, sorry,' said the assistant cheerfully. 'It's them
drawers – bloody antiques they are, weigh a ton, an' who's
got to oil 'em all? You 'ave to yank, see, it's the inertia.
No lightweight, is 'e? That okay?'

'Fine, thank you,' said Hal, leaning over to look inside.
For a moment he said nothing. His face might have been
carved in stone.

'This is just Hell's Angel rubbish – Nazi trash. *Satans*,
what do they see in it? But he has one of the replica

bracelets from the Museum Shop, and – what is this?' The thing's head lolled on its left shoulder, obscuring the mark with a ragged fringe of red beard. Without a moment's hesitation Hal reached down, grasped the beard, and pulled the ruined head free. Bone grated and flesh made soft liquid suckings as it turned. 'Look here, Inspector – on the shoulder. You see the tattoo?'

'I see it,' said Ridley between clenched teeth, leaning closer because he was a hard copper and not a soft college type. 'Means something?'

'I don't like this,' said Hal, releasing the head. It settled back with a squelch. 'This survivor – he is conscious? He has spoken? I need to see him – cannot say more until I have. All right, you can put this one back now. I can wash my hands somewhere?'

Ridley stood by while Hal scrubbed with disinfectant. 'How come that didn't bother you? How d'you manage it, all of a sudden?'

Hal stared at his hands as he slowly and methodically dried them. 'I thought of him as a specimen. As something I might find on the site. I cannot think of Paul Harvey in that way.'

The doctor who emerged from the little hospital's intensive care facility was a gangling, olive-skinned young man with an unidentifiable foreign accent. He was rubbing his hands with an air of horrid gusto that made Ridley want to strangle him.

'Inspector? I am Dr Lehmann. The lad's just regaining consciousness, but I'm afraid he'll slip back into coma before long. Your sergeant's talking to him now. We're patching him up, making him comfortable – lovely neat job, but even a respirator won't do much good now. Abdominal injuries on that scale, it's only a matter of time, though chances are the brain damage will do the trick first. Depressed fractures, you leave them too long, all sorts of nasty things happen underneath –'

'Thank you. Sure you're right,' mumbled Ridley, and plunged through the swinging door.

100

It was hardly an escape. The room assaulted their nostrils, and not only with the normal hospital smell. Over it there hung a taint of vomit, blood, and something worse that Ridley tried hard not to think about. Curtains screened out most of the room, and the light around the only occupied bed was dim. A frame held the sheet high over the twisted shape inside. Harshaw levered his bulk off the steel chair by the bed as they came forward, carefully avoiding the few thin tubes that threaded out from under the cover to the laden trolley nearby.

'Hallo, Charlie,' said Ridley softly. 'What happened to you, then? Fall off yer bike?'

'Fuckin' coons . . .' wheezed the dim figure in the bed.

'What did he say?' whispered Hal. 'I don't understand his accent.'

Harshaw grunted. 'Summat about some, er, blacks. What blacks, lad? Been duffing 'em up again?'

'They came . . . while the kid . . . 'n they came . . .'

'The kid?' rasped Hal. There was cold fury in his voice. 'What did you do to him?'

'*Nowt!*' whimpered the biker. The head tossed to and fro on the pillow. 'Weren't gonna do nowt. Just fool 'round a bit . . .'

Harshaw leant closer. 'Fool around, lad? Scare 'im, you mean? Bit more than that, wasn't there? Same as the girls you took up there?'

'No . . . girls're different. This for the men . . . warriors.'

Harshaw grimaced at Ridley. 'Been talking, this one. Right high jinks they've been 'aving oop in their little snuggery – load o' bloody arse-bandits.'

'No! Weren't like that! We 'ad bints okay . . . like wi' brothers . . . bond . . .'

'Sounds like the Hell's Angels thing right enough,' whispered Ridley. 'Read about it somewhere once. Swing both ways, but what goes on in the pack is special.' He made a face.

Hal frowned. 'Many cultures had something similar, especially masculine, aggressive ones – the Spartans, the Afghans, your Oliver Cromwell's army –'

101

'The Vikings?'

'Oh yes. We know it was part of some Norse cults – Jomsvikings, unless they are a fairy tale. Berserkers, too –'

'B'serkers!' coughed the biker, struggling weakly to move. 'That's us! 'S what Jay said. You're 'is boss, right?'

'That's right,' said Hal softly, 'and I know what he knows – maybe more. He said you were berserkers – warriors, servants of Odin. He marked you with Odin's sign, showed you Odin's rites . . .'

'Ay . . . showed us what t'Odd Dance really were . . . what we'd done . . . all forgotten . . . brought it back. 'E was a berserker – 'ow 'e got 'is strength . . . make us all like 'im.'

'Did he go berserk? Did he hurt you and the others?'

'*No!*' howled the biker, so loudly he almost choked. The doctor came forward and swabbed at his mouth, then drew back shaking his head. 'He *fought.* Fuckin' Kingfield, *he* jus' did 'is nut. Screamed 'n ran.' He gave a ghastly chortle. 'Serve'm right. Straight over, 'eard 'im go down, wheee-splat! Me, I tried t'fight . . . fuckin' bitch jus' chucks me at a rock, 'n Jay comes chargin' over, pulls 'er off, then 'e goes for t'other . . . dunno, didn' see . . . back hurts – and me belly . . . gotta . . .'

'The boy!' rapped Hal. 'Paul! Did Jay kill him, Charlie?'

Charlie Boot stared at him for a moment – then heaved himself up on the pillow and burst out laughing. Hal recoiled, and Ridley swore under his breath. 'Kill 'im?' yelled the biker. '*Kill 'im?* Fuck off, mister, you can't pin that on us! We weren't gonna hurt a hair on 'is pretty little 'ead! Rope was just straw – wouldn't choke a fuckin' gnat! Nor t'spear, neither – didn't throw proper, did it? Just t'little stick 'e throws, see if the little booger shits 'imself, right? Did it all t'me and I'm still 'ere, right? Anyhow, kid's one of Jay's lil pets, ain't 'e? Fancied 'im, right?' The biker's voice was running down, gargling in the back of his throat. The doctor hovered, ready to push the others aside. 'Wouldn't – hurt . . .' He stopped, threshed, stared wildly out at something he alone could see. The voice rose to a screech. 'It changed . . . it *changed!*' He fell back, retching, bubbling. His eyelids closed and fluttered. Even in the dimness Hal could see the shadow settling on them.

'Out!' said the doctor. 'That's it. Just a matter of time now.'

The three men straggled out into the warm, clean corridor, shoes squeaking on the polished vinyl floor.

'Phew!' said Harshaw, 'glad t'be out of that.'

'Aye. That was evil,' said Ridley. 'Get anything before we came in?'

'Didn't I just. Not a dying declaration, though – tried to read 'im t'words, but 'e wouldn't take me seriously. Couldn't bloody well force 'im, could I?'

'Okay, Bill. Bloody stupid process anyway. So what'd he tell you? What's all this crap about blacks and buggery? Let's park on that seat while you give me a playback.'

Ridley listened attentively, but Hal's fingers were writhing on the scuffed plastic of the chair. Harshaw read out the biker's story as if he were giving evidence at the coroner's court. Its broken fragments painted a weird, half-formed picture: the ritual, the dance, the arrival of the two figures in the clearing, and the hint in the biker's last words: 'It changed . . . it *changed!*' Only Harshaw's flat, emotionless voice made any of it even remotely believable – that, and the grisly evidence they had just seen for themselves.

'Well, Prof?'

Hal started. 'I'm sorry. I was listening, of course, but – what was Jay trying to do?'

'Jesus Christ, Hansen, you want it in writing or what?'

'I know. I have shielded him, and I blame myself. These things – these terrible things . . . but no killing. Not if we can believe that unfortunate fellow. Paul – Jay shares the responsibility for that . . .'

'But?'

'He tried to stop what was happening – to save his friends. You heard.'

'He's right,' said Harshaw. 'Seems to be these blacks we should worry about, and they must've taken soom stopping. Big lad, Colby – 'e could've gone over the cliff like Kingfield, and been swept out.'

'All right, forget Colby,' said Ridley, with the air of a

man struggling to hold onto thinning sanity. 'Prof, I can tell when you've got one of your ideas, and you have. Give.'

'There is a legend – the best single authority for the Odin rite. A king, Vikar, was chosen by lot as a sacrifice – so his followers tried to save him with a mock sacrifice.'

'Like Colby's, you mean – and he knew the story?'

'From one of my lectures, if nowhere else. The noose was of soft cowgut, the spear a blade of grass. But at the moment of sacrifice they *changed*. Became real. And the king died.'

Harshaw swallowed, and said nothing. Ridley stared. 'Listen, Prof, there was no sign of tricks or gimmicks, if that's what you're driving at, but we'll take another look. Stuff is all back at the station. Should be some photos ready, too – the whole bloody mess as we found it. You mind coming down?'

'*Skidt og løj!* You think I could stop now?'

'No,' said Ridley, with the ghost of a smile. 'I don't believe you could.'

'Shouldn't sniff too hard at that, Prof, or we might have to haul you down off the ceiling. Cocaine. Very pure.'

'I know,' said Hal, 'though I cannot say I care for it.'

'Not your brand, eh?' Ridley's mockery held a trace of genuine amusement. 'Well, out here in the backwoods we aren't quite as picky as your faculty chums.'

'You're feeling better,' said Hal.

The policeman sighed. 'Suppose so. Couldn't've felt much worse. All this on a so-say quiet patch. Hasn't hit the papers yet, thank Christ – tabloids'll have the place under siege. Them and the bloody sightseers.'

'I know how you feel,' said Hal, sorting vaguely through a bundle of painted staves. 'It is the same with me. One moment a great success, more than I could have dreamed of, and now – who knows? The price I must pay for being blind. I knew that Jay was a little crazy, but I am a little crazy myself. This ritual – for an archaeologist, you understand, it is a dream come true, a chance to put flesh on dead bones, to understand something vanished, something lost. A secret cannot choose where it is hidden . . . Those bikers. Would I have behaved any differently in his place?' Ridley gave him a sideways look. 'I don't mean the drugs, the schoolboy homosexuality – but the Dance itself . . .'

'It really is that old, you reckon?'

'There were many sacrifices on the tree. You saw them. It is old – and more than ever I am angry with Jay. A discovery like this – he had no right to keep it secret. What was he trying to do? What did he hope for?'

'Mmh. You know, I've been wondering if he brought in his own supplies.'

'The drugs, you mean? Yes, I imagine so – he would have many opportunities in his work for me. Among the dig equipment, the chemicals – *ja, for fanden!* There, too, I have been at fault.'

'Stop whipping yourself, Hansen. He might've bought them somewhere else – London, maybe. I've been thinking – there's a USAF base down Scarborough way. We're always picking up airmen from there on dope charges, plenty of 'em black. Maybe Colby had a little disagreement with his suppliers.'

Hal shrugged wearily. 'I don't think so. I don't know. All this – it is too much. Perhaps you were right. Perhaps he simply ran amok – why not that, when he has done so much else?'

'Maybe, but I'm keeping an open mind. Only if I don't wrap this up PDQ I'll have more than the papers on my back.'

'How do you mean?'

'For a start there'll be the Chief Constable. Then there'll be the little bloody Hitlers on the Police Authority – and all of 'em breathing heavily down the back of my neck. They might send help – or they might chuck me right off the thing. Handy scapegoat. C'mon, let's take a look at those photos.'

'Clear, aren't they?' said Harshaw a little later.

'Great,' said Ridley, spreading them out across a rickety table. 'See the real thing before breakfast, then get it back on jumbo-sized technicolour glossy prints just in time for lunch. What do you make of it, Prof?'

He had to repeat the question before Hal answered.

'This tree – it was being used before Jay or any of the others were born. See how the weight of the sacrifices has bent it – and some of the ropes have grown into it. How wide is the trunk, would you say?'

'Bloody massive. About six feet. Looks like a new tree growing inside an old one.'

'That would make it – hm – at least two hundred years old.'

'You're kidding.'

'No. There is an ash tree in Ireland almost three hundred years old.'

'How come you know all this?'

'Dendrochronology.'

'I'm sorry I asked.'

'Using wood to date an archaeological layer. Not so easy. But the formula for a living tree is simple enough – an inch of girth to a year of growth.'

'Isn't science bloody wonderful. Think Colby knows that?'

'Dendrochronology is a special interest of his. It can be particularly useful in ship excavation – Jay wanted to try out some new ideas on the Saitheby timbers.'

'Wasn't all he was trying out.'

'Meaning just precisely what?' said a voice from the door.

'Jess!' Hal's voice had just the wrong amount of surprise in it. 'What are you doing here?'

'Looking for you. And maybe one or two answers. Like what's happened to Paul Harvey, and why your inspector friend is so damn keen to find Jay. That kind of thing. What the hell is going on? And what are . . .?' She looked down at the table and the words seemed to die in her throat. Hal had never seen the blood drain out of someone's face before, so he hadn't believed it could happen. But it was happening to Jess, now, as she caught sight of the photographs from the clearing.

'You – you . . .' She struggled to catch her breath.

'You're trying to pin *this* on Jay? Jesus Christ, even you can't believe he'd do something like this!'

'Try me,' said Hal bitterly. 'Just try me! For years I have been shielding him, protecting him, convincing myself he was a victim, someone to be cared for, encouraged, helped. And the end of it all is a clearing full of smashed human bodies, a young volunteer – Paul – brutally murdered . . . And you, how many times have you told me to be patient, to trust him, to give him just one more chance? Are you happy now? He *ran* from this! Would an innocent man run away?'

'He might have done, Prof,' said Ridley.

'What?'

'There's no denying that Colby's involved somehow – but the killings could be down to the others, the ones Charlie talked about. In which case he'll be hiding from them. I reckon he might come to you, Miss Thorne – and if he does, the best thing he can do is give himself up.'

'If he does, Jess, you will *Satans* well get some help for yourself right away!'

'I don't need help, Professor Halfdan Hansen sir – yours or anyone else's. And if it's gonna be the kind of help you're giving Jay right now, you can stick it up your ass.'

Hal seemed to ignore her. 'You will not be needing me here now, Inspector?'

'We can manage,' said Ridley. 'Harshaw'll drop you anywhere you want.'

'Thank you. I must go and tell young Paul's parents what has been done to their son. I am sure they will appreciate your deep sympathy, Jess.'

Three short strides took him to the door. As he wrenched it open a gust of icy air from the corridor outside swirled into the room, riffling the photographs on the table and slamming the door behind him with a shattering impact. Jess stared after him for a moment, clenching her fists. Then she banged them down on the table, and the photographs scattered across the room.

CHAPTER SIX

PRU SIGHED, and let her arms sink to the bench. She looked up for a minute, blinking. The brightness of the bench light only made the shadows outside its intense little circle that much darker. The high Victorian room had always managed to look gloomy and cold, even with light streaming into it; now, with the end window still a mass of boards, it was so dark it might have been underground, an ancient castle vault or a cathedral crypt. The long rows of benches could be ancestral tombs, the hummocked shapes under plastic wraps and dust covers the sculpted forms of their inhabitants, in cold stone drapery. The dank, musty, sea-bed smell from the bags of wood fragments and the wild howling of the wintry wind outside completed the illusion. She put down the fragment she was cleaning, wiped her hands on her jeans, and rubbed at her weary eyes. It seemed to help a little – she blinked once or twice more then bent forward to her task again.

Gripping the slender steel dental pick firmly in her long fingers, she jabbed with grim delicacy at a corner of the pattern on the fragment, complex, intricate, as tangled as seaweed. The pick held an instant, then flew off at an angle with only a tiny piece of encrustation attached. She pursed her lips, turned it round, and attacked it from a different angle. Not much more this time. A bit of patience, that's what they'd said – just a bit of patience and she'd have the knack. In a day or two. She jabbed again, viciously. The pick found no footing, bounced off with a clink, and scratched her finger. She swore into the echoing roof. It had been a week now –

Then, as the last echoes were dying away, she froze. She had heard what were surely footsteps crunching into the gravel of the Museum drive, strong footsteps with a

108

long stride. Once she would have found that a welcome sound when she was on her own in this great lino-tiled mausoleum. But just a day or two ago a man had died outside that high, blind window . . . She got up quickly, ran over to it, peeped out through the gaps at one side – and almost laughed with relief. The day seemed so much brighter out there, grey and windy and chill though it was. And it was only Hal coming up the drive. She grinned, and went to fill the kettle, hearing the front door slam and footsteps echo across the empty exhibition hall. Welcome company, after all.

But she jumped, all the same, as the lab door crashed back with unnecessary force and Hal stopped, almost in mid-stride, looking suddenly rather foolish.

'Er – oh. Hallo, Pru.'

'Hi,' she said, and waved the kettle. 'Coffee?'

He closed his eyes for a second. 'Yes. Yes please. The cold out there . . .' He shook his head. 'I must have been walking about for . . . never mind. I am sorry for my grand entrance. I did not think anyone would be here on Sunday –'

Pru laughed. 'Well, I could always go if you'd rather be alone.'

'No. Please. We need all the overtime that we can get. I was surprised to find you here alone, that is all. Why are you not out having some fun, with Wilf?'

'Wilf?' Pru squashed a lump of milk powder in her cup. 'Oh, he's away for the day. Out with Tom Latimer, trying to work up a script for that pilot film of theirs. Wilf's barrows again – honestly, Hal, will they ever make anything good out of that?'

Hal's fingers drummed uneasily on the bench. 'Well . . . Since you ask – I do not like to discourage him, but I cannot think it is really something that *Timescape* will be interested in. There is nothing new, nothing very exciting, even where the burial chambers are intact.'

'I know, that's what I keep telling him. But he's so ambitious, and he keeps saying that Tom thinks it's good – he would, the amount of beer they get through together. Anyway, that's why I came in. Thought somebody else

109

might turn up – anyway, I'd as soon be alone here as up at the Farm. At least I can get on with something useful – at least, I could if I wasn't such a butterfingers. Anyway, what brings you in? Why aren't you out and about with –' She stopped. Hal was on his feet again, his face turned away from her.

'Why did I come in? I am not sure. To see how things were looking, how much Wilf and the others were able to salvage yesterday. I don't know.' He swung back to face her. 'And what does that mean, "butterfingers"?'

Pru smiled wryly and waggled her fingers. 'These tentacles of mine. Who said long fingers were good for delicate work? I'm going gaga – and blind – trying to clean up one of these box clasps.'

Hal smiled, and Pru thought how worn he looked. 'Let me see them. Ah yes, the clasps. Snaky little creatures, these. I had hoped to get them from the box intact, but *saadan er livet*. Show me what you were doing.' She sat, and he leaned over her shoulder, staring into the little pool of light. 'Yes, I see. But it is not the butterfingers, your problem, it is the way you hold the pick. See – like this.' He reached out and took her hands in his own, deftly angling them, guiding them. The crust on the clasp flew away in flakes as he worked carefully around the thin lines. She could feel the strength in his hands, lean and wiry and precisely controlled. The probe stuck for a moment, and his arms pressed against hers – it felt as if a static shock had passed. She tensed, and so did he, and abruptly he let go of her hands. 'Well – like that,' he said lamely.

'Yes,' she said, looking up at him. 'Thanks. I see. I'd been doing it rather the hard way. Thanks for the master class.'

He shrugged. 'Everybody has to learn – even the masters.' His voice was oddly breathless, and he ran a hand through his already dishevelled hair. Pru stared at him a moment, then hooked out the chair beside her with her foot, turning it to face her. 'Hal – sit down a minute. You look awful, really. I thought it was just the cold, but – you're really upset, aren't you?'

He sat, heavily. 'Young Paul is dead. Paul Harvey. You would have heard soon enough . . .'

'How? Not like – like *here*? And there's something else, isn't there?'

'More and worse!' He rested his head on his hand for a moment, staring at the ground between them. 'Others died. Yes, like here. I did not know them. But Paul – that was different. I had to identify him . . .'

'Oh, Hal –'

'There is more – you will hear it later. Everybody will. It may have been Jay who did it.'

'Jay? Are you sure?'

'The police think so. They are looking for him. He was definitely involved, and he has vanished.'

'Yes, but Jay – he wouldn't –'

'No? You wish to take his side as well?' The bitterness in his voice shocked her – and then she began to understand.

'Hal, don't talk like this. Try to relax for a minute. You mustn't blame yourself for any of this. Not for trying to help Jay, even if he does turn out to be – well, involved. You couldn't have known.'

'I made myself responsible for him. After that first time – that was an accident. At least, I thought so then, and so did the college authorities. Just – over-enthusiasm, one would call it. It was not the first time something of the sort had happened. I wanted them to ban fraternities at Rayner, you know? The way they have elsewhere – not that the alumni would have permitted it to happen. I was so ready to put the blame anywhere – except the place it belonged!' He slammed a fist down hard on the bench, and the clasp leapt into the air. 'And so I – made – this – possible!'

He half rose, but Pru reached out a long hand and put it on his shoulder, pressing him gently back down into the chair. 'You said he was involved, and he might have done it – are you so sure he did? You don't have any proof, do you?'

'Well – not of the killings, no.' He sighed. 'But the rest is bad enough, and there is no doubt of it at all. He is more than a little crazy, Pru – like a Holy Roller or a snake-handler, if you have such things over here.'

She smiled. 'No, we don't – sort of religious nuts, aren't they? Anyway, I think all archaeologists are a bit crazy. Goes with the job.'

Hal's mouth twisted. '*Touché!* But we do not all set up sacrifices to Odin.'

She shuddered. 'Oh Jesus, did he do that? Yes, I see what you mean – crazy. But Daddy's a JP, a magistrate, and he's always saying people are innocent until they're proved guilty. So –'

'All right, Jay has not been proven guilty. But does your father ever speak of circumstantial evidence?'

'Yes, and I'm still not too sure what it is. Anyway, it was you I was thinking about, not Jay. You're torturing yourself before you know all the facts. I mean, Jay might just have been stupid – I bet it was something like that. He might've brained somebody by accident when he was drunk, or *bored* some poor girl to death, but tearing – well, *you* know. He just wouldn't. And I'm not taking his side or anything; I can't stand him, actually.'

'Well – perhaps you are right. I do not know all the facts. But I cannot think that they will look good for Jay.'

'Wait and see. Don't let it gnaw at you. He's a grown-up, after all. And anything nasty he's been up to here, he'd probably have done somewhere else, too, in a different way. Come on, you can work for your coffee. Have a go at the other bit of that clasp.'

Hal grinned. 'Okay, *froken*, I hear and obey. But still – that *forbandede* ritual . . .' He shook his head and picked up the clasp. Selecting another pick from the box, he began flaking away the corrosion.

Pru laughed. 'I blame the temple, myself. It's having a bad effect on people. Look how the papers went on when we found the thing – the Vikings didn't really sacrifice slave-girls, did they? With all those sexy bits?'

'Well – yes, they did. At least, the Rus did.'

'The who?'

'*Rus* – Viking settlers who founded Russia. But they

112

were all Swedes, and with the Swedes, *Gud bevare os*, anything is possible! But they only did it at funerals, when a girl volunteered to follow her dead master. There is an eyewitness account – an Arab traveller. It reads like one of your Sunday newspapers.'

'Mmh. Maybe I've been doing Harry an injustice, then.'

'Harry? Our Harry?'

'Who else? You obviously haven't heard about his latest trick.'

'No . . .'

'Well, he's been picking up all these little tourist girls and taking them up to the temple site – priming them with all sorts of stories about slave-girls and sacrifices and fertility rites, gangbangs with the priestesses, all that kind of thing. Then he drives them out to Harbord Wood in that horrible old Cortina of his and – well – sort of demonstrates.'

Hal threw back his head and roared with laughter. 'I am sure he does! That man – he has hidden depths, you know. There is a story like that, about Viking orgies in a church, in an old Irish chronicle. No one takes it seriously now, it reads like IRA propaganda, but some books still quote it. He must have read it there –' He ducked aside from the spray of blonde hair as Pru shook her head.

'No, I don't think so. He probably got it from his granddad – old Hardwicke was our gardener, you know. He used to tell us some pretty X-certificate fairy tales when we were little, and there was one about a wizard – or a witch – who did – well, things like that. Maybe it was both – wizard and witch, I mean. You could ask Jess, she knows about things like that –'

Hal's pick scraped violently across the clasp he was cleaning. He glared down at it, muttering to himself, then put it down very carefully on the benchtop and dropped the probe back into the box. 'Sorry,' he said, 'still a little jumpy, I think. I had better go home. I am doing little good here.'

Even more light dawned on Pru. *I have the idea*, she thought, *that I have just dropped a special green brick . . .* Aloud she said, 'You didn't come by car, did you? I'll

113

drive you. No really, I don't much fancy staying here on my own, not now it's getting dark so early. All right?'

Hal was still folding his long legs into the front of Pru's white Alfasud as she went roaring out of the drive in a spray of half-frozen gravel and onto the road, turning right, uphill and away from town. 'You don't mind if we go round the long way, do you? I'd have to go slowly all the way through town. Daddy's said he won't pay for any more speeding tickets, and it's so boring, and I can get round just as fast this way, honest!'

'I am sure you can,' said Hal, holding on for grim death as she sent the little car charging up the steep road. At the top she swept regally onto and across the deserted main road, and surged away along it in grand defiance of the speed limit signs and the occasional patches of slush. He watched her pale hair flutter and stream out in the icy draught from the open window, leaving her profile clear against the grey sky: a swan-necked, delicate face, for all the firmness of nose and chin, managing to look cool and intense at the same time. *Like Boadicea*, he thought. *Any day now she'll be putting blades on the hubcaps*. She caught his look, and met it with a quick smile.

The road ran close to the cliff here, and they could see the town below through occasional gaps in the trees. Lights were already coming on, though it was only late afternoon; clouds hung heavily over the land, and the airflow through the window was rapidly getting unbearable. Pru touched the winding button, and a minute later the heater. 'I must be going soft,' she said, as they came to the turnoff for the southern route into town. 'Shivering in September! Probably seems tropical to you.'

'Hardly,' said Hal. 'You forget, I have lived in Texas for the last five years – *I* have gone soft. This is cold even for Scandinavia, though – surely it is unusual here?'

'For as long as I can remember, yes. But Granddad Ravenshead used to say they had some terrible winters when he was a boy. Maybe it's a cycle or something.' The southern route led them away from the town, out towards Oddsness and then back along the seacliffs. Hal could feel the wind buffeting the little car, and imagined a winter

114

storm powerful enough to pick it up and whirl it back over the edge like a dry leaf. Ahead of them, the road climbed into a wide stand of trees extending almost to the edge of the cliff. Their foliage was swept back by the prevailing winds to form a dense canopy that arched across the road. Pru slowed down as they approached the patch of gloom, peering along the road ahead and then into her mirror. Impenetrable-looking hedgerows loomed over the road on either side, but without warning she twisted the wheel and sent the car hurtling towards the one on the right. Hal made out the narrow opening just a split second before the car plunged through it with a rasp and rattle of twigs, and went humping and bumping onto a narrow, rutted track.

'Don't try bringing that great brute of a Range Rover through here,' panted Pru, wrestling with the wheel. 'You'd take half the hedgerow with you and make it too obvious. Haven't been here before, have you? Thought I'd show you 'cos we were passing – whew! – the woods. There's a nice view.'

The track ended in a wide clearing, sheltered by bushes but open at the far end to the unfenced cliff. An angry orange sun sank free of the clouds, flooding the clearing with long shadows and a brief melancholy warmth, staining the wind-driven whitecaps far below. The car bumped to a halt, and Pru switched off the ignition. Sounds of wind and sea closed in around them in their slow, ancient rhythm. Hal realised he could hear Pru's breathing, in the same soft sequence as the waves. He turned to her, but she was looking straight ahead, with the sun flaring on her cheeks. He reached out to her, but she caught his hand. Then her fingers twined tightly with his own and pulled him to her.

She rose to him, and their lips met. In a single simultaneous surge they grabbed at each other, her hands sliding under his heavy jacket, scrabbling at his shirt, his hands at her waist, sliding under her cashmere sweater to find warm skin above her jeans, up and around the slender waist to trace out her spine. Her hand swept in slow circles over his bared back and downward – his found her bra and followed it caressingly round, fingertips tracing the

115

curve to its peak. Her tongue lashed and writhed around his, reaching, and he slid his fingers back and under the taut fabric, then forward and up till her blunt nipples nuzzled against his palms. She fell away from him, gasping, but he kept his hands where they were.

'Oh God,' she gasped, 'the back –'

'Don't the seats fold?'

'Broken. Oh God –'

Separating, they stumbled out on either side, Hal shedding his jacket, the wind whipping his shirt. They swung open the back doors and fell in. Pru yanked her sweater over her head as Hal leant forward to kiss her, so he kissed her breasts instead. She held him for a second, wrestling with his shirt, hauling it down off his shoulders and dabbing them with quick, hungry kisses. His thumbs rubbed over her nipples, and the kisses became bites. Her waistband yielded to his fingers, and they stroked slowly downwards, twining in the soft, flattened curls, lingering in moisture and warmth. Her breath hissed through her nostrils as they kissed, fluttering against his face and then against his neck as she hung there; her long, delicate fingers traced, opened, sought and found. With a gasp of effort she arched her back off the seat, sliding jeans and panties to her knees, then to her ankles, and slumped back. His lips slid from hers to her breasts, her navel, and past; she gasped, as if in panic, and clutched at him. Then her back arched, and her bright hair flew out in an arc across the seat-back. The smoky light tinged her body for an instant longer, and was eclipsed as he moved over her and down. She rose to him, and their lips met. The rhythm of their breathing moved ahead of the sea and the wind, swelled and drowned it in a fast, insistent hiss. He drank in her scent as her body butted at him with cramped, demanding urgency, and felt his own response surge up and out and overwhelm him. The two cries came from a common agony, a shared violence that tore only at itself. Gulls screamed an echo, and the sea-sound washed around them once more.

'Mmmmh,' said Hal.

'Mmh yourself,' said Pru, and then yelped with pain.

Hal shifted hastily aside, rose, and slumped down on

116

the seat beside her, rubbing his left thigh. 'Hey, *kaereste*, what's worrying you?'

'Owww. About the same thing worrying you. Nearly put my hip out of joint – and that bloody armrest must've been sticking into me the whole time.'

'Ah,' murmured Hal, reaching over to rub, 'I wondered why you were making all that noise.'

'No, dear, that was something *else*.' She shook her head suddenly, as if to clear it. 'Oh my God, Hal, we must've been out of our minds!'

He tilted her chin up with a gentle hand. 'There are worse ways of going mad, I think. Let us say we were upset, and lonely, and we – found each other. I only hope you do not regret it too much –'

Pru bubbled into laughter and swung her hair across his face. '*Regret* it! Hal, darling, it was *fantastic*! I mean *really*!' She draped herself around his neck and kissed him demurely on the nose. 'No. I mean having it away in this silly little car instead of somewhere civilised! I mean, I'm not exactly a teenager any more –'

'And I am old enough to be your father –'

'Only if you were a really active sixteen-year-old. Which given the way you do it now is certainly – Oh come on, Hal. Don't you think you could *find* me again, hmm? Tell you what – come up to the farm tonight. I could fix you dinner, something really super – well, better than you'd get at the Ravens anyway! Oh come *on*!'

'Well . . .'

'Eight tonight, then. I'll drop you back now. Give us a chance to get a bath and – catch our breath a bit . . .'

'But it was kippers tonight, Professor!'

'Well, I am sorry, Mrs Robinson, but I am sure you can freeze them again for tomorrow night. I have some urgent business to attend to up at the farm. I may be back late, but I have my key. So long!'

Hal felt years younger and pounds lighter as he swung himself up into the battered Range Rover's high driving seat. He chuckled with pleasure at the soft, smooth throb

117

under the bonnet, and revved up a couple of times, remembering the sports cars he had left unexpectedly standing. *Like me*, he thought, and chuckled again. *Faster than it looks!*

Four-wheel drive was made for Saitheby streets, and the savage headwind hardly held him back as the car climbed steadily up through the town, heading inland. Once above the cliffs, though, it seemed to claw at him from all angles, and grew worse the higher he climbed. He passed the turn-off to Jess's van without the slightest qualm. Let her wonder where he was, what he was thinking. He had no idea what would happen tonight, or tomorrow, or after, and for once he didn't care. Right now he'd had his bellyful of caring in that particular direction, for Jess and her refusal to commit herself. And Wilf seemed to be just as bad for Pru, in much the same way. Poor Pru! That was the one care he must have in all this, to see she wasn't hurt. For the rest . . . He gave a deep, luxurious sigh, both in memory and in anticipation, and slowed the car as the Fern Farm signpost came into sight, leaning as drunkenly off-centre as it had the first day he saw it. But as his headlights played clear across it he stared, and then braked violently. The hummock at the base of the sign was new. And if it was what it looked like –

The figure's outflung hand was cold and lifeless, without a trace of a pulse. It had fallen at the base of the post, sliding down it, perhaps, as if reaching out for something. Hal put his hands under the shoulders, flinched at the touch, then nerved himself and heaved the dead weight over onto its back, baring the face to the headlights' glare. It was nobody he knew, and he was angry at himself for feeling relieved. A man's face, round and ordinary, gaped up at him with the slack-jawed idiocy of death; a pair of glasses hung askew, one lens starred with cracks. The pallid skin gleamed wetly from the damp grass, with no mark on it. Hal glanced across at the road. It was easily two metres away, the farm road even further. He had seen a hit-and-run victim before; anyone flung that far would have some kind of scraping or bruising even if they

118

were dead before they hit the ground. Something warmer than dew trickled across his hand; he looked down, and wiped it hastily in the grass, shuddering. The man's over-coat collar was folded in oddly, as if by an impact, just above the breastbone, and the blood, no longer pumping, was seeping slowly along the creases. Hal looked around wildly, and saw a dim gleam in the mirk – the phone box, of course, about fifty metres on down the road. He scrambled up and ran towards it. Then, halfway, he stopped and turned. The dim shape in the grass seemed to be pointing at him. Had that man, too, seen the box, and run towards it – but been overtaken? Hal hurried on.

'Police? Inspector Ridley, please – yes, it is urgent! This is Professor Hansen –'

A new voice came on the line. 'Prof? Harshaw 'ere. Inspector's out, I'm afraid – what's the bother?' Hal could almost hear the sergeant wincing at the word *body*. 'Jesus, not another – bang go our bloody crime figures! Right, we'll 'ave a patrol on its way up now. 'Appen the inspec-tor'll be out, too, if we can get 'old of 'im. You just 'ang on till they get there, eh?'

'Of course. Or, no, I had better go on up to the Farm. The house, not the site. You cannot miss the –'

'No. Well, all right, that's not far. But we'll need to talk to you –'

'Gladly. Goodbye.'

Hal felt suddenly very alone in the box as he put the phone down, and almost reluctant to step back out into the chilly evening air. But he didn't want Pru coming down looking for him, and finding the body and his empty car. He strode back down the road, flapping his arms to keep warm and refusing to look at the huddled shape as he passed, or as the headlights again swept across it. He swung the big car onto the farm road, tyres drumming on the rougher surface, and climbed as fast as he dared on this twisting road towards the top of the ridge.

There the main gates of the manor house stood silhou-etted against the dim sky, the Victorian carved gateposts blending oddly with the shredded clouds. The gate was open; he was expected. He found himself able to smile

119

again. But as he turned down the drive and the house appeared from behind the mass of rhododendrons by the gate, the smile faded as quickly as it had appeared. Over the low, wide frontage of the red-brick building darkness hung; not a single window showed any light. As he pulled up outside the central portico, where even the outside light was off, Hal remembered the other side of his young love-life, namely being stood up.

He grimaced wryly and got out all the same. He couldn't really blame Pru if, on mature reflection, she had chickened out. Or maybe Wilf had turned up unexpectedly; she might have left him a note. The sound of gravel scrunching underfoot reminded him of teeth grinding with frustration. His shoes slapped at the hard stone of the steps. But he was just about to reach for the bell when he saw that the big oak door was not in fact closed; it was just ajar, showing a thin line of blackness between it and the post. He stared at it for a moment, wondering if Pru was playing some peculiar kind of game, and then pushed it open a little further. The hallway was solid darkness. He called out 'Anyone home?' and then 'Pru?' and heard nothing but the echoes. But the air was warm; somebody had been in the house recently, at least. Hal swore under his breath, called out again, and fumbled at the wall for the light switch. He found a whole bank of them, and clicked on several at random. But nowhere was there the least glimmer in the darkness. Alarmed now, he clicked all the other switches, and called Pru's name again. Nothing changed.

He knew a moment of intense alarm, and then almost laughed aloud. He had run head first into the reason he was here at all, in this country. The power supply at Fern Farm was notoriously primitive and unreliable; it was during work to upgrade it that the temple had first been uncovered, and that work had since had to take second place to the excavation – one reason the senior Ravensheads were presently spending so much time abroad. And now he was hoist with his own petard – the damned thing had gone and failed again at just the wrong time, and Pru had probably gone to chase up an electrician,

120

leaving the door open for him but, in the heat of the moment, no note. Well, he could forgive her that. Sooner wait in the dark than in the car. If he could only find a chair somewhere, he'd be quite happy; if he remembered the layout of the house, the main drawing-room ought to be at the extreme right of the hall, and reachable just by feeling along the wall.

He set out, running his fingers over the smooth panelling and feeling as if he had suddenly gone blind. But the wood was pleasant to the touch, and he was just beginning to get confident when he barked his shins on something hard and almost fell. He stopped for a moment, and it was then that he realised what was making him uneasy. There was a strange smell in the air, not so noticeable by the open door but increasingly strong over here; it was not a pleasant smell. He thought of burning electrical insulation; it didn't smell like that back in the States or at home, but maybe these old British setups used something different. *Parchment, probably* he thought, and chuckled. But it could be something serious. European current was far higher voltage than American – if Pru had shorted something, or given herself a shock, she and the house could be in real danger. If only he had a flashlight –

It was then he remembered his lighter. He was always forgetting to refill it, so the gas would be low, but it was a lot better than nothing. He tried to remember whether the Ravensheads kept candles around, but couldn't. He fished out the slim ovoid and pressed the button. Adjusted for his pipe, the flame leapt high, flickering in the breeze from the door. He found himself almost in the corner, facing the end wall of the hall and ready to turn left towards the drawing-room door. What he had fallen over was the corner chair, missed by his outstretched fingers because it lay on one side, overturned. Had Pru followed this route to get out?

He turned. He was so stunned by what he saw that he forgot to shield the flame; the chill breeze caught it, and it wavered high and was gone. He snapped frantically at the button, but nothing happened. The hall was a mess, as if not one person but several had gone stumbling and blundering through the middle of it. The heavy hall table was overturned to one side, and the worn oak settle pushed out from the wall. The central rug, immensely old, heavy, and threadbare, was rucked up as if feet had been tangled in it, in a tremendous arrow of creases that pointed across the bare glossy stone floor to the stairs.

Hal paused only a second to fix the picture in his mind before he stalked out into the darkness. He managed to cross the hall without problems, and rested his foot very slowly and carefully on the lowest step. It was stone, and he made no sound. But at the first low landing, where the stairs turned right, they had wooden centres, and he had to make his way very quietly up the edge, taking great care never to lean on the wooden banister. As he climbed he felt in his pockets, but found nothing except his large ring of site keys that would do as a weapon. He thought of going back to the car to fetch a spanner or wheelbrace, but if he did that he could hardly avoid making a noise. If there was anyone here, they would be ready for him then. Whereas now – well, if he couldn't see in the dark, neither could they.

The smell was getting stronger, rank and rubbery and unpleasant. He was almost at the landing when something brushed against his sleeve. He lashed out, but hit nothing; whatever it was was small and hanging from the wall. He touched it gingerly, then flicked back his fingers as if it was hot. It was the wall light-fitment, and it was hanging loose by its wires. Ten to one this was what had blown the power. If Pru had been trying to fix it, failed and perhaps fallen as she went downstairs – That was possible. Likely, even. In which case there wouldn't be anyone up here.

Still, he'd better take a look.

He reached the landing, and was surprised to be able to see a little. The curtains must be drawn over the hallway windows, but here the great arched window at the corridor end was left bare. Trees outside obscured it, but let enough light in for his dark-adjusted eyes. There were plenty of doors visible, some open. Looking in those first would be quietest. He padded softly down to the first of them and peered in. A bedroom, tidy and anonymous. The next two

122

doors were closed, but were probably a bathroom and another bedroom. The next opening was half a double door, obviously a cupboard. The smell was giving him ideas about sneezing, but he repressed them firmly and moved across to the other side of the passage and the next open door. He peered in, and felt the breath catch in his throat.

It was like looking into a dream or a fantasy, beautiful but eerie, unsettling, and wholly unexpected. Against the grey-steel glimmer of the sky beyond the window a woman's form stood silhouetted, tall and willowy, obviously naked. Hal hesitated, almost afraid to speak and break the spell. Slowly, very slowly, she turned her head in his direction, the long hair sweeping across the shoulders and freeing her profile, straight-nosed, strong-chinned. As her body turned her breasts, too, showed clear, small, firm, high-set.

'Pru?' whispered Hal, throat dry, almost aching with the beauty of the image.

He saw long, slender hands lift and widen as she reached out her arms to him and stepped forward. He tried to reach out in turn, but found himself trembling, leaden-footed, as if the vision had plucked up some deep-rooted primal terror from his mind. *The man who gazes on the goddess naked* . . . The distant sound of a car seemed hardly to lift the weight of silence, and the dark swampy scent filled his head like a drug. She was closer now, arms outstretched, quivering, taut as if with longing, making no sound, floating through the still blue-grey light like an image from under the sea.

The light changed abruptly. An irregular golden patch flashed onto the wall, a distorted projection of the window by headlights from the distant road. It swept across the wall as the source turned, and gleamed for an instant on the woman's flank and arm. Hal stared, unbelieving; fear blew through him like a forest wind. In that moment of light her skin shone, not pale but dull slaty dark. Reflex flung out an arm to ward off that dark embrace; he missed, overbalanced, staggered to one side. She was not so close to him as she seemed in dim silhouette – simply far taller,

123

a head and more above him. She was easily seven feet high.

Choking, he stumbled back, caught his balance, then almost lost it again as his foot struck something soft on the floor, soft yet heavy. A sound caught at him, faint and fading, an anguished sound. A voice, wordless but laden with pain. Pru's voice.

He bent down to her, then fell back barely in time to avoid the long hand that scythed across an inch in front of his face. The speed of the woman was terrifying – now she was between him and Pru, and all he could do was back out onto the landing, watching the shadow gather for another leap. The moment he was out of the door he turned and ran, and knew that the thudding at his heels was death, the same death the man on the road had fled from, and in vain –

Only the stairs saved him, because in trying to turn too quickly he stumbled and half fell down them, out of control but far faster than he could normally have run. Mercifully he stayed on his feet as he thudded into the banister at the landing and down the last few steps into the hall. He lurched against the overturned table, grabbed it, and with cracking shoulder muscles hurled it into the path of what followed, and stumbled for the long pillar of light that was the front door – and through it, wrenching it shut after him. But even as he turned to run, it exploded out in splinters behind him, bowling him off the top step and out onto the forecourt, gravel chewing at his face and hands. Winded and dizzy, he heaved himself upright and staggered a few steps towards his infinitely distant car. Then the gravel lurched and rose to meet him. His out-thrust arms only rolled him onto his back, staring at the sky, unable to stir. A patch of dark loomed darker than the night, towering over him. With slow, unhurried grace it stooped to him, long hair tumbling over its face, long fingers reaching out till the tips touched his cheeks. He jerked like a hooked fish – the touch was like cold iron, the marsh smell choking him. Slowly the fingers clamped down and closed.

Again the light changed, into a sudden, agonising blaze.

124

For an instant Hal thought it and the roaring sound were inside his bursting head, but as he wrenched it desperately to one side he saw the car that had come rumbling up the drive brake violently, lurching on its suspension. Its lights played full on him – and on his attacker.

She crouched there like a startled beast, the figure of a tall, slender woman, quite naked, her whole skin the colour of an old bruise, mottled and stained like charcoal. A dark, straggling mass of hair hid her face. She was rising slowly to her feet; he could see the tension quiver in her long flanks. Her hands clenched and unclenched, revealing long fingernails darker even than the skin around them. Beneath it the muscles flexed and corded in a terrible interplay of strength, like meshed wire hawsers.

For a moment, half crouching, she seemed to hesitate, making no sound save the crunch of gravel under her feet. Then, without warning, she charged headlong at the car.

The door flew open and Ridley's burly figure spilled out, thrusting both arms straight out across the top of it, hands clasped. There were two flat cracking sounds, and the woman went down sprawling in a great shower of gravel. Ridley sprang out and ran towards her – then had to fling himself aside as Hal shouted a warning. The woman bounded back onto her feet in a single movement and sprang. Ridley pounded frantically back to the car and round it. She cannoned into the bonnet and fell across it, clawing out at him on the other side, almost reaching him. Hal struggled to haul himself upright, managed it, and staggered towards the car as she rolled right across it and after Ridley again.

He was faster on his feet than he looked, dodging desperately from side to side, keeping the car between them. But he began darting to the back of it, trying to get at something but never quite managing it before she was on him. Hobbling closer, Hal scooped up a handful of gravel and hurled it at her, shouting furiously. Her head turned for an instant, and Ridley dodged right under her arm. Her hand came crashing down an instant too late – a window exploded outwards as the car roof dented under the terrible impact. But Ridley had reached the tailgate,

125

and as she bore down on him he flung it up right in her face. She staggered back, and he stooped inside and yanked out something Hal saw only as a metallic gleam. Clutching it to him, Ridley stepped back a few paces, the revolver absurdly small in his outstretched hand. Hal stopped dead as the woman turned her head to him for an instant, then back to Ridley. The policeman made no move as she stalked lightly towards him, graceful, terrible, wiry arms outstretched.

Then he lifted the gleaming object and flung it in her face. She flicked up a contemptuous hand and swatted it to the ground at her feet. Ridley's hand spat fire straight into it, and the night lit up.

The exploding petrol can knocked Hal off unsteady feet. Looking up, he saw the woman rolling across the gravel, limbs flying, wreathed in flames. She sprang to her feet with one arm ablaze, flailed at it wildly, and rushed off into the darkness dripping fire like a comet. All without the slightest sound – Ridley ran after her a little way, stopped and fired again, then lowered his gun. He came trotting back towards Hal, who was hanging onto the car for support.

'Off like a rocket,' he grunted, waving the little revolver around to cool it. 'No stopping power, these things. Practically antiques. Thames Valley boys've got Magnums –' There was no tremor in his voice, but Hal could see the whites of his eyes too clearly. 'Well, are you okay? And what the bloody hell was that? Can't say I care for your choice of lady friends –'

Hal raised his eyes to the darkened house, to the second floor. 'I'm all right,' he said harshly, 'but for the love of God get on your radio, call an ambulance . . .'

CHAPTER SEVEN

THE LONG blades quivered and cut at the dull air, their
wind whipping up little rills in the powder snow. Hal
shivered. They reminded him of the blades in the Odd
Dance – which, come to think of it, must just be getting
under way for its morning performance about now. If
those prancing idiots had the least idea what they were
really acting out! But then he had to duck away from the
sudden blast of the helicopter's rotors, sending all the
half-thawed top snow scattering and streaming out in a
wide circle, obliterating the stretcher team's narrow trail
of footprints. The engine bellow rose to an almost unbearable pitch and the machine leapt unsteadily into the air.
It rose vertically, hung an instant wobbling and wavering in the sudden buffet of wind, then spun on its axis
and chattered off over the whitened roofs of the town,
heading straight for the rimed cliffs. At the last moment
it hopped up over them and vanished into the grey. The
little knot of doctors and porters straggled back towards
the warm indoors.

'Well,' sighed Ridley, 'at least that's that.'

'But I wonder, will she be all right?'

Ridley looked askance. 'As well as she can be, with a
broken back and a fractured skull.'

'I mean in that helicopter!' snapped Hal. 'When they say
even microscopic injuries could make all the difference!
Surely it would have been smoother by road?'

'Ah. Mmh. There's no alternative, really, not after the
snow last night. The roads are open, yes, but another fall
could really gum them up. She'd be a lot worse off stuck
in a snowbound ambulance, I can tell you. Better she gets
to Pinderfields – Spinal Injuries unit there's as good as any
in the country, even Stoke Mandeville. She'll get the best

of everything. They fixed up a lad of ours a treat after his motorcycle prang –'

'Did he ever walk again?'

'Well, no. But I gather her chances sound a bit better. She's lucky to be alive, anyway. If you hadn't showed up at the house like that –'

'But for me she wouldn't have been at the house! It was her first night back for a fortnight.'

'Still just as well. Means they were probably keeping an eye on the place, doesn't it? Sooner or later she'd've gone back anyway – only you mightn't have been there. So don't worry too much – at least,' he added hastily, 'not about that. God knows, we've enough else. Such as just who we had our little run-in with last night. A pretty pressing problem, in the circumstances. Any suggestions?'

With an impatient gesture Hal swept the snow off one of the benches ringing the hospital's little lawn, and sat down. Ridley joined him, carefully arranging his coat flaps to protect his trousers, but Hal sat silent, staring at the dents the helicopter's undercarriage had left in the lawn.

'Well,' repeated Ridley quietly. 'A woman – all too obvious. But that's about all that bloody well *is* obvious. That tall, that strong – left dents all over my poor old car –' He gave a short sharp laugh. 'Knew I should've taken a patrol car. What do I put on my insurance claim form?'

'How about Act of God?' muttered Hal.

'Not *my* idea of God, that. More like the other fella.' Hal smiled thinly, but saw no answering amusement on Ridley's face. The policeman rubbed his hands, mottled with cold, and then looked down at them again as if they reminded him of something. 'Remember her skin?'

Hal grimaced. 'I would hardly forget. Horrible. Black. Or leaden, rather – as I thought leprosy must look, when I was a child.'

'Right. With streaks and patches of a sort of dirty yellow here and there – the forearm, right? And the thigh?'

Hal nodded resignedly. 'What of it?'

'Plenty. You can check me with the doctors if you like, but I remember that from path. class – pathology to you.

128

That yellow, that's fat decaying, turning liquid, beginning to seep through the skin.'

'It sounds horrible. What sort of illness causes that?'

'Don't ask me! Heavy bruising, maybe. But all over like that? Decomposition. After you're dead. I don't know of anything else.'

'After – *Satans*, man, talk sense!'

'Well, suppose you try and explain it?'

Hal snorted angrily. 'I thought that was your job!'

Ridley sat back, looking completely unruffled. 'Not any more, it isn't. Remember what I was saying yesterday?'

'Ah – they are sending you some help then, your bosses?'

'Help be damned!' said Ridley crisply. 'Taken it right out of my hands. Bound to happen, really, once the papers got hold of that little mess on the cliffs. Special squad set up, couple of CID big bugs brought in from Leeds, the lot. They're busy setting up a mobile incident room outside town right now –'

'Outside town?'

Ridley gave a cold chuckle. 'It's a sort of bloody great mobile home thing, they can't get it down the hill into town in this weather. Anyway, my face doesn't fit, it seems – not enough experience or something. I get the local knowledge jobs – protect outlying villages and farms, see nothing more happens, that sort of thing.'

Hal nodded. 'The dirty jobs, huh?'

'That's it. Oh, and while I'm about it, find Colby – who by their brilliant deductions is the boy to blame, of course . . .'

'But –'

'Ah. But we know different, don't we – now? So what're we going to tell them?'

Hal started to speak, stopped, frowned and knotted his fists slowly. The policeman nodded, as if acknowledging something unspoken. 'So explanations have become your job now too, haven't they?'

Hal breathed in a great gulp of the icy air and sat for an instant as if it had frozen him solid. 'But what – how? What I saw, you saw. I cannot account –'

'And I've been pining for a university education all these

years! Some bloody good it must be! Not a single idea? Not one tiny –'

'Nothing you would believe.'

'Try me.'

'It is stupid, it could not be – I could not believe it myself!' He jumped to his feet and began stalking off towards the car park, with Ridley padding after him like an angry bull terrier.

'Why? Because it's something supernatural?'

Hal glared down at him. 'You said that, not I! So you can save your sneers. Whatever you think of academics, I am a practical man – I cannot go believing in spooks and spectres, any more than a policeman can!'

'Can't he? Think about it a moment. Who's more likely to run into the supernatural than a cop? It's a funny job this – day in, day out, you're being asked to find answers, explanations for all kinds of questions, problems, mysteries even. And then one day, you run right into a mystery that doesn't have any answer. It's about then you begin to wonder . . .'

Hal stopped dead. 'You are not serious!'

'I'm deadly bloody serious! Listen. Back when I was new on the beat in Brum, I got called into a house, grotty little council affair it was, because things were being flung out of an upstairs window. In I go thinking it's just another domestic. Husband and wife tiff, that sort of thing, dead easy to sort out – just lace into one, and half the time the other gets all protective. Anyway, I go in, and the whole family's running about like wet hens, and nobody seems to be doing the throwing. So I open my mouth to say something and this bloody great rug just comes snaking up like it's alive and wraps itself around me, wup! Moment I get free, I'm out that door and running, I don't mind telling you.'

'A poltergeist,' said Hal musingly. 'I have heard of similar cases. But surely some natural explanation –'

'Any explanation's natural once you find it. Seems this house was well known on our patch – the station sergeant just rang up some Father O'Malley and told him to get down there on the double. So after last night I'm keeping

130

an open mind – and I suggest you do the same, Prof. But open needn't mean empty . . .'

'You need not labour the point,' said Hal drily. 'One thing – whoever, whatever, was solid enough to be burned. So –'

'I get the idea. Put out the word to watch out for severe right-arm burns, that sort of thing. Just in case.'

'Just in case.' They had reached Hal's car, and he began searching abstractedly for his keys. 'But opening my mind – *Herre Gud*, once you admit the supernatural, anything is possible, ideas are not the problem. The trouble is, they are all crazy. Except –'

'Aye? Spit it out –'

'I don't know. But the things that were taken were solid enough, too – they had to go somewhere . . . And there's something I seem to remember, some legend . . . It might be worth searching – *ah, fanden i helved!*'

The hospital's front door popped open, and Wilf Jackson shot out. He came trotting down the steps, gesturing urgently to them.

'God damn it to hell,' Hal muttered, 'I was hoping –' He didn't finish. He'd been hoping he could avoid Jackson. He wasn't in a fit state to face the inevitable questions about what he'd been doing up there with Pru, not just yet. He felt like jumping into his car and roaring off, but he knew he'd only be making it worse. Jackson came scurrying between the cars, and he braced himself for the worst.

But when Jackson arrived he was breathless and not in the least hostile. 'Whoof! Glad I caught you!' he panted. 'Lift back to town – the Museum, if you're going that way?'

'Well, it's easy enough to drop you –'

'Thanks! Meeting Tom there – quarter past – just on the phone and he said he wants to make an early start, with the weather like this –'

Ridley blinked in mild astonishment. 'You – er, were seeing Miss Ravenshead off?'

Jackson looked startled, then smiled. 'Oh hello, Inspector, you coming back with us too? Yes, I saw her go – not that she knew I was there, poor girl.' He sighed, and shook his head. 'A frightful business! Who would want to – well, that's your job, of course. You've still no idea –'

'We're pursuing a particular line of inquiry,' said Ridley calmly, looking at Hal, who was fumbling nervously with his pipe. 'That's all I can say for now.'

'I understand. Well, there's not much more I can do for her, besides worry. Couldn't go with her in the copter, after all; she's in the best possible hands, they won't want me hanging about till she comes round – if then. So –' He shrugged. 'Life goes on. Hal, we'd better hop it . . .'

'Er – yes, sorry,' Hal stammered, hastily opening doors. 'So you are, er, going out filming, then?'

'I can't just sit around all day chewing my nails. And Tom's been pestering me to do this for a while. As part of a pilot, for *Timescape*.'

'Oh, yes,' said Hal drily, looking over his shoulder to reverse the Range Rover out of the narrow parking space. 'Your project on barrow burials, wasn't it? Actually I was just thinking of having a word with you on that –'

Jackson writhed a little on the back seat. 'Well, actually it's not entirely barrows. Tom felt that might be a little too – too intense, you know? Too academic? It's more an overview of the whole archaeology of the area – a general piece –'

'But including barrows?'

'Oh yes,' Jackson chuckled. 'As many as possible, in fact. There are all kinds of different types in the area –'

'Yes, I read your thesis. But listen, Wilf, there is something else you can be doing –'

Jackson leaned forward in instant protest, but lost his balance as the big car bumped out onto the snow-covered road. 'Now, come on, Hal, you don't own me, you know – and there's nothing doing on the dam, and this is the only time Tom's got –'

'No, no, Wilf,' Hal said soothingly. 'It need not interfere with your filming, and it is something you should know about anyway. The inspector and I were just talking over all this theft business, and we reckoned there is half a chance that the stolen stuff might still be stashed away in

132

the area –' Ridley looked sharply round at Hal, but said nothing. 'Now, the usual places, the sheds and barns and so on, the inspector's men can cover. But these swine obviously had some kind of archaeological knowledge – and they might just have chosen some of the open barrows around here, the ones that nobody ever goes near –'

'God, yes,' whispered Jackson, 'that would be brilliant!'

'Well, there you are. We thought you would not mind keeping an eye open for us, maybe even looking over some of the likely ones, and calling us in the moment you see anything suspicious . . .'

'Aye,' said Ridley, picking up Hal's cue. 'You'd be doing yourself some good, after all –'

'Yes . . .' breathed Jackson. 'If we found something, it'd be one in the eye for them, from Pru . . . and a magnificent hook for the film –' His face fell. 'But there are so many potential sites, and most of them not very close to each other. We couldn't possibly cover them all in this weather . . .'

Hal thought for a moment. 'Suppose you and Latimer cover half? I can manage the rest, with the inspector if he is willing.' Ridley nodded. 'Right then – if you could mark them on a map . . .'

Jackson pulled off his beret to scratch among his curly hair. 'Better than that, I can run you off a map on the computer at the Museum – if someone's there to operate it . . .'

Somebody was – Jess, looking pale and thin-lipped, with smeary shadows under her eyes. She said little or nothing to any of them, but followed Jackson's instructions crisply enough, calling up an image of the standard road map of the area from the database onto the big screen of the main terminal and helping him to superimpose details of the various sites. When that was done he called up a duplicate map and scattered a second set of glowing green points over the coloured background of the map. Jess, still silent, fed the two map images to the colour printer, and they came rolling out bit by bit, the screen colours duplicated by minute electronic ink sprays. Jackson ripped the first one free the moment it was done and handed it to Hal, but folded the other gingerly to avoid smearing the ink and stowed it away in his pocket.

Ridley looked at him dubiously. 'Now remember, Mr Jackson, these people are dangerous, as you very well know. I'm grateful for your help, I'm chronically short of men at the moment, but I'm making this an official warning. The first suspicious thing you see anywhere near any of these barrow places, the first sign of any recent disturbance, you don't hang around, you run like hell and call the police, and they'll call me. No poking around, not even for a moment, and no heroics – none! And don't so much as go *near* a barrow after it gets dark.'

'He's right, Wilf!' said Hal. 'That is when these thugs seem to move around. Not even a second look – just high-tail it out. We will be doing exactly the same thing, don't you worry. In fact –' He glanced down at the crowded map, and sighed. 'We had better be getting on with it –'

'On with what?' Latimer's tanned face, discoloured by touches of red around nose and ears, peered around the door of the dig office. 'Don't tell me you bastards're going out to that bloody dam in this weather? Jeez, what a summer, I thought I was just getting used to this climate –'

'Well, I did tell you to wrap up warmly, Tom,' smiled Jackson. 'Come on, we'd better be on our way too – I'll tell you on the way out to the car . . .'

Ridley moved to follow them, but Hal lingered a moment, looking at Jess. She turned to face him with a stare so bleak it was like a slap. He looked quickly away, but walked out evenly enough, and shut the door softly behind him. It was only his car door he slammed.

'There goes a man with troubles,' chuckled Latimer, sitting in his car and watching the Range Rover sweep out down the drive in a spray of gravel and slush. 'Still – if you will screw around with ball-breakers you'll end up losin' your nuts. Speakin' of which, Wilf, you might at least have used your nut a bit when you were doing those maps! Christ, I mean, what a bash if we were the first to find the stuff, we'd scoop the flamin' pool, the evenin' news headlines even – You could've sent them harin' off after all the dud sites and kept all the likely ones for us, couldn't you?'

Jackson's moustache twisted as he smiled his largest, smuggest smile. He tweaked the map out of his anorak pocket. 'What makes you think I didn't, Tom my old mate?'

Latimer let loose a rebel yell and grabbed the map. 'There's more to this than they're lettin' on, you know that? They must have some sort of sure-fire idea that the stuff's there – and why aren't they getting the ordinary dicks to do the searchin'? They're tryin' to keep somethin' quiet, you bet! It's all a cover-up – and we're goin' to blow it!'

'You could be right, Tom,' said Jackson thoughtfully. 'And if it was something to do with Colby – that'd explain why Hal was so nervous . . .'

'Yeah, shame 'bout him,' said Latimer. 'Nice enough bloke – but this is a cruel hard world, Wilfred my lad, and we've got our own careers to look after.'

'Yes, we have. But still – they were right enough about Colby, or whoever this is, being a killer. We're going to have to be rather careful . . .'

'Never you worry, my lad,' grinned Latimer. 'Uncle Tom will look after you, yea, with this –' He snapped open the dashboard locker.

'Good God!' Jackson exclaimed. 'Have you got a licence for that?'

'Licence?' laughed Latimer. 'They'd stick me in the slammer just for havin' the bloody thing!' He fingered the enormous revolver lovingly. 'Smuggled it in in my camera gear. Bought it off a refugee Afghan gunsmith, little village near the Khyber Pass. Those *mujaheddin* boys can copy almost anything, did you know? This is a spittin' image of a Colt Python – what most folk'd call a Magnum. It'll rip holes in a car engine, this little lady, or stop a chargin' elephant. Want to lay odds on your mate Colby?'

Later that afternoon Jackson was suffering cold feet in every sense. He'd cleverly decided the likeliest barrows

135

had to be large, with open or accessible burial chambers – but they would also have to be off the beaten track. It hadn't occurred to him what that would mean in this weather. He and Latimer had spent the whole day stumbling and scrambling through snowbound woods and hedgerows, over slippery, unstable stone walls and across endless freezing fields, full of potential pitfalls covered up by the snow. Within the first hour his anorak had proved inadequate, especially when he tripped and fell over; now it was soaked and stiffening in the chill wind. His walking boots had also begun to leak; now they were caked masses of slushy snow, and they too were beginning to freeze hard. Afraid of frostbite, he tried to keep his circulation going by waggling his toes, but they were so numb now he wasn't sure whether he was actually moving them at all. The only time he felt anything was when he stubbed them. He kept his muttered complaints to himself, however; Latimer, plodding along under the weight of his camera gear, had long ago given up even pretending to be sympathetic.

'Barrows!' grunted the cameraman. 'Your bloody barrows are the most bloody boring set of subjects I've ever bloody well run into, bar none! Just a load of fucking featureless humps, and the most interesting thing we've found in any of them's two empty crisp packets and a used flamin' –'

'You'll like this one better, Tom!' Jackson panted.

'You've been sayin' that all day! And this is the first time you've been right! And d'you know why? 'Cause it's the last! And after this I never want to see another useless bloody barrow again, I never even want to hear another flamin' word about them – jeez, what'm I doin' here when I could be back on Bondi! *Barrows!*' He made the word sound obscene. Jackson bridled at the insults to his favourite subject, but he didn't want to alienate the cameraman any further. He might still do him some good with the media – and anyway, the Australian was a lot bigger and tougher. So he swallowed his outrage and stumbled on. Latimer swore again as he caught his ankle on a snow-blanketed tree-root.

136

But then suddenly they were at a wall, and a gate, and at the far end of the large field was the barrow, a long low dome in the snow.

'There!' said Jackson helpfully.

'I've got bloody eyes, haven't I?' grunted Latimer.

'I mean, wouldn't that be a good shot? The way the sun's tinting the top pink?'

Latimer paused, stared, tilted his head on one side. 'No. Never see a thing on the box. Just a lump. No good. C'mon.' He thrust hard at the gate, scattering snow from its upper rim, and it hissed and skittered out across the snow, piling up a small hummock and leaving a wide fan-shaped scrape. Together the two men trudged across the field of unbroken whiteness, Jackson circling around to find the opening he remembered.

'There were two steps down to the entrance chamber – not original, Victorian restoration – and a rusty old gate.'

'There's a gate down here,' called Latimer, 'but it's padlocked – hey, no it isn't, it's been forced! And put back so the break doesn't show . . .'

'Common enough in these out-of-the-way places,' sighed Jackson. 'Saves us the trouble. Come on, let's go in, at least it's out of the wind. Got the torch?'

Freed from its little heap of snow, the narrow grille gate was forced creaking back. Stooping to manoeuvre himself and his ENG camera through the narrow opening, Latimer halted.

'Wilf – what's this down here?'

Jackson crowded past him and scooped up the gleaming fragment. 'Glass – thick glass, maybe – Tom! Yes! It could be that armour-glass stuff Hal ordered for the Museum –'

'Keep your voice down!' grated Latimer. He unshipped the rig from his shoulder and thrust it at Jackson. 'Drop that and I'll flamin' well kill you! Now –' He yanked out the enormous revolver, hefted it a moment, considering. 'Yeah, well, it could just be an ordinary bit of glass, couldn't it? Still . . . what's the layout in there?'

'Layout? A – a sort of sloping tunnel, a bit low, so mind your head – a small funerary chamber off it, then the main chamber at the end, big and wide. If anyone's in there, that's where –'

'Okay, I'll lead – gimme the torch, dammit! And don't bang that camera on the bloody walls!'

Latimer's face had drawn back into a hard mirthless grin. He ducked quickly through the low doorway and into the shadow beyond. Clutching the awkward rig, Jackson had to wrestle himself through, barking his knuckles on the projecting stones, ice-cold and nitrous. The floor was earth, over great boulders laid as flagstones, and in this sheltered place it wasn't quite frozen; it drank in the sound of their footsteps. Their breathing was the loudest sound, Latimer's cat-quick panting and Jackson's nervous snuffles. He felt a sudden draught, saw a patch of darkness somehow darker than the rest, blinked at a quick flicker of Latimer's torch. The opening to the little side chamber, and he was making sure it was empty. Nothing moved but the slow drops of moisture falling from the irregular stones. Then the light went out, and the darkness wrapped itself around them again. Jackson moved forward, then jumped as he bumped into Latimer, unexpectedly close.

'Watch that fuckin' camera!' hissed the Australian. 'Jeez!'

Jackson heard him pad quickly away down the tunnel, turned to follow. It curved slightly just here . . . He bounced off the unseen wall, feeling his anorak scrape and snag, clutched the camera to his bosom and scuttled frantically on. Only a few steps later he cannoned into somebody again, and squeaked with fright.

'Jeez, will you –'

'What'd you expect, just standing –'

'Where's the bloody main –'

'Go on! *Go on!* Just ahead –'

Latimer snarled something incoherent and plunged on. Jackson followed, hit his head a ringing blow on a project-ing roof stone and almost dropped the camera rig. But only a step or two further on he felt the air change around him, the deadened footfalls begin to echo slightly. It felt less close, less still, but something hung in the air, a taint . . .

'Where's the bloody main chamber?' Latimer repeated angrily, only half whispering.

'Can't you feel? You're in it! Use the torch! Use the wretched torch!'

It flickered on, but revealed only Latimer's furious face an inch or two from his own. A trickle of blood ran down from one temple, and Jackson realised why the cameraman had been standing still. He must have caught his head on the same stone, rather more severely by the look of it. Jackson reached out for the torch, caught the gun barrel instead and let go hurriedly. He swung Latimer's hand around to sweep the beam across the chamber floor beside them – and felt the cameraman jump when he did.

'Jesus Christ!' said Jackson, who seldom swore.

'Bloody . . . hell . . .' breathed Latimer.

Just next to them, so close they might have tripped over it, was a very ordinary carved wooden stool, and beside it a small table, equally rough and nondescript. In themselves, nothing. But both men recognised them at once; they had been part of the cottage reconstruction at the Museum. Latimer raised the beam slightly, and a scatter of objects glinted on the tabletop – plain domestic objects, some replicas, some real, snatched from the shattered display cases. Crude knives, wooden platters, a large cracked earthenware jug – and beside it an oddly shaped cup Jackson didn't recognise. Almost absently he reached out for it, felt it weigh cold and heavy in his fingers. He rubbed it with his sleeve, and saw ornamentation like tangled leaves gleam up at him. Latimer peered down at it.

'Looks like silver, that. Nice. Might be worth a bob, eh?'

'Worth more than a bob,' Jackson murmured. 'And not just because it's silver – it's priceless, unique. Scandinavian, early Urnes style – but I've never seen anything quite like it before. Where . . .' Then it hit him. 'Tom – this must be something that was in the chests!'

'Yeah . . .' whispered Latimer, awed. Then he stiffened, as both men remembered exactly what that implied – and also that they hadn't yet looked behind them. Jackson saw

139

the gun swing up in Latimer's hand, and then the light dance wildly over the walls as he spun around. Jackson, encumbered by camera and cup, turned more slowly – and stopped when he saw the taut animal mask of Latimer's face.

'What is it? What's –'

The torch flicked out. 'Gimme that rig, quick! Gotta get some proper light –' The camera was snatched out of his hands and he was left to endure minutes of feverish switching, clicking, connecting sounds in the darkness, no word from Latimer but half-voiced oaths. Jackson sensed something had rattled the cameraman, and badly; the air stank of fear, and not only his own. And beneath it that putrid, bitter taint –

A cold sun flared in the night, and he was blinded. He flung an arm across his eyes, too late to blot out the glare. For long moments he cringed in utter helplessness, blind to everything but scarlet streaks and blotches. 'You might at least have warned me!' he protested.

All Latimer said was 'Look!'

He stared, blinked, made out a blurred outline, blinked again as the streaks faded from his retina. A shape – a bed, the tall carved bedstead from the house display – and on it . . . He yelled aloud at the sight.

The bitter greenish glare of the ENG rig's lighting filled the wide chamber, glancing off the low roof, highlighting every hollow and outcrop of the ancient stones in the walls with stark shadows. The rich carvings on the bedposts stood out in high relief, and the posts themselves threw long dragon shadows over what lay beneath.

There were two of them in the bed, naked, slumped in a limp parody of sleep, one figure on its face, the other on its side with its back to them. Choking with shock, Jackson stumbled forward, but Latimer held him back. 'Better not get too close, Wilf,' he muttered, in an un- usually mild voice. 'You wouldn't like it. Me, I've seen this sort of thing before – too often, bloody sight too often. They're dead – been dead quite a time, too, I reckon.'

'That smell –' Jackson whispered.

'Yair. World's worst. Caught a whiff when I came, but

140

I never thought – Must be the cold in here that's kept 'em this whole, or we'd've smelt 'em sooner. God . . .'

'But who . . .' Suddenly Jackson dropped to one knee, staring at the long muscular arm that lay draped over the edge of the bedstead, hand palm uppermost on the floor. 'That arm – look at the size of it – it looks like Jay's!'

'Relax!' grunted Latimer. He stepped forward and bent over the bed. 'Yeah, thought so, his hair's black. Never seen this guy before – though the way his face is, his own ma might have trouble . . . All blown up, jeez . . . And the other – *Christ!*'

Jackson was happy enough to stay where he was. 'What is it?'

'A girl – a woman, who can tell? Shit, these murdering bastards!'

'You think –'

'S'obvious, ain't it? That's a couple more deaders old Ridley can chalk up on their slate. And they don't bloody hang 'em any more!'

'Two more . . . but why?'

'Well, I don't bloody know, do I? They're just lyin' here stiff as boards – no use askin' them! Innocent bystanders or something – maybe a pair of gippos who saw too much, or hippies sleeping rough, they look a bit like that. These bastards'll kill anyone in their way, we know that.'

'And just leave the bodies here? With their loot?'

'Wouldn't worry some people. Couldn't bury 'em in frozen ground – not that the sods've ever buried anyone. Just kill and leave 'em lyin', like the Afghans did the Russkies – bof!'

With an effort Jackson choked down the rising acid in his throat. 'Well . . . we'd better go and call Ridley . . .'

'Hang on!' protested Latimer. 'I haven't got any piccies yet!'

'What? You want . . .'

'Yeah. That's what we were looking for all this bloody time, weren't we?'

'Yes, but . . . this . . .'

'Well, I wouldn't hang it on my bedroom wall, but it's what the news is all about, eh? Isn't it?'

141

Jackson shook his head frantically. 'You can come back with the police – come *on*!'

'No! Bloody hell, the cops'll never let me get any film. It'll only take a minute – you go phone!'

'But if *they* come back –'

'Oh Christ – look, c'mon!' The cameraman swung the rig around and prodded Jackson up the short tunnel ahead of him till they reached the gate. 'Look! See! One bloody great bare field. Past that there's that scrubby little copse, the marsh on all the other sides, and more open field every which flamin' way you look – see how far back you can see our tracks in the snow? Anyone shows up headed this way, you'll see 'em half a mile off – just give me a shout and we can eff off out of it at speed, okay? Right –'

Jackson stared at the sinking sun, reddened and angry against the lifeless sky. 'But it'll be dark soon. You know what Ridley –'

'Better bloody well get on with it then, hadn't I?' grunted Latimer obstinately. 'Look, it's not going to get pitchy the moment the sun drops, is it? We'll have time to get back to the car. You hang on there an' shut up unless you see something, you hear?'

Jackson shut up. He was afraid to stay, but more afraid to go back on his own. Latimer had the torch and the gun, too. He'd have to wait it out. He shuddered, hugged himself for warmth and comfort, and realised he was still carrying the cup. He tucked it into his anorak pocket as far as it would go, and thrust his hands into his trouser pockets. He meant to keep a minute watch, but a few minutes of scanning an empty field of snow became boring; he took to glancing occasionally down the tunnel to where Latimer was disengaging the lighting units and setting them up for maximum spread, creating weird flickering shadows on the wall. It made Jackson think of the grave rites that must have once been performed among these very walls, and he shuddered again. Even the Vikings, a people much more sophisticated than the original barrow-builders, had thought of the grave as a kind of dwelling or home. The Museum had had that carved bed copied

142

faithfully from one they'd found in the Oseberg ship burial – grave furniture, he thought uncomfortably, only too appropriate now . . .

Quickly he glanced out over the fields again, but they were empty and still as ever, and no new tracks had appeared. Looking back, he could just make out the bed's high shadow on the curving wall, and that of Latimer moving around beside it, reaching out as if to tilt one of the dead faces towards camera. Jackson's stomach turned. He looked hurriedly away, taking a deep breath of the chilly air, and saw the sun spill its last scarlet light across the low hilltops. Then it dipped, sank and was gone, and the colour drained out of the landscape. Shivering, he turned to call Latimer, and saw a sudden rush and flicker of movement reflected on the tunnel wall. He heard Latimer's voice raised, and scuttled down the tunnel towards his only security. But almost at once he stopped in his tracks, shaking. The patch of light was wiped out, eclipsed by an immense shadow that slid across it. Then it passed, the light blazed – and went out in a shattering of glass. He heard, unbelieving, a high hoarse yell, a scream almost in which only one word was clear, his own name, and barely recognised Latimer's voice. Then in its echo another voice, echoing crazily from wall to wall around his head, the deep slamming report of a pistol, twice. And then, as the echoes died, a slow horrible sound like dry wood snapping and mud sucking, and the short sharp blow of the butcher's cleaver. Something fell with a liquid slump and a soft, gargling rattle. Jackson yelped like a beast and ran – up, out, through the low entrance, never noticing as he grazed his head, and up, away into the open whiteness.

But outside the barrow the field had vanished, sunk into swirling grey as if the clouds had come dropping down to bar his way. The icy mist closed and weaved around the barrow, mixed light and darkness, deadening sound. He gulped it in regardless, and it froze his lungs, he staggered into it and lost all sense of direction, knowing only that he had to run, bolt, anywhere but here, to be anywhere else in the world but here. He managed only a few steps

in the snow before colliding with a solid form. He clung
to it to keep from falling, looked up – and gasped with
incredulous relief.

'Oh God,' he babbled, 'it's you, thank God, I thought
– you've got to – we've got to – come on, let's go!' His
voice faded and ran down like a clockwork toy. Strong
arms reached down to help him up, and he tried to wheeze
out a grateful word. But the newcomer was looking not at
him but over his shoulder; Jackson squirmed around to
follow his gaze.

There were other forms in the mist, strangely distorted
by it, peculiarly tall, lithe outlines that seemed to slip in
and out of its coils, only gradually coalescing and growing
clear. He saw the first one – huge, half-naked, leaden-
skinned as if he had the mist for blood. And behind him
a woman, face hidden, quite naked – a lean, high-breasted
nakedness he somehow seemed to recognise, but as if he
saw it in a distorting mirror. Metal, pale and cold, glinted
among the shadows on their bodies, among the dark
tangles of their hair. And still more shadows, inchoate
still, slithered and writhed in and out of vision behind
them, and the mist was full of faint sounds.

Frozen, transfixed, Jackson saw the tall man reach out
an arm, sinewy, massive. The motion revealed a shadow,
stain or hollow in his side, deep black against the dull
skin. The huge fist opened, and a finger, ridged and
black-nailed, pointed straight at him. He opened his mouth
to scream, but felt the hands which held him lift him up,
up, bodily, and keep lifting; they grew tighter, harder, till
the fingers seemed to be biting right through his clothes
and tearing into his flesh. He tried to kick out, and found
his feet already free of the ground and flailing at the elusive
mist. He was suspended by his outstretched arms, sagging
between them and twisting with the pain in his shoulders,
and the more he twisted the more it hurt. He yelled and
squirmed to show them it was unbearable and they had to
stop, but somehow, impossibly, unbelievably, it wasn't
stopping, it was getting worse and the hands that held
him tighter yet. They were clutching harder, harder, with
impossible strength that bent his bones and ground them

144

together till hands and wrists seemed to be swelling like balloons. He heard his clothes tear, and then something terrible happened in his shoulders and an agony like liquid fire erupted in his chest, a searing that bent him backwards like a bow so he stared up into the face he had recognised, relied on, and saw it staring coldly down at him. Someone was shrieking with lunatic laughter, and he never knew it was himself. The tall figure swam into his reddening sight, and the hollow in his side seemed to glimmer, as if the mist beyond shone through it. Still kicking vainly, he felt the cup leap from his pocket and strike his leg as he fell, and then a seam of icy agony ripped across his mind.

The cup lay half sunken in the snow. There was a sound like a splitting branch, and liquid splashed and spattered across it. Something was dropped to one side of it, and an instant later something else, much heavier, that fell and lay like a sack. The steaming fluids cut channels in the snow, and the cup filled to overflowing.

CHAPTER EIGHT

AGAINST THE door of the Two Ravens saloon bar fantastic shadows materialised, shapeless shimmers in the hammered glass panels, shading from grey to black. Then it was thrust open, and out of the early evening dimness the two figures seemed to solidify and take shape. They let the door sink to on its spring behind them, but a wisp of icy air licked through and followed them like an uncomfortable memory. They stopped to kick the caked snow from their boots, saying nothing, as if the silence outside had sunk into their bones as deeply as the chill.

'Evening, Harry!' said the landlord. 'Evening, Nev! Usual, eh?'

Neville nodded listlessly, and Harry, hopping up on a bar stool, hastily filled the gap. 'Not 'imself – been like it all day. Ah c'mon, you gloomy booger, cheer up!'

The landlord leaned on the pump lever. 'Weather getting him down, eh? Me too, an'all! Look at the place! Open half an hour, and there's only the three of you in 'ere! I thought you diggers wouldn't be put off by the snow, even if everyone else seems t'be.'

'Ah, nobody's got the 'eart for it, Fred,' sighed Harry. 'All this business – that lad Paul, and now Pru, and t'Old Bill from Leeds grillin' us half the day – we're all right friggin' fed oop. I mean, look at Laughing Boy 'ere –'

'Or her,' said the landlord, tilting his head slightly towards the chimney corner. From long experience the men glanced, not around, but up into the big wall mirror behind the bar shelves. They saw a figure hunched over a table, staring vacantly into the gas-log fire and toying with a half-empty glass, and they knew her at once by the bright tartan shirt and the tangle of damp dark curls.

146

'Ey-up, Jess!' said Harry brightly.

'Hi,' she croaked, without turning her head.

Harry raised his eyebrows to the others. 'Fancy a jar wi' us – maybe a bite t'eat, an'all? Hey?'

The shoulders lifted wearily, and she still didn't turn around. 'No thanks, Harry. 'Nother time. Sorry . . .'

'Ee,' said Harry, hopped off his perch and trotted over. He risked touching her shoulder, and felt it quiver under his fingers. She turned her head away sharply. 'You all right, flower?'

'No! Okay? Shit, will you just leave me alone?' She whipped around to face him, and he was shocked speechless to see her eyes reddened and puffy over damp cheeks, the normally firm line of her mouth pursed up and trembling. It was like seeing a statue cry. 'Just go'way, huh?' Her head snapped back, her glass lifted and clanked down on the copper table-top, and she surged out of her seat so fast Harry skipped back like a scared sheep.

'Ee, where're you off to –'

'Home!' She yanked her anorak off the seat beside her, scooped the case that held her precious computer terminal off the floor beneath, and walked a little unsteadily to the door. The landlord winced as it crashed open against the panel, there was an inrush of cold damp air, and she was gone.

'God!' snorted the landlord. 'Great heifer – what's eatin' her?'

Harry, left staring, shrugged helplessly and strolled back to the bar. 'Well, from what I 'eard she's 'ad a dust-up –'

'Stow it, Harry,' said Neville sharply, and pointed out of the side window, into the pub car park. An incredibly muddy Range Rover had just pulled up.

'Oops,' said Harry, fishing for a cigarette. 'Speak of t'devil –'

A door banged viciously, and voices were raised under the window. Then Harry's cigarette flared red in another blast of freezing air as Ridley and Hal Hansen stalked in. They looked almost as gloomy as Neville.

'– an incredible waste of time,' Hal was saying. 'He must have done it deliberately! And when I get my hands on him – good evening, Fred! And Neville and Harry, too. Has Wilf Jackson shown up yet?'

Neville shook his head. 'Nope. Off on a field trip or something, wasn't he?'

Ridley and Hal exchanged glances. 'Near sunset,' said the policeman significantly.

Hal stirred uneasily. 'They should have been back before us. This weather would surely not stop Latimer's truck – I hope they have not been stupid . . .'

'Bit much t'ask wi' Wilf, ain't it?' Harry joked, and was ignored.

'Get some drinks,' suggested Ridley. 'And something to eat, for God's sake. I'll put out a call for them, just in case. But surely . . .'

'*Draugar . . .*' murmured Hal.

'What?' asked Ridley.

'Maybe I should have warned them more clearly . . .' muttered Hal. 'But then they would not have believed the warning at all . . .'

Ridley pounced. 'Aye, Prof? About what? *Drow-gar*, what's that then? Eh?'

Hal shook his head irritably. 'It's something . . . years ago . . . creatures, I can't . . .'

'Creatures?' asked Harry. 'We got a circus in town or summat?'

'*Quiet!* C'mon, Prof, spit it out!' growled Ridley fiercely. 'Never mind just getting it all academic-intellectual spick and span – people are dying, damn it, being murdered! And now you've even sent those poor bloody idiots off blind into God knows what danger –'

'They are in no danger if they have done as I told them!'

'Without knowing why? Look, I'm not asking you to commit yourself even –'

'You are asking me to make a public fool of myself! If you think anybody would pay any attention to –'

'Don't worry about us, Prof,' interrupted Harry. 'Nev an' me, we'll just slope off down the bar if you want some quiet, like –'

'No, stay, Harry,' said Hal angrily. 'We will try this out

148

on you two, and let Mr Ridley see whether I am believed or not!'

'I'm in no 'urry to laugh,' said Neville quietly. 'Not at either of you two.'

'Very well,' said Hal. He looked up and down the empty bar, and took a deep breath. 'You understand, it is not that easy to explain . . . You know that last night Pru was attacked, most seriously – what you do not know is that I interrupted the attack, and encountered the attacker –'

Neville's round face set hard, and his eyes narrowed. 'I wish I fuckin' well 'ad!'

'Oh no you bloody well don't,' said Ridley tersely, and began telling them about the encounter.

'Running round starkers?' breathed Harry. 'Ee 'eck!'

'Too much of an 'andful even for you, by the sound of it,' grunted Neville. 'So who'd you reckon she is? What's 'er game?'

'Scarpered from a bin or summat?' suggested Harry.

'He means,' translated Ridley for a puzzled Hal, 'is she an escaped lunatic? I almost wish she was. But we both saw –'

The listeners fell silent as he went on, and at the end Neville let out a long slow whistle. 'Bloody 'ell! Listen, I know I said I wouldn't laugh or anything, but . . . you're both grown men, you're educated like, and 'ow you can sit there talking about ghosts, spooks, spectres, things as go bump in the night – it's beyond me!' He glanced across at Harry, who could only shrug. 'Well, like the man said, I weren't there, I'm not gonna open me mouth . . . But there's more, is there? You think you know what she, it was?'

Hal shook his head. 'No, I do not –'

'Then what was this morning all about?' snapped Ridley.

'A – a guess, a gamble – something I read many years ago – legends in the Icelandic sagas –'

'Icelandic? You mean Viking?'

'Well – yes, for these purposes. Something, some legendary creature that looked something like that . . .'

'Uh-huh. And what else?'

'Almost nothing – except that they were very dangerous

149

– and connected somehow with graves. And I remembered how the Icelanders, like so many primitive peoples, thought of the grave as like a home, to be furnished – and I thought of the furniture that was so pointlessly taken . . .'

'I see now,' breathed Ridley. 'And what were these creatures, you called them something, didn't you . . .'

'*Draugar.*'

'Well?'

'I remember little more – just that they were very hard to get rid of . . .'

'Great,' muttered Ridley with a twist of the mouth. 'Horror films – ever go to one? No, you wouldn't, of course. Load of old rubbish, but I used to quite enjoy 'em. They always have some wise old Professor Van Helsing turn up, a real occult expert who knows all the folklore and stuff about vampires or whatever. And all I've got is you. Any chance you could find out some more?'

'Well – I do not have all my books here, you understand. I might have some general references, no more. I could find something in a good university library – York, perhaps, or Leeds – Tom Shippey is professor there, with McTurk and others, they would have the literary sources. But it would be faster if I could get through somehow to the computer at Rayner . . . Oh.'

'What's the matter?'

'We would need a suitable remote terminal, and an operator. Really, we need Jess, because she is also a folklore expert. But – as you know – we are not speaking at present, she and I. And I do not know where she is . . .'

'We do,' said Harry ruefully. 'On 'er way 'ome . . .'

'What? How do you know?'

'You just missed 'er. 'Ere – not too 'appy – said she was off 'ome . . .'

'Home? That tin trailer, in *this*?' Hal seized him by the shoulders. 'And you let her go?'

' 'Ere, listen, she's a big girl now, she can do what she likes! Could *you* stop 'er? Any'ow, she'll just 'ave 'opped on t'bus, they're still running –'

150

'Just,' said Ridley. 'If she changes her mind she won't be able to catch one back. And a mile walk up to her trailer – All this when she knows there're killers loose in the area – it's no bloody wonder so many Yanks get murdered . . .'

Neville grinned. 'Give 'er some credit, Inspector. She can look after 'erself.'

'The number of times I've heard that!'

'Normally it would be true,' said Hal ruefully. 'At least as well as most men can. But against this –' He stood up stiffly. 'I must go bring her back –'

Neville pushed him down onto his stool. ' 'Ang about! The mood she's in, you'd likely just push 'er the other way. Anyway, you need your dinner, and 'ere it is. I'm not doing anything, and all this supernatural crap's got me baffled. So Harry 'ere can run me up in 'is old banger, and we'll get 'er back if we 'ave to carry her!'

'Thank you,' said Hal, awkwardly. 'I –'

'You sit down an' eat. C'mon, 'Ardwicke –' Neville more or less frogmarched Harry through the doors, and as they closed his voice drifted back. 'And whatever you do – *don't* call 'er *flower*!'

For a few minutes there was silence around the end of the bar. Hal obviously didn't want to talk, and Ridley was quite happy to attack his dinner with concentrated force. Hal ate hungrily too, at first, but he slowed down until he was only pecking absent-mindedly at his food. 'Van Helsing . . .' he muttered. 'Folklore . . . If something had happened here . . . Ridley!'

'Mmmh?'

'Do you know of any local history or folklore enthusiasts?'

Ridley swallowed his mouthful. 'No, but then I'm not a local man. Fred!' He gestured to the landlord. 'D'you know of anybody around town who knows about local history, legends, that sort of thing?'

The landlord scratched his head. 'Can't say as I do, now you mention it. Funny, that – think there would be, wouldn't you? But then old Mr Braithwaite, he'd have covered all the ground too well, him as was vicar up at

Oddsness. Fact, it was him had the place renamed Odds-ness –'

Ridley looked sardonically at Hal. 'Thought you said that was a Viking name –'

'Ah, well,' said the landlord, 'Oddsness, that was the old name, it seems, and he dug it up in the Domesday Book or some such place and had it put back. Folk had been calling it Turness –'

'Which is also a Viking name,' said Hal, surprised. 'Thor's Ness – for the Thunder God, the Friend of Men. Interesting . . . and this vicar . . .'

'Ah, well, sir, he's gone now, forty years gone, and he were close on ninety when he went – 1903 to 1950, he held that living as you could in them days. I can just mind him from when I was a lad – right old character, always ferreting out all the old family stories and scandals and who was related to who. Songs, too, even the ones the little girls used to sing at their skipping games. Seems he'd known that fellow who collected songs – Sharp, I think his name was. And the other one, who wrote the hymns as well, Vaughan Williams. See, it was mostly him as dug up the Odd Dance and got it restarted. Real scholar he was, Oxford man like yourself – said he was going to write a book, but he never did.'

'But did he leave any notes – any papers?' Hal demanded fiercely.

'Wouldn't know about that, sir. But there's been two vicars there since, and the one now, Mr Thirkettle, he's a no-nonsense type. Runs a youth club and teaches boxing. So I don't suppose . . .'

But Hal was already striding to the phone. Ridley glanced wryly at the landlord and set up another couple of pints. While they were filling he pulled out his radio. 'Control? Ridley. Nothing new? No, nor me. But there's a chance the dig mob might come up with something; I'm sticking round here to see – the pub, yes, I know, *very* convenient. But I want the patrols to keep an eye open for two of the dig types and their car – description follows. Green Toyota pickup, very dirty –'

Hal's conversation was animated but short, and he came

back twisting his fingers nervously. 'There are some old papers there, but not many. Just a box. This man Thirkettle knows nothing about them himself. There may be some older documents – I will have to see . . .'

'Good God, you're not thinking of trekking all the way out there in this weather? Probably be a complete waste of time!'

'I agree – and we have none to spare. But I find I cannot sit still, not and worry about – never mind. I have got through worse in a Danish winter. I will not be long, an hour or two. If . . .' He paused. 'When Jess gets back, tell her to get onto the Rayner computer.'

Ridley stared. 'Rayner? In Texas? How?'

'She will know. I will pay. I will start a search when I get back – meanwhile she can be raking through the databases for any local history and legend from this part of Yorkshire, perhaps run a theme and motive collation and analysis –'

'Just a mo', I'm writing that one down. Greek to me.'

'She will cotton on – is that an English expression? Oh, and she is to use the international link if she needs to. Excellent. Well –'

Ridley plunged after him. 'Hey, hold on, you slippery . . . That name you mentioned – *dr*-something – you still haven't explained that!'

'*Draugar* plural, *draug* singular – *Satans*, I cannot take the time now! Jess will get that for you too. From *my* Dr Van Helsing. *Farvel saa laenge!*'

The snow had begun to cake around Jess's boots the moment she stepped off the bus, and was soon soaking through. She plodded on, the terminal swinging on its strap and dragging painfully at her shoulders with every long stride. Shifting it from shoulder to shoulder didn't seem to help; her right side tired more quickly, and she was beginning to get a stitch. If she could only put the goddam thing down, just for a minute – no chance. The terminal was guaranteed rugged, but snowdrifts hadn't been mentioned and this was no time to experiment. So

153

there was nothing to do but go stomping on and try to remember how it felt to have toes. And of course it didn't help to reflect that she'd only herself to blame. Storming out like that was a kiddie trick. Not that she hadn't been provoked, but why the hell sit weeping into her beer and then take off like a sulky teenybopper? Self-pity, that was all it was – coming down to a man's level. And why refuse Harry, for crissake? He surely hadn't meant anything, he was just trying to be kind in his blundering way. Just being male, was all. Not his fault.

The cold gnawed at her lips, and her mouth tasted foul. Fatigue poisons, she thought, and spat with malicious accuracy at a shrivelled nettle drooping above the snow. Her boots were caked masses of ice by now, and she stopped to kick them clean. At least there hadn't been another fall since last night, though there probably would be soon, as the sun set and the clouds came sweeping in off the sea. Still, here was the new access road to Temple Dell, and those were the trees of Temple Covert ahead; only a bend or two in the road to go, and then her field, the shabby comfort of her trailer, and a good hot drink. Not paradise – right now that was Berkeley, Cal., and a tequila sunrise in the shade – but near enough to get by.

She stopped to think. In these conditions it might be quicker to take the new road up through the Dell site, cutting out one bend. And it would certainly be more sheltered, the way the wind was rising. She turned and began plodding up the slope.

The way was quicker but steeper, and she was already breathing hard as she reached the trees. She did not want to linger in the wood; well as she knew it, from her time on the temple dig, it was an alien place under the snow and the dismal twilight, and she was disturbed by the wide gash made for the road and the power lines that ran alongside it. Large signboards flanked it, put up by the company the Ravensheads had brought in to landscape the temple site for opening to the public. But like it or not, she knew she would have to rest for a few minutes at least, and as she emerged into the temple clearing she looked for somewhere to sit.

154

The Dell clearing was a wide uneven dip in the hillside, like a tilted bowl; on the downhill side it was more or less level, but on either flank it sloped steeply upward to a crest crowned with the trees of the covert. Towards the uphill end these thinned out, leaving a gap like the end of a horseshoe opening onto the bare hillside. The temple itself lay directly below this, just where the slope flattened out, but it was almost hidden by the snow now. Towards the front of the clearing were some odd hummocks in the snow, spoil-heaps from the excavation, and a cosy-looking portable works hut put there by the landscapers – and irritatingly well padlocked. Jess found a tarpaulin folded across one part of the temple wall, kicked it back and slumped down on the patch of clear stone, easing the terminal gently down beside her. Gingerly she massaged her aching legs, and tried to ignore the chill creeping through her parka to the seat of her jeans. The wall was really too low to sit on comfortably, simply stone foundations for wooden walls like those of the oldest churches in Scandinavia. It might even have had the same rows of fantastically carved pillars, the strange roof of scale-like wood tiles, the same rearing dragon-heads on its gables. In this timeless white landscape it wasn't too hard to imagine that – but it had all perished now, in a fire whose charcoal fragments she had dug out of this very ground, crumbling between her fingers as she worked. Jay had been with her then, quarrels forgotten in the excitement of discovery, and he had rebuilt the temple around her with the force of his enthusiasm, the sweep of his gestures, had made her hear the hiss and crackle of the flames, feel their heat – she shuddered. She could use some of the heat now. Hal, too, had brought things to life around her – but more slowly, more methodically, so that they rested on surer foundations; his fires burned darker but deeper, consuming the very heart of the wood.

Jess shifted uneasily on numb haunches, but the ache in her legs was still too sharp to go on. Something was making her nervous – perhaps a certain sound half sensed, half felt in the instants when the wind dropped. She looked around at the deepening shadows, but nothing moved.

155

And yet the sound had a continuous patter, like falling water . . . She looked up, and almost laughed. It was the continual faint sizzling of the small pylon that carried the famous power lines up across the site to Fern Farm and its tenant farms, the lines whose installation had uncovered the temple. But she still felt nervous; something more than the sound disturbed her, something intangible, a presence . . . Angrily she scanned the blank rows of trees. If some asshole was lurking in there, let him lurk; she wasn't going back that way, and nobody could sneak up on her in an empty snowfield. She hauled herself upright, ignoring the ache, and rubbed her rear end vigorously to try and restore some circulation. She chuckled; it was the kind of thing a man was handy for. Jay would like it; he always had a kind word for her butt, how neat and bouncy it was. Hal never noticed – or never said anything much; he was too goddam prim for that sort of comment . . .

She stopped and looked down at the patch where she had been sitting. The tarpaulin had evidently been placed deliberately to protect something, a carving in the solid stone – a set of chiselled ridges that seemed to resolve into a knot-like shape, three triangles linked and overlapping. She knew it well, an Odin-sign; one of her first computer jobs had been to record the temple carvings. They must be cleaning this one up for the public. Well, her weight wouldn't have hurt it any. She lugged the terminal back onto her shoulder, where it immediately chafed, twitched the tarp back and with a last glance round at the watchful woods she set out uphill, with the setting sun at her back.

At leg-aching last, there was the familiar rickety fence and unkempt hedge, huddled and deformed now under its snowcap. The wind came howling down to greet her, whipping snaky lines of powder snow across the smooth curves of the drifts to cake on her front and sting her face. The way it felt she'd only just be home in time. Another of those nights, then, when the caravan shook in a soughing gale, when the thin walls thrummed and pressed inward under giant fingers. Not so good. Better when you had company, even fun when you could huddle together and find ways of sharing warmth. But alone you'd find yourself

156

awake and doing interesting calculations, such as the exact weight of you and the van, the exact wind force it would take to just scoop you up and over that neat little hedge and over the handy-dandy cliff back there. About three in the morning you could come up with some odd answers . . .

Jess pulled herself together. The hell with that, and with company. If your independence was worth a damn you had to keep it in hard times as well as easy. Sleeping-bag, Scotch-and-hot-water and, say, *The Sword In Anglo-Saxon England* to chase the bogeys away –

She stopped in her tracks, so abruptly the terminal dug a corner into her thigh. She didn't notice. There was her trailer, squat and grey under its snowcap like a lump of fallen cloud. But across the gusts of wind a sharp repeated thumping came to her, as if someone was knocking loudly, urgently, or . . . A few paces more, and she could see its door flapping in the wind, open and closed again like a slow hollow handclap. The door she knew damn well she'd locked.

She remembered to leap the snow-hidden ditch before the fence, but the terminal's swinging weight almost yanked her back into it. Swearing, she clambered over the wire fence, but in manoeuvring the terminal she snagged her jeans on the barbs. With an impatient yelp of rage she ripped free, grabbed the terminal strap and looped it carefully over the stoutest fencepost. No throwing that carelessly aside, even if all her books and money and letters and all the decent clothes she had along were in that thing, that sardine-can on wheels that she might've known wouldn't keep out the local gooks for five minutes and if whoever it was were still in there he was due one very big surprise indeed –

The wind came howling in off the sea, sweeping across the Oddsness road in great gusts. The suddenness of it almost made Hal swerve off the road: he had to fight the heavy car back in line as it slithered over the caked surface of the old snow. He thought of Jackson and Latimer, and

157

cursed himself for ever involving them. If they had got caught in this . . . At least his Range Rover had four-wheel drive. They could get stranded, with more to worry about than the cold. And Neville and Harry, chasing after that idiot of a girl – that obstinate, posturing, pig-headed girl, and all her *Satans* half-measures. Finished with Jay but still trying to mother him, sleeping with Hal but refusing to commit herself, making a big deal of her independence while expecting him to be unquestioningly loyal and patient . . .

Something rattled across the windscreen like a fusillade of bullets, and suddenly he was driving head-on into a white wall. He almost reached for the brake – but it was a wall of snow, hurtling towards him across the bare moorland as fast as the seawind could throw it at him. Even with the wipers at double speed he could barely keep his windscreen clear, and the Range Rover's powerful foglights were almost useless. For a moment he thought of turning back, but with two miles to go it hardly seemed worth it. Had he really gotten through worse than this back home? He must have. All the same, it was strange. Both wind and snow he had expected – but neither so sudden, a curtain flung savagely across the sky. Already the road ahead was covered, and the car was sliding as fresh snow packed down into ice under the tyres. He changed down and slowed again. Too much of a hurry on this road and he'd go over the cliff. Besides, a storm like this would soon blow itself out – September was hardly a month for blizzards, even in Yorkshire. Even so, reaching Oddsness now would be a matter of luck – if the storm broke, or passed, if the snowfall eased a little, if it didn't drift too high.

The ghost of a signpost loomed out of the night like the answer to a prayer. Inland, away from the coast – there, surely, the wind would be slowed, and he would have a chance to escape. The Range Rover skidded into the uphill turn, and he felt the force of the gale punching at the side of the car, struggling to turn it over, fingers of ice and snow scrabbling across the roof and windows, its voice howling in triumph. A picture flashed into his mind, a book from his childhood: the North Wind, a huge creature

158

of spirals and swirls and outstretched arms, flattening all that lay in its path, driving all before it. Only now there was a car in its path, a toy car, so small as to be almost beneath contempt.

And then, suddenly, unbelievably, the wind had turned to face him, drowning the windscreen in snow, hammering, slowing, driving him back in a blind fury where it wanted him to go. He felt the wheels slipping, the car sliding backwards down the slope, out of control, saw a fencepost looming in the rearview mirror, swung the wheel to escape it, and cursed as he found himself rolling back onto the coast road. At least if the wind had changed he might still get through that way. But as he wound down his side window and knocked the caked snow off the windscreen he felt the wind lash round again, and a chill grew within him deeper than anything merely physical. The spectre of Pru rose before him, two faces superimposed – one flushed, lovely, floating in the tense serenity of flooding passion, the other stark white, swollen, bruised and blood-caked, the face above the blanket on the stretcher.

The battle had already begun. He was being hunted – and already he was trapped here in the cold and the dark as surely as Pru had been trapped in the stone prison of Fern Farm. Could he believe that? He had to. His encounter with the woman had already taken him into the twilight, and now his invisible enemy was herding him like a helpless animal . . .

With an angry curse he shifted gear and swung the car into a violent U-turn, heading back the way he had come. He felt the back swinging, skidding out of control. Too fast. No matter. If the drive didn't kill him, the wind would do it. No point in caution now. Fingers of ice and snow, lifting him, trying to hurl him down the cliff – and then, just as before, the wind was ahead of him, the snow driving into the windscreen like a hail of gravel . . .

A heavy impact, hurling him forward till the safety belt pulled bruisingly taut across his ribcage and his neck snapped back against the headrest. The engine whined and stalled.

Snow. A solid wall. As though the air itself had frozen

into a barrier. For a moment, something like silence. And then the sounds that the engine had concealed – ice scrabbling around the car, searching for cracks, clawing to find him, hammering at the windows. The North Wind come to call, enfolding him in snowdrift arms. Caught in his enemy's spell. What was the word? Sending. Caught in his enemy's sending. They would be coming for him now, as they had for Pru. He smashed a hand down on the wheel in bitter frustration. 'Well I won't, d'you hear me? I will not sit here and die!' The wind howled a mocking reply as he zipped up his parka, wound his scarf around his face, and sprang out of the car, feet crunching into the frozen surface crust of the snow. The clutch of tiny houses at Oddsness was less than two miles away, though in this weather it might as well be a hundred. Even so, there were many ways to die tonight, and snow might be the cleanest. He staggered forward, blinded, ice already crusting his beard and eyebrows. At least he knew the way to go – against the wind, always against the wind, fighting the raw power of his enemy's sending. Burning with fury he staggered into the darkness and gave himself to wind, and snow, and emptiness.

Jess ran towards the trailer in great bounds, kicking free of the clinging snow, aches and chills forgotten in a sudden blaze of adrenalin. She'd show the lousy bastard, she'd show the whole goddam crew of them – they weren't so used to ladies fighting back around here – and Jesus, were they ever about to learn! The small wooden step lay splintered in the snow, but one leaping stride shot her through the opening, left fist bunched and ready. Then she stopped, staring, and all but fell back out.

He was still in there, all right. In fact he was calmly sitting at the far end of the trailer, sprawling among the tangle of rugs and cushions that was Jess's bed, a shadow outline against the drawn curtains of the end window. Jess's eyes narrowed. If the creep was actually waiting for her –

'Hey!' she bawled. 'Hey you!'

160

Slowly, unhurriedly the head turned towards her, and for an instant the profile stood out sharply. She sucked in her breath with sheer disbelief, and then smashed a fist down on the flimsy worktop in a frenzy of exasperation. 'Jay, you utter asshole! That does it, this is the goddam limit! You get mixed up in some crazy goddam riot, you screw off Christ knows where for days, then you just mooch 'long back and think you can smash into my damn trailer – well, that's it, you hear? To hell with covering for you, you drunken jack-off, I've had my bellyful! There's a cop wants a word with you, you know that? And we're going to go call him right now, both of us, got that? But first I'm gonna settle with you for about one hundred things I never should've let pass, I owe myself that and I'm gonna enjoy it, you hear, enjoy it! So just kindly shift your ass right out of my bed and –'

The bed creaked loudly, the figure moved, rose, and Jess's fist clenched tight in a transport of rage. Then it froze in midair, crept up to her mouth and jammed hard against her teeth. Something had plucked at her nerves an instant before he shifted, a faint musty scent that bristled the hair on the back of her neck. Now it grew stronger, a reek like ancient parchment and mouldering fruit and the taste of blood from an abscessed tooth, an essence of corruption that tainted the clean sea air from the door.

The door! Suddenly she couldn't think of rage or pity, of helping Colby or hammering him or both. Nothing but getting out, out, away –

The huge left hand seemed to move with her thought, and her leap almost carried her straight into its grip. Off balance, she landed on one heel and toppled sideways. The fingers closed on the inner edge of the flapping door and yanked it shut with such force that it bent and wedged into the frame. Jess slumped against the narrow washroom door, staring aghast at that hand. It was visibly coarser, thicker, and the nails on it were long and blackened. The skin was dead white and waxy, with nothing of Colby's tan, and mottled with patches of sickly colour, yellow and brown and bluish black, that spread like fungus right up the arm. But beneath the skin the muscles were swollen

161

to tautness, rippling and bulging with life, and even the hairs that bristled over it seemed thicker and coarser in their turn, full of fearful vigour.

The shadow seemed to keep on rising, like some monstrous snake uncoiling, until it loomed over her. The caravan's peaked roof was low: Colby had always had to bow his head. But now his shoulders crashed into the flimsy ceiling, rattling the orange plastic skylight, before he was even standing straight.

Somehow he had become more solid, till he looked like some ancient weathered statue, cast in dark metal and larger than life. His clothes fell in rags about him, his massive arms bare. They hung apelike, fingers twitching restlessly, eagerly. His long blond hair, lustreless now, fell lank over his forehead, but Jess could see the gleam of his eyes. The steady, unblinking gaze of concentration jarred horribly with the eagerness in those twitching fingers. Its calmness was maddening, as if nothing beyond that even gaze was worth an instant's attention.

She had no more time to think. The hand swept out towards her again, the other rose to meet it, to encircle her when she made a panicky leap for the door. Only she didn't, but stood her ground and chopped down viciously with a blade-stiff hand. It was like hitting a stone wrapped in leather, cold stone, but the arm jumped, bent back, lost its impetus. Ducking under the other hand, she fumbled at the little door behind her. The washroom had a little window, the only one he wasn't blocking –

The arms flicked out again, she dropped – then gasped with pain as they closed on her shoulders. But she used the grip as she'd been taught – steadying herself on the attacker's arm, balancing on one foot and unleashing a terrible kick with the other, aimed right below Colby's breastbone. The heavy Bean boot connected with a force that should have ruptured Colby's diaphragm and possibly stopped his heart. All it did was rock him back slightly off balance, unable to tighten his grip.

Jess gave a single desperate twist. She felt the long nails rip through her thick parka and wool shirt and tear into the flesh beneath, claws of edged ice that left fire in their

162

track. Then the parka ripped around her and she was twisting free, leaving it and half the shirt in Colby's grasp. The air chilled her bared side, but the little door swung free, she ducked desperately through, stumbled over the crude shower fitment, breaking it, and slammed and bolted the door behind her in a ridiculous moment of relief. Ridiculous, because a child could break it down. Then she grabbed for the window catch – and tripped over the broken shower tube, lost her balance and tumbled onto the water-sprinkled floor.

It cost her the split-second she had. Sprawled helpless, she saw the panel above her bulge and splinter – then, with a tearing screech, the whole front of the partition was ripped away. Colby held it poised for a moment, as if uncertain what to do with it, then placed it carefully to one side. It was so like his normal finicky habits that Jess almost shrieked with laughter. She tried to scramble up, but the tube tore free in her fingers and Colby's long hand was on her. But it lingered an instant before it closed, rough cold fingertips brushing the bare skin of shoulder and breast. It was her mindless animal reaction that jerked the broken tube forward, a sudden upsurge of violent revulsion, but it had all her weight behind it. The jagged rim tore deep into the palm and went slashing up the arm, ploughing up the flesh like soil.

Colby bellowed and wrenched back his arm, almost taking the tube with it. Then he simply stood there an instant, looking at the wound. He looked down at her, and smiled, livid lips revealing teeth set in dark, shrunken gums. 'You fight well,' he said suddenly, and his voice was a dry parody, a rasping, dead-leaf rustle. 'I'm real glad about that.'

'Why, Jay?' she managed. 'Why're you . . . glad?'

'Stands to reason. Go out fightin', that's always the best way, anytime. But 'specially for *Him*.' There was no mistaking the emphasis in the barren voice. 'Proves you're brave – proves you worthy. No matter you're a woman . . . Hell, he doesn't mind. Long as you're no quitter, no candy-ass. An' I know you wouldn't be, Jess, wouldn't let me down. You'd fight.'

163

Jess shook her head as if webs entangled it. 'Jay . . . Why . . . what happened to you . . . why'd you – come back?'

'Oh hey, Jess, haven't I always told you?' The papery voice was soft, cajoling. 'I love you, honey, I love you. No life nor death's gonna change that –'

It was almost too much for her. 'Same old Jay,' she gasped, half-laughing through clenched teeth. 'Same old naked ego! Just fuck around anyone you care for, however you like, and it's all just peachy 'cause deep deep down you really love them – *what are you doing to me now?*'

The stained lips settled into something like a tolerant smile. 'Could say I was draftin' you, baby . . .'

'What for?' she spat. 'More games with little boys? You want us taking turns at them or somethin'?'

'Jess! Jess-i-ca!' Under all the pleading tones lay something else, a dark pool of mockery. 'You don't know what you're *sayin'*! This's life I'm offerin' you! And strength! Limitless, both of them – *Age shall not weary* them *nor custom stale* . . . Tread the road just once, with honour, and then there's no more dyin'! Never fade, never age – just growin' stronger – growin' – and followin' Him –'

The mocking note was gone, the whisper almost rapt, trancelike. Jess whispered in her turn, 'F-following who, Jay?'

He swung his head around sharply. 'The High One. The Ruler of Battles. The Lord of the Slain – oh, He's got a whole heap of names. Some of them you better be damn careful how you use, too. Some's for the summonin', some's for the sacrifice, some . . . Well, they don't mean a thing till the time and place are right. Then they're runes, real runes of power.' He chuckled harshly. 'Me, I didn't know that. I'd always felt it, though – felt I was born to somethin', never sure what, never belonging . . . But drawn to the old tales, the old knowledge, always, but always too far away, trying to make them live again but I was in the wrong time . . . And then I came here to excavate the temple, and I saw the Dance. Just a shadow, near a skeleton, livin' on in the shadow lives of shadow men and no true heroes to answer the call. It could've

164

come to guys like Hal, who'd only turn it into dry print –
but it came to me. Then I knew what I'd been born for,
what I was – a hero, a berserker, the last of His servants
living who could bring the old rite back. And so I did.
And I knew, when we found the ship, that He had heard
me – but I didn't know what else. I didn't know it brought
Him other servants. He sent them, the King and Queen,
to accept the sacrifice, cast out the unworthy into darkness
and choose the worthy. And I alone fought well – I alone
was chosen.'

Jess fought to keep her grip on a world that seemed to
be slipping away from beneath her, like a tide going out.
Was this thing that grinned and spoke like Jay Colby
nothing but her own insanity, a mirror to her inner self?
The familiar interior was a shell of shadowy nightmare,
the world beyond it infinitely remote. She had walked
through silent whiteness, alien, hostile, sterile. What way
had she come? Had she fallen exhausted in the snow, and
trodden a darkening downward road?

He was looking at her, into her, and the hiss was
contemptuous. 'You don't understand, do you? Hal would
– should go ask him. And maybe you'll get your chance
after you join us – if you ever really cared for him. That's
the way it is with us – the *einherjar* look after their own.
That's why I came back for you – why you'll go with me
now –'

'Jay – *no* –'

The whisper rose to a fierce rasping whine. '*Yes!* Yes, I
love you, can't you even see that, you stupid bitch? I want
to save you! There's no other way! The King's loose now,
the long winter's coming, the Winter of the World, the
Fimbulwinter! You'll die like the rest of them, the herd,
the thralls! And that's waste, you're not like them, you're
like me, a berserker born, a shieldgirl, a valkyrie! I chose
you –'

'I know what I am!' yelled Jess, half crazy with fear of
this creature that wore Jay's shape, that raved in whispers.
'I'm nothing of yours, nothing for you! You don't own
me, you can't choose me, save me, take me – whatever
you think you want to do to me –'

The mocking smile broadened. 'What's ours we take, by right. Fight all you want, that's as it should be. You'll thank me for it, you'll lose nothin' but the fear of death. The *einherjar* have any pleasure they want. For the taking.' The arms lifted, the huge hands opened – slowly, almost caressingly, as if moulding in the air the shape they would be touching. Colby took a step forward, and the floor groaned and creaked under his weight. The fingers caged around Jess's head, dropped to her throat.

With a wild yell of sheer loathing she jabbed her make-shift spear at the shadowed eyes; Colby fell back a pace, twisting his head away. For an instant the hair swung free of the bloated neck.

Jess stared, then her legs began to shake beneath her and she needed desperately to scream madness and wake up. Only all her throat allowed was a hoarse dry croak, and she knew damn well she wasn't dreaming. Her knees gave, she felt her jeans damp at the crutch and she shrank down into the corner under the window, unable even to think of trying for the catch, unable to trust her very mind or senses. On Colby's broad throat, like the mark of a terrible halter, were the bloodshot bruise impressions of two huge hands, fingers wide, thumbs meeting in the centre over the Adam's apple. It was a crushed mess, small ends of bone gleaming through the broken skin. It was not a wound a man could survive, she knew that, and yet Colby was turning towards her again, reaching out to brush aside the slender metal spear that was the only barrier between them.

The terror that shook Jess was beyond her understanding, seeking to strip off her humanity and leave her a helpless howling ape in the dark, trembling before the jealousy of the dead. The hidden eyes seemed to suck the very warmth out of her; she couldn't move, she could hardly breathe for the sickening stench of death. The spear fell from her fingers, and the out-thrust hand closed around her throat.

But the fingers, the fingers as cold as metal, did not close. They slid down, spread out, tracing the lines of muscle and tendon that stood out rigid from her shoulders, and down, down to span her breast. The other hand snaked out; the index finger hooked into the neck of the shirt and tore downward. The thick cloth parted like paper, the black nail traced a bloody furrow in the skin, snagged her belt and burst it and ripped into the fabric of her jeans, clawing them brutally open. Then it leapt to her throat, and she yelled once before it lifted her bodily off the ground and the shadow surged down over her. A vast cold weight, like a statue carved in dead flesh, flattened her threshing body against the creaking wall, bore down her frantically kicking legs and thrust brutally against her. The hand tightened on her throat, her jaw was jammed shut and the stinking weight of the body ground into her face, cutting off her breathing. Her neck was a band of agony, her head buzzed and there was a high-pitched shrilling in her ears; blood flooded her nose and rushed choking down into her throat. The force of the vast body twisted her splayed hips almost to dislocation, the bones of her pelvis ground and creaked under the sheer weight of it as she twisted and squirmed frantically against its assault. A foot caught a cupboard side, she kicked sideways but the vast body moved with her, sliding her off the wall and bending her backwards over the edge of the worktop till her spine creaked and her legs fell open to a tearing thrust –

There was a crash. Light exploded into her pounding head, and for a dizzy instant she thought it was death. Then the weight was gone, she fell in a limp heap and saw the shadow over her swing around, the door open and a dazzling light flood in. Harry bounded into the van, and drew up so suddenly that Neville cannoned into him.

'*Jesus –*' he shouted, seeing as Jess did – Colby rearing up in the torchbeam, Colby a vast bloated parody of himself. A huge, hunched, slavering, tumescent brute, a minotaur not a man. A rampant thing, near-naked, bruise-skinned, smeared with blood and filth – and in the time it took to shout that word it was on them. The rush of it bore them back, smashed them against the end wall with a force that made the van creak and rock on its supports; the bricks under the legs broke, the van seesawed and rolled back towards the fence. But the legs drove into

167

the ground, tilting the van forward, and the floor snapped and splintered under Colby's giant weight. Off balance, he went stumbling back with one man on each arm, hammering and kicking furiously at him as they were rattled and dashed against the cupboarded walls. In the open they would have been shaken off in seconds, but in the narrow space Colby could not swing his arms enough to free himself; he stood like a baited bear, battering his assailants against the splintering wood. Things spilled out of the cupboards, packets and bottles and clothes and books, all caught up in a whirling maelstrom; the floorboards smashed to matchwood under Colby's feet.

Jess clawed herself half upright against the ruined partition, clutched briefly at her aching body, then fumbled for the broken shaft of metal. She couldn't find it. He was stronger and heavier than all of them together, he'd been toying with her before . . . She dragged herself up on aching legs and staggered forward. Her weight tipped the van, it seesawed again and tipped sharply back. The fighters lost their balance, the men were flung off as Colby's arms windmilled and he staggered back down the sloping floor, smashing into the remains of the bed. Jess caught the rim of the fanlight for support, and the feel of her fingers closing around the rim awoke a memory, or something less, a reflex from her gymnastics classes. In a single polished movement her arms tautened, her back tensed and her chin tucked in, and her stiffened legs swung free of the floor, kicked back and went slamming forward straight into the centre of Colby's chest.

It was like kicking a mountain. But she still had her boots on, and all her own weight was behind the blow. It shot Colby off his precarious feet and straight back at the caravan's end wall. His vast weight cannoned into it and through in a tearing screech of metal and tinkle of toughened glass, making jagged teeth that ripped and tore at the toppling body. It smashed through the flimsy fence and hedge behind, and landed with a shattering crash at the cliff edge.

The three others slid forward in his wake, landed in a tumbled heap at the torn end wall, saw the huge half-mangled thing scrabble at the frozen earth and fight to rise, its head, part severed, lolling on its shoulder. Then there was a soft, tearing crack, a rustle and patter of little stones falling, and a small patch of the overstrained cliff edge crumbled and slid away under it. The shape twisted, bounced, and for an instant a dark arm, hand out-thrust, showed against the swirling clouds. Then, quite silently, it was gone.

Neville scooped up his lantern, still working, and half clambered, half crawled through the open gap, shuddering as he brushed against the dark moist shreds that hung from its teeth. He crawled very deliberately towards the cliff edge, at a point well away from the recent fall, and shone the beam downward. Harry followed, and so, to her own surprise, did Jess, clutching her ripped jeans around her. The three lay there together, not speaking, staring down into the abyss. The tide was just coming in, and the thing that had been Colby had fallen into the shallows, onto the narrow spines of rock leading out across the beach. The pale surf was washing the shattered body back and forth across them, like the teeth of a saw, stone completing what steel and glass began.

Jess turned her head violently away, and the others ushered her back gently. Harry draped his old coat around her shoulders. 'Nowt broke then, flower?'

'No. No – thank you. Both of you.' She was shivering violently. 'He – it – was trying to . . . Oh Jesus . . . Poor Jay.' She sobbed a little. 'Poor fucking Jay.'

'Aye,' said Neville in a shattered voice. 'Poor Jay. 'E's long gone. Whatever that bloody thing was, it weren't 'im.'

'Saw yer computer thing 'ung on t'fence,' said Harry drily. 'Knew you wouldn't 'ave left it there normal, like, so we were ready for a barney. Not that, though. Not that . . .' He shivered violently. 'Snow's coomin' on 'arder. Get 'er soom togs, Neville, if there's any left, and we'll 'ead for the car. And thank our lucky stars if we make it back t'town.'

*   *   *

'No, dammit!' Ridley glared furiously at the telephone. 'Not a chance! That's three more we've got listed missing now – plus the deader. No, not ID'd yet, but there's no doubt who it is – Wilf Jackson. Yes, another of the archaeology mob. How? I'd put the mobiles onto their car, is how. Tango Charlie found it and followed some tracks. Outside one of those big barrow affairs – empty, right. Real video nasty, apparently – torn in two. And his mate Latimer's missing – Tom Latimer, TV type. Unhuh, quite well known.' He shot a despairing look at Neville. 'Then another archaeology bloke. Hal Hansen – the boss, right. Set out for Oddsness two hours ago, hadn't got there before the phone lines went down. Aye, it's bad! And it's going to get worse! Every road's closed, in or out, I've only got two cars still operating and they're both miles away. You'll have to stick it out – or get over to Grimsdyke Farm, about a mile up the side road – yes, there. They'll see you right. Okay. Watch yourselves.' He dropped the phone contemptuously back in its cradle. 'Ass! Gets snowed up in that mobile HQ thing and expects me to cripple what policing capacity we've got left to come dig them out. At least you three are back –'

'No news?' croaked Jess. 'Nothing?'

'Nothing I wouldn't have heard first. I'm sorry. All we can do now is wait till morning. When the snowfans clear the roads, we'll be able to start a proper search.' He put a hand gently on her shoulder, feeling the tremor in her and glad there was nothing worse. Another girl might have ended up a stretcher case. Perhaps he was seeing in her now something of what Hansen saw, a unique blend of vulnerability and strength – shattered, worried sick, but still desperately ready to help.

'Jess . . .' She did not answer, but he persisted. 'Look . . . ordinarily I'd say there's nothing you can do, get some rest like the quack told you to. But – well, you might be better for something else to think about, and there *is* something . . .' She looked up fiercely, and he held up a hand. 'Not to help Hal now, not exactly. But something he wanted done, something to help us all . . .' He pulled out his notebook, flipped over the pages. 'There – I don't know if you can read that, but . . .'

She slammed her hand down on the bar. '*Jee-sus!* Yes! Of course! Why didn't I think of that – Neville hey Neville –' He lumbered over, swinging the terminal from one hand. 'Careful with that, dammit!' She slid off the bar stool and grabbed it. The two men, half a head shorter, exchanged amused glances. 'Oh, crap! It's full of snow here – I hope to hell that's okay – guaranteed waterproof but I can't remember the temperature parameters – has that phone got a socket? No? Hey, landlord – and Harry, Neville, I'll need a socket, a power point and something to stand this on –' The mask of sick pain and fear seemed to fall from her face, though the pallor remained. A few minutes later, by drafting everyone within earshot, she'd installed the terminal on a card table in the parlour. She hobbled over and sat down very gingerly in the worn old armchair, unlocked the case and tilted back its hinged lid to reveal a typewriter keyboard and a bank of controls. 'Hey, somebody turn the lights off, okay? Plasma display – works better in low light.'

The landlord hovered anxiously as she flicked at the controls. A blank plastic rectangle inside the lid lit up with a row of dusty green characters. 'Here, Miss, where were you going to call with that thing? An' how much . . .?'

'Oh, no more'n a phone call,' said Jess. 'It's got a modem – fits any standard phone line. I'm just calling Texas.'

'Texas! Here, hold on –'

Ridley waved him quiet. 'This could be bloody life or death, man!' Rows of green characters were flickering across the screen.

```
**RAYNER COLLEGE COMPUTER DEPARTMENT**
PLEASE STATE THE FOLLOWING:
*SERVICE REQUIRED
*NAME
```

```
*USER-ID
*YOUR AUTHORITY
**SINCE THIS IS AN OVERSEAS CALL, DO YOU WISH
TO CHARGE CALL TIME?
```

The keys rattled under Jess's fingers.

```
*MAIN DATABASE
*FULL ACCESS AND VIRTUAL SEARCH FACILITIES,
MOST URGENT
```

She filled in her name and an enormous number, then
added:

```
*ARCHDEP PRIORITY, HANSEN
*ALL CHARGES TO ARCHDEP, PERSONAL ACCOUNT
PROFESSOR HANSEN.
```

The landlord sighed.

Ridley watched in silent fascination as the small green
cursor line flew across the screen like the shuttle in a loom,
weaving a fabric of codes and commands. He could just
about use the police computer system himself, but this
went far beyond his experience. 'What I'm doing,' said
Jess, answering everyone's unspoken question, 'is access-
ing the main database – sort of a reference library, only
it's held on videodisks, computer disks, tape, that kind of
thing. You can get the whole *Encyclopaedia Britannica* on
two disks. It's got most of our library in it, plus unpublished
notes, research, all kinds of bits and pieces. Most universi-
ties have something like it now, paralleling the book
library. Just set out what you want to know and it'll dig
out the info for you – one hell of a research tool if you
know what to do with it. God, can somebody get me a
beer, my throat's on fire!'

Harry blinked doubtfully at the compact terminal. 'Ee,
you mean that little booger can 'old all that crap?'

'God, no – but the phone lines are hooking it up to the

172

big computers at Rayner. And now I've got them looking up your local legends, like Hal suggested.'

'Will your computers have that kind of stuff?' asked Ridley.

'Sure. My department – Anthropology – it's pretty big on folklore, even got a new classification system going, miles better'n the old Aarne-Thompson. I'm using it now, setting up a thematic search – sorry. Sorting through stuff from this part of Yorkshire for recurrent themes – stories that appear a lot. Then we give them a motive analysis – thanks!' She stopped and gulped at the lager the dazed landlord had brought.

'Think I liked 'er better worried,' muttered Neville, looking equally dazed.

'I *think* I see,' said Ridley. 'You're looking for any memories of something like this happening before – and how they dealt with it.'

'Yeah, or at least how it started – hey, we're getting something . . . quite a lot.'

The screen emptied, and then, one by one, lines of numbers and letters began to appear. The men craned over her shoulders.

```
R.2224/70/V15 (A-T 1170) Sale of Soul to Devil
R.4527/33/V4b (A-T 3000) Scholomance (Sorcerers
study with devil)
R.4510/33/V4b (A-T 3026) Magicians' Contest
R.4579/12/V6c (A-T n/a) Sorcerer Lord
(Pengersec etc.)
R.2835/12/V7c (A-T 1571) Servants punish Master

R.2647/56/V4b (A-T 1537) Man killed more than
once
R.1225/12/V4a (A-T 565) Sorcerer's Apprentice
(Magic Mill; Magic Storm)
R.98/39/V1d (A-T 363-5) The Walking Dead
R.1179 (A-T 501) The Wild Hunt (Sir Francis
Drake; Jan Tregeagle; Herla; Woden/Odin)
R.1535/5/V22? (A-T 766) The Sleeping King
R.90/95/V20a (A-T 325) The King of the Black
Art
```

'Bloody 'ell!' said Neville.

Jess nodded agreement. 'I'm getting a very bad feeling about this . . .'

'Let me get this straight,' said Ridley, clutching his head. 'These are all local fairy tales?'

Jess shook her head, winced, and massaged her neck. 'Not exactly. They're themes that turn up in folktales from this part of the world. See, most folktales have common roots – you can make a date with Cinderella anywhere from Norway to Indochina, with a stopover for the North American Indians. But when some themes keep turning up in a particular area more often than others, it may be 'cause they fit in with some real history – the way the true stories of heroes like Hereward the Wake and Owen Glendower get mixed into folktales about legendary figures like Robin Hood, say, and King Arthur.'

A few extra lines appeared on the screen, like footnotes, and finally a flashing line that read:


```
*SEARCH COMPLETED
*RETURN TO MENU?
```


Jess hit a key and a long list of options filled the screen. She chose one and called up a display consisting, so far as Ridley could see, entirely of incomprehensible questions. 'So you're trying to work backwards – read the history through the legends.'

'Something like that. Crazy, huh?'

'Aye,' agreed Neville. 'Unless you've just gone five rounds with a legend.'

'You really expect it'll tell us anything?' Ridley asked plaintively.

'God knows.' Jess was only half-listening, absorbed in entering her answers to the questions on the screen. 'But

174

Hal thought it might.' The green glow betrayed the momentary flicker of anguish in her face. 'Right. That's it.' She leaned back in the chair, stretched, and gasped with pain. 'Oh God, I need a chiropractor. And a masseur. Or maybe just a new body.'

'What's happening now?'

'Hard to explain. Motive analysis –' An echoing snore cut her off. Harry, dead to the world, was recovering from the fight in his own way.

Ridley chuckled. 'Never mind him. Motive analysis.'

'Yeah. See, when these stories were written down, they were analysed in detail and the various story elements noted – incidents, characters, backgrounds –'

'Like *Malevolent return from the dead*?' said Ridley, catching sight of the phrase as it flickered past on the screen.

'Yeah, like that. Jesus. Anyway, I've got the Rayner computers checking through all those stories, sorting out common elements that turn up everywhere, picking out unusual ones that might be peculiar to this area, and seeing if there's a pattern.'

'What sort of a pattern?'

'Well . . . if we're lucky it might – just might – come up with the pieces of a common story. And if it does we should be able to put at least a few of them back together.'

'Get some idea what it was about?'

'Right. Then we could even compare it with the history books.'

'Books?'

'Computer files. Same difference.'

'Not to me. How long is all this going to take?'

'A while. Might as well relax and – *damn!*'

'Trouble?'

She slumped back from the screen. 'Uh-huh. Not enough data in good ol' Rayner's files. References are there okay, but we need *all* the details, so the programme's hung up.'

Ridley was getting involved. 'Well, my God, there must be some way we can get them!'

Jess hesitated. 'There's a new international network,

UNET – kind of a long-range hook-up between university databanks. Trouble is, it's expensive, and I've never used it. If I foul up, we could lose all our data.'

'I know what Hal would say.'

She flashed him a thin smile. 'Okay. Here goes my fellowship –'

Her fingers picked slowly and carefully over the keys, the screen filled with text – and went black. 'Christ!' hissed Ridley. Suddenly the word

    *OXFORD

appeared in the top corner.

'Jesus! It's calling back to England!' Jess was fascinated. A few lines of text flickered across the screen, too fast to read, and then the name changed to

    *OREGON

Another jumble of words, then more names –

    *HEIDELBERG
    *AARHUS
    *CALCUTTA
    *OSLO

– each contributing its own piece to the jigsaw. 'All over the world – just for footnotes, I think. Don't seem to be getting much more'n that. The result had better be worth it . . .'

Again the screen flickered and went blank. Jess sucked in her breath, then sighed audibly as the scurrying words reappeared.

'All right?'

'Think so. Something shaping up – what I've seen doesn't make much sense, though. Black magic, defiling churches, and something about burning at the stake. Don't expect too much.'

176

The scurrying stopped. Four words appeared.

```
*ONCE UPON A TIME...
```

'Programmers,' muttered Jess. 'Lousy sense of humour.'
Ridley hardly noticed. He was riveted. Line by line, rolling
up the screen like credit titles on a film, a story was
beginning to unfold.

```
There was a King (Variant: King Raven) who came
from over the Sea (R.316/55/V12a)


And conquered a Town for himself.  (R.316
/55/Variant local)


He was a Pagan, and sold his soul to Satan to
learn Black Magic (R.452/33,34,82/Variant local
in this combination)


And so hated Christ that he defiled (destroyed)
the Church (Local variant--cf hagiographical
incidents?)


(He built a temple to Satan where) He and his
wife and their evil followers held terrible
rites (human sacrifice) (R.90/95/V20a/Extreme
variant local, cf ogre and wife stories
R.525/ff.)


Until Saint (Hilda/Oswald/other local saints/a
brave young priest) defied him (resisted his
magic) (R. 3407/ff.; A-T 303 ff.)


And he and his wife were burned at the stake
(hanged and burned/lynched and refused
Christian burial/stoned and buried as pagans by
```

their own followers (Historical Witchcraft
refs., esp. 17th and 18th centuries)

Neville whistled softly. 'Could put the porno writers out
o' business, that. Frederick Forsyth, an' all. Just like a
bedtime story, eh?'

Jess was staring, open-mouthed. 'But – it shouldn't be
like that! It can't be! Folktales just don't fit together that
way!'

'Unless they happen to be true?' suggested Ridley. 'How
about checking the history books?'

'Files,' said Jess, with an unsteady smile. 'I still don't
believe it, but here goes nothing.' Nervously she keyed
another set of commands into the terminal, then sat back
in the big chair, biting absent-mindedly at her finger.

'Now what?'

'I've got a sweep going for anything which might match
that story – anywhere in Europe. Could be an import, you
see –' The screen flickered, and the words

```
*TRINITY DUBLIN
*KOBENHAVN
*TRONDHEIM
```

appeared and vanished in quick succession. 'Jesus, we're
still on the net! I forgot!'

'Let it go,' said Ridley.

'More the merrier,' said Neville, as

```
*MOSKVA
```

appeared. 'Gawd, not the bloody KGB, is it?'

'The Russian colleges have some good specialists,' muttered Jess. 'Especially – wait a minute.'

```
*REFERENCE: Monastic Archives, Kiev (now in the
Hermitage, Leningrad): Monastic chronicle,
```

178

Spanish, 11th century--MSS fragmentary;
marginal note added to account of 11th-century
English kings; corrupted Latin (derived from
unknown Anglo-Saxon original?).
Modern English rendering follows:
*In this year, when the pagan Hericus was
finally driven from Eboracum, that vassal of
his named Herafenius, also called Rimaconerius,
likewise met his end, and his wife Aodana, who
had made their rule abhorrent in the North by
defiling the church of Christ with pagan
obscenities, claiming thereby to rule the
fertility of the land and the fortunes of
seafarers. But their cruelties so stank in the
nostrils of the Lord that when Hericus could no
longer aid them the oppressed arose against
them, and slew them, and all those of their
followers who did not repent. And they were
given no Christian burial, but by the will of
their repentant followers, being in great fear
of their evil souls, disposed of like carrion.*

NOMENCLATURE
Hericus = Eirik (id. Eirik Bloodaxe, king of
York AD 948-954)
Eboracum = York (Jorvik)
Herafenius = prob. Hrafn (Raven)
Rimaconerius = meaning uncertain; compound?;
-conerius conject. *konungr*, a king or prince;
Rima- meaning uncertain
Aodana = prob. Aud
*POSSIBLE SOURCE REFERENCE--Irish Chronicle:
War of Goidhill and Gael: Chieftain Turgeis
(?Thorgeir) and wife Ota (?Aud) try to
reestablish paganism: defile church and hold
obscene rites on altar; defeated and drowned.
All major authorities agree account wholly
legendary
*REFERENCE ENDS

Ridley took a deep breath. 'Do they now?'

Without a word Jess leaned forward over the keyboard and tapped a series of controls. The screen image split in half and shrank, and the folklore analysis reappeared on the left-hand side to lie parallel with the chronicle account. Neville whistled. 'Reckon you just struck gold, love!'

But Ridley frowned. 'Gold? Look, it's all fascinating, this, but we haven't found anything to help *us*! I mean this – this Raven character got the chop in – in –'

'In the tenth century,' said Jess. 'Yes! And then he was burned, or buried, or something. What the hell's he got to do with what's happening here now? So there might be a connection – how do we find out what it *is*?'

' 'Ey, what's all the racket?' demanded a sleepy voice behind them. 'Can't a bloke get a decent night's kip . . . ey-oop, where'd you dig up this lot?' Harry was staring at the computer display with a slightly sheepish expression. 'Could've told you this meself. Heard it from me grandda' –'

Neville snapped his fingers. 'Right! That's the bloody story you've been using to shock all those naive little tourist bits!'

'Just like that,' agreed Harry cheerfully. 'Right up t'end – buried like pagans. 'Appen that meant they just choocked 'em in the sea –'

He stopped, appalled, as Jess grabbed him by the shoulders and shook him. '*No!*' she yelled. 'Christ, I'm a turkey, Hal'd kill me. Pagan burial! Balder's funeral! Scyld, in *Beowulf*! That Arab traveller's account! The Vikings didn't always bury their upper classes, the rich men and the kings. When they could, they gave them a classier funeral – they burnt them! In a ship!'

Ridley gave a sudden growl of understanding, and Neville's jaw dropped. 'You mean – pushed 'em out to sea with the ship on fire? Then the chests –'

'Right! That's why they were covered in pitch!'

'So they'd burn!' said Ridley. 'But they bungled the job.'

'We almost found 'em!' breathed Neville, aghast.

'Bloody 'ell, almost. An hour or two earlier and we'd have been opening the first chest on the spot –'

Ridley shook his head. 'Pity you didn't! Him in the first chest tucked away in the lab tank, her in the second – free to escape, flatten the guard, and come release him. It fits, but –'

'He – Jay,' Jess swallowed. 'He said something about finding the ship because of him. Because of what he'd done. The ceremony, he must have meant. And he said – he said that the King and Queen came to the clearing that night.'

'Meaning our friend Raven and –'

'Aud.'

'Right.' Ridley scowled. 'So it *is* them. Aud I've met. Can't say I care for the lady. He didn't say anything else that might help us?'

'Nothing good. Something about *Fimbulwinter*, I think, whatever in hell that is. Could be I had other things on my mind at the time.'

'Could be. Why not check it out now?'

'Huh? Jesus, we're still on-line!'

'So pay by instalments. Or I will. Right now I could use some answers.'

Again the keys clattered and rattled under Jess's fingers. Harry started humming *'Them bones, them bones, them dry-y bones!'*

'Fimbulwinter. Hope I'm spelling it aright. Hang on, I'm getting something . . .'


```
*FIMBULWINTER?


FIMBULWINTER (Old Norse fimbul-vetr: found in
Voluspa (c.9th–10th century AD) and cognate
sources). The 'winter of the world', an
infinite time of cold and darkness before the
RAGNAROK (q.v.)
```


'Ragnarok?'

'That one I don't have to look up. It's the last battle

between the Norse gods and their enemies – the end of the world. Kind of a Viking Armageddon.'

Ridley stood up stiffly and walked over to the window. He pulled back the curtains; orange light flooded the room, from the street lamp outside reflected in the thick snow. 'Still snowing,' he said quietly. 'You know, in this modern age all this – these creatures – shouldn't be half the terror they are. Not when burning scares them off. Not in summer, with hours of daylight. It's winter gives them their real power – when we can't cope, can't go whizzing around in cars or planes or any of our modern marvels. It takes us back to being savages in huts, squatting around the fire.' He turned away, as if there was something he did not want to see.

'Hey, Inspector!' Jess's voice was puzzled. 'There's something else on your pad here. I can't make it out – there! That anything?'

'Aye – that's what Hal was calling these things. Dunno if I spelt it right – drow-gar, he pronounced it.'

'Draug-gar? Doesn't mean much to me. Hal's the Old Norse freak, I always have to look these things up. Hang on, I'll input alternative spellings, just in case. If I don't get it wrong, ten to one the bloody programmers have.'

'God,' said Ridley, 'I hate it when that screen goes blank.'

'Yeah. Big databases, though. Takes time to find something I can't spell . . . Jesus, if I don't move I'm gonna lock up.' She eased out of her chair and went, as Ridley had, to the window, rubbing her eyes. But she stood there silently, staring out into the darkness lurking just beyond the streetlamp, and did not go back.

'It's through,' said Ridley. 'Jess?'

'Oh, read it out,' she said, in a curiously flat voice.

Ridley peered at the screen. '*Draug* – d-r-a-u-g; something or other . . .'

'Etymology. Origins of the word.'

'Whatever you say. A – God above! A malignant ghost, or living corpse, of Icelandic folklore; similar to superstitions in many other countries, notably Vampire (q.v.) though without feeding on blood. Descriptions occur in

182

many Old Norse sagas, notably Grettir's Saga; Viga-Glum's Saga. Draugar appear as dark, bloated, creatures (resembling corpses buried on marshy ground) who haunt their own families and the places where they are buried. At first they kill domestic animals, and frighten the household by shaking the roof, or battering doors and shutters. Later they attack and kill human beings; such victims may become draugar (possibly subservient) themselves. In saga accounts draugar are almost invulnerable, but are wrestled to death by a strong hero and destroyed by burning. Most likely to return as draugar are those who have been evil in life, especially those who practise the dark arts of – what's this? Sey-ther?'

'*Seithr,*' said Jess. 'Sound familiar?'

'Not to me.'

'Nor me,' said Neville. 'Feels like we've got all the bloody pieces, but 'ow the 'ell do we put 'em together?'

'Try this one,' said Jess. 'An evil black magician, so evil that even when he's killed by his Christian enemies his own late followers are afraid he'll come back from the dead; they try to stop him – and screw up. So evil that hundreds of years after he's gone there are stories of plagues, dead fish, dead birds, endless winters. Then one poor goddam lunatic called Jay Colby tries to bring back the past, and gets him instead – as a living corpse, so he can finish what he started a thousand years ago.'

'I don't get it,' said Ridley.

'I didn't, not at first. But look outside.' She pointed. Beyond the gap in the curtains, beyond the thin glass pane, they could all see the rush and swirl of the snowflakes in the wind. The miniature mountain range along the bottom of the window was growing almost as they watched, climbing upward, and a film of pale ice was forming on the inside of the glass. 'We know his name – Hrafn, Raven. And what else he was called; Rimaconerius – Rimkonungr. Rime-king. Rim, rime, it's the same word. In English and in Old Norse. It means ice.'

'Raven,' said Ridley slowly. 'Raven the Ice King. You're saying – *An infinite time . . .*'

'Why not? Ever known a winter like this, this early, this

bad? You said it yourself – it's the winter that makes him so terrible. And there's no better place to start it than here – Saitheby.'

'I'm not with you,' said Neville.

'I already told you!' said Jess darkly. 'They've been wrong all along about the name of this place. This is Saitheby – goddam it, don't you see? *Seithr-by*. The Town of Black Magic.'

CHAPTER NINE

THEY WERE hunting him – hunting, with the blizzard baying on his heels. Twice now he'd glimpsed them, undisturbed by the snow and the scything wind. It bit through clothes and skin in great chill slashes that left him gasping for breath, breath that sucked the warmth out of him. The snow it drove at him crusted like lead armour in his clothes, flayed his cheeks and caked solid in his beard. Icy trickles, melted by his breath, ran stinging over his cracked lips and down his neck, soaking his pullover till it rubbed his throat raw. His feet were numb weights he lifted, dragged and let fall with only the remotest tingle of pain. And all the while he had to wrestle with the howling air as though it were a living enemy, clawing and buffeting him. Exhaustion embraced him with dreamy promises of warmth, tempting him to slow down, lie down, forget, so easily –

Hal bit down savagely on his cracked lip. That was one way of staying awake, anyway. Not because he had any real hopes of help, not with night fallen, the roads closed – the only people abroad would be strays like himself or . . . or others he did not want to meet. This was their storm, their sending: give in to it, fall down and sleep out his life in a dream of comfort, and he gave in to them, now and forever. They were not the only menace the snow hid; he had been stumbling around for so long he might easily have gone right past church and houses and be wandering around the edge of the Oddsness cliffs. But that hardly frightened him: if nothing else, it would at least be a cleaner death . . .

He bit his lip again, hard, and tasted warm blood. People were relying on him. He had no business thinking about dying, not yet – not while he could still stay up or awake, that way or any way. He *had* to.

185

Suddenly something icy clutched painfully at his half-numbed legs. He stumbled and floundered into a slope of snow that rose in front of him – a drift-wall his feet had sunk into. He took a deep breath, feeling the icy air dance like glass fragments in his lungs, and began to scramble up it with desperate haste, wading, kicking, shovelling the snow aside. If it was only high enough to give him a little shelter on the lee side! Even a minute free of the blast might help, maybe even let him get his bearings, though his eyes were snow-stung and half-blind. By the time he reached the crest he was almost on all fours, hands and arms as dead as his legs. He stood for a moment to get his breath – and in that moment the wind swirled sharply round, as it had against the car. It lashed hard at him from one side, whipping powdery snow off the drift and across his eyes. He staggered, fighting furiously to keep on his feet, afraid to fall in case he couldn't get up again; then, freed from wind pressure, the slope under his feet cracked, crumbled and spilled out, sending a small avalanche pattering down into shadow. He slid with it, arms flailing wildly for balance or a handhold, and finding neither he toppled . . .

Gud i himmel, the *cliff!*

His numbed fingers scraped on something, slithered, clutched – and held. Frantically he twisted round, grabbed with his other hand and hung on, half crouching, while the snowfall slithered out into darkness. Under his fingers he felt a sharp edge of rock, cold, dry and infinitely welcome. When everything was quiet he hauled himself painfully up and leant there, gasping. He was out of the storm here, all right, but it was too dark to get any idea of just where 'here' was. The wind sounded distant and strange, and after a moment he realised why: it was mingling with the sound of the sea, rising from below. He shuddered. He had been too near the cliffs, right enough – as good as dancing blindfold on the edge of them. Sheer chance had led him into what must be one of the deep gullies leading down to the beach. He could just as easily have gone right over.

He still might, too. He couldn't just stay here, safe as

186

it seemed. The chill rock seemed to have drained the last heat out of him; he felt as if he'd never be warm again. If he could only make it down to the beach, though, the tide should still be out; he might just be able to get round to Oddsness village by following the cliffs. A better chance than the unsheltered clifftops offered, anyway. And there were still the hunters . . .

Carefully, but not too slowly, he began to feel his way along the rockface and down the steeply sloping path.

In places it was more like an irregular natural stair, and he would have to crouch on each step and feel cautiously around for his next foothold. Once, when his feet barely reached it, he had to give up and just risk the drop, not knowing whether it would be firm or wide enough. Sand squeaked between rock and shoe as he landed, but it was all right. He stopped for a rest, though he no longer felt so exhausted, and wondered about Jess. At least she ought to be all right: Neville and Harry would surely have got her back. But somehow he couldn't see her face, however much he tried. It was Pru, always Pru – and far too clearly.

The sea sounded louder in his ears, louder and closer. Had he really come that far? Maybe. He was losing his sense of time here in the dark. But even as he thought of it, he realised he could actually see something now. A faint, glimmering wedge split the night in front of him – an opening. He seemed to be in a great cleft in the rocks – one that led out onto the beach. And it was definitely getting lighter. Maybe the clouds were breaking at last, and the moon was coming through. Certainly there didn't seem to be a flake of snow in the air. He stumbled eagerly forward, and had just time to feel the sudden yielding of sand underfoot before he tripped on something in it – a stick, maybe – and fell flat.

In the giddy instant of falling, light came, and a greying sky whirled above him. He landed on his back, staring upwards, dizzy and disoriented. Shadow-cliffs loomed over him, looking far too high from this angle. There were no cliffs that high at Oddsness – no cliffs that high anywhere. And above them great dim outlines among clouds, gnarled, fantastical, like chains of rounded hills, almost spilling over the edge . . .

Dazed, uncomprehending, Hal rolled over and clutched at his head, squeezing his eyes tight shut as if to force out the strangeness. But when he opened them again, he saw the sea.

Vast, dark and empty, it stretched out before him to the horizon. Nothing broke its surface but the grey crests of the waves that came rolling steadily in to shore – far too steadily. No gale or blizzard drove these slow, steady breakers that came rumbling up the beach like some huge thing breathing, tossing and turning salt-bleached flotsam where they broke. Sea and sky grew out of a horizon hung with leaden, unmoving clouds; they stretched like a carved curtain across the whole sky. The light on them was too bright for moonlight. It was more like a grim winter's dawn, pale and sourceless. But unlike dawn, it was un-changing.

He looked down, and saw what had tripped him, sticking up out of the sand. He reached out gingerly and pulled it free. Light and dry as driftwood in his fingers, it was no stick. He flinched slightly at the feel of it, surprising himself: he handled bones enough in his line, even human bones. A lower arm bone, an ulna – he noted that in a detached, dreamy kind of way, and that it was longer than his own; it had belonged to somebody very large indeed. He laid it gently back on the sand and stood up, shakily. On either side those lowering cliffs curved outward, unbroken, into the hazy distance, forming the arms of an immense bay. He could not see to the limits of it. But as far as his vision reached there was no life, no movement, nothing except that gently rolling sea, the waves and the flotsam. He took a few steps down the beach towards it, feet grinding into coarser shingle – and stopped dead. At his feet, near the damp margin of sand, lay another bone, much eroded but recognisable – near it another, and then another. Those were vertebrae, almost certainly human. He stared down at the sea, unable to take another step. A wave broke with a soft rumble, and out of the surf rolled something rounded and white, tumbling up the beach to rest as the water fell away again. For an instant it sat there, grinning mockery as empty as its eyes, and then the next wave snatched it back like a disobedient child. Hal looked wildly from side to side. All the tumbling flotsam was – He stooped, dug in his fingers, then quickly dusted them clean on his coat. Now he knew what the shingle was, too.

The light wind tasted bitter on his lips. He turned and bolted for the cliff, hearing the bone fragments pop and scatter under him. But as he neared it he faltered, slowed, stood. The cliff towered above him, a citadel of smooth black rock, unyielding, unbroken. He reached out, to make sure it was no illusion. The stone was hard and cold, but the chill in him was deeper still. The crevice he had come through might never have existed.

There was a sudden, violent judder in the rock. He felt it twitch like the flank of an animal. Through earth and sky rang a deep, vibrating groan. His body throbbed with harmonies he couldn't hear, deeper than the deepest organ chords. Hanging onto the cliff, he twisted round and saw that smooth sea become a rippling, boiling cauldron. Behind him the tormented rock quivered and cracked like a cannonshot. He threw himself aside as debris pattered down, and a moment later a massive boulder spun almost idly downward to thump into a fountain of sand where he had stood. Afraid of others, he looked up and saw that the heavy clouds were stirring at last, tearing and parting. Light shone through the gaps, slanting down in great rays through the icy haze in the air. But it was no wholesome sunlight. A stark, intense blue, it laid a steely tinge on seafoam and sand, deepening the shadows where it did not fall.

One glaring beam swept down the beach around him. Just where he had first fallen, he saw the sand convulse. It scattered aside as something thrust up through it, a dark stalk growing like a seedling in a time-lapse film. It writhed and twisted upward, swelled and spread at the top – not into a flower. A human hand raked at the sky. Beside it another arm thrust up, and a little way off another, and another, and still more. The beach rippled and surged as if a nest of burrowing things writhed in panic beneath it.

Sudden pain lanced into Hal's leg with a jerk that almost overbalanced him. Crab-claw fingers, withered and dark, crooked out of the sand to grip at his ankle like the last handhold of a drowning man. Even as they clutched they grew, the withered muscles filling out like feeding leeches. With a strangled cry of disgust he tore free and staggered back, barely dodging another hand that came inching feebly out of the sand, beckoning, entreating. The whole beach seemed to be sprouting around him like some obscene parody of a cornfield, everywhere dark grainstalk arms rising and swaying in a dead wind. The harvest – Around the first outflung arm a squirming outline took shape in the sand.

Hal turned on his heel and fled through the rippling mass, staggering over things that leapt and twisted underfoot. A hand plucked at his clothes, tripping him. Black nails raked his cheek as he landed. He scrambled back on his feet, and in a fury of loathing kicked and trampled both hands back into the sand. He stumbled a few steps further, and no hands clutched. He was beyond the nimbus of the ghastly light. But where he had been, the beach was blackened now, a seething, beseeching mass of arms.

From the heart of it a single figure heaved itself upright, swaying uncertainly, and raised its arms to the opening in the clouds. That was closing now, narrowing as if to focus the light. The figure shimmered in the intensity of it, and it seemed to Hal that it turned for an instant to look at him. Then the light flashed into an unbearable blue-white arc, blinding him. Another tremor lashed the beach, flinging him to his knees in a welter of bone fragments. By the time the seared streaks of colour faded from his sight, the clouds had healed, the sea was calm and the beach was as empty as he had first seen it. Stark as it was, it was peaceful again.

Hal slumped back onto the sand, head hanging. The worst, the very worst thing was that he couldn't believe he was dreaming or schizoid. He was *here*. Whatever happened to him here would matter. If, for example, those hands had held him . . . He looked away –

And sprang back, scrabbling frantically to get up. The

190

dark figure beside him made no move. It simply stood, tall and still, in a great cowled robe the colour of the stone. No face was visible. He felt strangely certain that this was not what he had seen rise out of the sand. That had sprung up in violence and turmoil. This figure's stillness and calm were at one with the world around him – and all the more awesome.

All it needs is a scythe . . .

It moved. Cloaked in shadow, it bent over him as he sprawled helpless. In the depths of the cowl he saw a glint like an eye, a gleam of gold. Light was growing, and a face swimming gradually into focus. A woman's face, framed in long blonde hair, one blue eye open. On that side calm, serene, beautiful – on the other, slack, swollen, puffy and blackened with suffused blood, the eye closed. A dead face. As he had last seen it –

He found his voice. 'Pru?' he croaked.

She hangs between life and death. That is my kingdom, so I speak to you through her face. Do you know where you are?

He swallowed. 'N . . . yes.' The worst shock of all was realising that he had known, and never admitted it to himself. 'Nastrand –'

Indeed. The Seastrand of the Dead. Do you know who I am?

Now he had to believe he was mad, and couldn't. 'You . . . you are Hela. You rule . . . in the myths you rule the kingdom of the dead.'

More, and less. But that will do. I need one who will know his way. I cannot leave this place. I am this place. And now it is being invaded – you saw. The face hung masklike before him, yet there was a terrible bitterness in the voice he heard. *My peace is broken – what I hold in trust is taken. Old powers are stirring, long, long past their time, beyond hope of good or gain. Only hatred and envy remain. And it is your world they threaten with Hela's stolen legions – all remaining that they can command. But as they breached my barriers, so also can I. I led you here before they could hurl you down as they sought, and so they have no power over you. You went looking for help.*

You would not have found it. I cannot give it – but I can send you as my messenger to where you will find it. Will you go?

The voice was less and less like Pru's, more like the sea, rolling out of an infinite distance. Hal felt his fists clench convulsively till the nails dug hard into his palms. He desperately needed something solid to hang onto. He lay on a beach that was not sand, calmly talking to a goddess out of legends he'd thrilled to as a boy, studied as a man, without ever really believing in them for a single moment. The beach, the sea, the bitter cold, the face that hung over him were the landscapes of a dream, a delusion – but as real as the bite of pain in his fists. It was his own world that felt like the dream. And in this one he had no handhold, no basis of reason or logic to guide him.

The einherjar of legend walk in your world, and threaten it and all that you love. Is that not reason enough?

He stared at the ravaged face for a moment. Then something flared up in him, driving back the deadening bonds of cold – a great anger. 'Yes,' he growled, 'it is. I will go.'

The hood drew back, and he clambered painfully to his feet before the figure. A fold of the robe lifted, gesturing down the empty beach to an outcropping of the cliff, great, jagged rock strata that stuck out of the sand like some perished giant's bones.

Your way is there. And your enemies.

He waited, but it said nothing more. 'You must tell me –'

You know enough. That is why I chose you.

Hal hesitated, then flung out an arm and flicked the shadowing hood right back, baring the hidden head and shoulders. Even in the dim light, Pru's hair gleamed, lifting a little in the light breeze. The face remained serene, calm, in its living half. On one bare shoulder he saw a red mark – his own mouth had left that. 'About her,' he grated.

She will live. Beyond that I know nothing, and I shape nothing. Go now.

He found himself backing away down the beach, unable to take his eyes from the half-ruined face. He had to know

192

more – or did he? He felt a strange kind of certainty, as if some unreadable inner self already knew where he must go, what he must do. Perhaps that eerie voice had told him more than he had heard. The figure seemed to be blurring with distance already, far sooner than it should. He saw the bare shoulders move, the hood rise again to cover the bright hair. Only for a moment he seemed to see something else in its shadows, a glimpse of dark curls – *Jess?* Suddenly she was clear in his mind again, etched sharp by anxiety. But he had seen no face . . . Then his foot slipped on rock, and he looked round sharply. He was already at the outcrop, and when he looked back again the great beach was empty.

He felt hideously alone and unsure of himself. The path that must lie ahead of him – in the myths there was only one way out of Hela's kingdom, and few, if any, ever passed it. He cudgelled his brain for more details, but they wouldn't come. That shocked him. It was the kind of thing any archaeologist absolutely had to know, to explain signs and symbols and images, and he'd always thought he did. But for years now his knowledge of mythology must have been slipping away from him, shrivelling up in a mass of dry detail – just one more thing he could always look up in his library. A lot of use that was to him now! Legend didn't come alive for him any more, not the way it did for Jess. Only now it *was* alive, and with a vengeance. She might know more. If only – He stamped that thought out sharply. This was the last place in the universe – or outside it – he should want to see her.

He stared up at the jagged slope and the gnarled ridge above it, straining his eyes. If he wanted her so much, that was his best – his only – hope of ever seeing her again. Was that why he'd been given a glimpse of her? As an encouragement? Or a warning?

'You and your goddamned threats!' he shouted furiously down the beach. 'You think I need them? Keep your claws off her!' But the soft wind whipped away his words before they could even echo, and the sea whispered on, unmoved. He could only turn and begin to climb.

The way was clear, in places a rough rock stair like the

one he had come down, elsewhere a path that wound through gloomy rifts and crevices in the rock, so deep and narrow that only the faintest streak of pale sky showed overhead. But the footing was easy, as if worn smooth by many feet, and he had other things to worry about. This was the Path of the Dead, and the Vikings had shrouded it in menace. And beyond it, what? His enemies, that was about all he could be sure of. The hunters would be on his trail again.

He walked on and on. Time lost its meaning in the unchanging twilight, the sheer mechanical action of walking, the rhythm of his footfalls grating softly on the dry rock. He never felt tired or hungry or thirsty, though hours or years could have been passing. Only the terrible chill stayed with him but it, too, was a negative thing, an absence of heat, and hardly bothered him now. He found it all too easy not to think as he plodded on, to let his mind wander off into vague memories – and all too dangerous. He concentrated, and traced an image on the darkness ahead – a special smile, lazy and loving, to bring the only kind of warmth he could expect in this dark place.

I'm not dead yet, kaereste – not by a long chalk. He sighed. He did want her here, despite himself. He couldn't help it. Once before, after his divorce, she'd salvaged his life when it was in ruins. *Now you are the last of it I can hang onto. I will get back to you yet . . .*

He looked up defiantly at the sky – and stopped short. When had it changed? High overhead there was something like a gigantic roof, an enormous tangle of matted shadow-shapes through which only a dim blue-green light filtered down. The cleft was shallower here. He could see most of the sky, and the massive web covered it all. And now he had stopped he could hear something, too – a remote rumble, like a continuous storm in the distance. He reached out to touch the rock wall, and felt the vibration in his fingertips. Whatever it was, it must be large. He shrugged sharply, and strode on. He'd find out soon enough.

Now the path grew swiftly steeper, and the sound of his

footsteps changed. He was walking over broken rock, even gravelly soil. Little avalanches rattled and skittered down the slope, sounding surprisingly loud even over the growing rumble ahead. Two high, jagged boulders leaned like broken gateposts over the narrowing path. He squeezed between them and found himself at its abrupt end – a steep cliff, its heights lost in the shadowy canopy. The lower levels looked climbable, but as he came closer he slowed, unwilling to believe what he was seeing, until at last he stood, dazed, at the foot of it, and reached out to touch the rough surface. He snatched his hand away as if it had burnt him, but it was not hot; it had the cool firmness of living bark. The sheer impact of the realisation left him gasping for breath. He knew now what the great vaulting was, and his thoughts withered away under the immensity of it, and what must lie above. He was no more than a mote, a tiny parasite clinging and cowering at the very root of the world.

'The Tree,' he whispered, clutching at the wood. 'The Tree – the World-Ash, Yggdrasil. Oh Jess, Jess, if you could only see *this* –' A faint tremor ran through the thick bark, as if in answer. The great tree of Viking myth, Upholder of Worlds, Pillar of the Universe . . . He stared up the vast arch of the root and saw faint bluish sparks dance and flutter there, like distant will-o'-the-wisps. Did he dare set foot on *that*?

Then out of the dark behind him drifted a sound that set the hair on his neck bristling, an eerie, distant howl as cold and shimmering as moonlight. Another joined it, rising and falling, a hungry, yearning sound it was not good to hear alone in a narrow place. And nearer, much nearer, just at the limits of his vision, there was a terrible grinding sound, as if one or both boulders were stirring like an awakened animal, stretching out stiff limbs across the gravel. Hal slid warily back into the shadows. Probably not his pursuers – more likely Hela's sentinels, back on watch. But either way, this was no place to hang around. He hoisted himself onto the great curve of the root and began to scramble upwards, very quietly.

Once at the top, he found he could stand and walk easily

enough. Like the rock below, the bark was worn quite smooth. The tormented twistings and gnarlings of the living wood formed a natural stair that led high into the hazy distance. Up here, the roaring sound was suddenly much louder – the whole air seemed to be quivering. And as he climbed he felt other, fainter tremors underfoot, echoing his steps as if he were walking across the top of a gigantic drum. The rocky path had seemed lifeless, sterile, but up here the whole place felt alive, aware. Of him? Maybe. Were those lights flickering again, high in the shadows above? It didn't matter. There was nothing he could do but stay on his guard.

That became difficult. The climb seemed as endless as before, and the sound was hypnotic. Thinking against it was an effort, and he found himself continually drifting off into waking dreams, formless images in which the sense of menace lurked like a monstrous shape at the limits of vision, always retreating as he came on, but always there. Then he would stumble, his foot slipping on the coarse bark, and be jolted awake again, tensed to face something that was never there.

And then, once, his foot slipped out into empty air, and he had to clutch frantically for a handhold as bark crumbled and slithered away under him. He hung there, gasping with the shock, and saw that the last turn in the path had led him too near the edge of the root. He looked down –

The world seemed to drop away under him. The gigantic root did not rest on the ground: it arched out like a bridge over an appalling gap, filled only with night and tumult. A glittering streak of water cut across the darkness under him and fell crashing into its depths, a waterfall deeper and wider by far than any he had seen or dreamed of, an immense green column plunging down a wide wall of rock like black glass. He could see no end to it. Sharpened by distance to a needlepoint, it plunged straight down amid foam and thunder into the secret heart of the world. Frothing spray erupted over the jagged rock walls on either side; it left them glittering with green phosphorescence, and filled the air with fine mist. The bark beneath him, the whole exposed face of the root, was wet with it –

Hal tore his glance away, clinging to the unstable bark. Panic could end only one way here. He felt carefully for a secure foothold, tested it, and slowly shuffled his way onto a safer part of the path, swearing murderously at himself for dozing off and doing his damnedest not to look down again. *Fanden i helved, I really do need Jess along – as a keeper! I am not fit to be out on my own* . . . He was at the top of the stairway now. Beyond it the root rose smoothly to a high, arching crest, and the path led right across the top of it. He stopped and looked warily around.

Out on either side there was nothing but the night, and the glimmering river. Looking back along it he thought he could make out its distant source, a great shadowy cavern-mouth hung with stalactites, like the jaw of some fantastic beast. He tried looking up, and was startled to see how close he now was to the great canopy. Through its loose mesh he could clearly see the vast grey wall it sprang from, curving limitlessly from one dark horizon to the other, and beyond. Against it even the great root he stood on looked absurdly small, a tightrope to a sky-scraper. Looking along it, he thought he could see where it joined the trunk. Not far now – at least, not compared to the way he had already come. If he could only make it that far without trouble.

He took a deep breath and stepped out into the open.

The moment his foot hit the wood it jumped and quivered under him like a startled animal, and the crash of a giant's footfall echoed through the emptiness below. Specks of blue light danced and flickered behind the crest of the ridge. Off balance, he stumbled forward. There was another ringing, rolling crash, and the bark shuddered, sending him sprawling. He struggled back on his feet, buffeted by echoes. If they would only stop for a minute, let him think! He knew what this place was – the bridge out of Hela's realm, the bridge that only echoed when – when . . .

A wisp of blue light crested the ridge and hung there, trembling in the vibrating air. Another joined it, another

197

and two more, and like wind-blown flames they came sweeping down the path towards him. He stood frozen, and they halted a few feet from him, blocking his path with a curtain of cold light like a winter aurora. Strange outlines formed in the play of the cold flames, half-substantial shapes of deep shadow and bright highlight that seemed to fade in and out of solidity. Human shapes, writhing, distorted, slack jaws open in soundless howls. Behind them, through them, he saw the upward path fade into darkness. The blue balefire turned his out-thrust hand stark and clawlike. Like the hands on the beach – like the creature at the Farm.

One of the shapes moved out of the line and glided slowly forward. After a moment's hesitation, another followed. Hal stood frozen, unable to form a single word. The ghastly faces, level with his own, he could see clearly, so clearly he could almost make out the features –

'Oh, no,' he breathed softly. 'Oh no – no, not you, too . . .'

The sunken cheeks worked, the mouth moved, the voice came like a distant, mocking echo. 'G'day, Prof,' said Latimer. 'Nice job you gave us, that one. Really appreciated that, we did, Wilf an' me.'

'That's right, Hal,' sighed the echoes. Hal shuddered as the sunken eyes met his own. 'Tom and me. They tore me apart, you know, Hal? Limb from limb, literally. The way you'd pull off a chicken leg, or something.' The twisted mouth fluttered. 'You got off lightly, Hal – as usual. Exposure, that's an easy death. But we got you, all the same. You're one of us now.'

Hal swallowed. 'Wilf – Tom – if it *is* you, I am sorry. I warned you as best I could. But you did not get me – Hela did, and I am her messenger. Let me pass and perhaps – well, perhaps all this can end.'

The echoes rang with harsh laughter. *'Hela?'* chuckled Latimer's voice. 'It was our storm sent you to her – you're ours by right. What's she got to offer but the Beach, anyway? Death. Not even that, not any more. You want to see your own world again? She can't send you – only the *einherjar* can do that. It's life we're offering you – new life, endless life, always renewed. And the power, the strength you've never had –'

A pale hand lanced out, clutching. He met it with his own – and was seized. A spurt of cold fire raced up his arm and fountained out into him like a million darts of ice. The blood in his veins, his very thoughts, seemed to gel and congeal. Frost clouded his eyes. And suddenly he was seeing, feeling, what Latimer described. A vision of fighting, taking, tearing, rending, endlessly glutting insatiable appetites – himself a hunter now, stalking live prey across an unliving white landscape, the chosen body broken beneath him and the hot, sudden brightness of blood on the clean snow –

'*No!*'

The prey was Jess.

A violent shock whipped through his body, and he fell on his knees, feeling the bridge sway beneath him. The river and the falls swung across his distorted vision, but he saw them very differently now. A river not of water but of human shapes, the falls' thunder a vast, discordant chorus of howling despair from the streams of souls as they fell threshing and tumbling over and down into the dark, to become scattered shreds of the identities they once had, washed up and eroded away into the sands of the Corpse Strand.

'Like it?' snarled Jackson's silky voice. 'That's the way you sent Tom and me.'

'The hell I did!' gasped Hal, struggling frantically against the icy hand.

'The hell you did,' said Latimer softly. 'But you, you get a choice. Wise up, Prof. There's just two ways you're gonna get off this bridge – with us, or with them!'

Hal kicked out furiously, fighting to stand.

'Be sensible!' hissed Jackson. 'Forget what you used to feel, what you thought was good or bad, that's irrelevant now! What other choice have you got? There's no going back – you're dead, man, *dead!*'

Hal felt the word echo thinly through the darkness around him, like a judgement. '*Dead . . . dead . . . dead . . .*' At last he managed to find his balance again and kick down hard. There was a crash of metallic thunder, the bridge bucked violently, for an agonised instant he felt his arm tearing out of its socket – and then the grip broke, and he was stumbling upright on the swaying surface. He saw the figures quiver with the movement, and felt a great laugh bubble up inside him, quenching the cold burning. He stamped again, hard, and the bridge swung and crashed under him like a vast tocsin, a great brazen clang rolling out into the chasm. The balefires bent and fluttered like candle flames in a wind.

'Dead, am I?' raved Hal. 'Thought I would forget – nearly made me forget! The Bridge of Echoes, yes – but only when the living pass! And *you*, my friends, make no sound at all –' The three other figures came rushing down on him, and he saw pale weapons spring up in their hands, axe and sword and spear. He plunged to meet them. Fingers clutched and weapons thrust, and the same heart-stopping chill skewered agonisingly through ribs and fore-head – for an instant – before it faded like a breeze. With the bridge thundering under him he passed through spear and spearman alike and sprinted for the crest. He turned to face his pursuers. 'You are the ones who cannot pass here! *Back to Hela with the pack of you!*'

The echoes caught his voice, and for a moment it sounded unlike his own, massive, rumbling, metallic. From infinite distance something answered it, a rising whistle of wind that came whipping past him on the un-steady crest and swept down on the advancing lights below. Then there was a mighty crackle, and the darkness was riven in two by a vast streak of glaring red-white light that came hammering down on the wood of the bridge and blasting across its surface. Hal was flung sprawling on his face, seeing only the abyss. Into it, like sparks from struck metal, fell a scatter of blue specks, slowly twisting and whirling away into the shimmering water far below.

Hal raised his head cautiously, a little dazed. What had he said or done to cause *that*? He stood up, shakily, acutely aware of how immense and alien the universe around him was, and how small and powerless he must be. He had been saved by something he didn't understand – by coincidence, perhaps even by mistake. It could easily have been him whirling away into nothing. After his brief moment of triumph all the laughter was knocked out of him. Whatever he'd once thought of Latimer and Jackson – He shuddered. *Nobody* deserved that. Could they be called up again? Probably. But what could he do to help them? He stared moodily down into the depths, back along the great river to its source –

And froze, staring. Out of the dim distance a pair of eyes stared up at him, immense eyes, awesomely aware. Ahead of them, shining in their own light, a vast expanse of shield-like scales, and two great pits just above the fanged cavern-mouth. They were nostrils. The cavern really was a mouth, in a serpentine head vast enough to swallow up falls, bridge and all. The river ran out from between the unmoving gape of jaws.

'*Fanden i helved!*' he breathed. 'The Serpent – Jormungand –'

The eyes blinked once, with slow reptilian malice, as if – there was no 'as if'. It knew he was there. The membrane flickered over the rounded green eyes, large as a mountain. The hiss of the river grew suddenly louder, and the same chill wind came whistling out along it and whipped around him once more.

A living tread awoke me. You go to give me back my rightful prey. Pass, creature – for now.

Hal turned and fled down the last slope.

It ended in a high, dark crevice, and he scuttled into it like a frightened animal, thinking only of shadow and concealment from that vast, cold, malignly intelligent gaze. He had encountered a power, and one that did not choose to cloak itself like Hela. Beneath those eyes he and everything human dwindled away to insignificance, no more than spray from a waterfall. It looked at him as he might at an ant in an anthill, or a microbe on a slide. There was nothing even remotely benign about it. And without its help what did his petty victory amount to? What chance did he have in this terrible world? He shrank back into shadow as if the weight of humanity was on his shoulders.

201

The crevice seemed to be in a high grey cliff, but the wall behind him was almost warm to the touch, rough-textured but soft and crumbling. It smelt musty and ancient beyond measure. Wood! Living wood, at that. On top of the shock he had just had, the thought made him slightly giddy. The Ash Tree, the Upholder of Worlds – here he lurked, like some maggot or bark-beetle, inside its trunk, and the wood of it crumbled in his fingers. 'Jess . . .' he sighed, and shook his head. What did it matter whether she would believe him or not? The important thing was getting back to tell her. He was alive, at least. He had some kind of chance. But if he wanted to keep it he had better get going.

The crevice opened deep into the wood behind; the darkness there was almost impenetrable, but he took a few steps forward and felt the upward slope of the floor. This had to be his way – into the heart of the tree. But the darkness of it daunted him. Compared to this, the gloom outside was dazzling. Yet there was nowhere to go but up, and the only other way would be to climb the bark outside. He bit his lip, swore softly, and began to walk.

Darkness. The warm air smelt resiny, stale, hard to breathe. Slight claustrophobia pressed in on his chest. He hoped the crevice ceiling was sloping to match the floor – he had visions of the tunnel closing in around him to an impassable point, forcing him to go back and climb the bark after all. And there were noises in the dark around him, little pattering sounds he ignored at first. He thought they might be wood fragments scuffed up by his feet, bouncing back down the slope – but they came too often, too clearly, sometimes from down the slope, some-times far ahead. He'd heard sounds like that before – where?

He chuckled. A kindlier memory came to him, a place of light and colour – the Vermont woods in autumn, and chipmunks scurrying among the fallen leaves. Naturally a tree this size would have little creatures scrabbling and nosing about in it. If they were going to be any trouble, they'd have done something by now –

The pattering rose to a sudden crescendo. He whirled

round, and saw an outline prance across the dim glow of the distant opening, a spidery, apelike silhouette, long arms held straight out from the hunched shoulders. In the same instant thin limbs whipped like a wire noose around his legs. He staggered where he stood, and something thumped onto his back and hung there, pinioning his arms. He tried to wrench it away; other hands grabbed at his and began forcing the fingers hard backwards, against the joint. Another weight hammered into his ribs with bruising force, and scrabbling claws clutched violently at the neck of his sweater, clawing through to the skin and twisting together sweater, T-shirt and chain with strangling force. For an instant, ice-cold, bitterly foul breath played across his face, then there was a yipping howl and that attacker fell free. With a yell of disgust, Hal twisted till his back was to the wall, then hurled himself backwards, hard. There was a thudding impact, a sickening, popping crunch, and his back was free. He flung up his hand and felt a body lift with it and go whirling away to crash against the wood. He grabbed downward, but his ankles were abruptly released. Something went pattering off into the dark ahead. He ran after it, kicked out, but connected with nothing. Faint blue glimmers hung in the darkness for a second, like the unblinking eyes of some nocturnal animal. Then they vanished, there was a single malevolent hiss, and nothing more. Hal lunged, collided with the wall, and fell sprawling in a cloud of wood fragments.

After a moment he got his breath back, sat up and shook himself, with a certain grim satisfaction. He hadn't had any help this time! And small as they were, these attackers had been a real threat -- that one clawed hand had ripped right through his sweater and his shirt. It could have been his throat next. He stood up, dusting off the worst of the wood. Too bad one had got away, gone on ahead of him, but now he'd be listening, ready. They wouldn't catch him off guard a second time.

He set off again, trudging on upward through the musty, stifling air and the unending night. The darkness was bewildering, depressing – he felt as if it was invading his mind, dimming memories of a time of light and open air.

He heard nothing but his own footfalls on the smooth tunnel floor; he smelt nothing but the wood around him. Only touch – his feet on the floor, his hands grazing the invisible walls – could tell him anything meaningful.

Slowly, gradually, he became aware that the floor was sloping more steeply. After a time – he only knew it was a long time – he began to think he could feel a slight leftward curve in the tunnel. But that might just be his imagination, filling in for his lack of real information. He was walking in limbo, far worse than the long climb up from the beach. There at least he'd had free air to breathe, and a feeling of space around him. Here there was nothing, and he could add nothing. He was used to humming or whistling on long walks, but here that would have been horribly out of place. Sound seemed to die stillborn in the heavy atmosphere, and too much noise might call who knew what down on him – another attack by those little monsters, probably. He was fairly sure what they were – *svartalfar*, dark elves, malignant little goblin-things that lurked in the shadows of the myths. He could remember other things there, too, worse things. With them he might not be so lucky. He trudged on, as quietly as he could, unable even to lose himself in daydreams. Everything he had once been, once known, seemed remote beyond recall, even the face he had followed till now. As years or centuries passed it blurred and faded, and there was only the leaden air and the relentless, lightless climb.

The sudden brush of cold air came like a slap in the face. He flinched at the shock and flung up his fists. Then he groaned. '*Satans ogsa*, what am I doing? Jess, Jess *kaereste*, I am coming to pieces, cracking up . . .' But he knew better. He couldn't crack up, any more than he could feel hungry or thirsty or tired – physically. He sagged back against the wall. It was further away than he expected, and he fell heavily on one arm. The tunnel was opening out. He clutched at his arm, and almost laughed. He could still feel pain, all right. It challenged the shadowy neutrality around him, anchoring him in the reality of one memory, at least – that night in the trailer, when he'd wrenched his arm . . . It brought her face back vividly, rapt with pleasure, biting her lips to keep back the faint, gasping little cries.

He looked up, unbelieving. He could hear them now.

Light. He had been without it so long he could hardly make sense of what he saw. Faint as it was, it dazzled him – a vague glow in the darkness ahead, sharply cut off along one edge . . . His eyes managed to focus. It was shining round a sharp bend in the tunnel ahead, a thin foxfire light with only the faintest flicker in it. That was where the sounds were coming from, too. Hal picked himself up as quietly as he could and stalked forward, nervous, alert. A quick glance round the corner first, to be sure it was safe.

What he saw rooted him to the spot.

The stark light threw hard shadows over the twisting, threshing bodies – a woman's, a man's. They lay some way along the tunnel, but not so far that he couldn't see them, all too clearly, the rider and the ridden. He could see the woman's thigh muscles hollow as she arched up and back, her ribs stand out sharply against the glistening dark skin. He saw her taut breasts quiver till huge hands rose to contain them, flicker over them, crush them. Her own hands resting on the wide dark chest, flexing, splaying, digging in and clawing. Her head tossing, the hands sliding down to rein in the sudden emphatic thrusting of her hips, the sudden convulsion lancing through both bodies as one. Her head thrown back, right back, her spine arched till her closed eyes stared straight back at him. Then they opened, and he clung to the crumbling wall for support. Laughter spilled from her lips, terrible laughter that rang like shivercd ice down the tunnel. He jammed his hands over his ears, his face against the wall, shivering violently with the shock. 'It is – not – true!' he whispered, and beat his hands on the wall, trying desperately to wake from what he knew was no dream. 'It's not true!'

Long fingers, cool, slightly damp, stroked his cheek gently. 'Oh yes it is – *kaereste*.' He couldn't close his eyes. Jess's face, against the wall, inches from his own, smiling slightly – smiling through thin, dry, cyanosed lips, in skin suffused with shadow, glossy and tight so the muscles

205

beneath showed clear. Her eyes sunken, overshadowed, no more than a cold glimmer like starlight on a lake . . . 'So what's all the fuss, hmm? Thought you wanted me here – all that mumbling about how I should see things, how I'd know my way around better. Thought you wanted me to come prop up that delicate little ego of yours *comme toujours*. Well, you got your wish. Aren't you glad to see me?' She chuckled lazily. 'Oh, uh, sorry 'bout the little scene, only we got so bored just waiting, Jay'n'me. Thought you'd –'

'*Jay?*' choked Hal.

'Sure – big boy with all the meat – *you* know. See, he came back for me. All the way, just for me. Kind of flattering, don't you think? So I've been drafted –'

Hal gave a wordless cry of pain.

'It's your own fault – *kaereste*. Shouldn't've let me go charging off on my own like that, should you? Very careless. You lose more ladies that way. But then you do seem to lose a lot of ladies, don't you, Hal? First Helga, now me. Let me give you a hint, kiddo. Where it matters, you haven't got it, Hal. It was always better with Jay, Hal. It's better *now*, Hal –'

He turned and screamed in her face. '*Shut up!*' He bounced off the wall and tried to plunge past her, but she stepped into the centre, darkened skin gleaming, and barred his way. He looked around wildly but there was no sign of Colby. 'Jess –' he gasped. 'Jessica – I can't, I don't want to hate you – let me go, let me pass –'

She smiled, smoothly, and shook her head. 'Afraid of hating me? Why? Hate has its uses. Never get to be *einherjar* if you don't know how to hate –'

'If – if you are *einherjar*, one of the warriors of Odin –'

The light flared blue, the wood around them trembled and groaned like a living thing. 'You watch how you use names, you hear?' hissed Jess.

'If you – you are one of his berserks, his immortals – well, I serve someone, too! Too late to save – what I care about, maybe! But I am still a messenger. *Let me pass!*'

'Like hell!' said Jess, and laughed. Cruel laughter,

mocking him, his feelings for her, everything he cared for, the weakness of human affection itself. The same terrible laughter he had heard when –

With a scream of pure agonised rage he flung himself on her.

She sprang to meet him. Her weight slammed into him, smashed him back against the wooden wall so hard that bits flew out around them. Chill fingers clawed at his throat, closed in an iron collar. But he was furious now, seething with fright, grief, jealousy and sheer churning horror, and it all came shrieking out. Fresh cold air whistled through the tunnel as if driven by a distant storm, and the biting edge of it, like a seawind, set his blood tingling. He struck upward with both arms – and broke the iron grip. Black nails gouged firetrails up to his eyes, but he was on her now, hammering at her wildly. It was like hitting a wall of cold marble, but it caught her off balance and they fell together, entwined in deadly mockery of an embrace. Clawing and wringing and snarling at each other, they went rolling over and over back down the slope into the dark. Her nails slashed through his clothes to the flesh beneath, tearing at his ribs, but now he had his hands locked hard around her throat, yelling with exultation as he squeezed, twisted, *wrenched* –

The body beneath him threshed convulsively and sagged, the hands fell away from his ribs, the head fell sideways. Hal fell on top of her and rolled aside, shuddering. For a minute he lay there, open-mouthed, staring, unable to take in what he had done. The face, the body he had loved – still loved – Panic swelled up to fill the emptiness left by rage, and idiot tears trickled down his face. His mind flailed and threshed like a captive beast, tearing itself against the bars of its cage. He dug his fingers into his hair to flood out his thoughts with pain. It steadied him, and he crawled over to her. He felt the chain and pendant she'd given him swing loose around his neck, a terrible dragging weight. Why had he ever hated these creatures so? Who was he to stand in their way? For all his smug self-righteousness, his show of civilisation, he'd found something worse, more vile, more brutal than any

207

of them lurking inside himself. And not so deep inside, either. The thing he had most feared they would do, he had been able to do himself.

His head bowed over the still breast, and the pendant swung and touched it –

A rumbling vibration, like infinitely distant thunder, shook the air. The cold light dimmed, guttered, reddened like a dying candle. The shadows on the still face flickered, deepened.

The slitted eyes flew open –

In a different face. Longer, harder, more aquiline, half-hidden under the great straggling mane of hair that over-shadowed those eyes –

The woman at Fern Farm.

Emotion was burnt out of him. He could only stare. But when those long hands snaked up at his throat his own hands met them, caught them – and slowly, effortfully, forced them back down.

'Not so strong here, are you?' he grated between clenched teeth. 'So you – *forbandede* bitch – you steal her face, make me think – drag me down – fight you all right, but no mistake this time, *nej* – and Pru – what you do to her I do to –'

She twisted like a snake under him, and an immensely long leg doubled up and slammed hard into his stomach and groin. His grip broke and he was catapulted back against the wall. He rolled, agonised, on the splintered wood, momentarily aware of nothing but pain and failure, waiting for the blow that would finish everything. It never came. He heard footsteps, running steps that went pounding off up the tunnel ahead of him. Somehow he staggered to his feet and, still doubled up, went limping after her. But when he rounded the next corner there was nothing but more tunnel, and stronger light. He sagged down against the wall and wheezed for breath. He realised his hands were still clenching and clasping automatically: he would have torn her apart if he'd caught her, not for showing him a lie, but for showing him a truth. About himself. She might have changed, but that hadn't. He had really believed –

208

He buried his face in his hands. How could he call them monsters now?

But after a while he raised his head, and let the cooling breeze play over it. More air, more light – he picked himself up, wearily. He might as well see where it was coming from. He limped unsteadily up the tunnel to its next corner, blinking in the brighter glow, turned it and scrambled up an uneven patch to a wide, irregular crevice. He stepped through – and stopped dead, scrabbling at the wall behind him for support.

The urge to go scuttling back into the tunnel for shelter was overpowering. Shelter from the sheer vastness of the shaft he stood in, perched on a narrow ledge in its jaggedly irregular walls – cliffs of wood, not stone. But the wood was no longer living. He stood at the centre of the universe, the very heart of the World Tree, and it was hollow, rotten.

He found himself crouching, cowering before it. Whether he looked up or down, distance held his eye hypnotically, an enormous weight of emptiness that seemed to be plucking him off his insignificant foothold. Insane urges warred in him, to rush wildly out or just as wildly back. In desperation he fought them down and fixed his eyes on the wall opposite. He could make out details on it, outcrops and openings, vast vertical rifts and smaller holes, nooks, crannies, clefts and openings like the one he had emerged from. And as he looked over to his right, relatively near him, he saw one fissure that spilled a narrow beam of light right across the shaft, onto the wall not far above him. Strong light, the colour of a cold winter sky – light that could come from the outside.

He was on his feet in an instant, scanning the ravaged face of the wall. From here he could just about reach another ledge, from there what looked like the edge of a natural terrace, and after that – He shrugged. It had been the same story all along. That had to be his way, because there was no other. Carefully, without looking down, he reached out and tested his first foothold. It held. He rested his weight on it, and began to climb.

The terrace turned out to slope like a steep roof. He

209

had climbed worse, but only with ropes and crampons – not to mention other climbers. Once or twice he slid, badly, but after that it was easier; he was level with the light, and it lit his way like a beacon. At last he swung across, right into it, and collapsed half-blinded on the fissure floor. Unlike the tunnel it felt damp, almost slimy. He would have to watch his footing. He sat up and looked around for a handhold. Some sort of large vine or creeper grew up through the fissure, its tendrils carpeting the floor and hanging in great loops from the walls. It was as slimy as everything else, but at least it looked strong. He caught hold of a loop and swung himself up – and it leaped like a startled snake in his grasp. He yelped and let go, and the whole vast mass of creeper tore free and reared up like a striking cobra around him. Beyond it, out of the darkness of the shaft, other tendrils rose and swayed. He spun round and threw himself forward up the steep floor of the fissure an instant before the whole mass of tendrils came crashing down where he had been. Then he was running for his life, head down, never stopping, never looking back. His hand burned where he had touched the thing, as if the slime were some sort of acid – digestive, maybe. He thought of the other tendrils, and the hollowed heart of the Tree. In the legends there had been some monstrous thing that gnawed at it – Nidhoggr, that was the name. As long as the Norns, the weavers of destiny, tended the World Ash, Nidhoggr had been kept at bay – but it must have broken through long ages ago . . .

Old powers are stirring, long, long past their time . . .

Suddenly cold leaves thrashed around him, enveloped him as he fought and ripped at them, tripped and clutched him. He fell headlong on his face. After a second he rolled over, gasping and winded. No vine-thing towered over him; a roof of branches, heavy with spearhead leaves, swayed and rustled in a cool, keen wind. A gust parted them for an instant, and he caught the briefest glimpse of cloud, steel-grey and scudding fast. There were leaves all around him, some kind of thicket. After the paths he had walked it looked almost unbearably safe, natural and wholesome. He sat for a moment, blinking in the light, and then heaved himself to his feet, pushing the lower branches aside. He could see more sky now, grey and cloudy – but not the leaden, motionless clouds over the Beach far below. Here the clouds were all shapes, all shades, from pure white wisps to great stormy ramparts, dark and lowering, and they raced and seethed before the rushing wind. For a moment he simply stood and drank it all in. He had always loved stormscapes, and this was the wildest he had ever seen. A thought struck him, and he looked around him at the branches – masses of them rearing and plunging as the wind whipped at them, but no trunk visible. He looked down at his feet. They rested not on hard ground but on bark, dull grey with thick interwoven ridges like the Bridge so far below. In his panic he had blundered right out through the fissure onto a limb of the great Tree itself. He looked around and there it was, rearing high over the tossing branchtops, a great jagged grey wall that blotted out half the angry sky. There was something about it, though –

The wind thrashed the branches again, and something among them caught his eye, something dark, bobbing and swaying almost overhead. He peered around cautiously before stepping out of the thicket for a better view, looked up –

It was a human skeleton. A few rags that might once have been flesh or clothing hung from the darkened, encrusted bones. One leg had gone, and the hands – the lower jaw, too, so he could clearly see the twisted thong looped around its throat. Between its ribs the ragged end of a blackened spear-shaft stuck out. Hal backed away shakily – the image of another glade was all too clear in his mind. He looked down the wide avenue of branches and saw other shapes dangling there, some human, some animal, some past recognition. From here alone he could see hundreds, naked, pitiful things that capered and shivered in the cold wind.

Sickened, he looked away hurriedly, back at the vast trunk. There *was* something – an image, a carving so immense his eyes had failed to take it in at first. The head and shoulders of a man, wreathed in a wild corona of

211

flowing hair and beard that merged into the rough bark. There might be more of the body, but it was hidden from him by tossing branches. The sculpted face was long and gaunt, with high, broad cheekbones and a great aquiline blade of a nose. It had nothing of the impassive statue about it: lines of pain were graven over every inch. The high forehead and thick brows were clenched tight, the tongue lolled slightly through thin lips drawn back in a tight rictus of agony. One eye was closed. The other was a sunken socket, ravaged and empty.

Hal stared, appalled. From cruder avatars in Viking craftwork, from the toppled pillar of the Fern Farm temple, he knew only too well who and what it represented. A god who, to regain a doubled power, went through the sacrificial ordeal of his own victims, the ultimate offering to himself. Who stooped from the Tree where he hung in ritual torment to snatch up dark power from the depths, creatures from the realms of the dead whom he gathered as warriors, *einherjar* to fight and fall for him and rise at sunset, healed, to fight once more. The image of Odin, Watcher, Wakeful, Wanderer, Deceiver, Lord of the Slain, caught in the shared instant of sacrificial agony, brooded over his offerings on the boughs below.

Suddenly a harsh, croaking scream cut through the air. Things wheeled there, high overhead, dark bird shapes silhouetted against the darkening sky, two huge black ravens that came spiralling down the raging wind to circle above him. They croaked again, and he felt the great Tree heave and groan and tremble under him. He looked around wildly –

Slowly, quite slowly, the vast image in the living wood was stirring, the lolling head lifting to turn blindly towards him. Unable to move, to speak, to breathe, he could do nothing but watch the tortured features, lined and grey as the wood around, lift and shudder like a moving mountain, the immense lips curl with the pain of effort. Nothing but consider, in some calm, detached fragment of his mind, a being who, in his unsparing, ruthless quest for power, hung for so long from the upholding Tree that it grew out around him – merged with him –

212

The vast eyelid fluttered open.

Hal gave a single throat-tearing shriek. He was bathed in a flaring, scorching blast of blue-white light that burnt the world around him to incandescent glare and shadow and sprayed agony like molten silver through his veins. The bones shone through the arm thrown over his eyes, and he felt the flesh begin to melt and strip away. The last shreds of strength and instinct sent him diving for cover, any cover that would shield him from that searing glance an instant longer. Back among the leaves he plunged –

And fell through. There was nothing beneath him, no branch. He scrabbled frantically, twigs lashed his blistered face, and then there was only empty air and a slow, sickening tumble. A whirling, dizzying landscape wheeled around him: leaves, branches, the vast trunk rising out of cloud, a dim, distant mountain horizon, a tall bank of stormcloud climbing above it, the last hollowness of final failure, absolute defeat. He had climbed, he had fallen, and all that he cared for fell to ruin with him, with a message that now, at the long end, he could never deliver.

The wind roared around him. Sheet lightning lanced across the horizon, a thunderclap came rolling and crashing out of limitless distance to shiver the very air around him –

I needed no message.

The wind came seething up under him, slowing the spin, slackening the fall until he seemed to be almost floating level with the tower of cloud. Lightning flared red-white within it, casting sharp shadows onto the mountains beneath. And in the glare he saw a glint of eyes, the shadowed outline of a face – one he knew, recognised, and yet struggled to name –

It was the messenger I had to have. I send no thralls to fight my battles. What is freedom, if they who fight for it do not have it? And once men called me their friend . . .

The cloud filled the sky above him, blotting out mountain and tree alike. With a last fragmenting crash, barbed light leapt out of the heart of it and came hammering down into him, shattering, reshaping. The last image was of his

213

own body glowing like molten gold, and above it that face, so enigmatic, that he knew and did not know –

The face was his own.

Darkness.

CHAPTER TEN

SLOWLY, SULLENLY, light returned to a world of winter. The sky resolved into streaks of grey, dappled with relentless snow. A grey plain crept out of darkness, scattered with bare, frost-blackened trees. The howling winds were still, but no sound had come to take their place; over the fields hung the uneasy silence of a dream. Then over the rim of a low hill erupted a roaring plume of snow. The roar grew higher, louder, and a snowdrift leaped skyward in one immense fountain as the snowfan crested the hill and went jolting and slithering on down the Oddsness road. Behind it, engine whining, came a Land Rover in police livery, skidding through the narrow furrow cut by the fan.

' 'E's doing it on purpose!' grumbled Harshaw as the Land Rover swerved into the side of the road for the third time.

'Just keep back from him,' said Ridley. 'Not his fault if the corporation use excavators instead of proper tracked vehicles. He can't help skidding any more than you can.'

'Nearly took me 'ead off wi' that ruddy back bucket!'

'Not his fault either. He has to keep it stuck out to counterbalance the weight of that bloody great fan contraption on the front. Just keep your distance.' Ridley glanced back at Jess, hunched in mute misery on the back seat. 'Snow looks a bit thinner out here,' he lied. 'Might've had a better chance.'

She shook her head. Her last hope had been the little houses and the church at Oddsness – but no one there had seen or heard of Hal. Now she could only pray that nothing worse than snow had overtaken him. The animal howl of the snowfan rang through her head, flaying the dead skin off the road, laying its black bones bare. She stared numbly out at the unchanging landscape that flowed past the side window, the strips of pale snow and dark sky framing a thin, black line of sea. Only the sea had a trace of motion – and something against it like the swoop of a dark bird . . .

'*Stop!* Please! Over there! *He's over there!*' Harshaw's broad shoulders jerked at the cry, and the Land Rover's brakes locked. It skidded and spun, barely missing the excavator's bucket as it settled into the heavy roadside drift and the shallow ditch beneath. Ridley swung around and grabbed her shoulders, expecting shrieking hysteria, but her face was alive with relief and hope, and as he too looked towards the cliff edge his hands and his jaw dropped. He made a grab for the side door, but Jess, clambering over the protesting Harshaw, was already out and bounding towards the approaching figure. 'Hal! Oh God, *Hal!*'

Then she slowed, faltered, stopped. Ridley, stumping after her, saw her put a hand to her mouth. 'Hal?'

Tall, dark, lion-maned, the approaching figure waved almost casually, without changing his brisk step. There was no sign of exhaustion, of a winter night spent unprotected in the open. Ridley found his hand straying to the pistol in his overcoat pocket as the man's confident, energetic stride brought him across the buried road and right up to Jess. He scooped her up effortlessly in a wide embrace that carried her back to where Ridley was standing, landed an immense, smacking kiss on her cheek, and burst out laughing. '*Hej, kaereste!* Glad to see me?' Jess stared wildly. His clothes were soaked, soiled and torn, his hair and beard dishevelled and windblown, yet he positively glowed with health and good humour – even his tan seemed deeper, the fire-gold glint in his hair more intense. Then she lost control altogether and sank sobbing onto his chest. He seemed to be holding her quite lightly, but Ridley noticed that her feet were off the ground. The inspector blinked.

'Well, Prof? Good to see you looking so chipper. Being brutally honest, I never expected to see you at all.'

Hal laughed. 'Nor did I! I tried for Oddsness on foot,

216

and had some bad times blundering about on the cliff. But I am only sorry to drag you all out after me.'

'No problem. Had to get through to Oddsness, anyway – make sure they'd had no trouble last night. Speaking of which –'

'Oh, they were hunting me, yes.'

'And you gave 'em the slip? Where d'you go?'

'The beach. And a cave – a crevice. I am not quite sure. It was a little harrowing.'

'Doesn't seem to have done you much harm. You look in incredible shape.'

Hal shrugged. 'Mostly it is not being worried any more.'

'Wish I wasn't. Hell of a night. First Jess was attacked –'

'Jay? Yes, of course.'

Jess looked up wildly. 'You *knew*? How?'

'The draugar prey on their own.'

'Oh great,' said Ridley savagely. 'We've just spent all bloody night trying to find out little things like that. Why the hell couldn't you tell us straight out?'

'There was much I did not know, or could not remember. Not then.'

Jess ran her fingers through her hair. 'Anyway, we found out more – things you don't know.'

'About Hrafn Rimkonungr and Aud? Do not be too sure.'

'But – but you never . . .'

'Never got to the church? The answer was not there. I will tell you more when I have had something to eat. A great deal to eat.' He turned towards the car.

Ridley caught his arm. 'Hey, hold on there –'

'Later, I said. There is anyway nothing you can do.' He grinned down at Jess and patted her bottom playfully. 'Come, *kaereste*, time to go home.'

She bridled and pulled herself away from him. 'Hal – what's happened to you? Really happened? Why're you so . . .?'

His face hardened. 'I am what I am. Later you will know. You have never quite trusted me, not really. It's time you began – now.'

217

'I – I never quite . . .'

'Oh, I cannot blame you. I never trusted myself.' He strode past her to the car, a light hand on her arm. When she resisted it he let her go without a backward look.

She stood staring after him, fighting for words. 'Insp – uh, Inspec . . . is that *Hal*?'

'You tell me,' growled Ridley. 'But I'm not letting him out of my sight, till I'm sure. And – Christ!' Jess started, followed his glance back the way Hal had come. His footprints led from a dark patch near the cliff edge – not a rock, as she had thought, but a wide circle of bright green grass, quite bare of snow, with an old, dead tree trunk at its centre. There were no tracks anywhere else at all.

The meal at the Two Ravens was a strange, strained affair for everyone except Hal, who merrily wolfed down everything that was put in front of him. Neville had come bouncing out into the chilly street to meet them, delighted to see Hal alive. By the end of the meal he was silent and wary. So was Jess. This tall, magisterial stranger had none of the doubts and quirks of the Hal she knew. In the car, his arm had been gentle on her shoulders – but too gentle, as though it could crush her like an eggshell. She had never known how strong he was. In love, in bed, she had fought him but he had never fought her. He had always been too controlled, too caring. And now – he still cared, but it had changed, as if he looked down at her from some enormous height. The thought grew inside her, harder and harder to keep down, like a scream swelling in her throat. *Say it, somebody! That isn't Hal!*

And then the tall figure sighed, sat back, smiled – and suddenly, astonishingly, it *was* Hal. 'I am sorry for my rudeness. I must have been burning much food last night. That cold – *Fanden i helved!*'

She could see the relaxation that spread around the table, tired backs slumping in welcome relief. Ridley smiled. 'Too right, Prof. Those stupid buggers in the mobile HQ nearly got themselves frozen in last night.'

218

'Made it, did they?' asked Harry solicitously.

'So I hear.'

'Pity.'

'Now listen, Hardwicke . . .'

'You will excuse me a moment,' said Hal. He got up and headed for the toilets.

'Mind you,' admitted Ridley, 'with them heading the official investigation I'm left free to deal with what's *really* going on. But I need help. Up to a point I can use my own lads – sorry, Jess! – under cover of rousting out poor old Colby. But I can't use them for the real hunt, after this precious pair. I can only rely on you folk, who know – who've seen. I can't make you help – but I hope and pray you will.'

'Yes!' barked Jess.

'These Murder Squad boys got guns?' asked Neville.

'Hm? Oh, aye – every officer with firearms training, as of yesterday. And I see what you're getting at. In emergency we can request help from members of the public who – er – just happen to have guns.' He gave Harry a hard look. 'Properly licensed, of course. Or certified, for shotguns.'

Harry looked hurt. ' 'Course they are. 'Cept for me poor old twelve-bore as wouldn't 'it a barn at twenty paces –'

'Because you've been using it to fire musket balls at sleeping pheasants. Off the record, haul it out. Good manstopper at close range. Could finish the pair of them.'

Neville shook his head. 'You're forgetting, they'll have a couple of recruits still. Don't reckon on guns alone. Garlic and crucifixes, more like. Or whatever'd scare draugar. Jess?'

'Don't ask me, ask Hal. Hal? *Where is he?*'

Ridley was already striding towards the door marked with a man's silhouette. He hurled it open with a crash, swore, and let it sink back on its cushioning spring. 'Went through the other door – to the saloon bar. Which just happens to be closed, so he had a clear route out. I bloody *knew* there was something off about –'

A shrill ringing cut him short. For a frozen moment

everyone stared at the payphone on the wall, then Jess dived across the room and caught the receiver out of Ridley's hand. '*Hal?* Hal, where –' Ridley heard the payphone tones, then the crackle of a voice, but he couldn't make out the words. Her hand clenched hard. 'Look, if this is dangerous I have a right to share it. Okay? Or don't I mean enough to you? Goddammit, Hal, you talk about trust –' She stopped, listened, her face twisting with frustration. 'Hal! *Wait!*'

Too late. He saw her face harden as the line went dead. She slammed the receiver back and swung to face him. 'Reckons he's got it all worked out. Has to handle it alone, he says. Okay so it's dangerous but we're all in danger anyhow and we'd only make things worse, so he'll see us tomorrow a.m. . . . And that's all! Just like that!'

'Like 'ell,' said Neville softly.

'Like fuck!' said Harry, not at all softly.

'I can't believe Hal would expect us to do nothing,' said Ridley, 'especially after last night. Not normally. And you feel the same way, Jess.'

'I – don't know. A minute ago, yes – I was so goddam angry – but now . . . That isn't *my* Hal, the one I know, but he's still . . . *Damn*, I don't have the words! It's like he's wearing a mask or – like someone's with him. But he makes me want to believe him!'

'If 'e's changed then we can't trust 'im,' said Neville coldly. 'An' I wouldn't take that from 'im anyway.'

' 'E's right,' said Harry.

'But – but maybe he's got something planned!' stammered Jess. 'An ambush or something! If we just charge in with a posse of cops we could ruin everything!'

'Good point, in its way,' said Ridley quietly, 'but can we afford to trust him blindly, Jess? We need to know more before we make up our minds. Right? He should have told us – *would* have told us, if this was the Hal we know. Just the same, you're right about not charging in, so how's this? We – just the four of us – find him, follow him, watch him till we know what's going down, and only mix in or call for help if anything's wrong or he's in real danger. How's that sound?'

The men nodded at once. Jess hesitated, then nodded an uneasy agreement. 'Okay, you win. But how'll we find him?'

'Ask a policeman,' said Ridley, pulling out his walkie-talkie. 'Control? Ridley. General alert for tall man, red hair and beard, in town area or outskirts, may be trying to move around unobserved – Professor Hansen. Most of you know him by sight. Do not, repeat *not,* approach or obstruct him. Just report time, location, and direction of movement, if any. Got that?'

'*Control,*' said Harshaw's voice. '*Knew there was summat screwy about 'im.*'

'Aye, well, keep it to yourself, Bill. And get WPC Macauley to break out some more emergency gear – parkas, skis, and that. Kit for five, and spares. Be down later to pick 'em up. Ridley out.'

He turned to the others. 'Any of you ever skied?'

'Three seasons in Aspen, and some cross-country in Canada,' said Jess cheerfully. 'Won a couple of races.'

'Ah,' said Ridley. 'Police course and a couple of week-ends at Aviemore, that's my lot. Harry? Neville?'

Harry grimaced. 'Me? Never. Sooner walk.'

'No chance, lad,' said Neville. 'We might need to 'op it fast, and your short fat 'airy legs make lousy snowshoes. I've done a bit. I'll see you right.'

'Right then,' said Ridley. 'I'll lay on a car, supplies – and your snowfan, Harry. That leaves weapons – Harry's twelve-bore –'

'Neville can 'ave me little four-ten, folding. Could find summat for Jess, too –'

'Not me. I hate guns.'

'You've got to have something!'

'There's big heavy mattocks in the dig store, pickaxe one side, spade-blade the other. Reckon one could take somebody's head off, easy.'

'Better than Ridley's ruddy little cap pistol, any'ow!'

'Aye. That's why I'm taking the Greener riot gun.'

'You what?'

'Magazine loading, huge charges, stop a ruddy elephant.

221

Souvenir of somebody's time with the Hong Kong riot squad; it's been lying around our armoury for years.'

'More likely you capitalist lackeys laid it in for t'miner's strike pickets! Well, 'appen t'workers learnt a thing or two then – like makin' petrol bombs, for a start. I 'ear these boogers don't like a nice cosy fire, eh?'

'Harry, I didn't hear a word,' sighed Ridley. 'Just for the love of God don't smoke, that's all.'

The Land Rover flashed its headlamps. For an instant the grimy yellow bulk of the snowfan stood out in the gloom, but it was already slithering to a halt, and Ridley had to pull in sharply behind it. He switched off the engine, and a sudden silence fell. 'Right. We're here.'

'You sure 'bout this?' grunted Neville.

'Two sightings – one patrol, one beat man. Both reckoned he was headed this way. I'm sure enough.'

Nobody seemed in any hurry to move. They sat staring out into the blackness outside, where tall shadow-shapes hissed and tossed in the chill wind – the trees along the outer wall of the Fern Farm estate. An endless moment of taut silence was abruptly broken by a sharp rap at the rear window. Harry wrenched the door open, muttering 'Jesus! Bloody brass monkeys!' and tried to scramble in. Thwarted by the pile of equipment in the back, he flung the door as wide as he could and started to haul it out into the snow. 'C'mon, c'mon, get yer fingers out! We've a job to do.'

It was the spur they needed. Jess, pale and large-eyed, swung herself out of the high front seat while Neville scrambled out of the back, pulling up his parka hood over his usual pork-pie hat and cursing as the inrushing cold air bit at his nose. Ridley was stacking the guns and Jess's mattock ready against the Land Rover's flank. Jess fussed for a moment over Harry's ski-boots, showing him how to clamp them onto the skis; Neville was already testing out his on the new snow near the turn-off to the temple site. She gave him a curiously quirky smile. 'That little spot of skiing – sport, or cross-country?'

222

'Mostly cross-country, love.'

'Where? Scotland?'

'Norway.'

'Ee,' said Harry, 'I didn't know you'd been there, Nev. Good place for a holiday, were it?'

'Might've been. I was freezing me balls off on winter exercises wi' the Territorials.'

'Since when,' said Ridley, 'do they send reservists out to Norway?'

'Well, the Territorial SAS they do.'

Harry whistled. 'Bloody 'ell, Battley, you're a fuckin' close one!'

Ridley, checking his massive gun, chuckled. 'Glad to have you aboard.'

Neville shrugged. 'That was a few years back, mind. Quickest way up's through that copse, I reckon.'

Jess had expected to have to lead the way, but Neville set out with such assurance, shepherding Harry, that she gratefully dropped back beside Ridley. Harry was an unsteady beginner, but his animal reflexes – 'and 'is low-slung arse!' as Neville pointed out – helped him stay on his feet. Ridley had no balance problems, but kept trying to ski as if he were on a sports piste, sailing ahead of the others on downward slopes and having trouble stopping. Only the wind-rush concealed Harry's ungainly clatter and Ridley's entanglements with trees and bushes. When the breeze dropped for a moment there were none of the usual small sounds of a wood, and no animals scuttling through the undergrowth – just the thump of snow falling from over-laden branches, and the faint, eerie music of rippling icicles. The wind bit more harshly as they began to pick up speed, but after a few minutes all of them were hot and sweating in their parkas, and the weapons hung like lead bars on their shoulders. Jess, more out of practice than she had realised, found the muscles behind her knees turning to red-hot wires, and was vastly relieved when Neville turned to signal a halt behind a heavy thicket. 'Reckon that's Temple Covert up there – that line of trees on the rise.'

Ridley, scarlet in the face, could only nod and put his

finger to his lips. Neville nodded back. 'Uhuh. Don't want to scare 'im off –'

'Scare?' grunted Harry, pulling his scarf back up over his raw nose.

'Or . . . alert . . . anyone . . . else,' panted Ridley. 'If he isn't there we work around – reconnoitre . . . if he is . . .'

'Use our ruddy initiative!' said Neville.

'*No!*' Jess flared. 'We wait, and we watch! We agreed, remember? We only show ourselves if he needs help, or . . .'

'Or 'e's not 'imself,' Neville nodded. 'Fair enough. Let's go. Stumm, remember, Harry.' Harry managed not to make a single sound until they crested the rise and came in among the gloomy knot of ash trees that was Temple Covert. Then there was a splintering creak and snap of wood. Neville rounded on him furiously. 'Broken your ruddy ski?'

'It weren't me! It were . . . down there, I reckon.' Everyone swung round, staring down into the gloom ahead, holding their breath to listen. There was another loud creak and crash, and a momentary flicker of orange light leapt up. Without another word they crept slowly forward, hunkering down on their skis among the sparse bushes. They came to the lip of Temple Dell – and froze, staring, as if the snow had run into their bones.

Within the shallow dip the snow had been cleared away from the low foundation walls of the temple, and brushed completely away from the huge altar stone. On this stone a tall man was working furiously, piling up stakes, pieces of wood and dig debris into a massive heap that was already alight. As they watched, he uprooted the landscaping company's signboard, broke the thick post over his knee and threw it onto the flames. Sap popped and sputtered in the raw timber. 'What's –' began Neville, but Jess clamped a hand over his mouth. The man turned, and in the firelight she saw clearly that it was Hal – or his double. He was pulling off his parka . . .

Now they had stopped moving the wind was whipping through their sweat-soaked clothes, and for the first time

224

Jess became aware of the ice caked in her eyebrows and in the hair that her skiing hat left unprotected. Neville's moustache was pure white. Yet Hal was calmly stripping to the waist. ' 'E'll catch 'is bloody death!' whispered Neville. 'That fire won't 'elp – I could use it right now, dressed an' all!'

'Maybe we should bring him in, Jess,' said Ridley in her ear. 'He does look, well, disturbed . . .'

'*No!*' she hissed. There was a moment's silence. Below them the fire crackled, damp wood sizzling and remnants of snow hissing away into steam. Then, far away in the wood, almost at the edge of hearing, came new sounds, as if something were awakening and stirring. They had heard no birds, but there was a sudden loud flutter of wings, a patter of falling snow, and a harsh caw from high above.

Ridley shrugged nervously. 'Okay. It's your show.'

Jess grabbed his arm. 'Look! What's he doing now?' Again the red-bearded man climbed onto the altarstone, paced slowly round the fire, and stopped facing the apex of the stone, the north end of the ancient temple. He spread his arms wide – and shouted. The wind was rising, rushing among the trees, but his voice, deep and resonant, seemed to ride it.

'Sounds like German or summat,' muttered Neville.

'Danish, maybe,' said Ridley. 'Must be raving.'

'Can it!' Jess pushed her woollen hat back off her ears. '*Morth-vig* – that's Old Norse he's shouting!'

Neville gaped. 'Old Norse? Viking? You understand 'im?'

'Not my subject – but I might if you shut your goddam mouth!' Neville touched his forelock, bowed, and shook his head at Ridley. 'Something about law – a murder – Jesus! He's calling a door court!'

'A what?' choked Ridley.

'Trying to remember – his lectures. A sort of Icelandic trial – no, like sticking a person with a subpoena, a summons. He keeps saying it over – calling someone . . .' Her voice died. They had all heard the name, howled aloud in a voice that rang with defiance and contempt, flung in the face of the bitter wind, the icy, deadened rows of trees, the sullen banks of snow. *'Hrafn! Hrafn Rimkonung!'* Raven, Raven the Ice King.

'Ek skora ther, Hrafn Rimkonung, til holmgongu!'

Jess was almost out of the bushes before Ridley could pull her back. She grabbed at his parka front with tearing strength. 'We can't let him! He can't – he wouldn't have a chance – not in a *holmgang* –'

'What the hell's that?'

'I've 'eard of it,' muttered Neville. 'Call it an Irish lawsuit – no 'olds barred. Trial by fuckin' combat.'

Ridley stared down aghast at the figure below, small against the rising fire. 'We'd better get him in. Like enough he's gone a bit gaga and nothing'll come of it –'

'Summat already 'as,' growled Harry. 'That bloody wind's gone and dropped. Just like that!' The air, suddenly stilled, was growing chill and clammy. In the silence, very faintly, Jess heard a soft, distant ring, a church clock striking an uncertain hour. The darkness seemed to grow heavier, to flow up and around the hill like a black wave. It gathered around the little circle of dancing orange light as if to overwhelm it utterly, but the man stood motionless, arms folded, looking down across the clearing into the northern slopes of the wood. Following his gaze, Jess saw the faintest flicker of pale light appear and grow, swirling like liquid moonlight. Harry swore softly. 'That's all we needed. Friggin' mist!'

'Not just mist,' said Ridley, and there was a deep shiver in his voice. 'Look . . .'

Not just mist. The trees stood out against it like a ghost of the fallen temple, shadow pillars supporting walls of vapour and a roof of darkness. And out of its billows, like swimmers striding from a creamy sea, dark shapes were rising, heads and shoulders lifting above the mist. It rolled past the barrier of trees and poured down in a silent waterfall to pool in the snowbound clearing. As it reached the altar fire the heat twisted it into fantastic rising spirals that bobbed and swayed in a grotesque parody of worship. Behind it, without the slightest sound, the solid shadows gathered, and the man faced them and did not move. The

226

watchers on the slope above could only stare. Jess, shaking violently herself, felt the tremor in Ridley's shoulder and heard the faint rattle of Neville's teeth. Only Harry seemed unaffected, the ghost of a grin lingering on his lips. He rose slowly to his feet, turned awkwardly on his skis, and suddenly he was away down the slope and into the trees to one side. Neville stared. 'What – you daft pillock! Come back!' But he did not dare shout.

'You blame him?' hissed Jess. They'd expected to meet two, or three, or four adversaries. But there had to be at least a hundred shapes spilling into the clearing below.

Not all of them were the same. Some seemed almost normal in outline, men and a few women, draped in ragged shreds of cloth. Others were monstrous, shapeless hulks that stumbled forward careless of obstacles in their path, or wiry skeletal figures that slipped between the trees like shadows. Most were naked, and the pale light glittered on their darkened skins and long, matted hair. Here and there it found tarnished metal, the encrusted remains of ornaments or weaponry, the glinting shreds of a mailshirt. But on the figures at their head the hot firelight awoke an answer, the fresh, cold gleam of copper, bronze and gold against the rags of the man, the nakedness of the woman. Serpent rings snaked up her darkened arms, twisted torcs clashed faintly under her shaggy mane of hair, glass beads shone at her neck, between her small, black-tipped breasts and around her waist, dipping over her belly to meet black curls. Rings and hoops shone on his swollen, black-nailed fingers, hung in tight chains from his massive arms, gleamed below the hidden ears. A jewelled belt clasped shreds of stiff leather about his waist. A thick-linked silvery chain looped around his neck under the thin beard, and from it hung a tarnished metal spearhead shape. His head was circled with a massive fillet of twisted gold which seemed not to weigh him down. Together, the two figures raised their arms, and the ring and crash of metal came echoing up to the watchers on the hill. They stood like ornamented effigies of a pagan king and queen – and behind them, silently, the draugar formed into a loose half-circle outside the firelight, heads bowed from their great height, gazing in and down at the figure they dwarfed, the man who stood, unmoving, as if he guarded some unseen bridge they still had to pass.

Jess had imagined herself running down the hill to join him at the first sign of an answer to his challenge. Now, her guts hollow and cold with terror, she found herself helpless, frozen with fear, struggling not to whimper aloud. Rising from below, far stronger than the feartang in her cold sweat, came the same stench she remembered from the trailer, but far stronger; beside her she heard Neville choke and a rasp as Ridley wiped a half-frozen glove across his mouth. She saw, and understood, the rim of white in his eyes. In that silent ring of undead shadows they were seeing themselves. They had all met and fought a single one of these creatures, and barely escaped joining them. Against such numbers, what chance did they have?

Ridley stirred himself with an almost visible effort and wrenched out his radio. 'Control? Ridley! Emergency, Fern Farm – temple site! Armed patrols – all patrols, every man, and fucking step on it!'

The radio crackled. 'Chief, t'nearest's out at Habthorpe's – five miles up –'

'Just get 'em here!' Ridley stuffed the walkie-talkie back into his pocket and swung the heavy riot gun off his back.

'Where'd this shower come from, anyway?' muttered Neville. 'They can't 'ave killed that many round 'ere . . .'

'No,' whispered Jess, 'but look at the armour on that one. From the King's time – maybe a follower who died with him. He's called up his thralls.'

'Maybe 'e's more powerful now 'is winter's taken 'old. Anyhow, 'e's scuppered us good and proper. Can't fight that crew, not just the three of us – well, four countin' Hal –'

Hal's powerful voice interrupted him. Again the ancient words of accusation and challenge rang among the trees, mocking the uncanny silence of the dark ranks before him, but this time the echoes died away at once, as if the mist and the power of the Ice King's winter had stifled them. For an endless moment the two antagonists stood watching

228

each other without a word or a gesture – yet the air seemed to prickle with tension, the red anger of the fire blazing against the chill, indifferent malice of the night. Then, abruptly, Hal flung his arms wide in a sweeping gesture. The King echoed it with ironic slowness. The Queen stepped back out of the firelight, and behind her the rows of draugar spread out along the ruined walls to form a wide ring round the altarstone. Ignoring them, Hal stepped lightly back to one end. Equally lightly, the King sprang up onto the other – but a thick billet of wood from the fire snapped and splintered unnoticed under his massive foot.

Neville gave a cracked chuckle. 'In the blue corner . . .'

Slowly, the King raised his arms and dropped into a wrestler's crouch, muscles hardening like dark serpents under his gleaming skin. Hal copied him, looking dwarfed, absurd. Fire struck flame in the tangles of his hair, and played runnels of molten gold over his bare flesh – but beyond his reach the orange flames were blocked by the living darkness that opposed him. An immense, bloated shadow reached back towards the watchers on the hill, bridging the circle of light, opening a way for the limitless night beyond. Suddenly the massive arm swept out in a contemptuous back-handed stroke – and was met, with a jolting shock.

'Bloody 'ell!' gasped Neville. 'He's holding 'im!' For a moment light and dark merged in a thrashing tangle of limbs – and then Hal was forced up, back, in the crushing hug of the King's left arm. Hal's knee strained against his enemy's ribs, hands clawing to keep the huge black-nailed hands from his throat. Together they toppled backwards, with Hal beneath, crashing to the altarstone inches from the edge of the fire. The King's hand whipped back and bunched into a boulder-like fist. With a tearing, terrible shriek Jess was on her feet, mattock in hand, sailing out over the crest of the slope and downward in a sweeping schuss.

In the shadows below, dark heads snapped around – and the Ice King's blow smashed into the bare stone beside Hal's head. Ridley shouted, but Neville was already speeding after her, shotgun in hand, swerving to cut between Jess and the shadows beneath. The draugar, the Queen at their head, were spilling out of the ruins, bounding through the snow with terrible energy to bar her way to the temple. Ridley's cheeks flared. He scrambled clumsily to the very edge of the slope, hefted the riot gun, and worked the lever.

Thanks to Jess, there was a way clear to the altar; he could see the massive form of the King lurch forward, threshing violently to avoid the fire, as Hal rolled free. Ridley took a deep breath and jabbed his sticks downward. He wobbled violently, then all at once he was flying along and gaining speed. Below him he saw Neville crouch on his skis and swing around in a great hissing shower of snow, right in the face of the nearest figure. The cold silence rang with a double explosion and the draug folded in the middle like a cardboard doll and flopped limply into the snow. Ridley yelled out his relief. Cartridges fell smoking into the snow as Neville flicked the gun open, but the dark wave was already turning and bearing down on him, and he had to swing away without reloading. A few stuck on Jess's heels. She swung her mattock, sent one sprawling, but almost lost her balance as two more leapt into her path. Without a thought for range, Ridley jerked up his gun and fired. The kick almost knocked him off his skis – Jess flinched as the heavy charge went past her ear – but the first thing's head exploded from its shoulders and the second fell in a heap and lay writhing horribly. Jess sailed free. Neville's gun banged again; Ridley saw him speeding clear of a ghastly loping figure with its side half blasted away, and then there was no time to see anything. He was swaying and ducking, fighting to slow down, to see with the wind in his eyes, to hang onto his gun and his sticks, simply to stay on his feet because at this speed God alone knew what a fall might do. He went whipping right past the altar, and saw it as no more than a glowing blur with a shadow at its heart. But he heard a shout, Hal's voice, a desperate yell of rage. *'No! Get away! Stay out! I told you! God damn you, all of you, i fandens navn you'll kill us all . . .'*

230

Then his raving was drowned in a sudden, terrible dragon-roar, a sound that shook the clearing, a dazzling, searing blaze of light. A shining shape arced through the air on a comet's trail and burst spattering among the draugar. Red flames danced and sizzled on the snow, and they fell back, scattering. The roar swelled to a climax, and with a terrible crunch of gears the snowfan rose bucking and lurching into the clearing.

In the stark sweep of its headlights the draugar stood revealed, like dark cave creatures frozen for a moment in a flashlight beam – horrible human things swollen to stiffness like overripe fruit or shrivelled to an awful leathery lean-ness, dark, discoloured, ghastly but shadow-quick. Harry swung half out of the cab, lighting another petrol bomb from the cigarette jammed in his teeth, but even as he threw it they scattered and regrouped, and it only spattered the stragglers.

Ridley, slowed at last by the slope above the temple, made a clumsy, skidding turn that brought him around behind the altarstone. He struggled to a halt, braced his legs apart and lifted up the gun, squinting down the sights at the locked, swaying figures of the fighters, firelit human flesh and black, gleaming hide. No chance yet of a clear shot – but a chance was all he needed. At the edge of vision he saw the tractor moving towards Jess and Neville, but the draugar were already sweeping across its path, charging straight towards it. There was something odd about it . . . It slowed, the fan began to spin, and – where was the safety-guard?

'Jesus Christ!' yelled Ridley.

As the bare steel blades of the fan met the first of the nightwalkers they simply seemed to vanish. There was a mincing, grinding sound, the fan slowed and the snow spraying out to the side turned slushy black. The tractor was through before the draugar could react, but it could not move fast with power going to the fan, and almost at once they wheeled to attack the lumbering excavator from the back and sides. Harry, trying to fend them off, veered it violently from side to side, and its powerful headlights swept blindingly across the altar. The King, startled,

231

reared up and broke free of Hal. Ridley held his breath and fired.

At such close range the charge hardly spread. It took the King in his right side, shattering his outflung arm – and Hal yelled with fury and despair. The King seemed to topple sideways, towards the fire – and then Ridley realised he was just reaching down, coming up with a burning fence-post in his hand. Something whirled momentarily before his eyes, and the night exploded into sparks of agony.

Jess saw Ridley fall as she scrambled onto the tractor. 'He's got him!'

'C'mon, lad!' shouted Neville, perching himself on the back with one leg hooked over the bucket arm. 'Shift yer arse!'

'I'm bloody tryin'!' bellowed Harry. By now the draugar were avoiding the fan, closing in from each side to grab at the tractor's two passengers. As Harry speeded up to avoid them he had to take the fan out of gear, and they closed in once again. 'Too many of 'em – if we can pick oop t'Prof and Ridley and fook off out of it we'll be bloody lucky!'

'We've got to get through,' Jess shouted. 'Look!'

Instead of meeting the King's great blows, Hal was dodging them, trying frantically to stay out of his opponent's reach. A backhand swipe grazed his arm – no more – and he was flung clear across one edge of the fire. The King closed in – then flinched back as Hal swept a shower of burning debris up into his face. Then he was dodging again, with the energy of desperation. Harry changed gear, and the tractor roared forward. One huge figure clutched at the slowing blade, slipped and vanished under the wheels, almost capsizing the tractor. Then Neville fired, swore and struggled to reload as a tall and terrible figure came striding out of the night. In two great bounds the Queen had drawn level with them and with a third she grabbed the trailing edge of the bucket arm. As she hung there the tractor bucked, heaved, and slowed to a crawl, its front wheels barely touching the ground. Harry jerked the wheel violently, trying to throw her clear, and

232

Neville's cartridges flew out of his hand. He yelled to Jess and jumped clear just as the Queen swung herself onto the back of the tractor. Then its racing front wheels struck the ground, and it leaped foward at full tilt. For an instant Jess met the pale eyes gleaming under the tangled hair – and with a scream she, too, sprang away and fell sprawling. She could see precisely where the tractor was headed, and what would happen, but she was winded, helpless, powerless to warn Harry of the black-clawed hand already reaching into the cab. Then, with a shattering crash and a screech of metal, the whole front of the snowfan went smashing into one leg of the power pylon. The tractor reared up and rebounded, the fan dissolved into a shower of twisted metal, and the pylon moaned and tilted slowly over at an impossible drunken angle. The impact flung the Queen from her narrow perch; she spun through the air, landed with a shattering crash and lay still.

Jess could see Harry staring back over his shoulder, his bloodstreaked face distorted with animal hatred as he pulled the coughing tractor clear of the pylon. Then the exhaust billowed smoke, the engine roared, and the whole machine reared up on its back props as the bucket swung out and down and bit into the snowbound soil. A massive scoop of earth and stone lifted skyward and went cascading down onto the Queen, burying her in a rain of debris – the bucket scooped again, and then went hammering down again and again, till the earth was flattened and still. The props retracted, and slowly, deliberately, the half-ruined machine went lurching backwards over the spot.

Harry waved wildly at Neville and Jess, making a Churchillian victory sign with his cigarette stub and gesturing out into the darkness. Silhouettes were moving swiftly between them and the altar fire, the scattered army of the undead massing to meet them.

' 'Elp me up, for Chrissakes,' gasped Neville, but Jess heard only the voice behind her – a low unsteady moan that grew inhumanly loud and high in an instant. They both swung round – and then Jess flung Neville backwards and threw herself down half on top of him as the buckled pylon leg gave up its struggle and the whole structure

233

toppled sideways. There was a lunatic screech of tearing steel and bursting struts. Its cables brushed the treetops into a rain of sparks and flame, then the whole mass of steel went crashing and jangling down onto the hardened ground, bounced, crumpled and lay still. In its wake came the cables, leaping and snaking, right across the little clearing, across the crippled tractor, and onto the heads of the draugar.

The bounding wires whipped the leaders aside in a rain of blazing sparks to lie charred and smoking in the snow. Others tried to leap free from webs of cable and fell in sparking ruin, tumbling their neighbours to destruction. Explosive crackles and hisses lit the whole clearing with flashes of stark blue flame. One huge figure bridged two cables and jerked upright in a ghastly aura – a spark leapt to his neighbour, and to another, and all three tumbled smouldering among the whitened scrub. Another touched one of the pylon's ruined insulators and was flung halfway across the clearing in a trail of fire. The mists vanished in wafts of stinking smoke, hiding the dangers of the wires; Jess retched at the stench of burning, rotten meat.

Neville saw the King rear upright on the altar, above the smoke, seeming to glance towards him. Then, as if following the glance, a shadow advanced through the smoke, picking its way across the wire as if some vestige of understanding remained. With a curse Neville wriggled forward to where his gun lay in the snow, scrabbling to find some undamaged cartridges. He rammed two into the breech and levelled the gun at the figure, now hardly ten feet away.

'Nev?'

He knew the voice even before he looked into the grey, ruined face, into the staring eyes of Tom Latimer.

'Gotta help me, Nev – can't help myself, not yet. See, we can beat this! I can tell you things! For – for the love of God –'

A hand closed over Neville's and squeezed his fingers closed. The gun exploded, and the body before him doubled up and went spinning back onto the wires. Sparks leapt from the fingers, the hair blazed, smoke erupted

234

from the nostrils and mouth, open in a last futile appeal, and the body was lost in flame.

'The legends said never to listen to them,' said Jess flatly.

'But it sounded like 'im – wanting help –'

'It sounded like Jay, too – *hey!*'

They both stared. From the tractor, right at the heart of the ensnaring wires, came a cheery shout.

'Harry!' bellowed Neville. 'You daft bugger, I thought you'd got yourself fried!'

'Me too, wi' this draped all over me – but they're always digging up power cables wi' these things, so they insulate t'cab!'

'Oh, Harry, Jesus, you moron!' shouted Jess tearfully. 'Hang on, we'll come get you out –'

'*No!*' roared Harry. 'Do that an' you'll ground me, an' we'll both go off like bleedin' Christmas trees! Get around this mess, rescue the prof, then phone Electricity to shut off t'juice! Christ knows why t'circuit breakers 'aven't gone already!'

'Will do!' said Neville with a grin. 'Don't go away!'

Harry replied with a spectacular gesture, then slumped back in the driving seat. This was one place those things couldn't get him. Tall shadows came and went in the smoke, as if searching. But just let them try and come any closer! Grinning, he fumbled for his cigarettes, then remembered the petrol. If any of that had got spilt in the crash – Bad enough, with all these sparks about. He looked around nervously – and stopped, staring wide-eyed at the scarred bare earth behind the tractor. It was rippling, swelling . . .

And suddenly, with the leaden slowness of a dream, he saw it bulge upward and burst around the Queen's bare torso as her arms flailed the earth aside. She sprang up at the tractor, her matted hair flying, her streaked breasts swinging, and a pale light gleaming on her lean dark limbs and flanks. For a moment, cowering back, he hung between lust and terror, as if a dark fantasy had sprung to devouring life – then the ruined cab door ripped open and he saw the hair spill back from her wide dark eyes, smelt an earthy, musky reek of decay, saw the slender, black-nailed fingers reaching out like a caress for his outflung hand –

The others heard the scream, and whirling, saw for a frozen moment the reaching and recoiling hands, dark against light – and the searing streak of blue that sprang between them. The tractor vanished in a cloud of flame. An instant later the night erupted in a brilliant flash and a blast that left them staggering, dazzled, and half concussed, ears ringing. A rain of debris pattered across the clearing, the dangling cables creaked and swung in the blast.

Then, with a terrible snapping creak, they ripped free from the next pylon at the summit of the slope, and fell looping downward. A huge pine tree burst into flames as they struck it, raining down torchlike branches that popped with exploding sap and raised answering fires in the dry underbrush. Huge sparks went slamming across the clearing as if an immense hammer was beating down on it. In the heart of the clearing the mass of draugar wheeled and plunged, mindless, as if a commanding will had fallen away, and went down in blazing, exploding ruin amid the entangling wires.

By the time the living could see, there was only a scorched circle with the collapsed, blackened hulk of the tractor at its heart, flames still licking around it.

'Oh my God,' stammered Neville through bloodless lips. 'Oh sweet Jesus. That fuckin' *p-petrol* . . .'

'Nev! Over there!' Jess grabbed his arm, pointed towards the altar. The King had sprung up, as startled by the blast as they had been. The smoke cleared. At his feet lay Hal, one arm dangling over the edge of the altar stone. Then came a crack, louder than a gunshot, and from the heart of the fire a wide crack opened and the whole stone split in two beneath the King's feet. He staggered – and Hal rolled clear.

With a bellow of pure hatred Neville charged forward, raising the shotgun, and Jess overtook him, brandishing a flaming branch. The massive form stooped towards the fire – then froze, at another shout. Beyond the fire Ridley struggled to his knees, working the action of his riot gun.

The King stood for an instant, glanced quickly around at the ruined battlefield. Then he sprang lightly off the altarstone and went loping away uphill into the darkness.

The pop of Neville's last cartridge mingled with the deeper roar of the riot gun; Ridley peered, fired again, cursed, and hobbled across to the altarstone to join the others. Jess was draped over Hal, hiding him, weeping uncontrollably.

'Hal – Hal, honey – sweet God, oh Hal, we're here, it's okay, please be all right, please, we made it, we saved you –'

'*Saved me?*'

There was a lashing anger in his voice none of them had heard before. Jess recoiled, eyes wide, as he struggled to sit up, towering over them all on the shattered altarstone. 'You – you damned fools! You interfering – sons – of – *bitches*! Can you do nothing you are told? *You have destroyed us!*'

He looked beyond them to the ruins of the tractor, and almost choked on his wrath. '*That* – It never had to happen! *You* did that! God damn you all!'

'I don't have to take any of that crap from you!' barked Neville. 'Harry knew what 'e was risking, same as us – and as for sitting tight, we might'ave done if you'd told us why! Instead of making out you were ruddy God Almighty or something. I reckon we've done all right, and Harry most of all!'

'Hal, please, he's right!' pleaded Jess. 'The draugar are gone, they're burned up –'

Hal looked up, and his face worked with fury. 'Gone? Oh yes, gone. *And what's to stop him bringing them back?*'

He stood up, flexed his arms, clenched his fists – and suddenly huddled forward on his knees, shivering. 'I had the power,' he whispered. 'I could feel it – the strength . . . I challenged him to *holmgang*, I was supposed to defeat him, and then they would all have faded away, even the Queen, she had not enough strength in her. He was the only one strong enough – it was him who brought them all back. And when you interfered, when you broke into the fair fight – then it went . . . I could feel it slipping away, and then there was only me . . . He caught me, flattened me, he would have killed me – if the Queen had not been threatened. He left me, used his strength to pull her back . . . He can do it again. But we can't, can we? Not for Harry. And he's gone free . . . to heal himself, gather his *einherjar* and . . . and begin all over again. Damn you! Damn you all! *To Hel and darkness!*'

CHAPTER ELEVEN

RIDLEY SNATCHED his radio out of his pocket. 'Control? Yes, I'm okay. Any patrols getting through? Okay, search of area around Fern Farm, general alert for escaping suspect – huge bastard, long dark hair, dressed in rags, visible arm injury. Bloody dangerous – don't approach, shoot on sight!' The radio crackled violently. 'You heard!' said Ridley darkly. 'Shoot. Or run him down. He's our killer – just him. He's more than a match for two men. Harry Hardwicke's dead.'

'Christ! Poor bugger. I'll warn the lads –'

'Make it stick. Patrol nearest the Fern Farm approach road to come pick up Professor Hansen at my car and see he gets to hospital. He's been badly roughed up. We're off on chummy's tracks. Ridley out.'

'I'm all right,' grunted Hal.

'No, you're not,' said Neville firmly. 'You're a bloody mess. What was all this about 'aving power, then? Power from where? What's got into you?'

Hal laughed weakly, clutching at his bruised ribs. 'I wish I knew. I thought I did, once, clearly. But it all seems so far away now . . .' He sighed. 'Something happened, that night. But maybe I was just . . . interpreting it . . . in my own terms. You could say I got some help. From the same place the Ice King got his . . . or not quite. But when the law was broken it was taken away.' He stood up suddenly, staring out over the lifeless emptiness of the clearing, its sterile snow melted and trampled to a brown slush. It steamed gently around the ruined tractor, the tangles of cable and the shapeless charred lumps that lay beneath them. 'Or was it? That pylon falling – like lightning – could a few cables really do that much? *Ha, det var noget!* Maybe he still wanted to make the odds a little fairer –'

239

'Don't know what you're bloody on about,' snorted Neville. 'Knock on the 'ead, I guess – better stay with 'im, Jess.'

She nodded, smiled weakly. Ridley had brought spare skis down from the top of the slope. Neville slipped on a pair and left the others for Jess and Hal to get down to the car. 'Switch on the radio there an' we'll keep you posted, right?'

'Sure,' sighed Jess. 'Play it careful, huh?'

'You know him,' said Ridley. 'Scared of his own shadow. He'll be careful.' They stomped up the slope, casting wary glances around them as they moved between the lines of trees. Jess retrieved Hal's abandoned clothes from a wall and helped him into them. 'Your undershirt's gonna stick to all those grazed bits – still, better'n letting you freeze.'

Hal grunted painful agreement. '*Satans*, I should have gone with them. This is *my* job –'

'Not any more it isn't,' said Jess, firmly. 'And I don't know what the hell you're talking about, either.'

Hal smiled. 'It could be that I shall tell someone, some day. You, perhaps.'

'Great,' said Jess crisply, tucking him into his parka. 'So I guess I'd better stick around.'

'It would help – *Satans*, woman, I can manage myself!' He fumbled at the zipper with torn fingers.

Jess looked at him sardonically. 'Gee, nice to know you're appreciated. C'mon, we better get back to the car, that fire of yours is getting low an' there's a wind comin' up.'

'Just a breeze. And not so cold. See? The clouds are beginning to break!' He grinned down at Jess, just a little more cheerfully. 'As you say, it is nice to know you are – appreciated. May I invite you to come walk in the moonlight, *kaereste*?'

'La, sir,' she said, curtsied clumsily, and sat down in the snow. 'Ah, crap –' Then she simply sat there, staring. Hal bent over stiffly to help her up, but she gestured impatiently, pointing past him. The torn clouds were sending scattered shadows racing across the bare white slope opposite, but among them, almost as fast, moved

240

something else – heading down towards the road that led back to Saitheby.

'He has doubled back!' hissed Hal. 'And look at the speed of him. Before they find him he will already be at Saitheby –'

'The car – the radio!'

'Too far. There is no time!' Hal seemed to straighten in his parka. 'We must follow him!'

'Hal, you're in no condition – and what'd we do if we caught him? We don't have any goddam guns!'

'I said we should follow, not attack. We could warn the town, at the least.' He was already stepping into his ski-clamps, wincing with pain. Jess followed suit, still protesting.

'Hal, that's dumb! I could get there faster –'

'Do not be so sure. Besides, *kaereste*, this thing is not finished yet.'

'Christ, are you going macho on me again?'

He laughed strangely. 'This is not revenge. I do not have to prove myself. But I gave a challenge, you must understand. You are coming?' He did not wait for a reply. By the time Jess was on her feet he was already skiing downhill, looking perfectly steady. Slithering desperately after him, Jess reminded herself that half of Denmark seemed to be born on skis. And at least the chase was lifting his spirits. The wind blew the hair back from his face, making it even more hawklike than ever; he gestured suddenly, and there was a hard, predatory glitter in his eyes she had never seen before. 'You see? There he goes, down across the fields – down to Saitheby. If we cut across to the road we shall have a clear run down the hill – no fences. We shall beat him there!'

Along the distant coast road car lights were moving, very slowly – police patrol, probably. At least the others would have some help. They reached the road, clambered awkwardly over a wall buried in snowdrifts, and went skidding and swooping down the sides of the steep road into town, alongside the deep cut left by the snowfan. Jess thought of Harry, and the same anger grew that had driven her to battle in the clearing. There must be no more

241

deaths. The bleak countryside flashed past her almost unnoticed; she kept her eyes on the tall figure just in front of her, alert for the least sign of weakness or wavering. Her own legs were aching, but she knew she could go on. And if it came to a fight, she had her own score to settle.

Hal was gesturing to slow down, skidding to a halt by the wall. 'I have lost him! There is the crossroads ahead – if he is heading into town he should take the left fork downhill, but I see nothing. *Fanden tag den!* If he has doubled back again . . .'

Jess looked wildly round, imagining a monstrous shadow slipping along the other side of the snow-capped hedge-rows. Then, far ahead, she saw a moving fleck in the instant before it vanished over the curve of the hill.

'He's there, dammit! The bastard's taken the back road, down by the cliff.'

'Good – then we have a clear run down to the estuary! Come on!'

'Okay, Hal, but be careful – this snow's too damn soft to go speeding on!'

'Yes. Interesting . . .'

And again they were sailing downhill with the wind biting at their uncovered faces, but now the flanking walls were becoming higher and more solid. A building flashed by, then another, the snow-choked forecourt of a garage with its pump lights turned off. The lightless windows frowned blankly down on the two skiers as they went bouncing and scraping by. *I should be shouting something,* thought Jess. *Like Paul Revere. Not 'The British are coming!' though! One light if by land, two if by –*

'Hal!'

The figure ahead of her swept sharply around and braked. 'What is it?'

'The bastard headed down to the estuary – you reckon he's after a boat?'

Hal pounded one fist into the other. They paused a second, peering through the dim orange street-lighting down to the harbour below. A dark thicket of masts stood out against the dim glow of moonlight on the water. Faint

242

sounds came drifting up on the breeze, the lap of choppy water, the soft, regular creak and scrape of fenders as it gently lifted the moored boats.

'Sounds quiet enough,' muttered Hal. Suddenly Jess pointed, wordless. One of the traceried masts was moving, rocking – and then it was blotted out by a shapeless, flapping shadow. Louder creaks and scrapes cut across the silence of the snow, and a rustling, booming sound. 'Jesus – *he's hoisting the sail!* There he goes!'

With a sudden surge, as if a massive hand pushed at it, the low mast was detaching itself from the rest, gliding out into the centre of the harbour. The wind caught it, and it bellied out with a crisp thrum.

'Come on!' snarled Hal, and plunged crazily down the last of the slope. Jess dug in her sticks and followed more cautiously, terrified of losing control and going straight into the water. But the snow had half-cleared from the square below, and Hal found himself bouncing and scraping to a stop on the bare cobblestones. Out in the harbour, less than a hundred yards away, the boat was only just wallowing its way out to the breakwater.

'He's – one lousy sailor – isn't he?' panted Jess. Hal peered out across the dark water. The boat showed as a dim outline, with a high, sharp prow and a steep stern transom, the stubby mast rising just in front of a small wheelhouse.

'*Satans!* He has taken a fishing smack! The sail is too small – it is just for steadying. No need to keep quiet now, damn him – another minute and he will start the engine.'

'Think he knows what an engine is?'

Hal turned to stare at her. '*Du – kaereste – barn!* I could kiss you!'

'So why not?'

'No time! Come on!' He had already snapped off his skis, and now he was slithering along the dockside, towards the jetties. Jess followed, trying not to run too close to the unprotected edge of the dock; even now, near high tide, there was a twenty-foot drop into cold, muddy water. Ahead of them the dig signboard loomed over the locked gate of the dig's own jetty. Hal pounded on the watchman's booth, but it was dark and empty. 'Kept away by the snow, I think. Let us hope I still have my keys . . .'

He had, for the jetty gate and the boathouse beyond. Ignoring the dig tender, he clambered stiffly down into the newer of the two dories and peered at its fuel gauge. '*Ah skidt!* Barely enough! And there is none in the big tank here – damned snow must have stopped deliveries. Well, we shall fill up from the tank on the dam if we must. Come on, *kaereste*, all aboard!'

Jess, standing shakily in the bows, unlocked and opened the seaward door of the boathouse, then sat quickly down as Hal gunned the dory's powerful diesel and sent it bouncing out into the harbour. Crouched down, she started to make her way back to him, but he waved her back. 'We are too lightly laden! You must sit in the bows – weigh them down a little! And put this on!'

He threw her a buoyancy jacket from the stern locker, and shrugged into one himself. The dory's flattened plastic hull hissed and bounced over the harbour wavelets, and the drone of its engine reverberated between the snowbound cliffs. In the houses near the harbour a window lit up here and there, sparks of warmth in the lifeless night. Jess felt ridiculously grateful. Looking at the rising ranks of steeply raked cottage roofs, at the stately Victorian piles that looked absurd against the natural majesty of the cliffs behind them, she thought of what this little place had so narrowly been spared – of what it might still face. If that wave of mist, those incarnate nightmares, had finally come stalking down these steep and silent streets in all their force, they would have had other noises to disturb their sleep.

The little boat passed the harbour wall and bounded out into the estuary, leaping across the choppy wavelets. The water drummed under its blunt, square-cut bows and flew up in sudden spray-plumes that drenched Jess. It made hollow, soggy slaps at the hull, and strange gurgles that her imagination turned into fountaining leaks. The combined fumes of fuel and exhaust began to play on her nerves. 'Shouldn't we have taken the tender?' she yelled. 'It's bigger –'

244

'Too slow!' he yelled back. 'Take us ages to catch him up!'

'You said we were just going to follow him!'

'We had no weapons then!' With a piratical grin, he held up something that looked like a short brass tube, and a fistful of smaller plastic ones.

'What the hell's that?'

'It launches distress flares. Just press the button at the bottom of the tube, and *pang!* Any sign of him?'

Jess crawled forward to hang out over the bouncing bows, and stared out into the night. She slumped back, shaking her head.

'*Fanden i helved!* Even with the motor, he could not have escaped so quickly! Has he capsized the boat, perhaps? We need to find out – and our damned fuel is low, too.' He pulled the boat hard to port, where the dam bulked black against the tag-end of the night. Reaching down into the steering pulpit he pulled up a small spotlight and clipped it to the rail. A section of jetty sprang into glistening life ahead, and as they came nearer he swept the beam up and down it. Rows of shining black fenders bobbed in the waves; there was no other boat in sight. 'Not here, at least!' he shouted. 'We can climb the seawall and look from there.'

'What if he tries to land here after us?'

Hal brought the dory into the lee of the jetty. 'We will see him coming long before. Can you make us fast?'

Jess nodded, and swung the line with practised move-ments. 'We'd better get up top PDQ. Could be he's turnin' back along the coast.'

The dam was an uncanny, dangerous place. Snow had gathered along the walkways, in some places frozen to a solid crust by the relentless wind, and black ice coated many of the metal stairways. They had to inch along with a firm grip on the rails, and once Hal slipped and almost toppled into the snow-filled excavation below. The pocket torch from the boat was almost useless, and every boom and flap from the tarpaulins made them jump. Jess, re-minded of dark sails, kept looking back at the jetty, but the sea around was empty. They reached the base of the seawall, and began to climb very carefully up the frozen steps.

'*Kaereste*, you should go first, that way I will catch you if you fall.'

'You kidding? I weigh a hundred and fifty pounds!'

'*Det var som fanden!*'

'Huh?'

'Never mind. Last stair –' Hal grabbed the stanchion and swung himself up, panting. Normally the climb barely quickened his breath, but now he felt drained. Jess joined him, putting an arm around his shoulders, and together they moved to the seawall and looked down. Below them, empty, half heeled over on the sandbank and bobbing gently in the eddy from the dam, lay the stolen fishing smack.

'*Satans!* He cast it adrift! He landed, and he let it drift!'

'He couldn't have! He couldn't have reached the far shore, not in that time –'

'No.' Hal's voice was strangely calm. 'He landed here before we did. He has been here all the time.'

Jess made a dive for the stairway, heedless of the slippery footing, but suddenly Hal thrust out an arm to bar her way. He stood an instant, staring down into the dark well below them. Then she heard it, too; the faint tortured creak of a stair under an immense weight, laid down with infinite care. She turned to Hal, saw him draw the flare-launcher from his pocket. He motioned her back, and unwillingly she retreated. For a moment she heard only his breathing as he strove to catch some movement among the shadows below. He held the launcher in both hands, at arm's length, his thumb resting on the button. Then there was a sudden scrabble from below, and his hand stiffened. With an explosive pop and hiss, a tongue of yellow fire licked down into the dark. Light exploded up through the trapdoor and Hal swung away, throwing up an arm to shield his eyes and staggering back into Jess. In the same instant a stanchion creaked and the platform timbers leapt under a reverberating crash. Silhouetted against the eerie glare of the dying flare, the Ice King stood before them.

246

He was an appalling vision. No semblance of majesty clung to him now; he was nothing more than monstrous, a lumbering nightmare with one arm that hung by skin and bone as ragged and splintered as his remaining ornaments. He no longer stood upright, but hunched to one side, bringing his left arm up and forward, the long, blackened fingers crooked into a diabolical clutching gesture, shadowing his lowered head. The gold fillet hung awry, unnoticed, meaningless now. He was a ruined thing – a king in exile, dispossessed. So much they saw in the split second before the King swung sideways, towards the massive fuel tank. His left arm hooked around it, and the whole hundred-gallon structure ripped free of its mountings, swung upwards, and hurtled towards them. Jess flung Hal aside and the tank glanced off her shoulder, knocking her spinning, smashed the railing behind them and toppled into the sea. Hal stumbled, and Jess crashed on her back an inch from the platform's edge. The flare tube rolled and skittered past her. Then the King was on them.

His huge foot cracked the boards by Jess's head, but he ignored her, closing with Hal as he had on the altarstone. His weight was his weapon as he bore down on his enemy, thrusting him back against the shattered railing – and the swollen left hand thrust out and pressed flat over Hal's face and upper chest, bending him backwards, trying to snap his spine. Hal's neck was grinding agony, his head buzzed, his chest laboured for breath under that unyielding weight. His tortured eyes could see only the huge shaggy head of the King against the turbulent sky, the shadow of something that not even time had wholly destroyed. And then the moon crept out from the clouds, shone full on the Ice King's face, and Hal met the gaze of the draugar. He screamed aloud. There was terror in that face – but no terror he had ever dreamed of.

The features were ruined, bloated, and this close the signs of decay were clear beneath the tautened skin; it was a shattered corpse-face, and the stench of it was choking. But it lived, it moved, it had expression, a stretching snarl of effort. And one part of it was most of all alive, and there the terror dwelt. The eyes he stared into were as blue as his own, clear, unstained, ordinary – human. And tormented. The gaze that fell on him was keen, intelligent, almost sad, for all the writhing mask around it. You peered into the depths of a hellish dungeon, beyond help or hope, and saw there an ordinary face – and worst of all, your own. For Hal it was like looking into a distorting mirror; beneath those puffy mounds of flesh and muscle lay features that had once been very like his own, the same hawklike Scandinavian cast. Viking looked at Viking – and Hal, in the crazy detachment of pain, found himself wondering about an intelligent, even intellectual man born in brutal times, turning to the darker side of a dark faith as his only means of survival, the only power he could gain to live his own life . . .

The cruel irony of it sickened him to the heart. What right had he to a better fate? What might he not have done, in the other's place? *We have met the enemy, and he is ourself* . . .

'Yes,' said the Ice King, and his voice was as cold and remote as his name, the wind calling bleakly over grinding ice-floes, the harsh yearning of a seabird through a chilly waste. 'That is our secret, you and I . . .'

'Hal!' screamed Jess, fighting to stand up. 'Don't listen! Remember the sagas – Grettir – he lost his courage –'

Then the cold eyes turned on her, and she shrank down from the terror of them. In that instant Hal could act, do all that was left him. In another minute he would be dead, and then Jess, themselves night-stalking horrors perhaps, suffering minds imprisoned in tombs of flesh. *What had the Queen's eyes looked like?* With all his strength he kicked out, throwing his weight and force the same way as the King's, backward against the rail.

And over.

Off balance, still clutching Hal, the King toppled forward like a falling cliff, and the two linked bodies whirled out into the air and were gone. Jess, struggling to get up, yelled with horror and threw herself forward. Her arms clawed at empty air, and staring down she saw the spinning forms strike the water with a resounding splash and fountain of water. It settled, and an iridescent, oily rainbow

248

sheen spread out over the surface. Something black bobbed into sight, but it was only the tip of the sunken fuel-drum. She sank back. Something knocked against her knee, and she clutched it violently. It was the flare-gun.

Then there was another splash, a violent turmoil in the water that went on and on. A shape broke surface for an instant, a flash of light skin, and then vanished again as a darker shadow surged underneath. Suddenly, Jess realised what was happening. Both adversaries had survived – perhaps the King had broken Hal's fall – and were still fighting. But the King would be too heavy to swim, perhaps unable to get a proper grip –

Then a larger, darker head and shoulders rose up in the sea, and behind it a fearful thrashing. The King was walking up the sandbar, to shallows where he could fight – and he was towing Hal with him.

Jess staggered up on shaky legs, poised for the long dive. But before she could make a move, Hal's body twisted violently, his head broke surface and screamed up to her.

'No! Don't risk it! Only way – flare – fire the flare –'

For an instant, no longer than a heartbeat, Jess stared appalled at the oily water. Then she held out the tube, shut her eyes and pressed the trigger.

On the slope above the town two skiers, careering madly along a trail of huge footprints, came skidding to a halt. Far out in the estuary a great scarlet light sprang and beat on their faces an instant, a low sullen boom shattered the pre-dawn silence. Then the light sank back, and the dam stood out starkly in a spreading ring of flames, dancing on the wavecrests.

'Bloody 'ell!' said Neville.

'The harbour!' yelled Ridley, and boosted himself violently away down the slope. But a minute later he was slithering all over the place, losing speed as his skis sank into the softening surface. Behind him Neville was already kicking his feet free. They began to run across the snow, but a few minutes later they were splashing through lumpy slush. And then, as they reached the crossroads at the edge of town and saw the patrol car come surging down the cliff road towards them, they found they were standing on immensely wet, extremely muddy green grass . . .

Jess never knew how she had made her way back down to the landing stage – a primitive instinct for self-preservation, perhaps, although the strong seawall was blocking off the flames from the dam itself. But the sea beyond was an inferno in which nothing could live, a rippling pool of flame. Numbly she turned her back on it, stumbled down towards the jetty. But she made no effort to get into the boat. She just stood staring at the reflections in the black water beneath, as dark and formless as her thoughts. After so much, to have endured so much, escaped so much, and to lose it all in the last mad gamble . . .

The sense of loss, the ache, was a vast emptiness inside her. Jess thought of herself as an intellectual, a realist. She had never considered the world as fair or unfair, any more than she could call a storm evil or sunlight kind. But if conscious powers of evil like the King existed – if there were other, deeper shadows behind him – then why didn't they have their reflections, their opposite numbers? Hal had found some help somewhere – but in the end what good had it done him? It was their own strength, human strength, that had brought down the menace – and at a terrible price. Too great a price. There were no powers of good, or if there were they were too weak to hold the balance fair against the shadows. And either way, what use were they? What use was anything, anything at all? The conscious thoughts were the merest echo of the bitter-ness and despair beneath.

She hardly heard the sound beneath her; she looked down almost unconsciously – and then recoiled, gasping, at the sight of the dark hand. Glistening with water, it clawed for a grip on the slippery metal flooring, clutched at anything, seemed to be falling back. Then, just as it made a last desperate grab at the air, Jess fell on her knees, clutched it, caught at the arm and pulled. There was a splash, a scrabbling on the slippery fender beneath and Hal came flopping and sputtering up onto the jetty. Jess fell sobbing on his neck – and then froze as she saw what had happened to his face.

Down the left side, from forehead to mouth, ran a great seared patch, blackened and blistered, crossing the eye. Darkness hid the socket.

'It is okay,' said a feeble voice, a croak. The other eye was open, conscious, looking up at her. 'Does not even hurt much . . . shock, probably. He was trying to drown me, Jess; he had got me right under just at the moment you fired. Then he let go – I only came up for an instant . . . got this . . . then enough breath to swim free, under-water. An eye for wisdom – Odin's bargain. Not a bad trade-off . . . don't think there's anything else serious . . .'

'Hush!' she said, and cradled him in her arms. 'I'll get you ashore, to hospital – in just a minute –' And then abruptly they huddled together like frightened night crea-tures. Through the heart of the flames, jolted free by the explosion, the fishing smack came gliding. Flames curled around its hull, smoke spouted from its wheelhouse and through its deck planking. And out of the flame-wreathed water, clinging to its gunnel, rose an immense dark arm. They saw it strain, flex, the boat dipped violently, and a great black figure, dripping flame, surged upward onto its deck. But the superstructure was already ablaze, and the new fire touched off the rest. The King stumbled on the deck, glanced against the mast; the fire raced up it, the sail vanished with a puff and roar and the tackle glowed in lines of red. The wheelhouse became an inferno, the mast cracked at its root and toppled, flames raced along the splitting deck seams and engulfed the King. A single shriek rent the air and echoed off the distant cliffs, a mad yell of greater agonies than pain – defeat, decline, unending darkness. Hal bowed his head. For an instant a shadow stood amid the fire, erect, defiant, and then crashed forward like a felled tree onto the erupting deck. A plume of fire shot skyward as the boat's own fuel tank caught, and it spun into midstream a vessel of flame.

Jess found herself giggling weakly, in a kind of feeble hysteria. 'Back – the bastard's back where he should've been all along . . . Just like Balder – or Beowulf . . .'

Hal sighed, and clutched her hand.

A warm wind was rising from the land, heavy and humid, rich with promises of autumn. It caught up the boat and the corona of blazing fuel, and swept it downstream, away from the dam, out into the estuary, out to sea. Along the line of the distant horizon the first faint colours of sunrise were showing; but above them clouds were massing, and the lightning flickered.

Then the warriors began to kindle
That greatest of funeral fires; smoke rose
above the flames, black and thick,
And while the wind blew and the fire
Roared, they wept, and the King's body
crumbled and was gone . . .
No man can say where that strange-laden ship at last
    found harbour . . .

Beowulf